Stories of the Islands

CLAR ANGKASA

HOLIDAY HOUSE  NEW YORK

To Mama,
for being the inspiration behind all this

To Ade,
for pushing me in more ways than one
(and because you asked for a dedication)

Printed and bound in June 2023 at RRD, Dongguan, China.
www.holidayhouse.com
First Edition
1 3 5 7 9 10 8 6 4 2

Library of Congress Cataloging-in-Publication Data

Names: Angkasa, Clar, author, illustrator.
Title: Stories of the islands / Clar Angkasa.
Description: First edition. | New York : Holiday House, 2023. | Audience: Ages 8-12 | Audience: Grades 4-6
Summary: "A graphic novel collection of girl-centered fantasy stories, based on Indonesian traditional tales"—Provided by publisher.
Identifiers: LCCN 2023006556 | ISBN 9780823449781 (hardcover) | ISBN 9780823455737 (paperback)
Subjects: LCSH: Tales—Indonesia. | CYAC: Graphic novels. | Fantasy. Folklore—Indonesia. | Women—Fiction. | LCGFT: Folk tales. | Fantasy comics. | Graphic novels.
Classification: LCC PZ7.7.A57 St 2023 | DDC 741.5/973—dc23/eng/20230213
LC record available at https://lccn.loc.gov/2023006556

ISBN: 978-0-8234-4978-1 (hardcover)
ISBN: 978-0-8234-5573-7 (paperback)

Table of Contents

Keong Mas

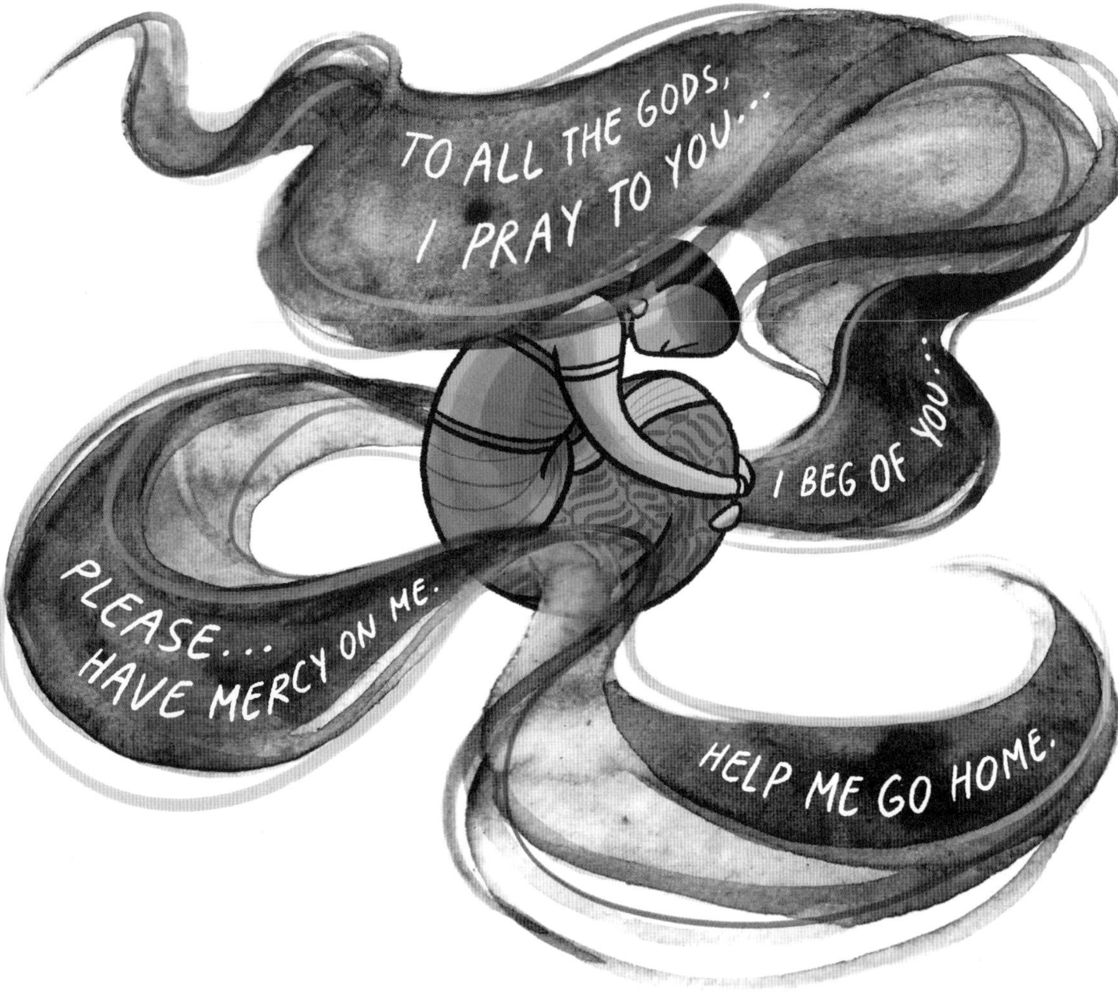
TO ALL THE GODS,
I PRAY TO YOU...
I BEG OF YOU...
PLEASE...
HAVE MERCY ON ME.
HELP ME GO HOME.

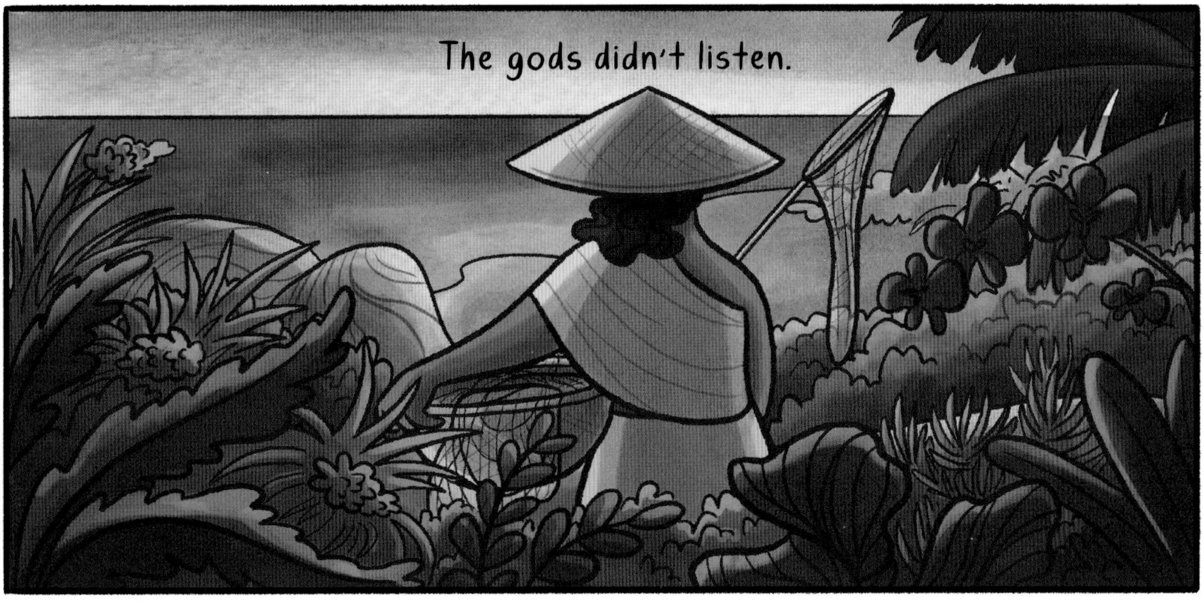
The gods didn't listen.

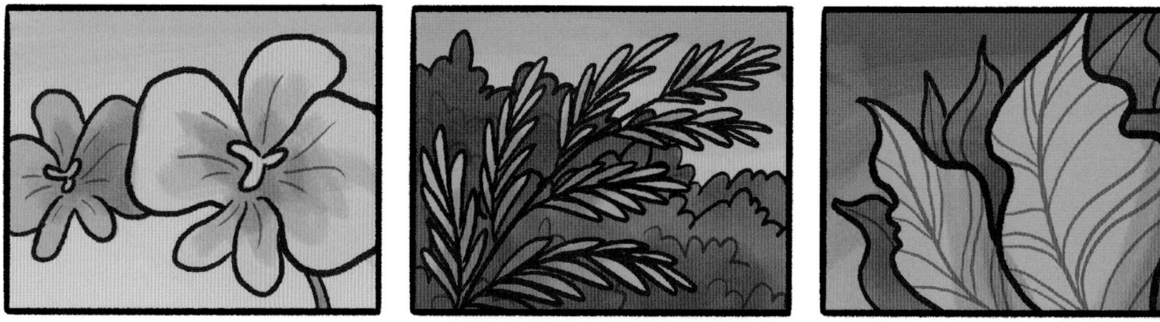

Every day is the same.

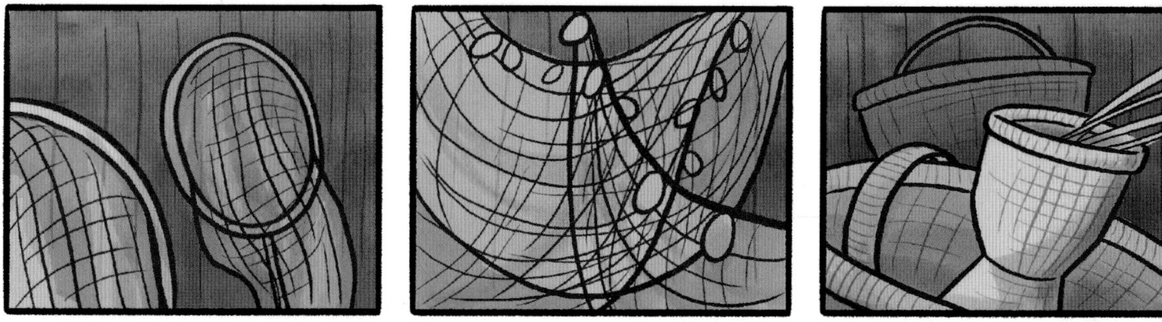

I keep thinking, when I wake up tomorrow . . .

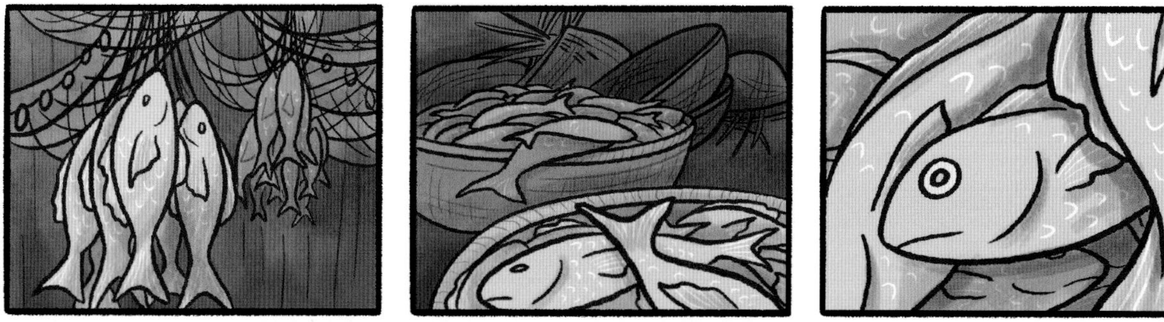

. . . maybe, just maybe . . .

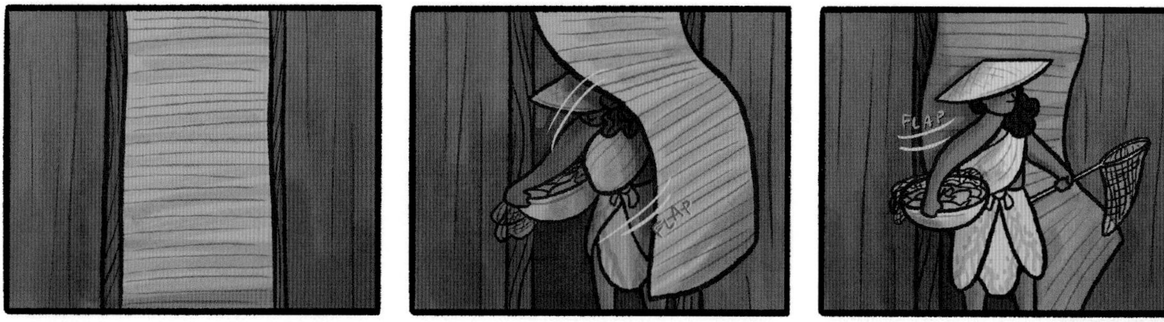
FLAP
FLAP

. . . I'll be home.

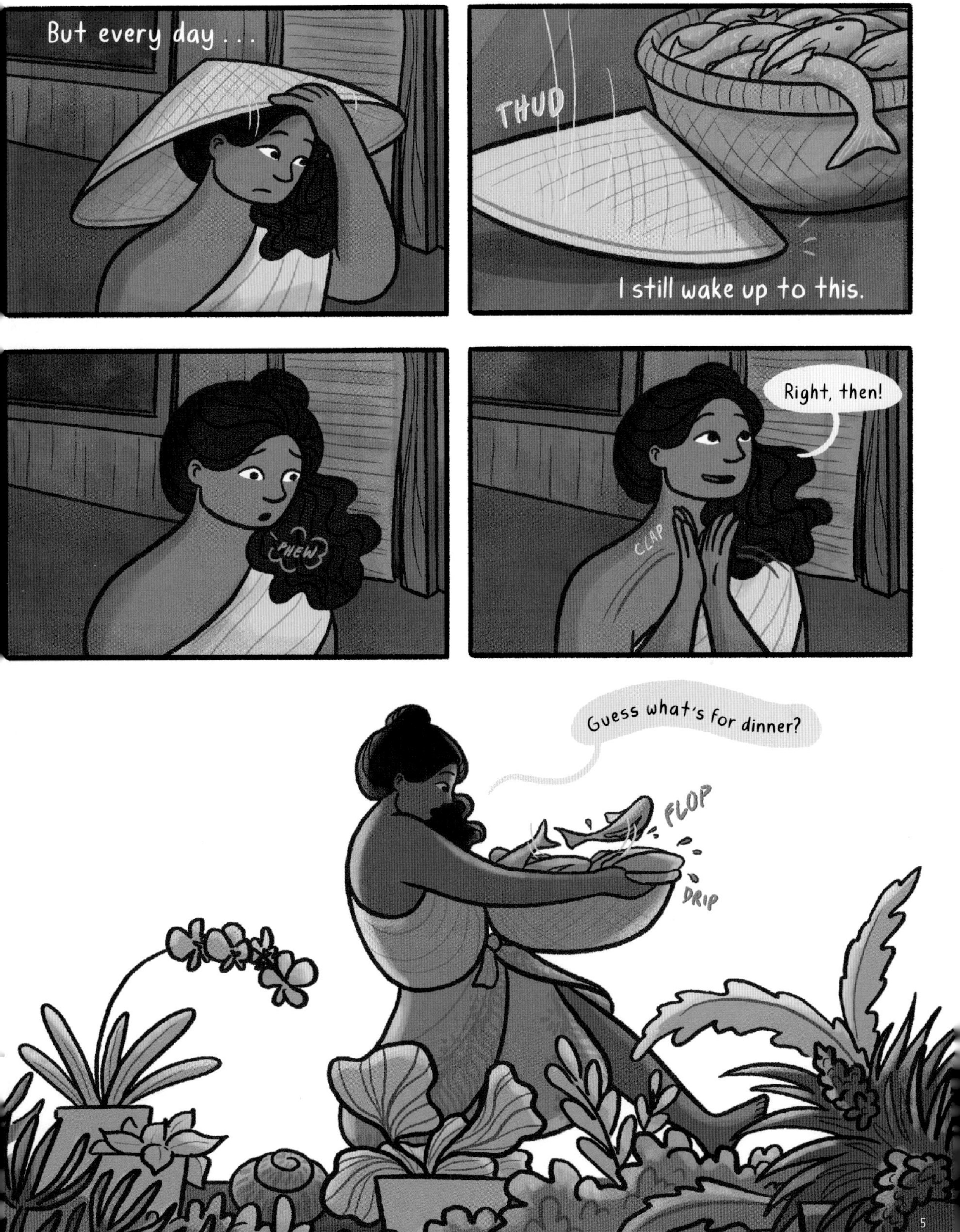

But every day . . .
THUD
I still wake up to this.
PHEW
Right, then!
CLAP
Guess what's for dinner?
FLOP
DRIP

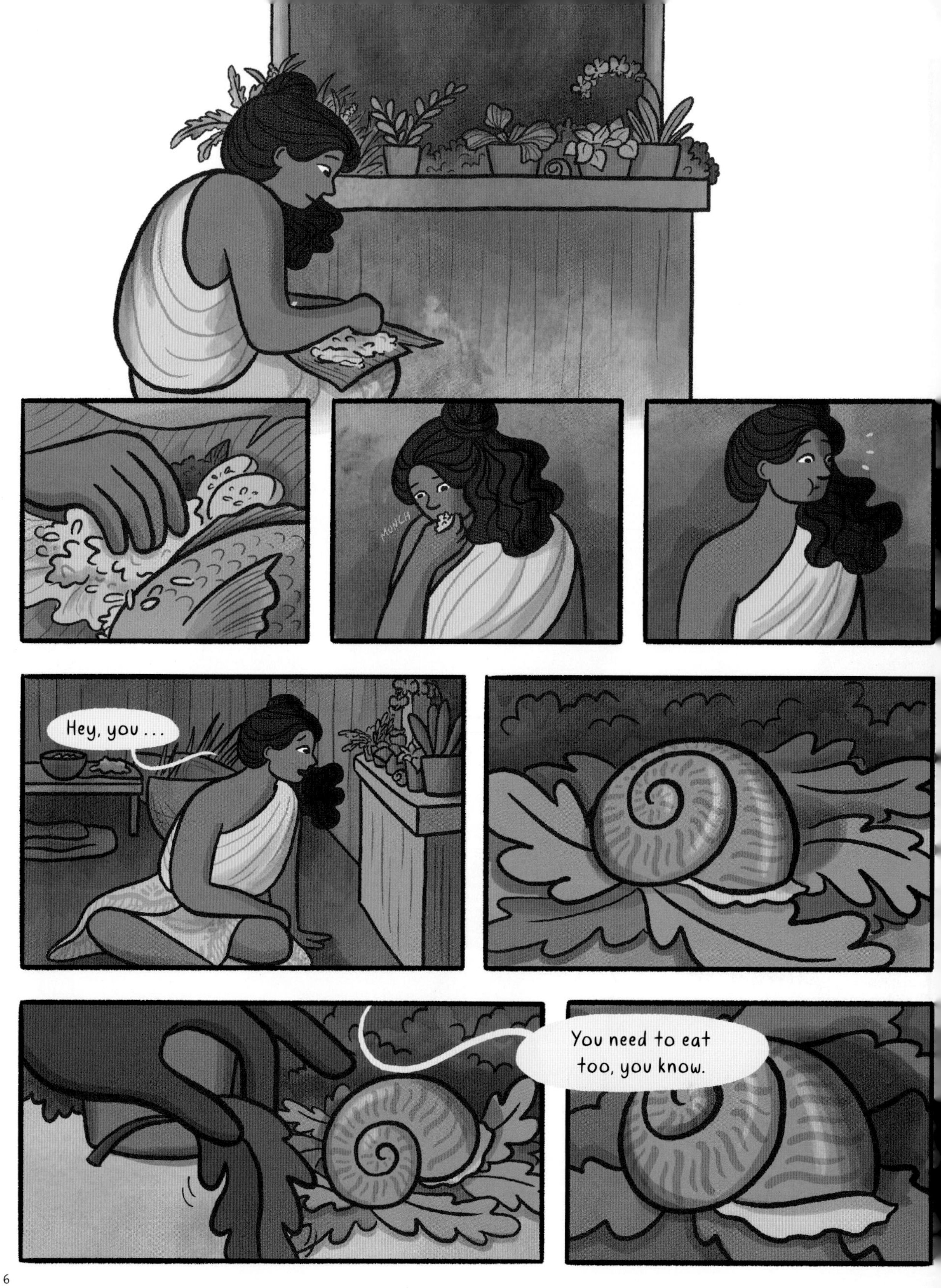
MUNCH
Hey, you . . .
You need to eat
too, you know.

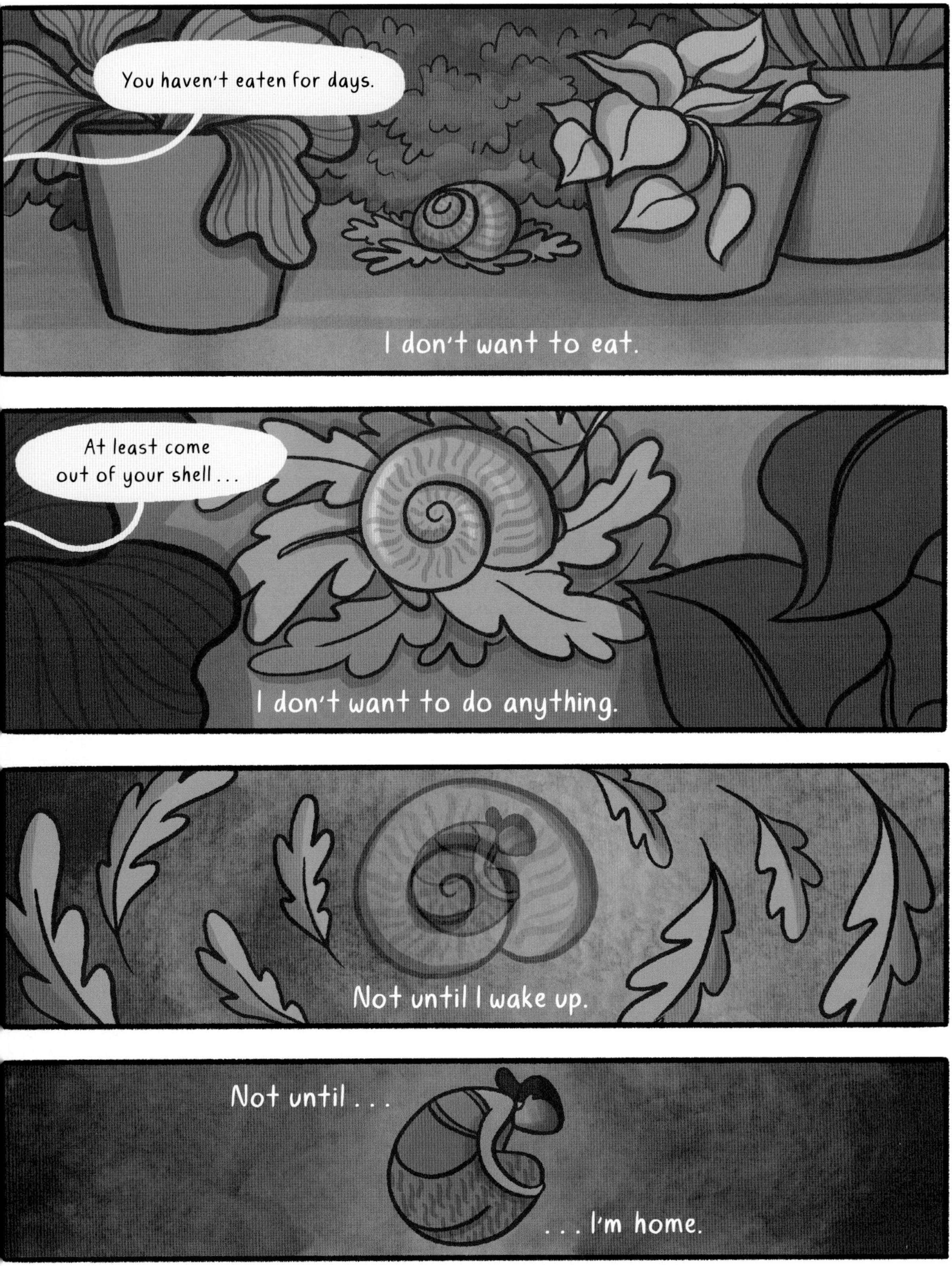
You haven't eaten for days.
I don't want to eat.
At least come out of your shell . . .
I don't want to do anything.
Not until I wake up.
Not until . . .
. . . I'm home.

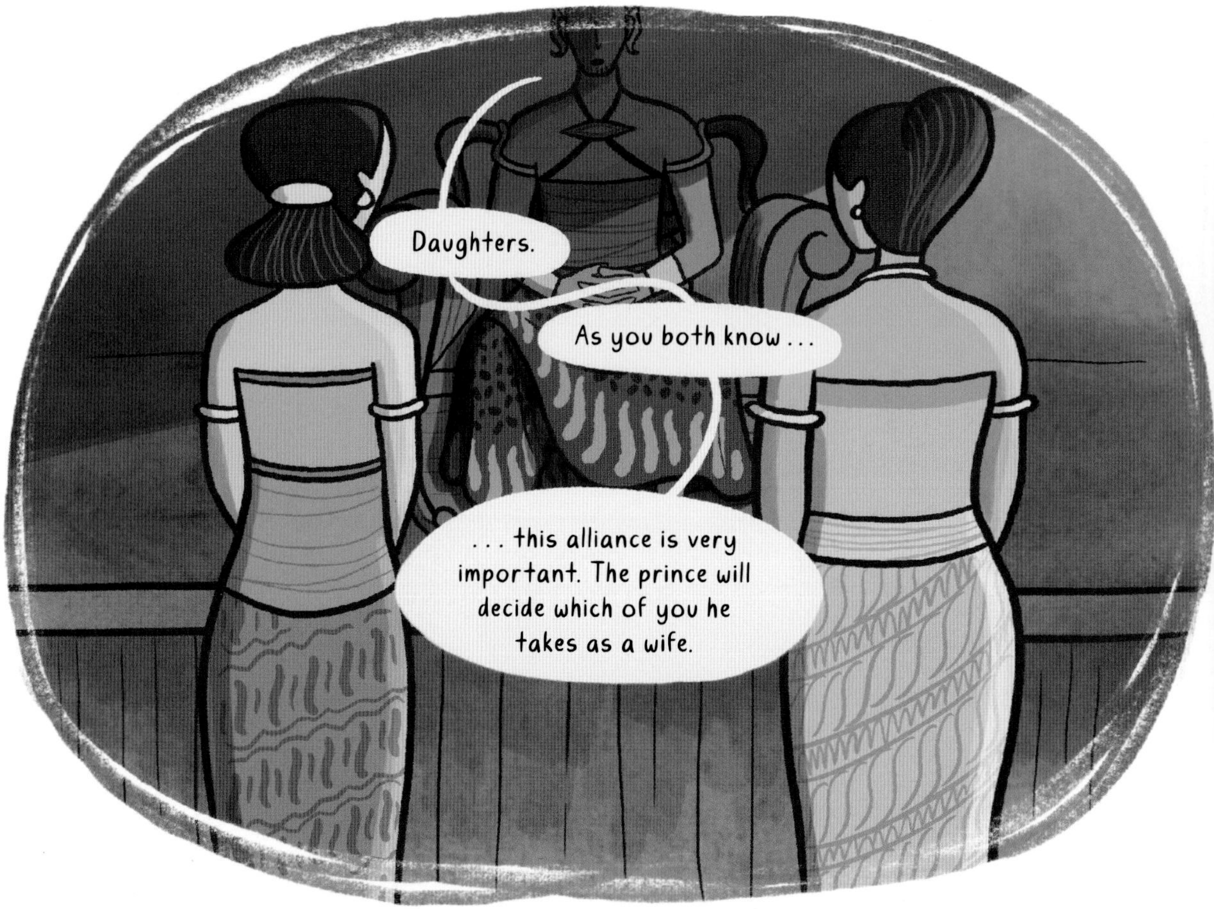
Daughters.
As you both know . . .
. . . this alliance is very important. The prince will decide which of you he takes as a wife.

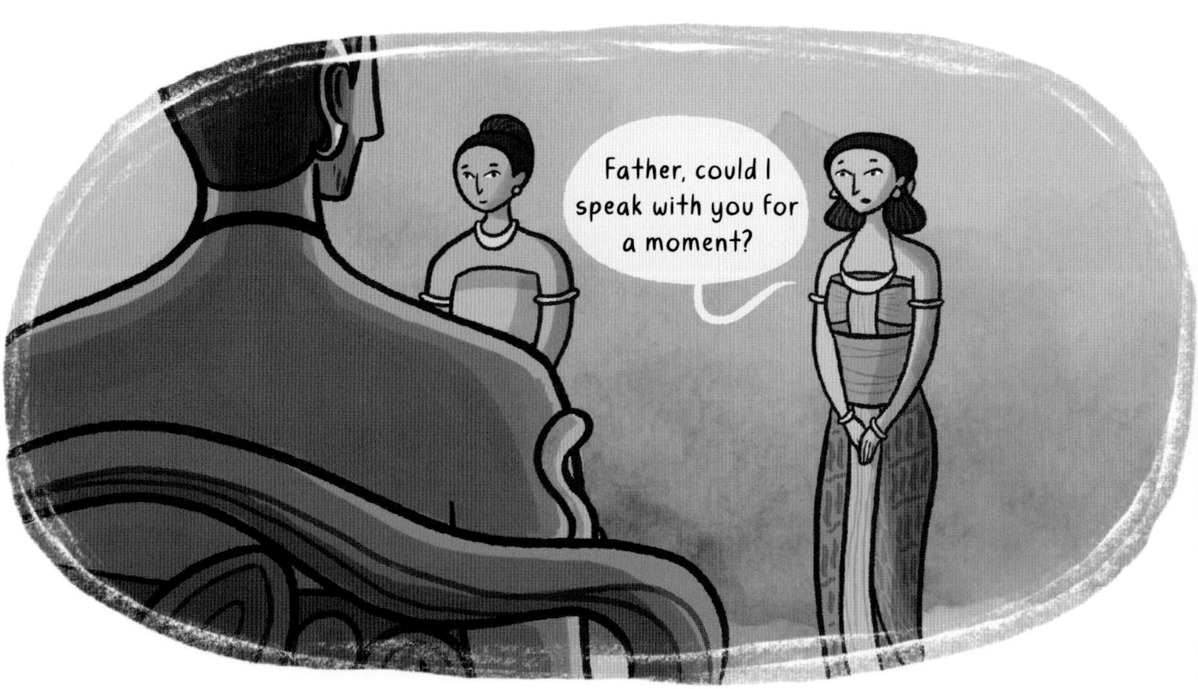
Father, could I speak with you for a moment?

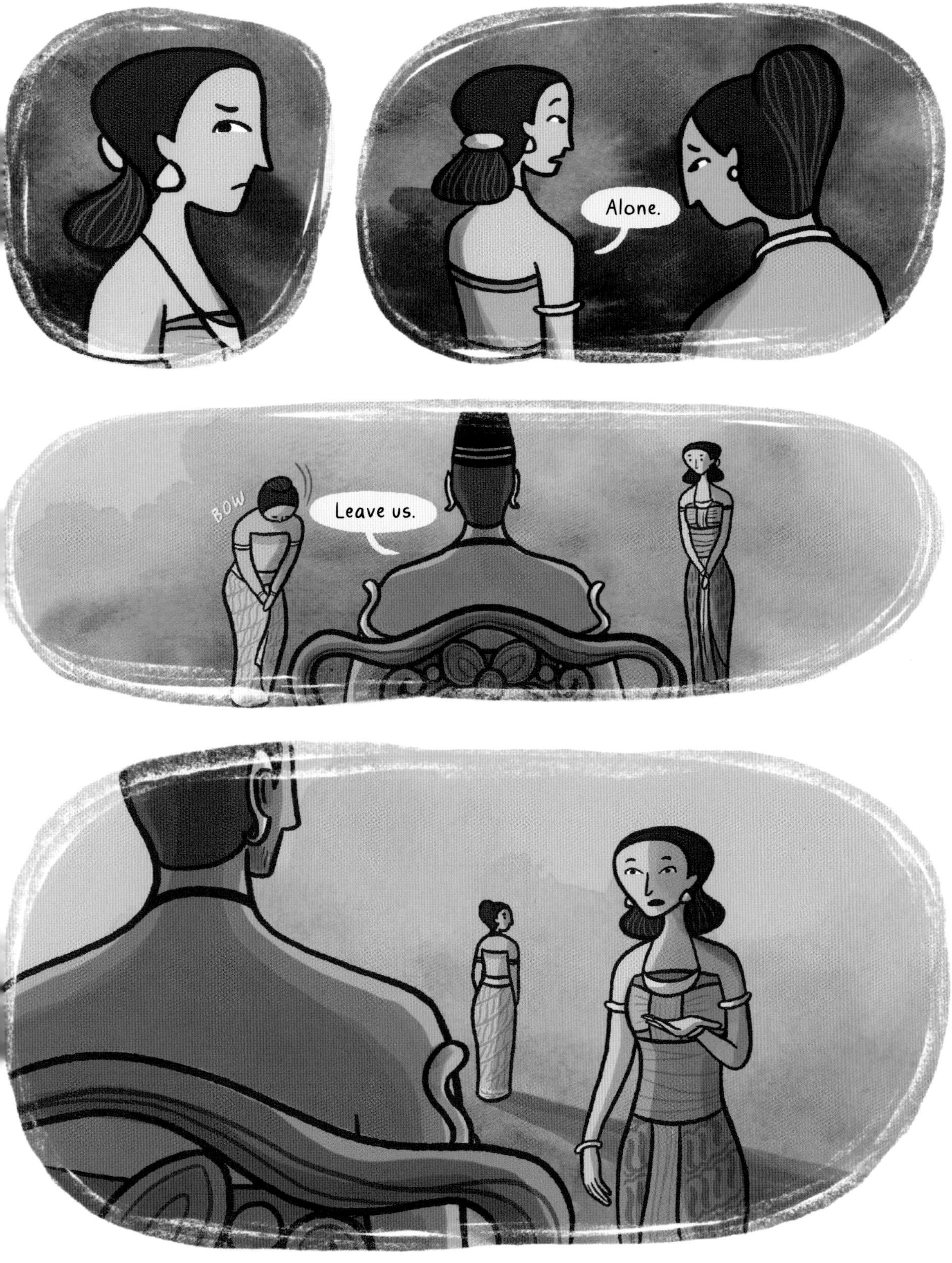
Alone.
BOW
Leave us.

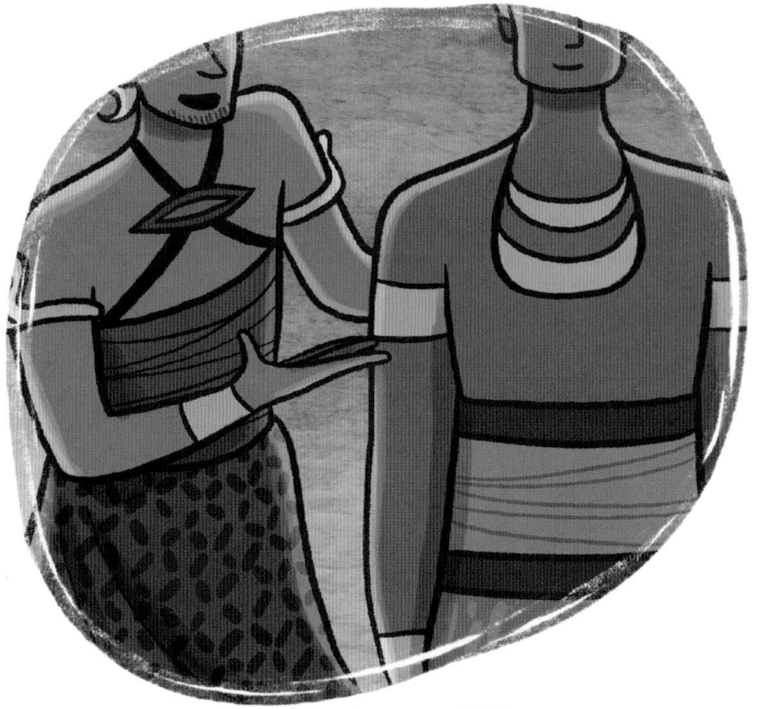
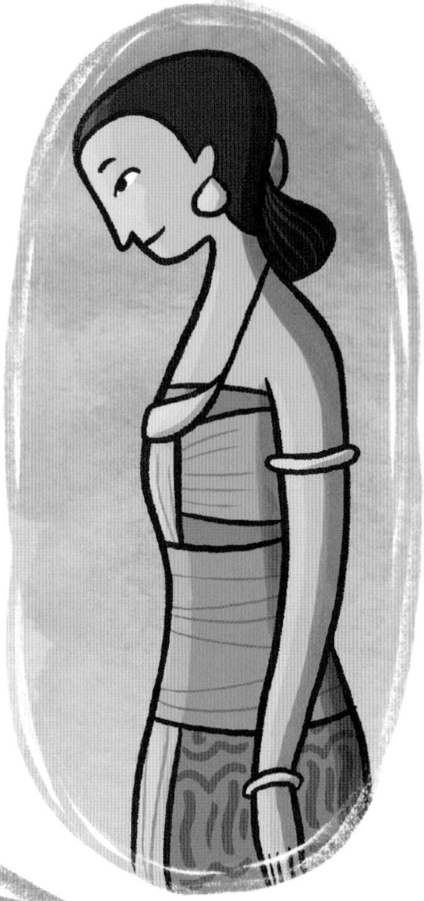
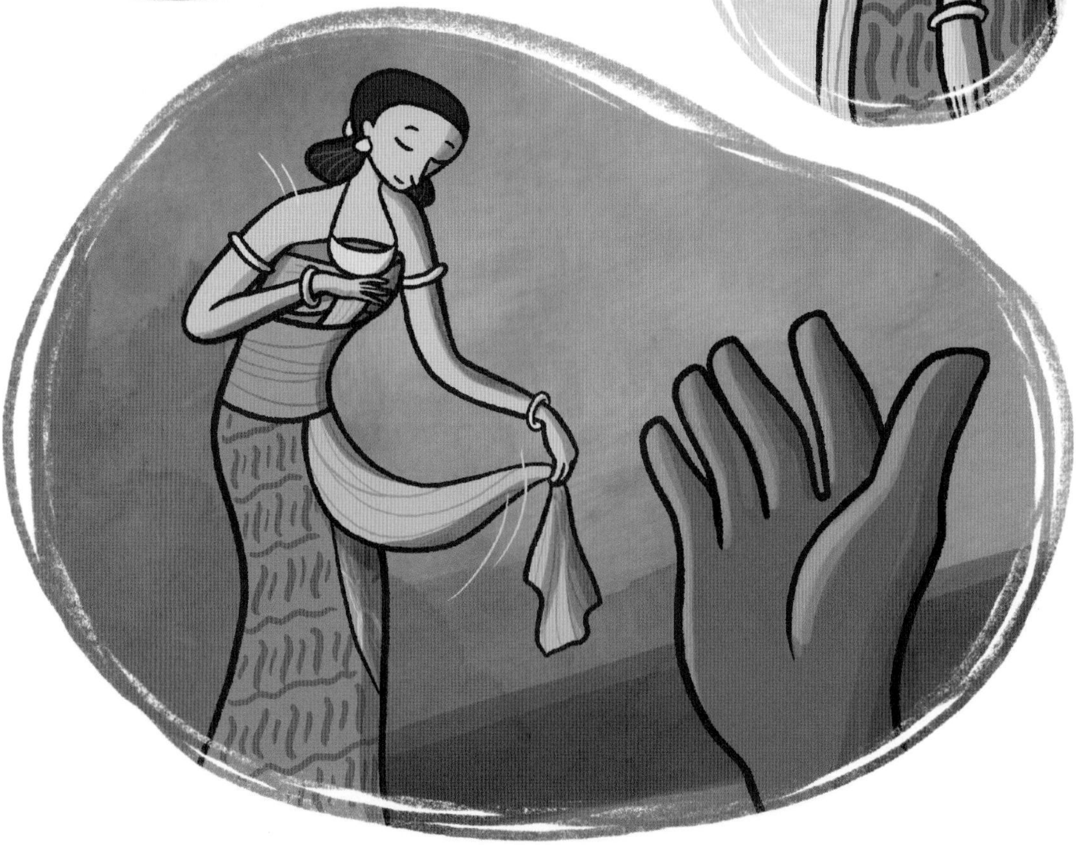

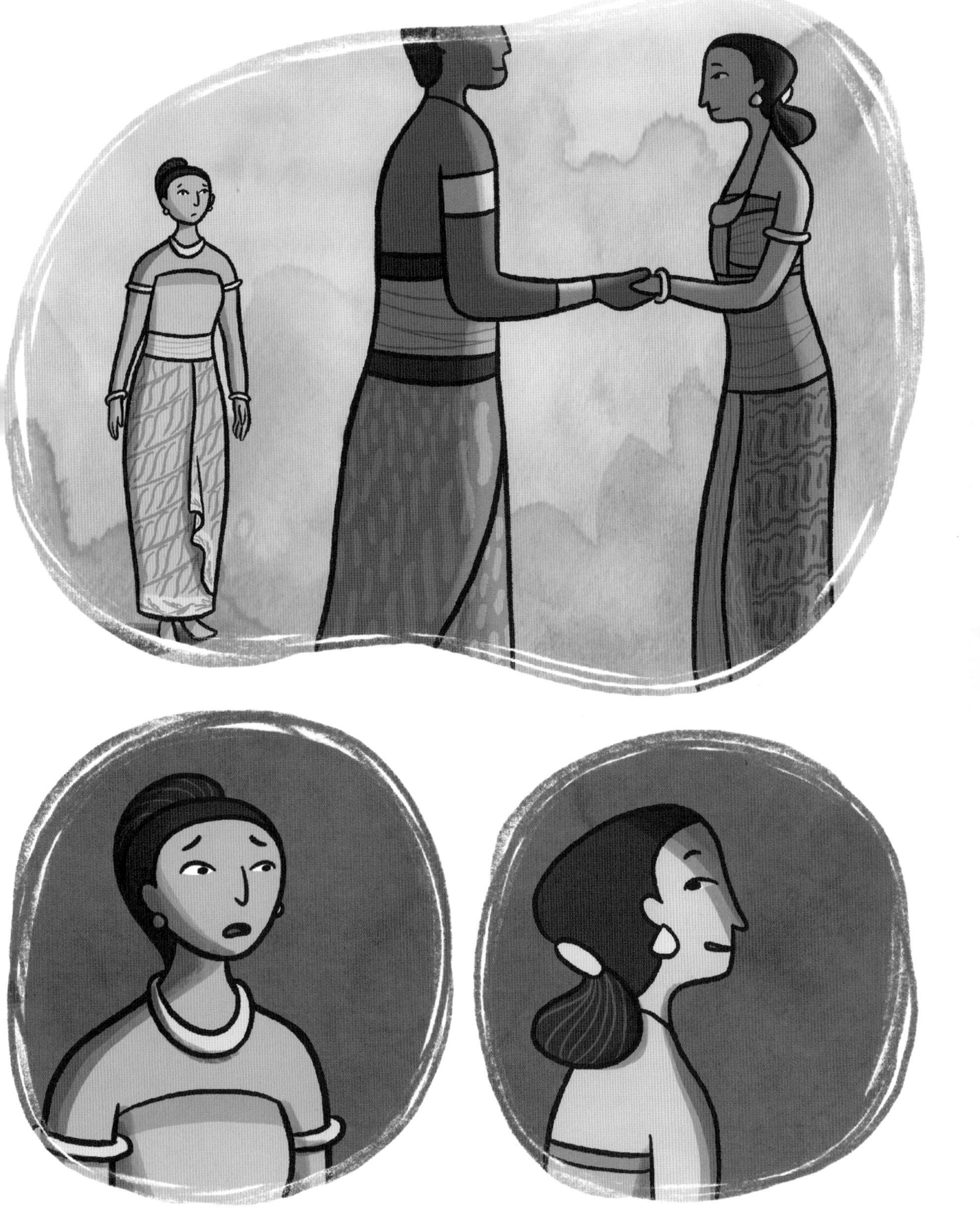

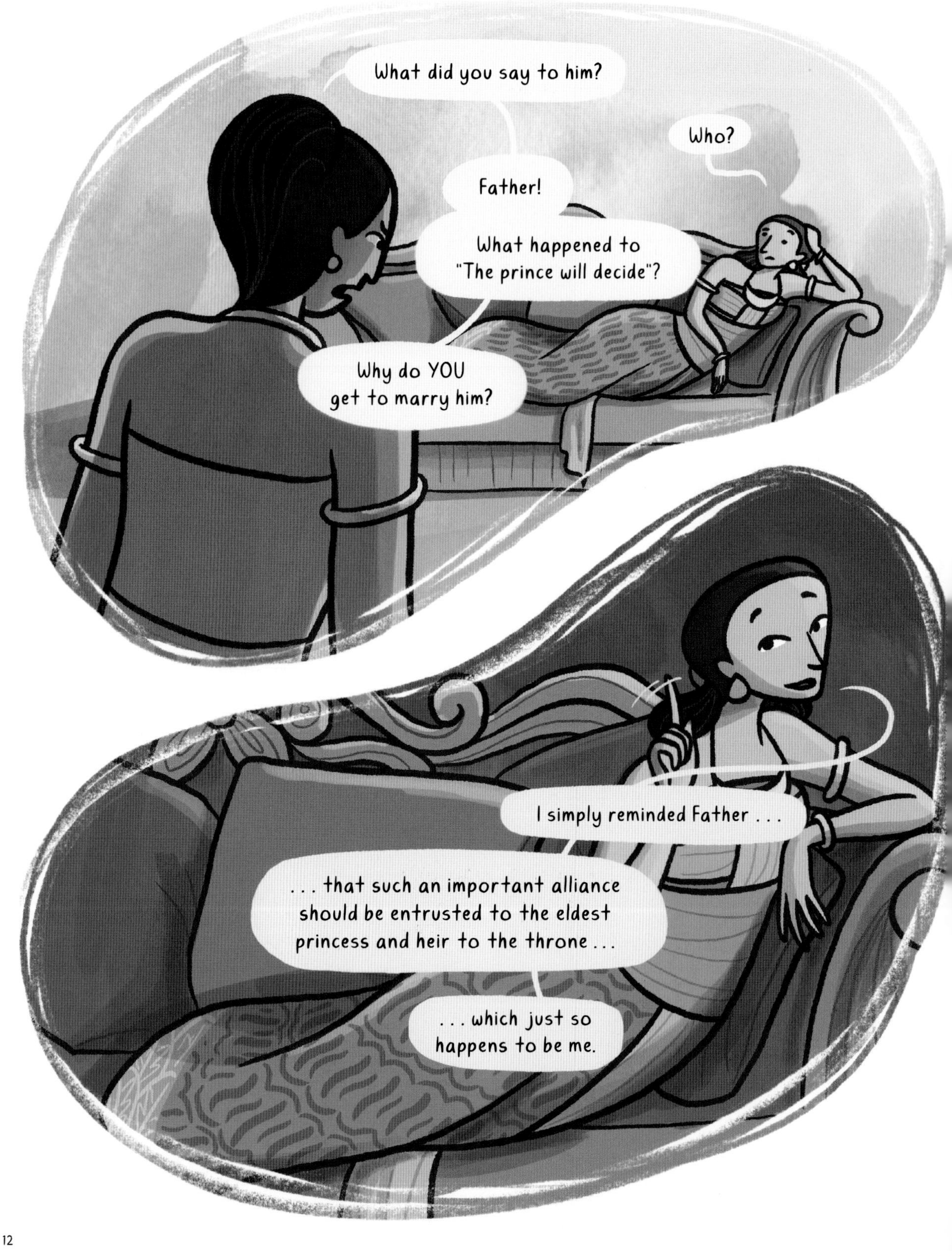
What did you say to him?
Who?
Father!
What happened to "The prince will decide"?
Why do YOU get to marry him?
I simply reminded Father . . .
. . . that such an important alliance should be entrusted to the eldest princess and heir to the throne . . .
. . . which just so happens to be me.

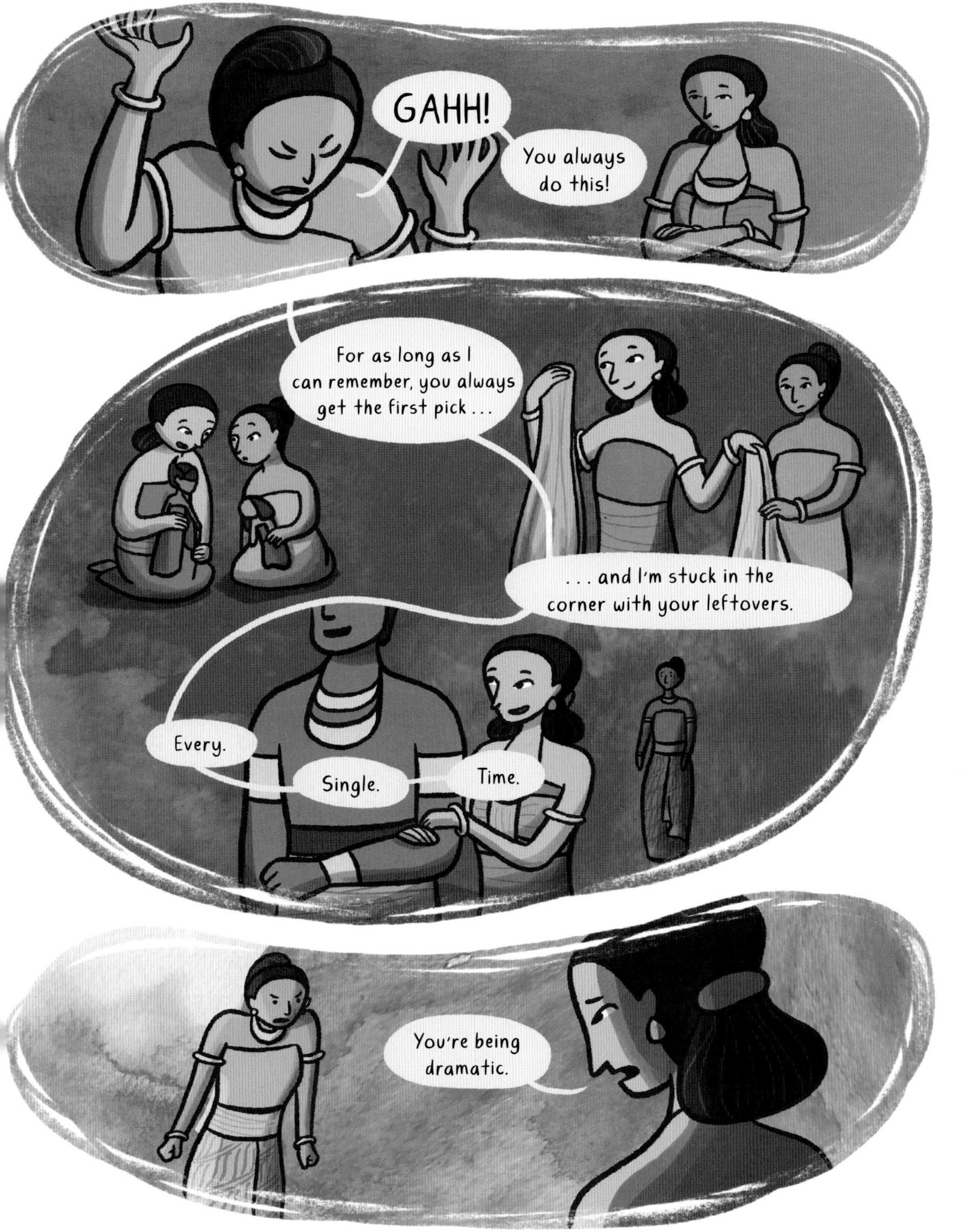
GAHH!
You always do this!
For as long as I can remember, you always get the first pick . . .
. . . and I'm stuck in the corner with your leftovers.
Every.
Single.
Time.
You're being dramatic.

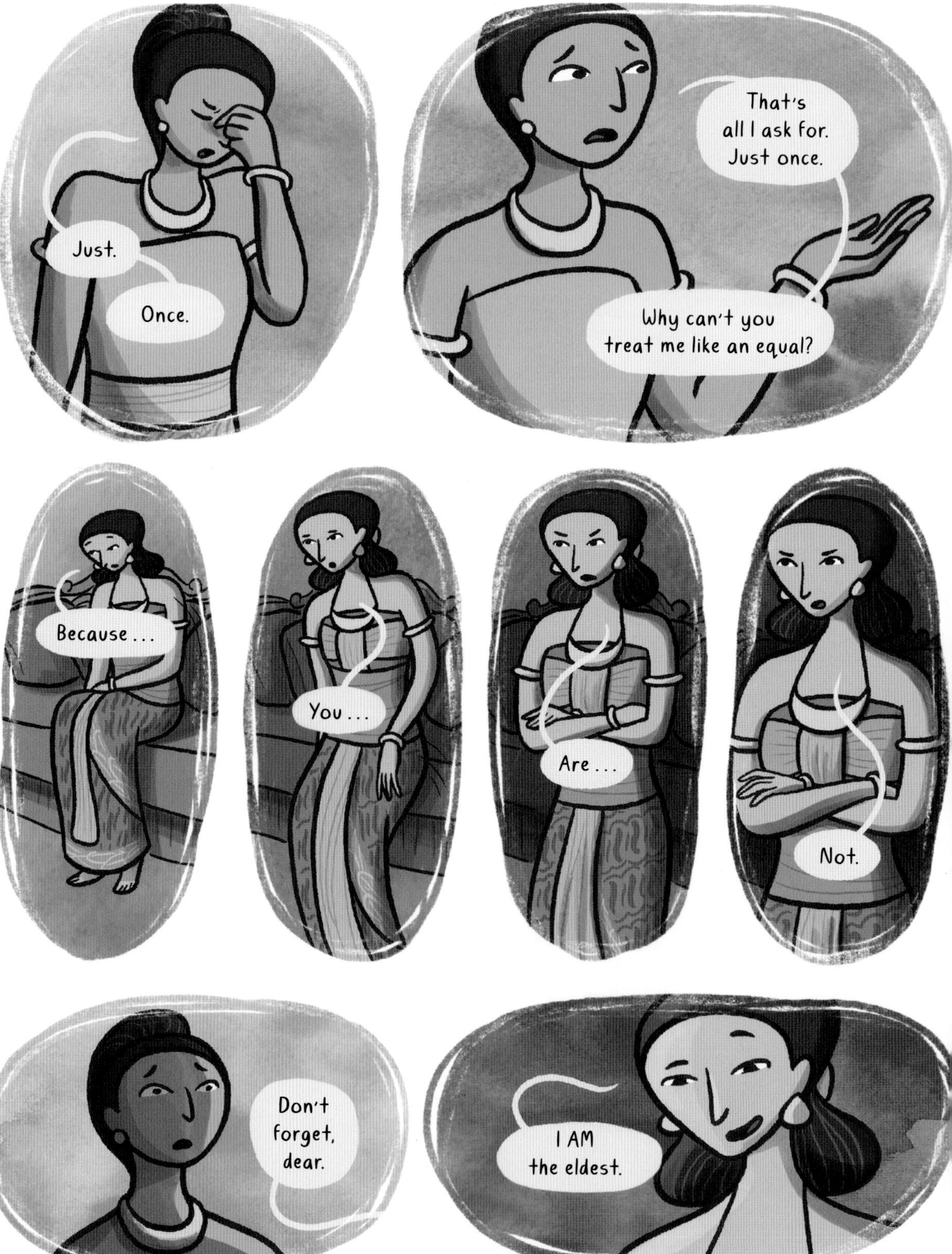
Just.
Once.
That's all I ask for. Just once.
Why can't you treat me like an equal?
Because...
You...
Are...
Not.
Don't forget, dear.
I AM the eldest.

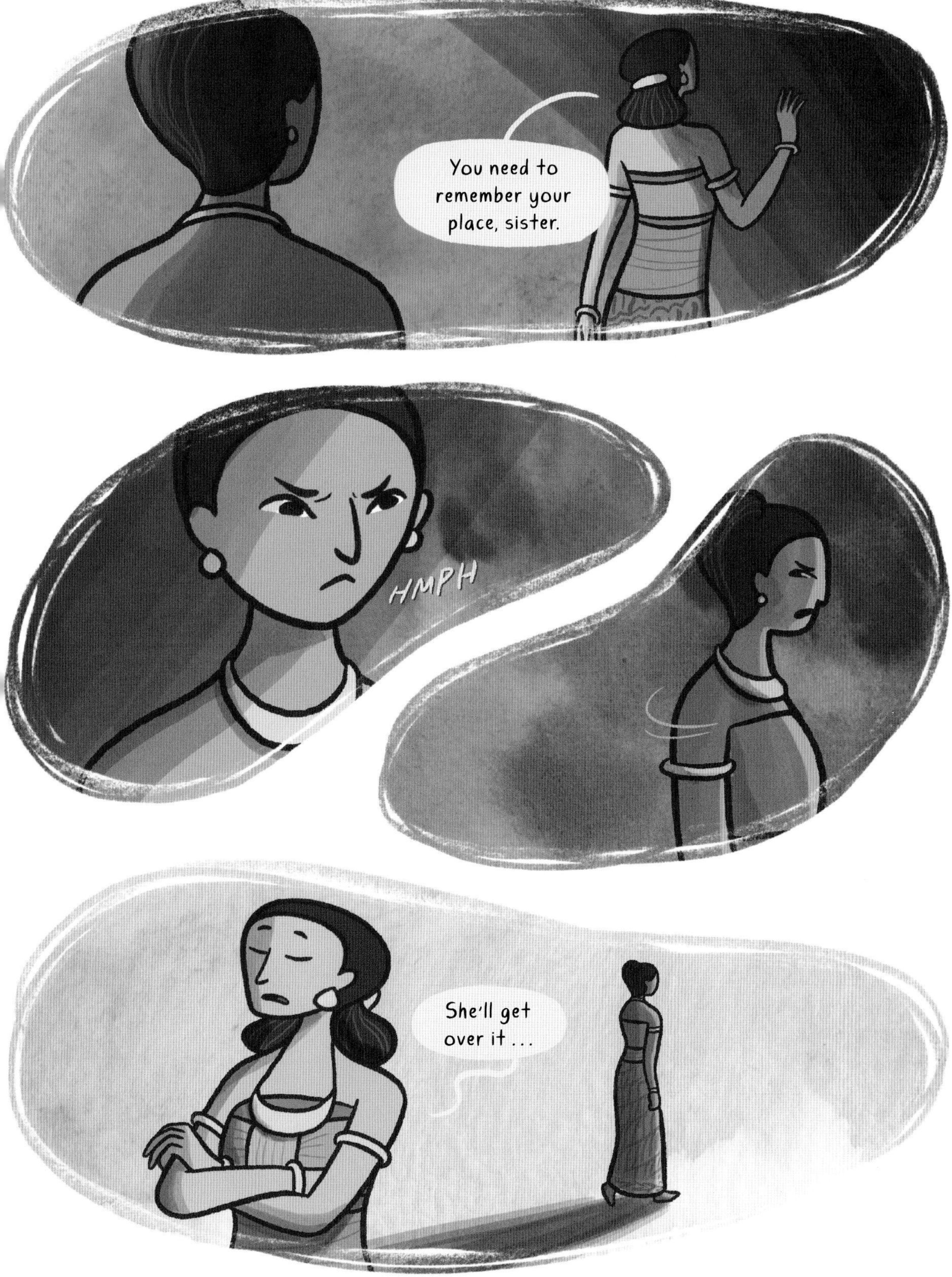
You need to remember your place, sister.
HMPH
She'll get over it . . .

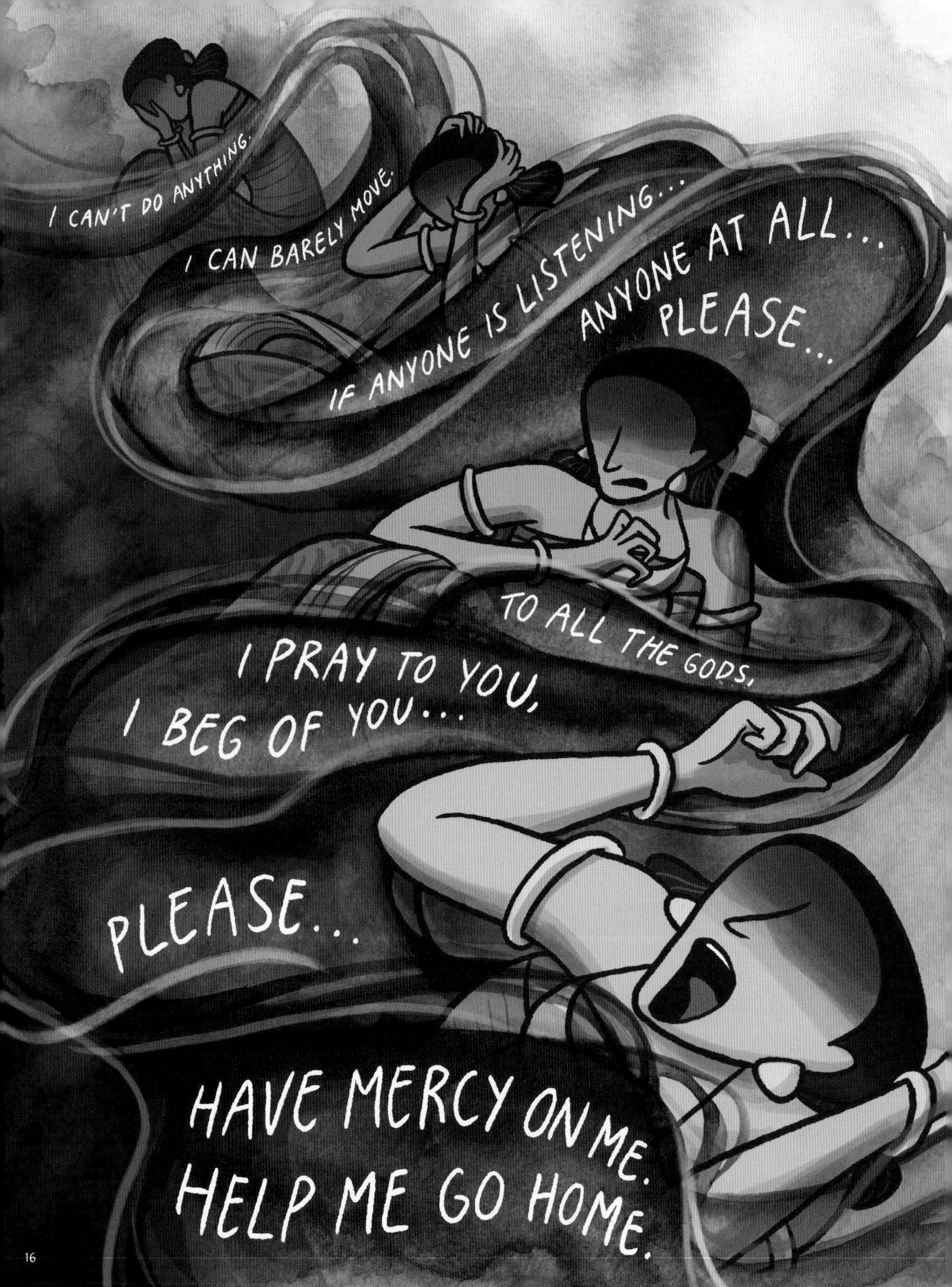
I CAN'T DO ANYTHING.
I CAN BARELY MOVE.
IF ANYONE IS LISTENING...
ANYONE AT ALL...
PLEASE...
TO ALL THE GODS,
I PRAY TO YOU,
I BEG OF YOU...
PLEASE...
HAVE MERCY ON ME.
HELP ME GO HOME.

The gods didn't listen.

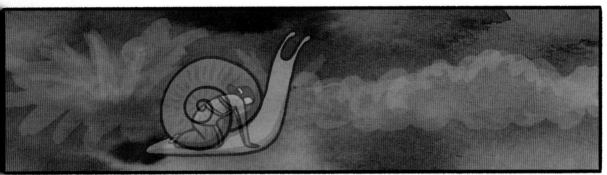

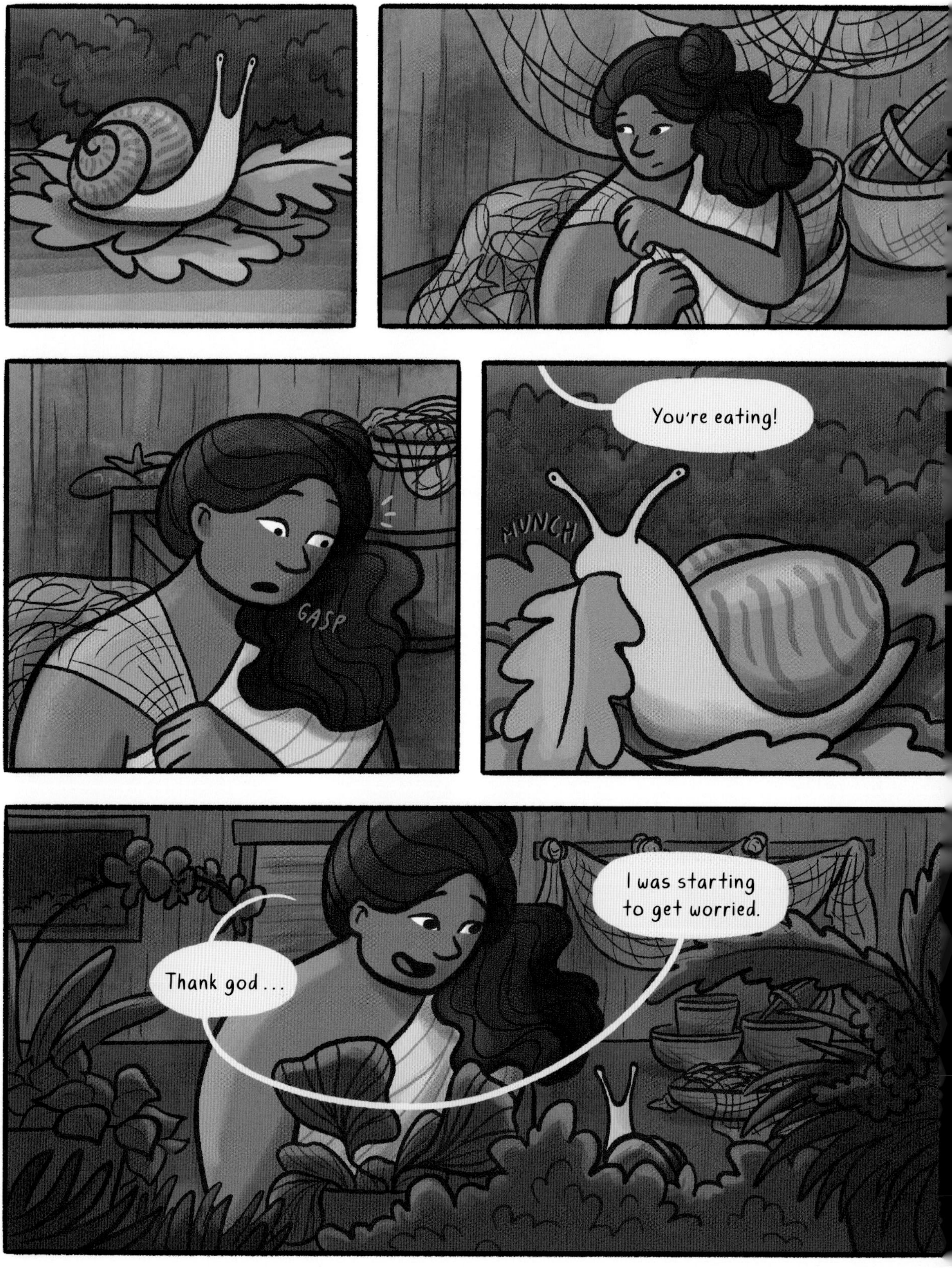
GASP
You're eating!
MUNCH
Thank god . . .
I was starting to get worried.

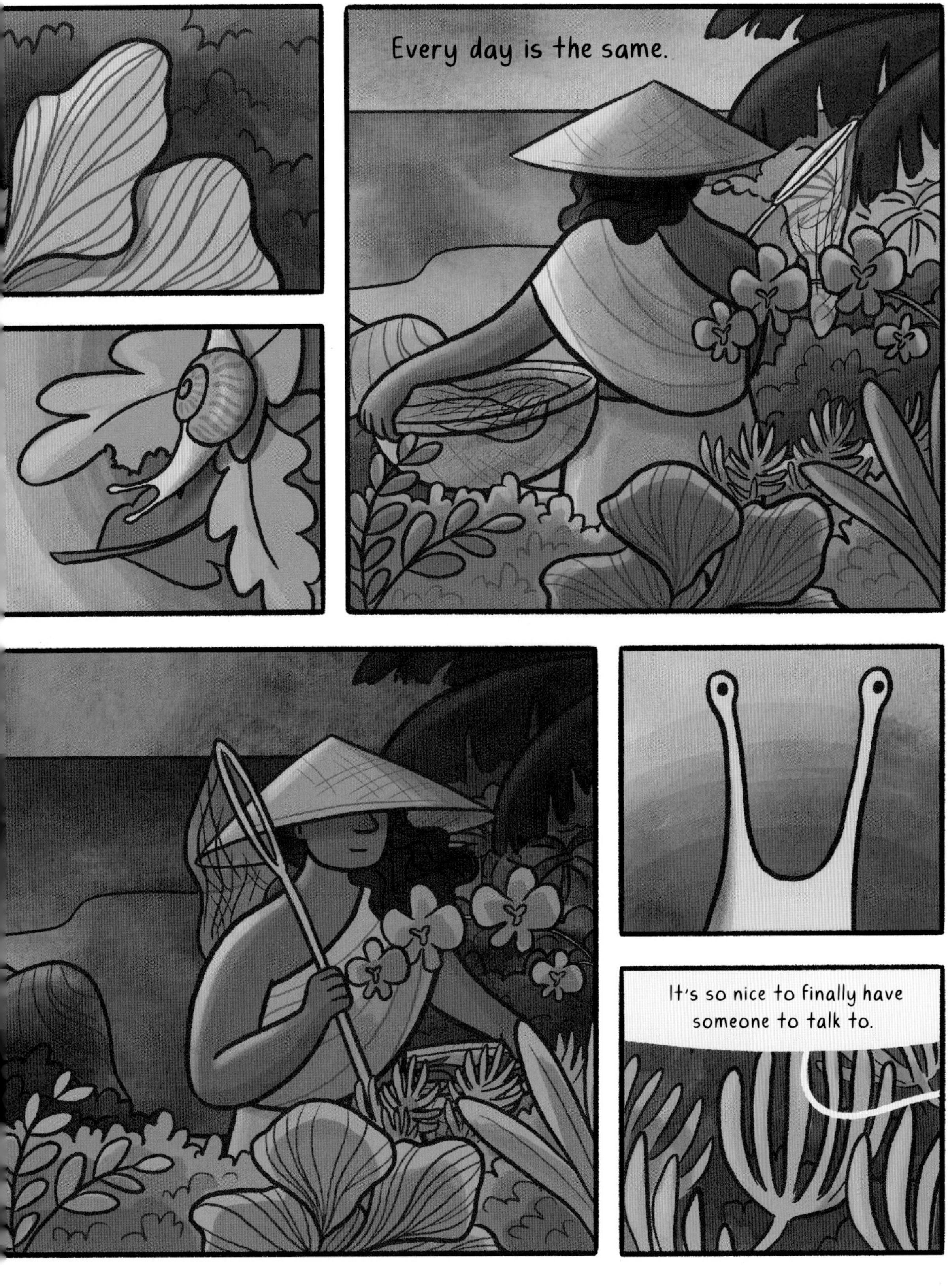

Every day is the same.
It's so nice to finally have someone to talk to.

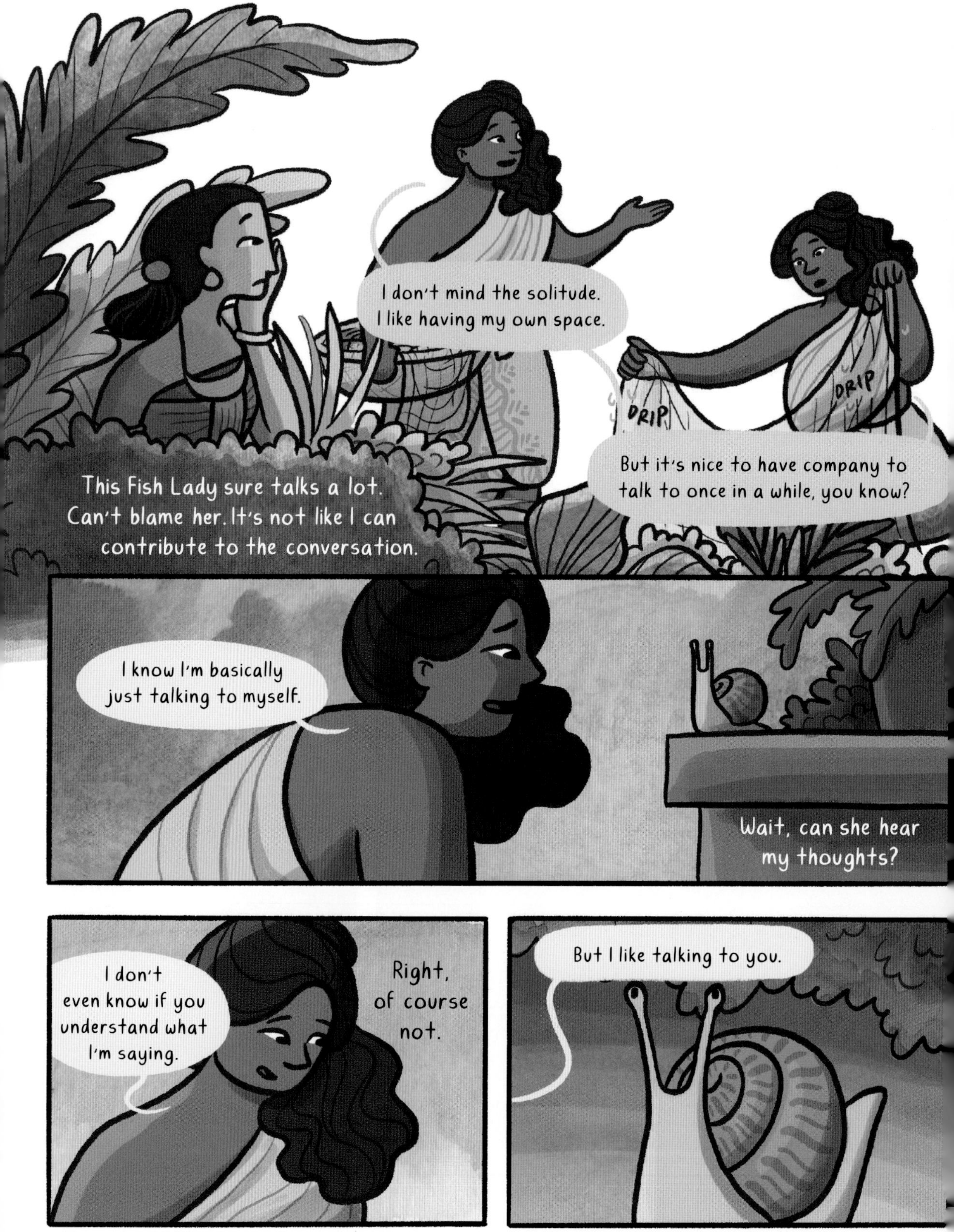
I don't mind the solitude. I like having my own space.
DRIP
DRIP
But it's nice to have company to talk to once in a while, you know?
This Fish Lady sure talks a lot. Can't blame her. It's not like I can contribute to the conversation.
I know I'm basically just talking to myself.
Wait, can she hear my thoughts?
I don't even know if you understand what I'm saying.
Right, of course not.
But I like talking to you.

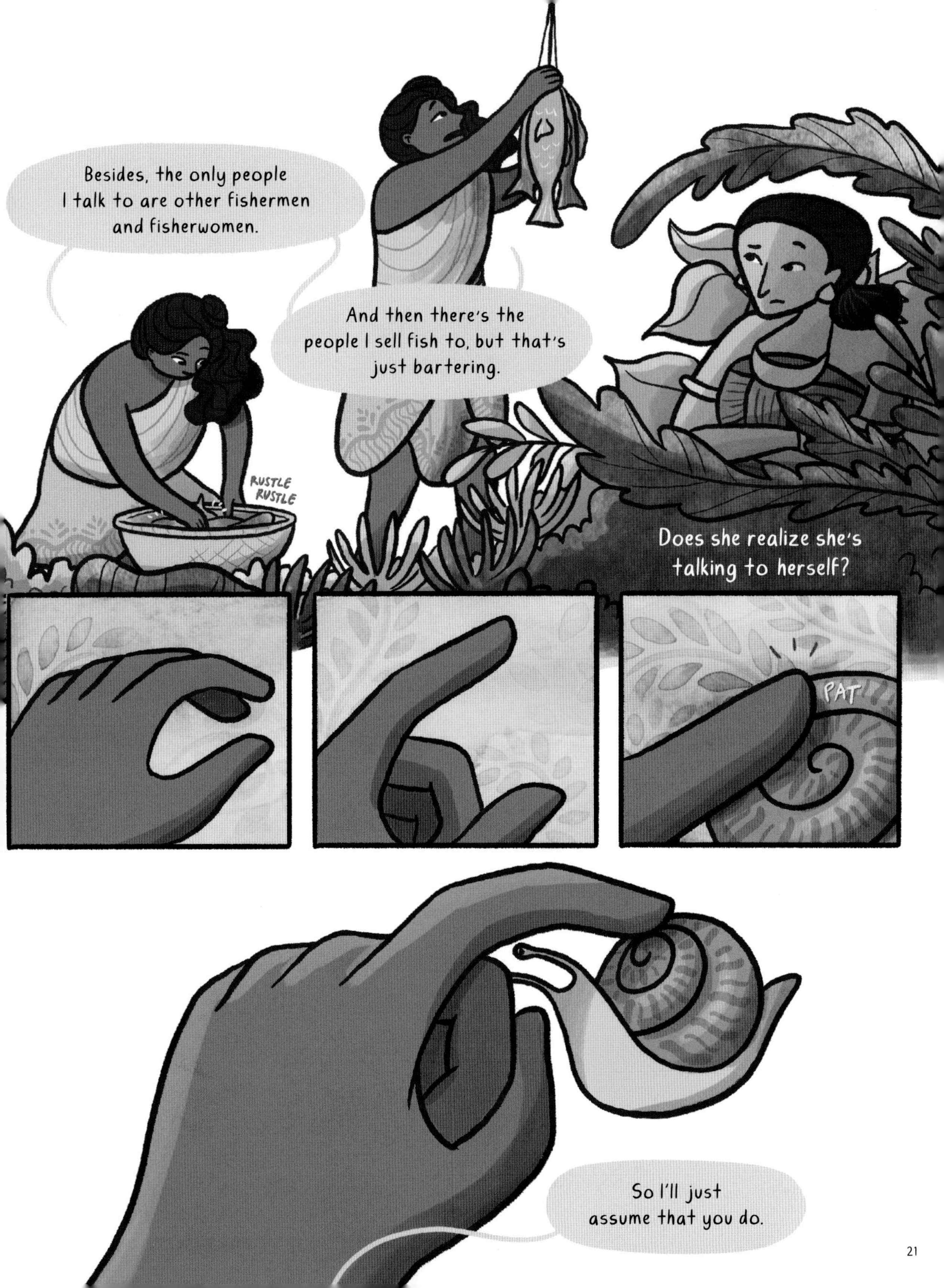
Besides, the only people I talk to are other fishermen and fisherwomen.
And then there's the people I sell fish to, but that's just bartering.
RUSTLE RUSTLE
Does she realize she's talking to herself?
PAT
So I'll just assume that you do.

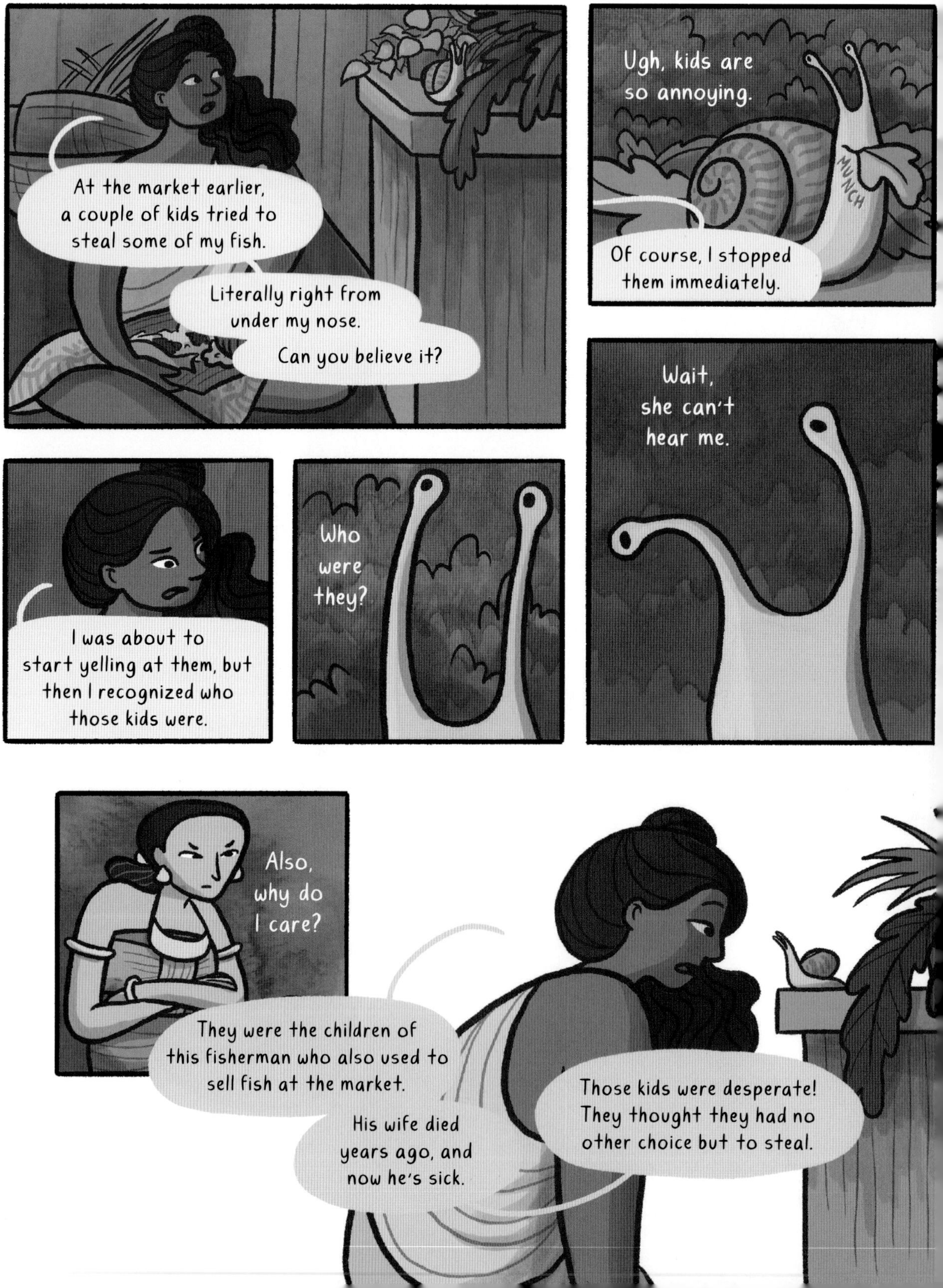
At the market earlier, a couple of kids tried to steal some of my fish.
Literally right from under my nose.
Can you believe it?
Ugh, kids are so annoying.
MUNCH
Of course, I stopped them immediately.
I was about to start yelling at them, but then I recognized who those kids were.
Who were they?
Wait, she can't hear me.
Also, why do I care?
They were the children of this fisherman who also used to sell fish at the market.
His wife died years ago, and now he's sick.
Those kids were desperate! They thought they had no other choice but to steal.

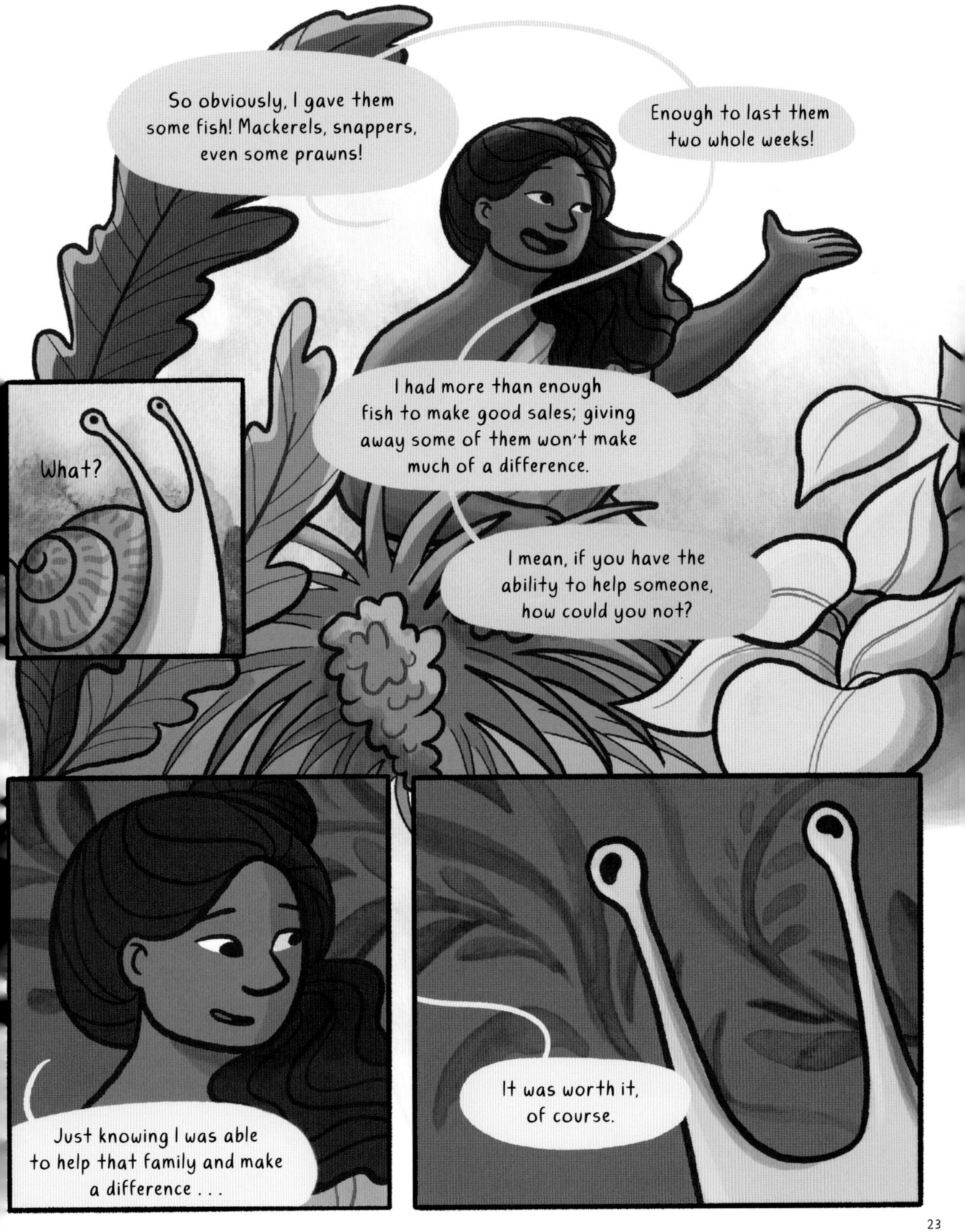
So obviously, I gave them some fish! Mackerels, snappers, even some prawns!
Enough to last them two whole weeks!
What?
I had more than enough fish to make good sales; giving away some of them won't make much of a difference.
I mean, if you have the ability to help someone, how could you not?
Just knowing I was able to help that family and make a difference . . .
It was worth it, of course.

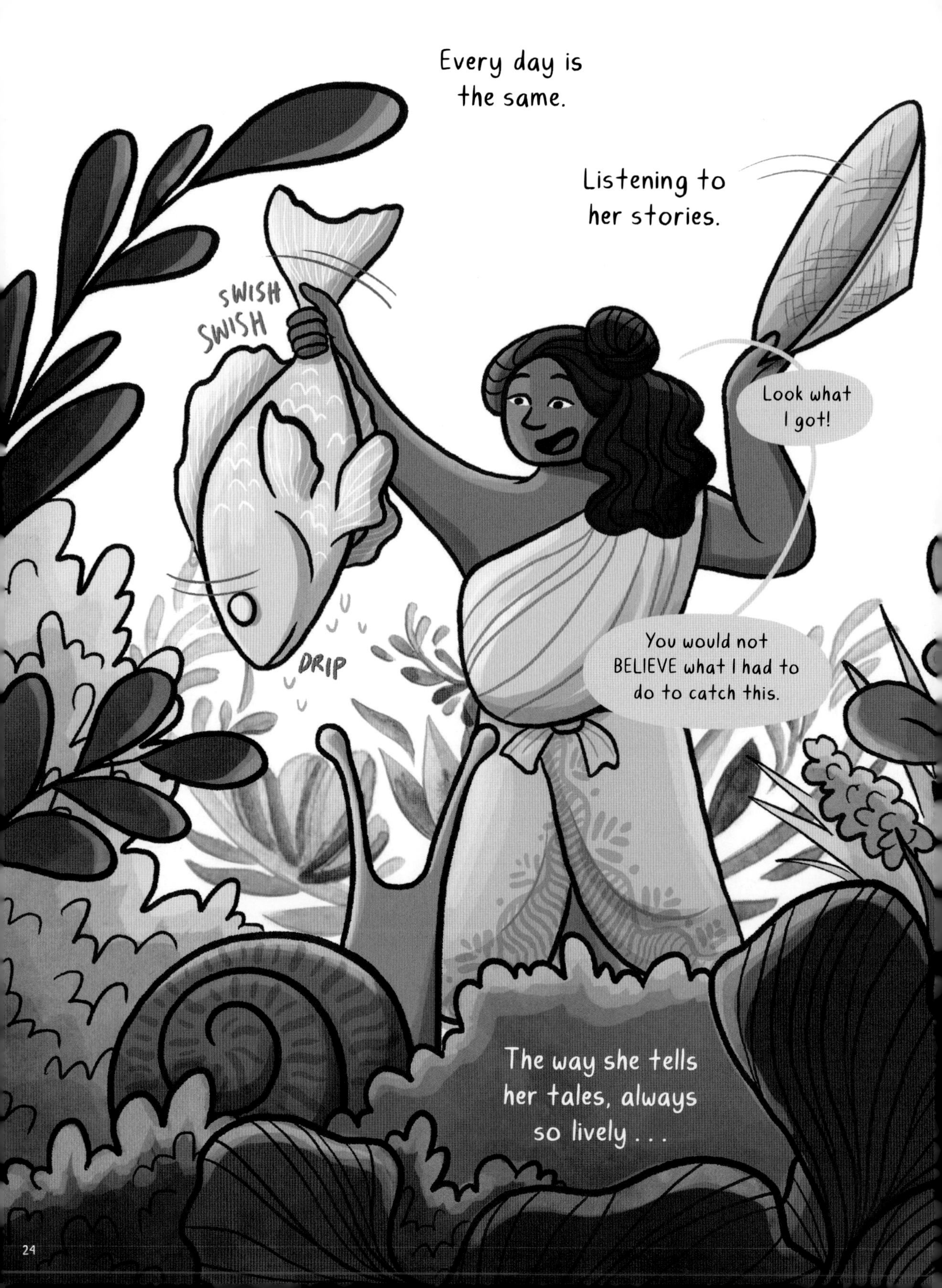
Every day is the same.
Listening to her stories.
SWISH SWISH
Look what I got!
DRIP
You would not BELIEVE what I had to do to catch this.
The way she tells her tales, always so lively . . .

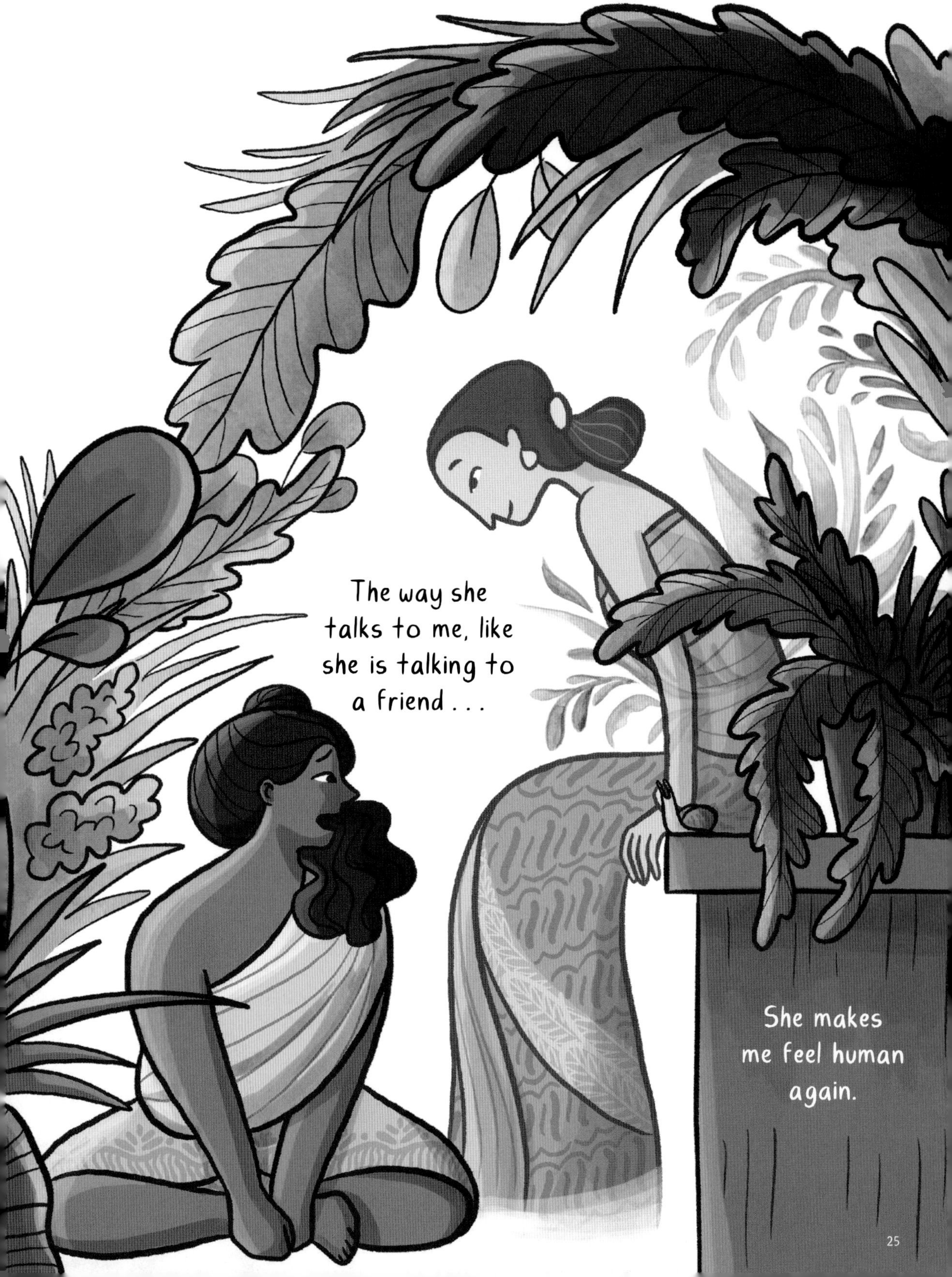
The way she talks to me, like she is talking to a friend . . .
She makes me feel human again.

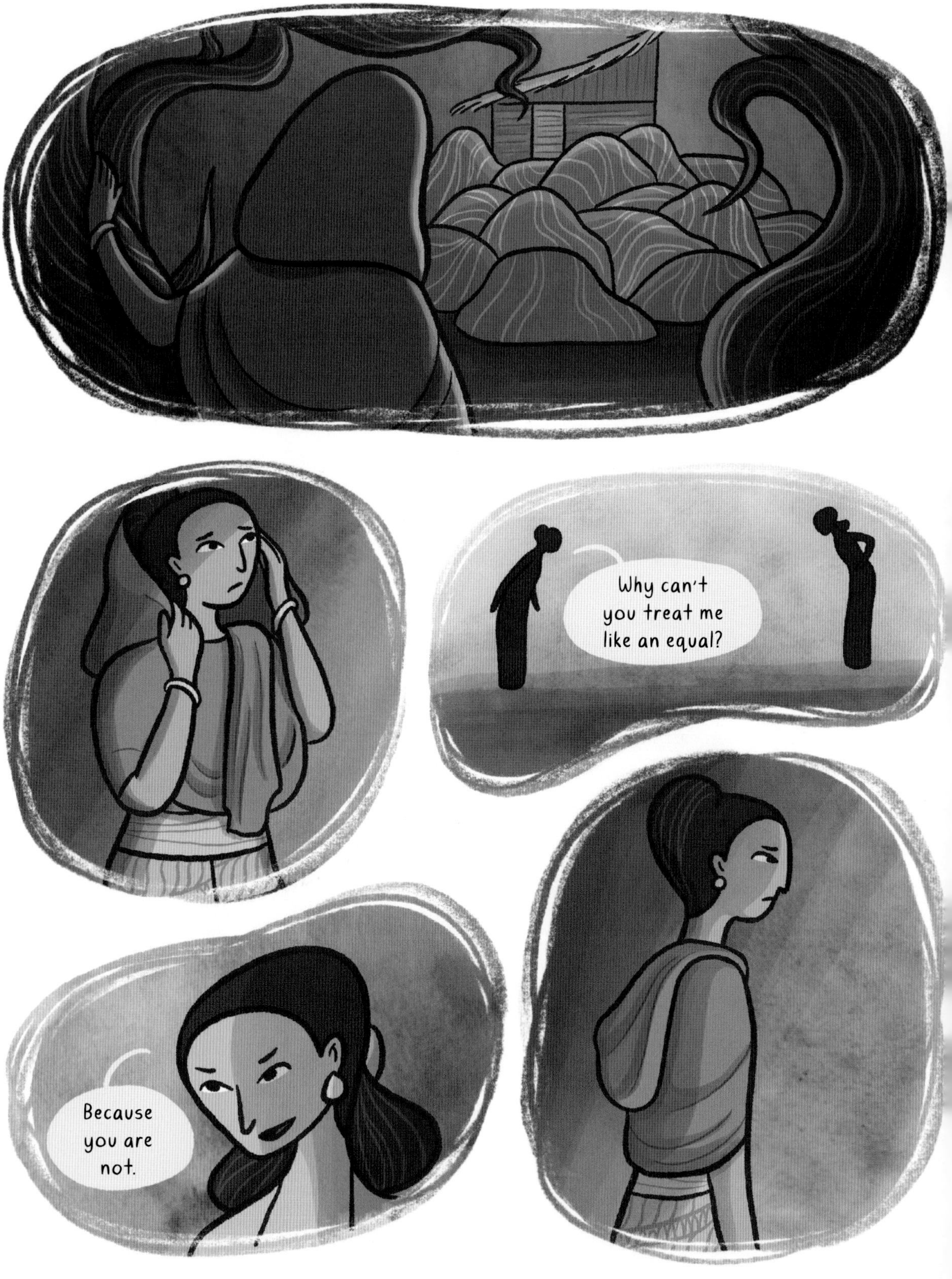
Why can't you treat me like an equal?
Because you are not.

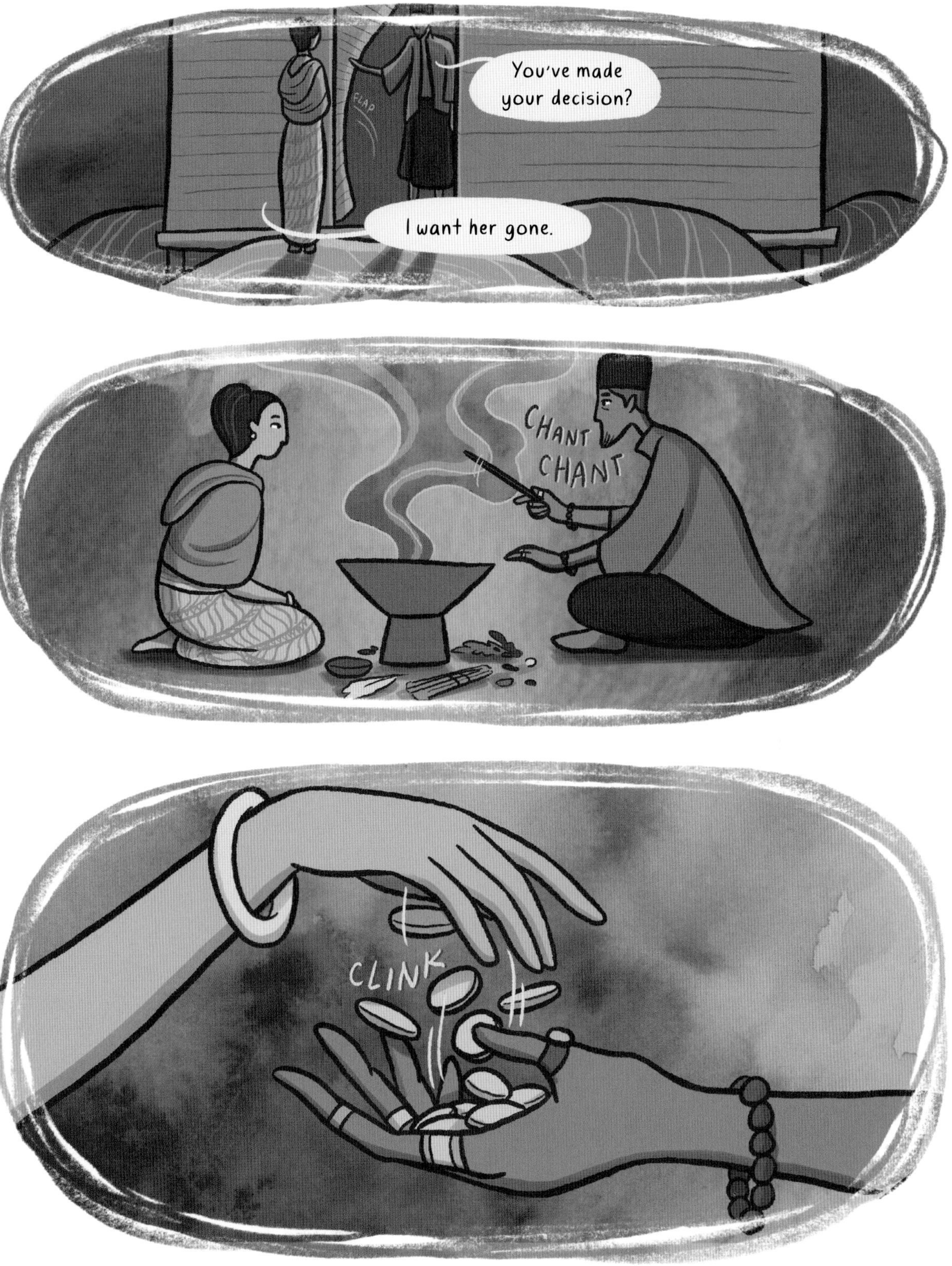
You've made your decision?
FLAP
I want her gone.
CHANT
CHANT
CLINK

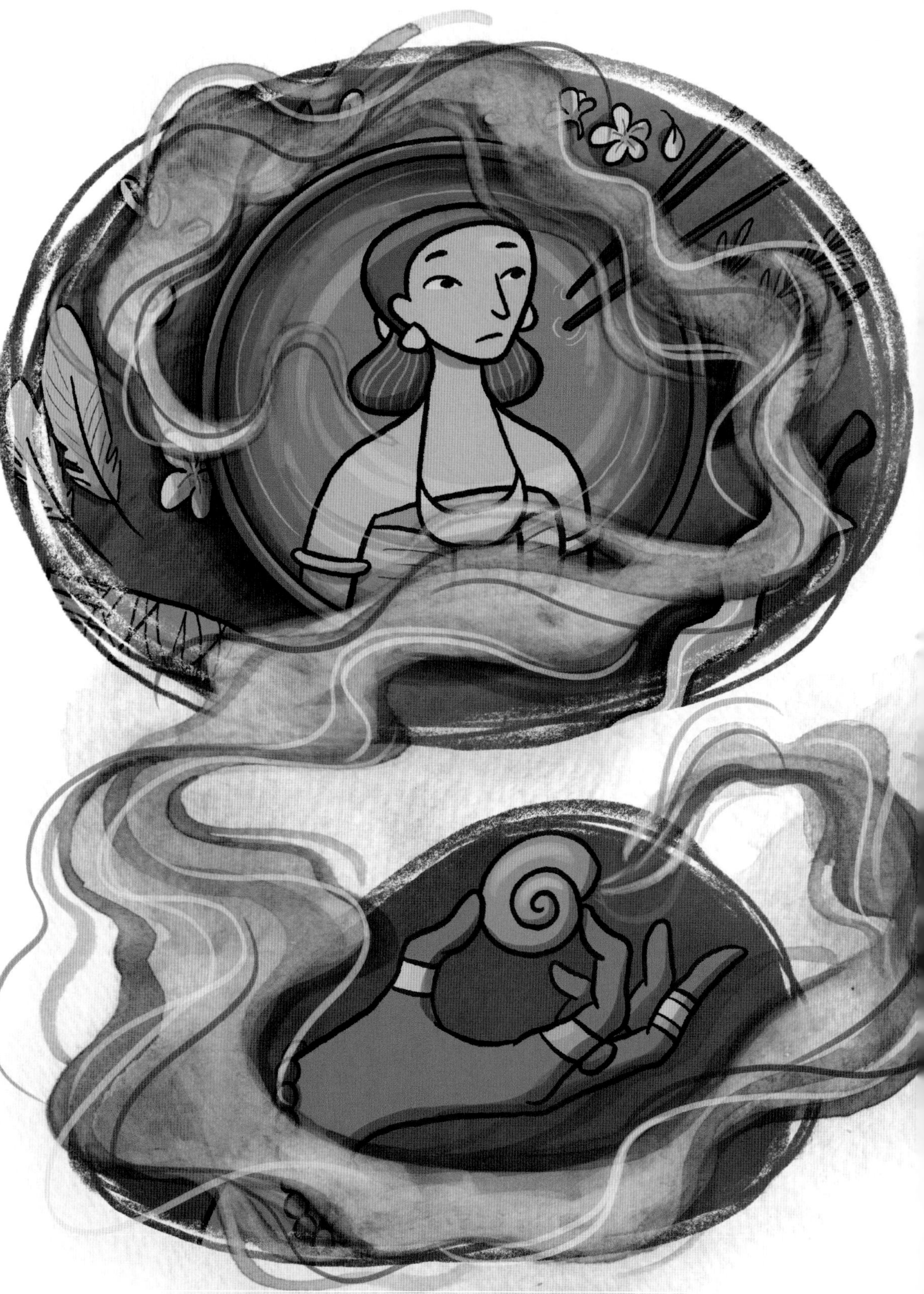

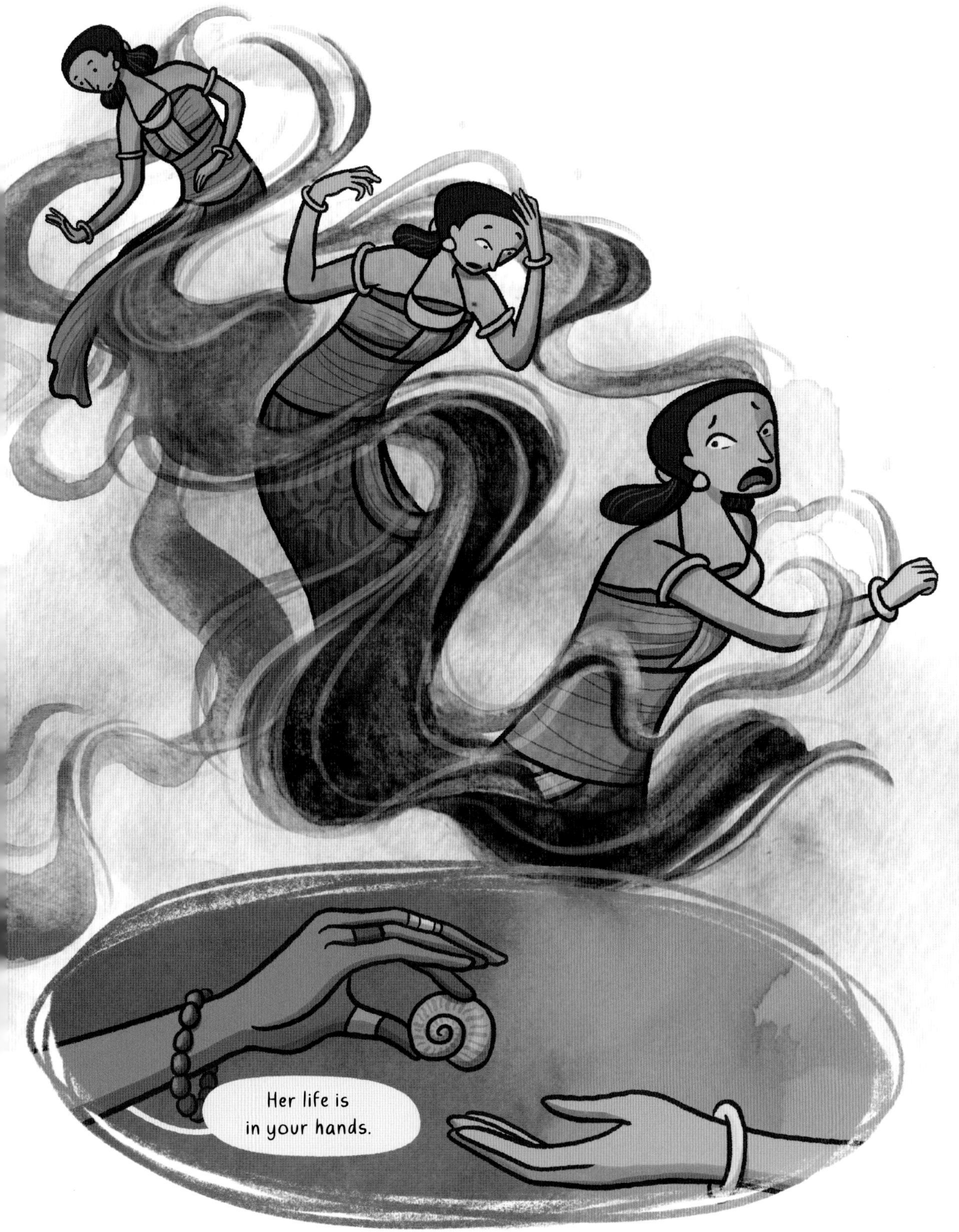
Her life is in your hands.

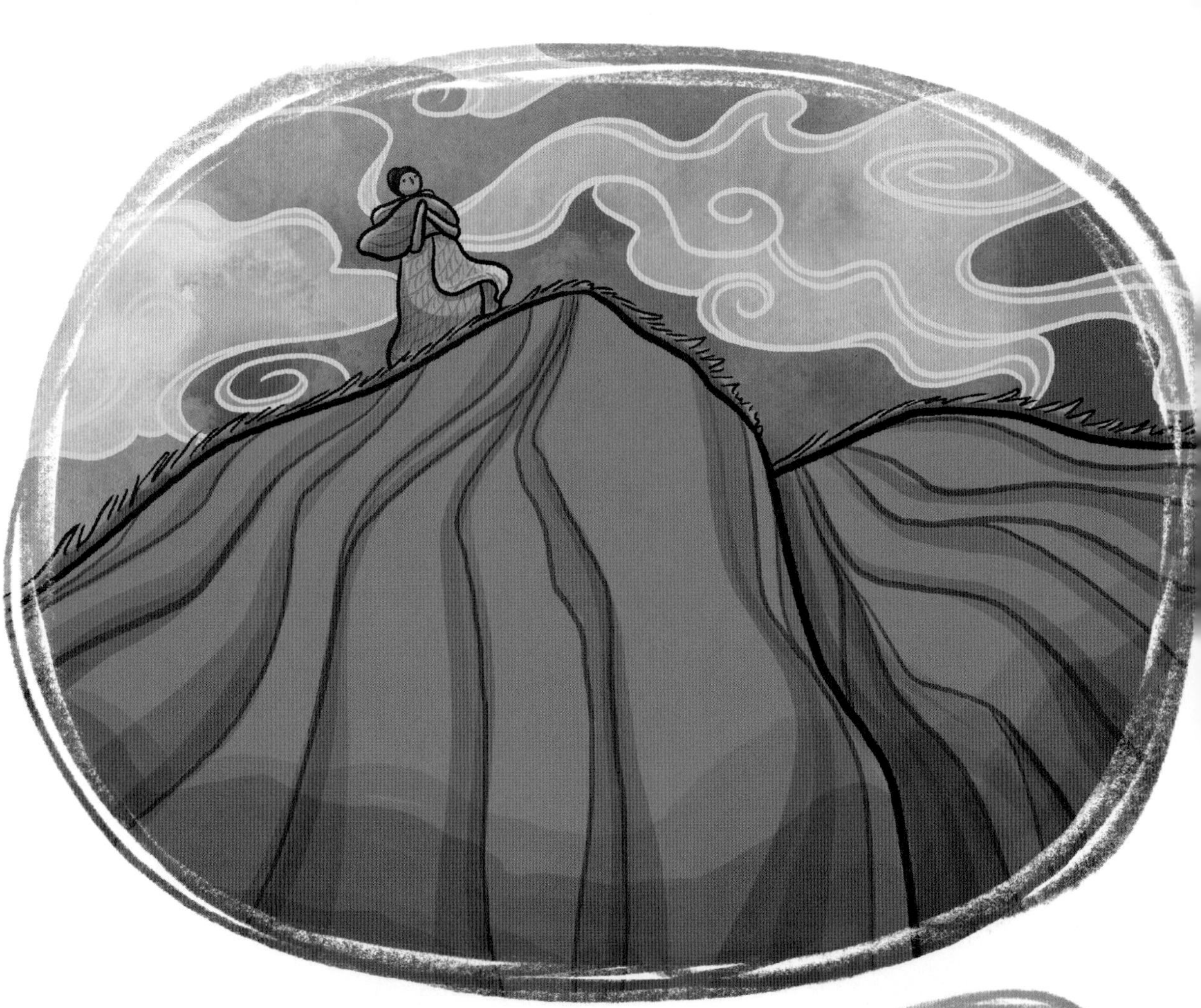

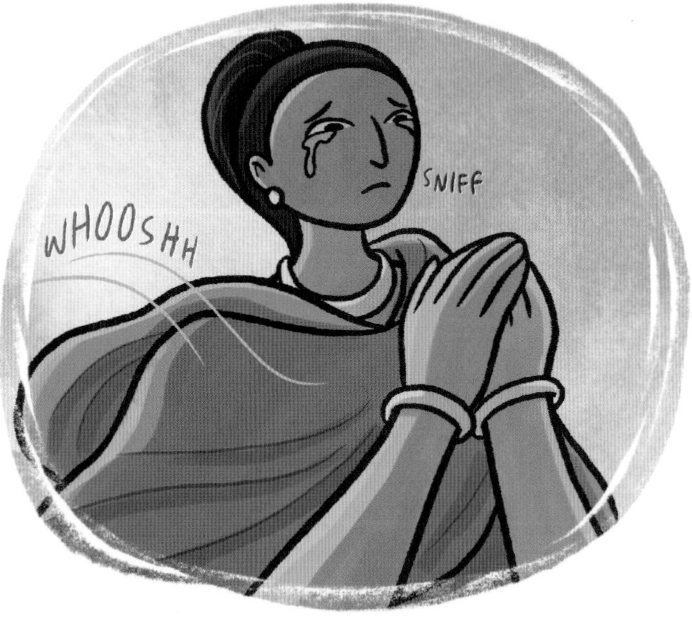
SNIFF
WHOOSHH

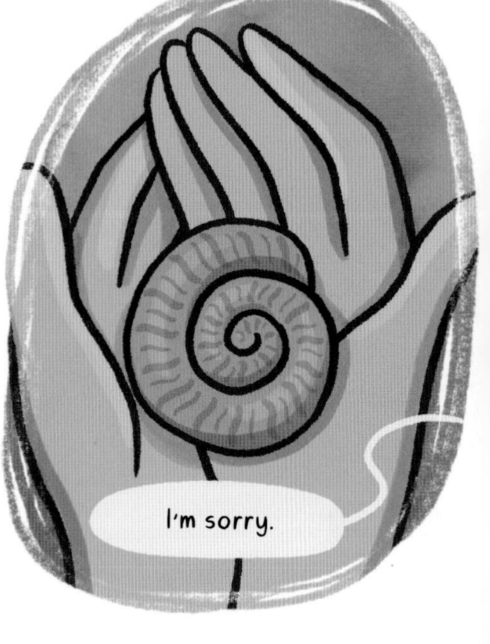
I'm sorry.

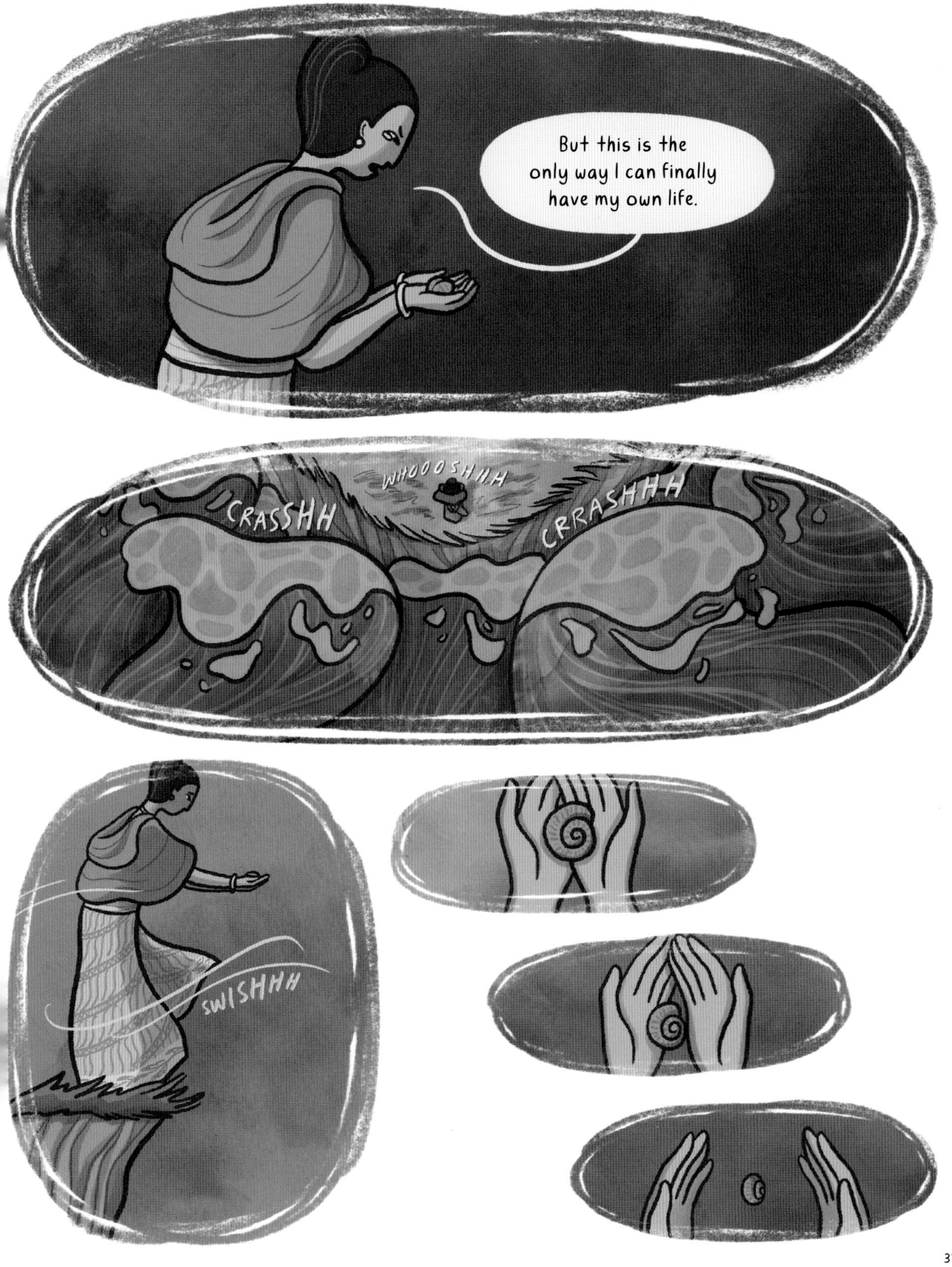
But this is the only way I can finally have my own life.
WHOOOSHHH
CRASSHH
CRRASHHH
SWISHHH

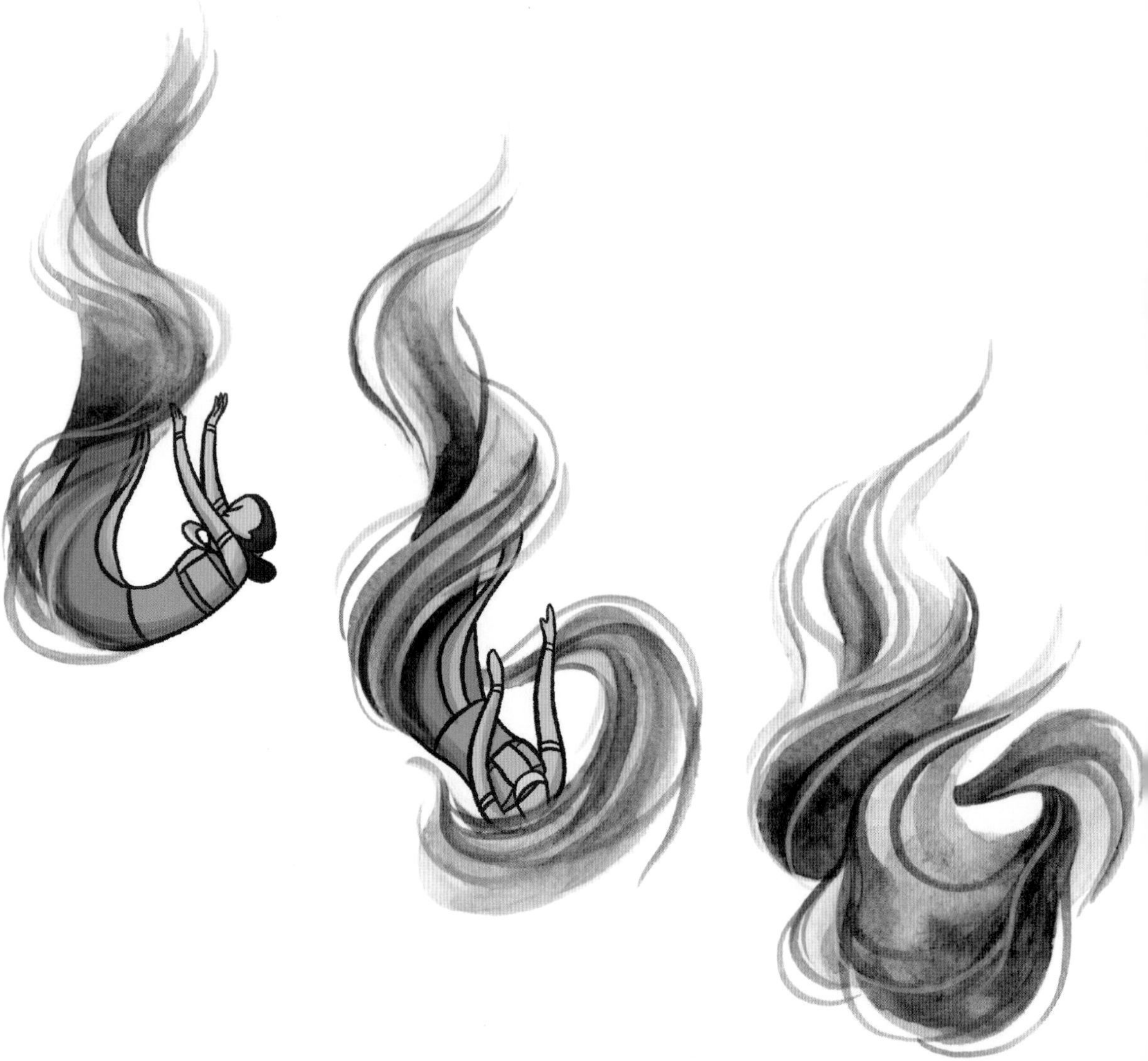

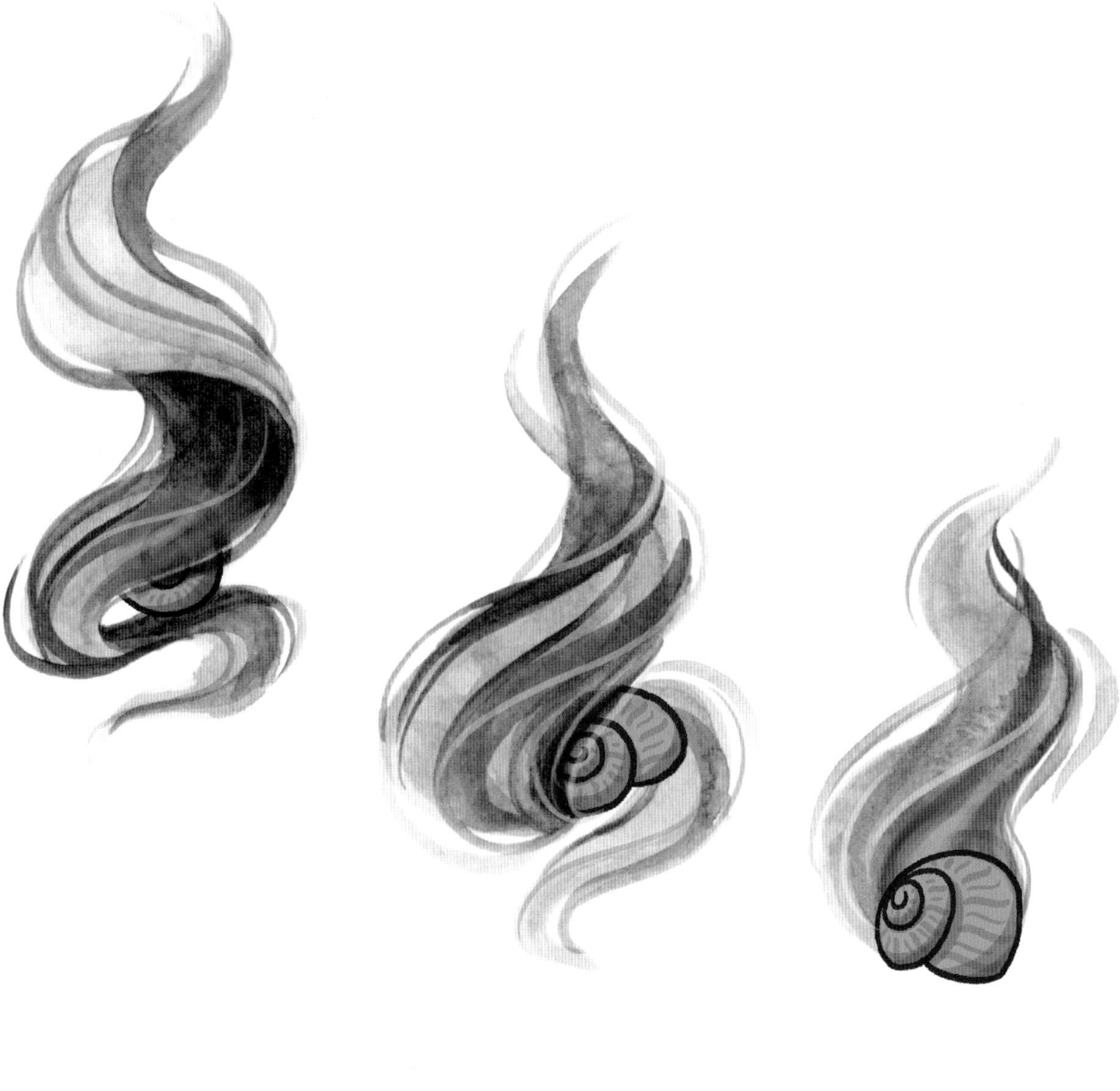

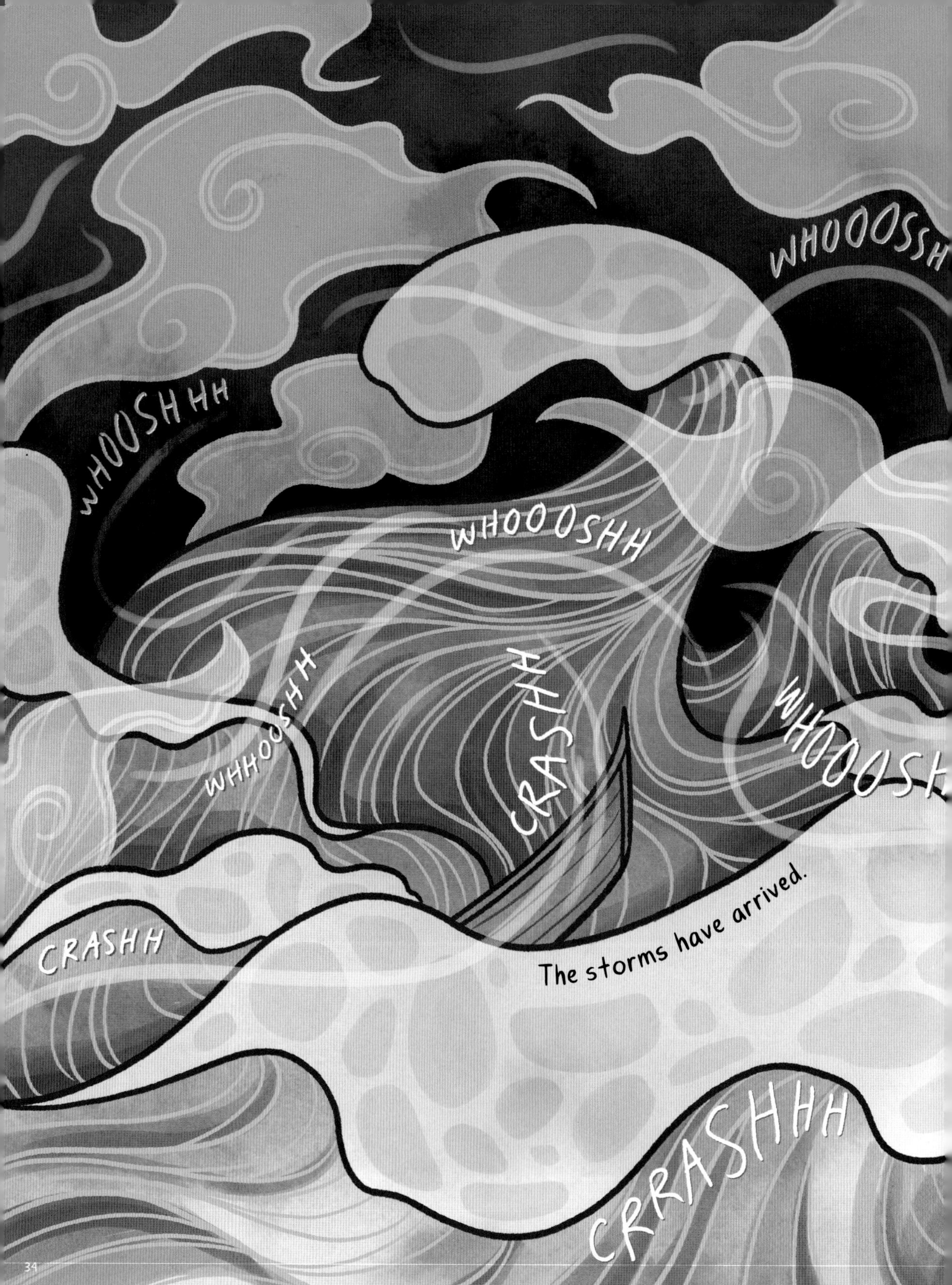
WHOOOSSH
WHOOSHHH
WHOOOOSHH
WHHOOSHH
CRASHH
WHOOOOS
CRASHH
The storms have arrived.
CRRASHHH

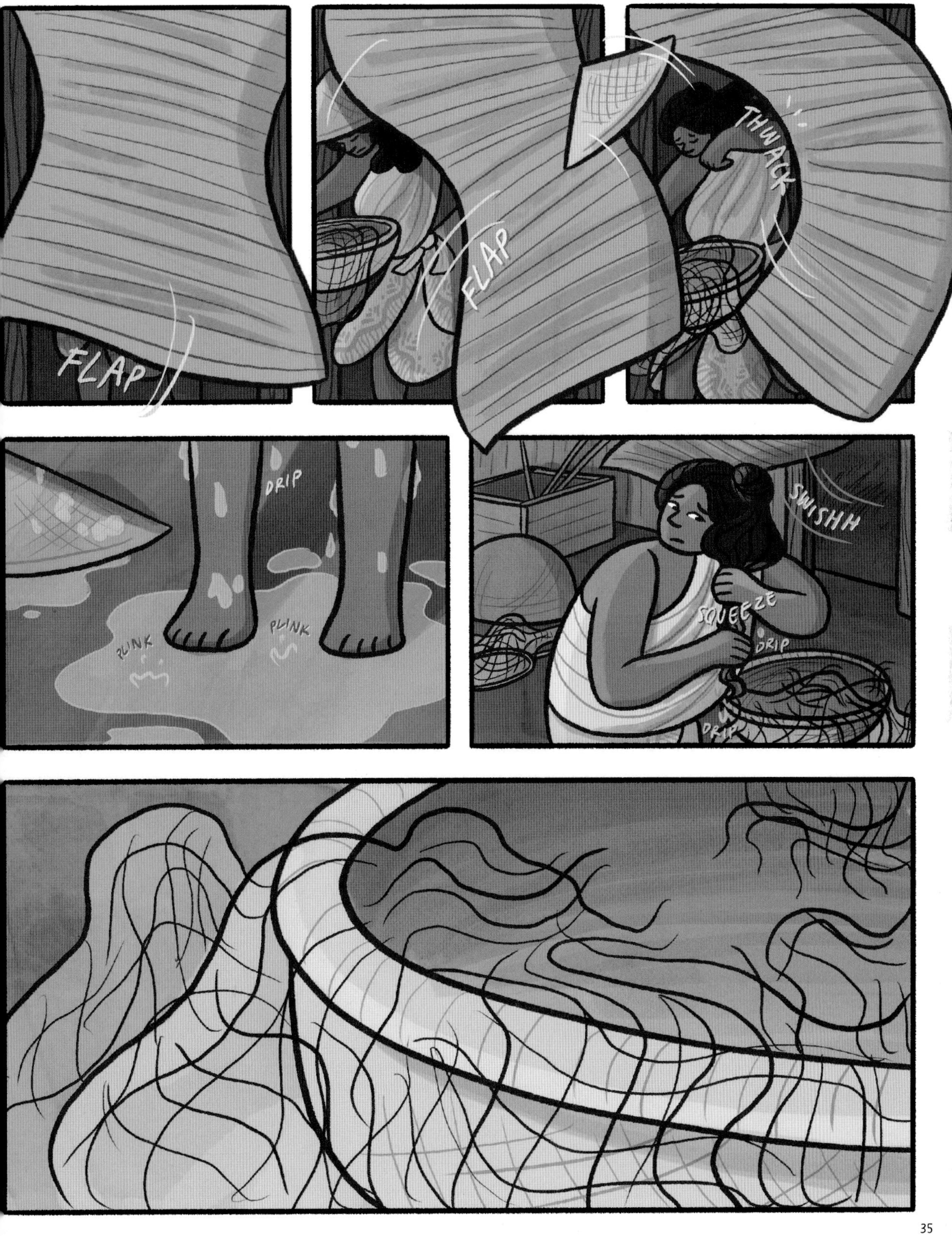
FLAP
FLAP
THWACK
DRIP
PLINK
PLINK
SWISHH
SQUEEZE
DRIP
DRIP

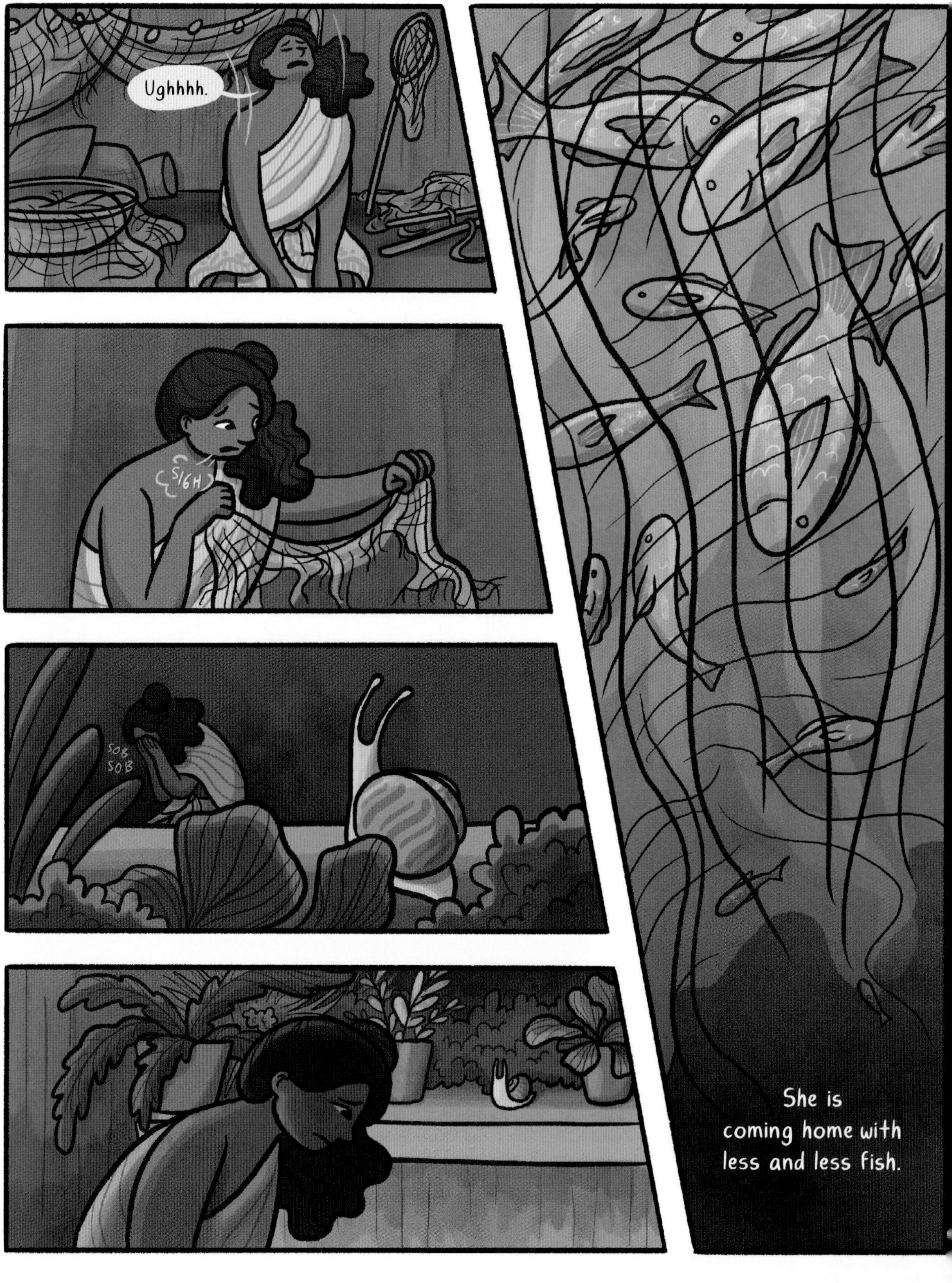
Ughhhh.
SIGH
SOB SOB
She is coming home with less and less fish.

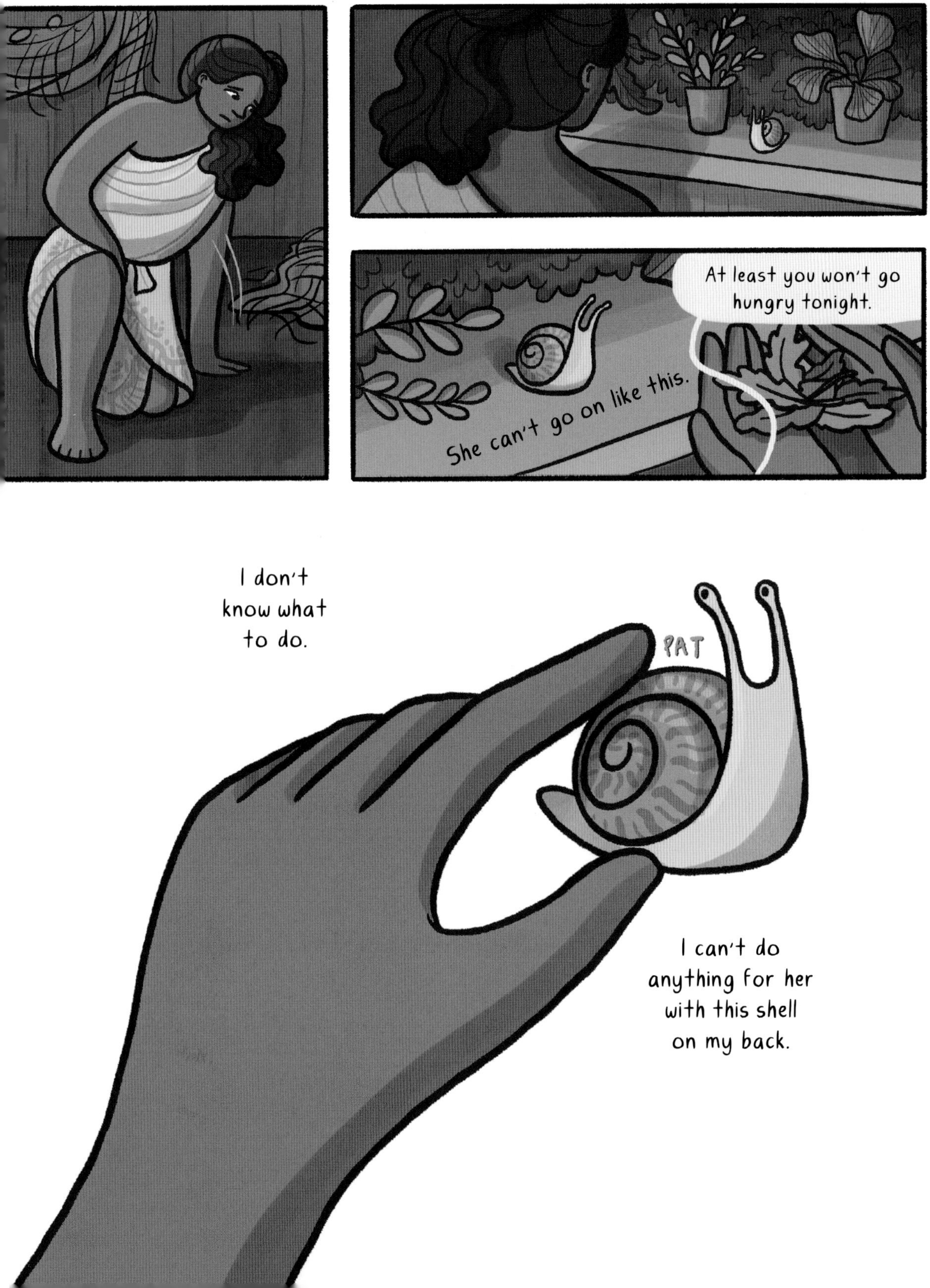
At least you won't go hungry tonight.
She can't go on like this.
I don't know what to do.
PAT
I can't do anything for her with this shell on my back.

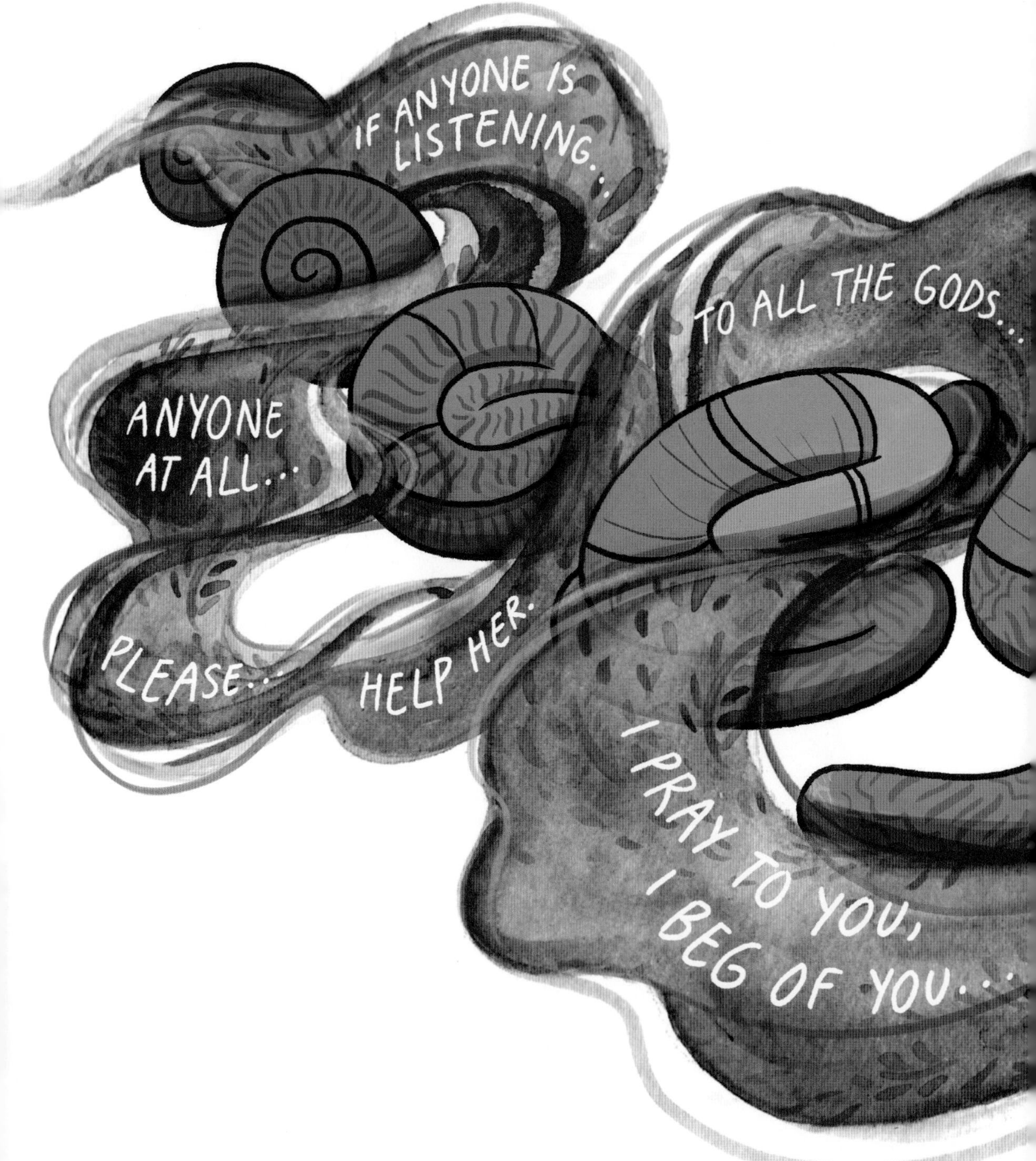
IF ANYONE IS LISTENING...
ANYONE AT ALL...
TO ALL THE GODS...
PLEASE...
HELP HER.
I PRAY TO YOU, I BEG OF YOU...

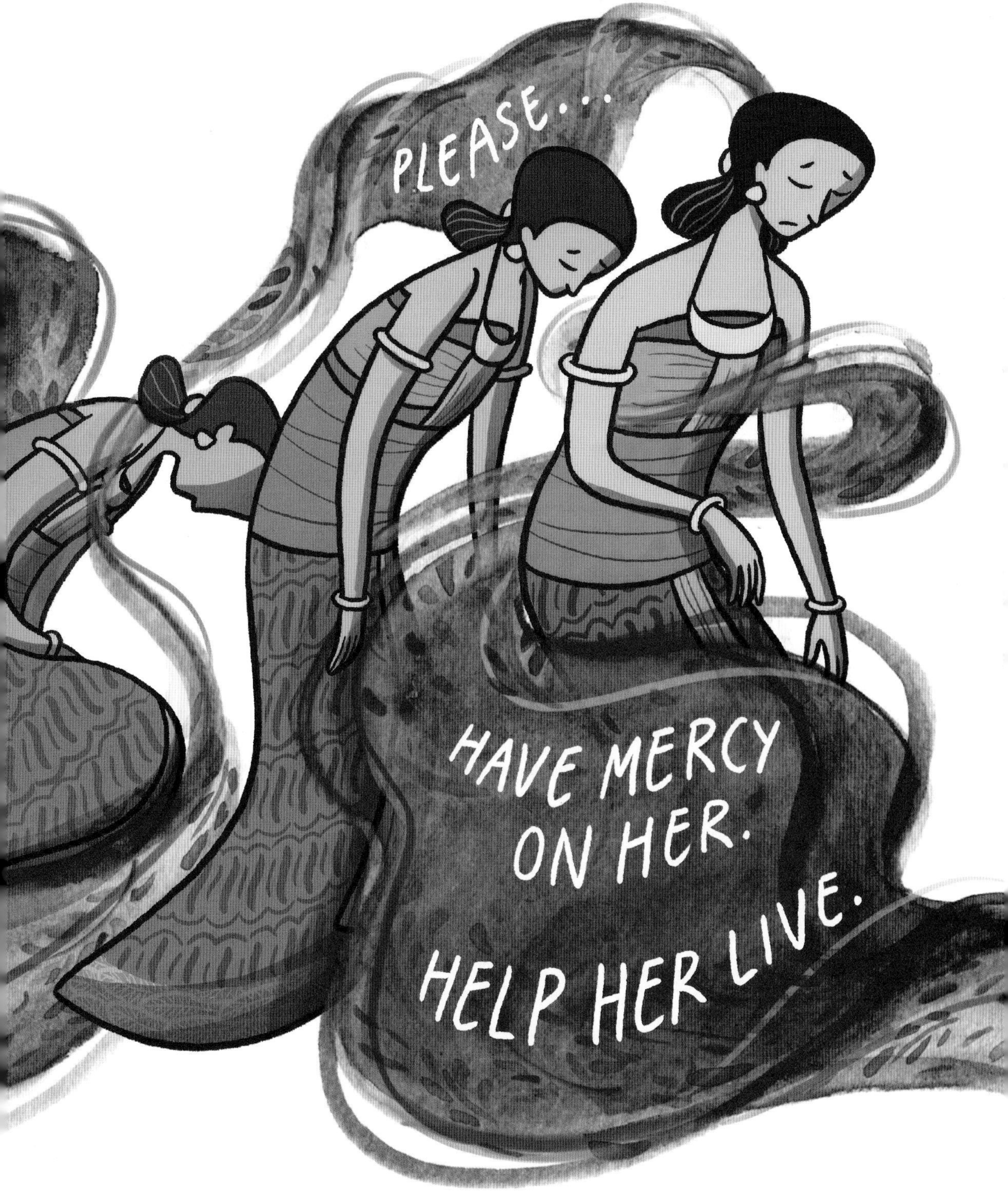
PLEASE...
HAVE MERCY ON HER.
HELP HER LIVE.

The gods . . .

THUMP

. . . they listened.

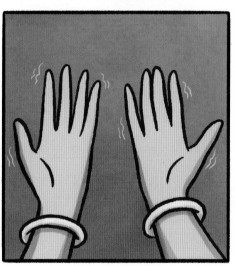

SOB

SOB
SOB

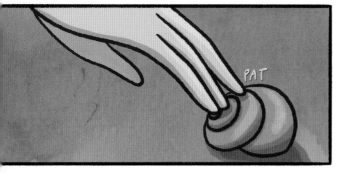

PAT

GASP

Fish Lady!

I have to help her.

But how?!

I don't know how to do anything!

FLAP

FLAP

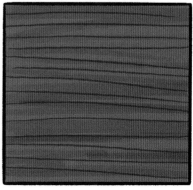

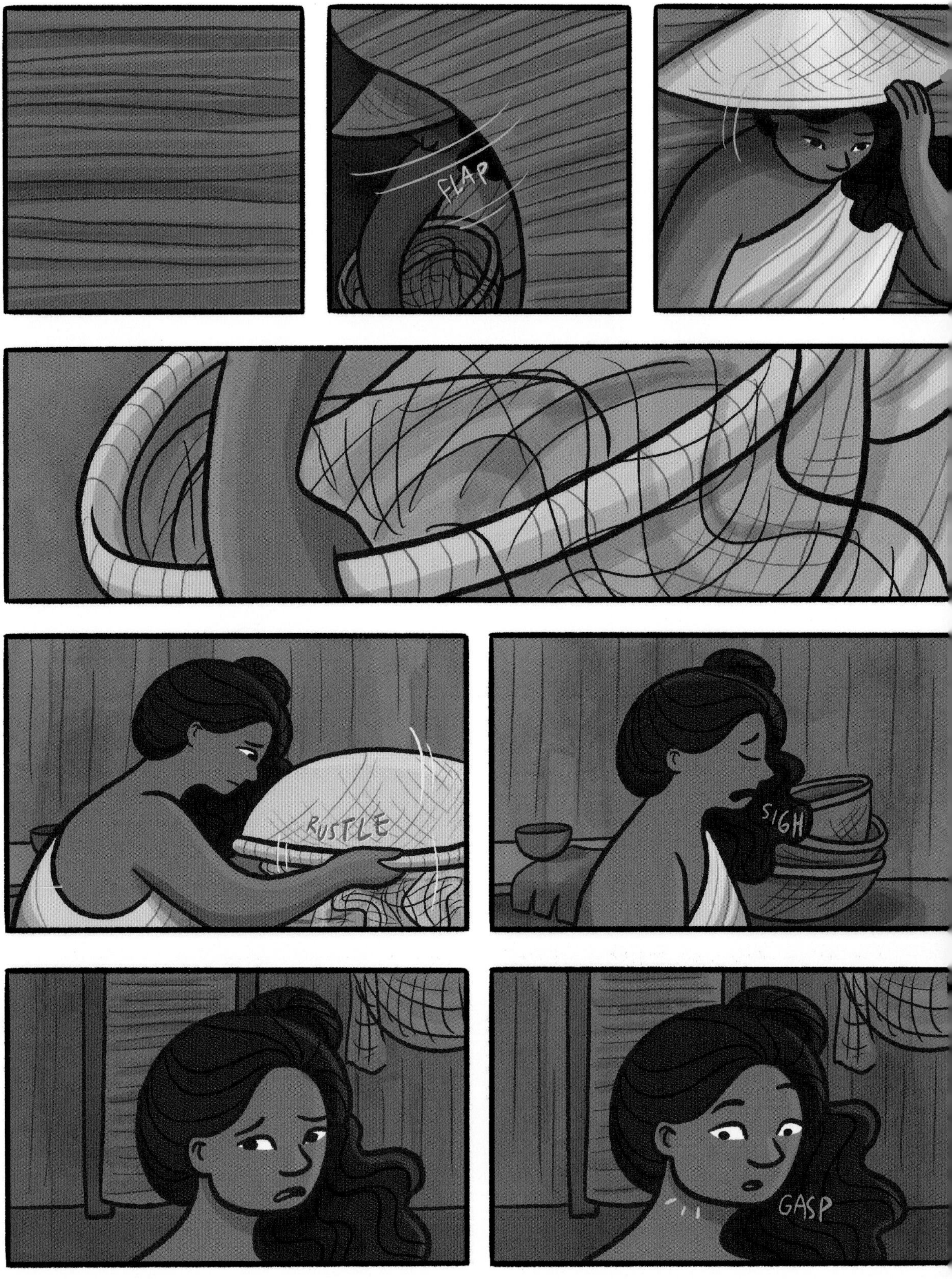
FLAP
RUSTLE
SIGH
GASP

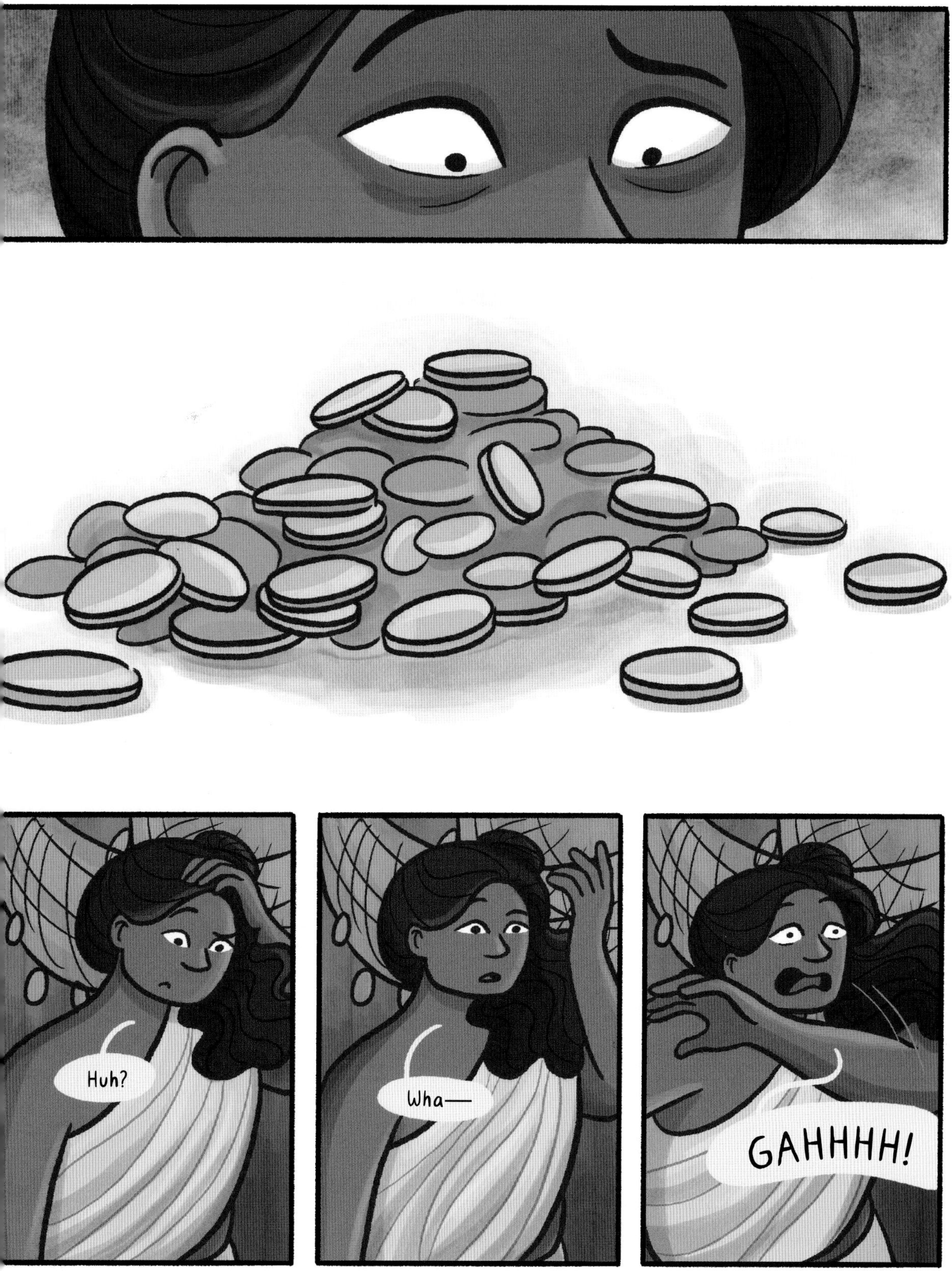
Huh?
Wha—
GAHHHH!

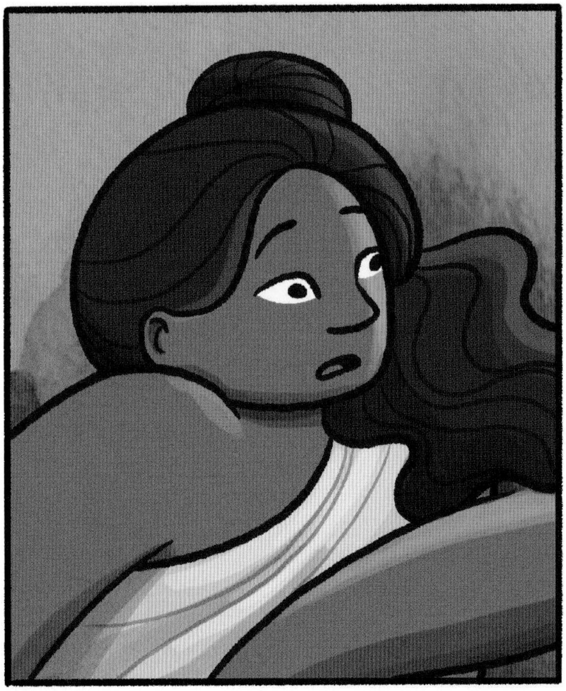

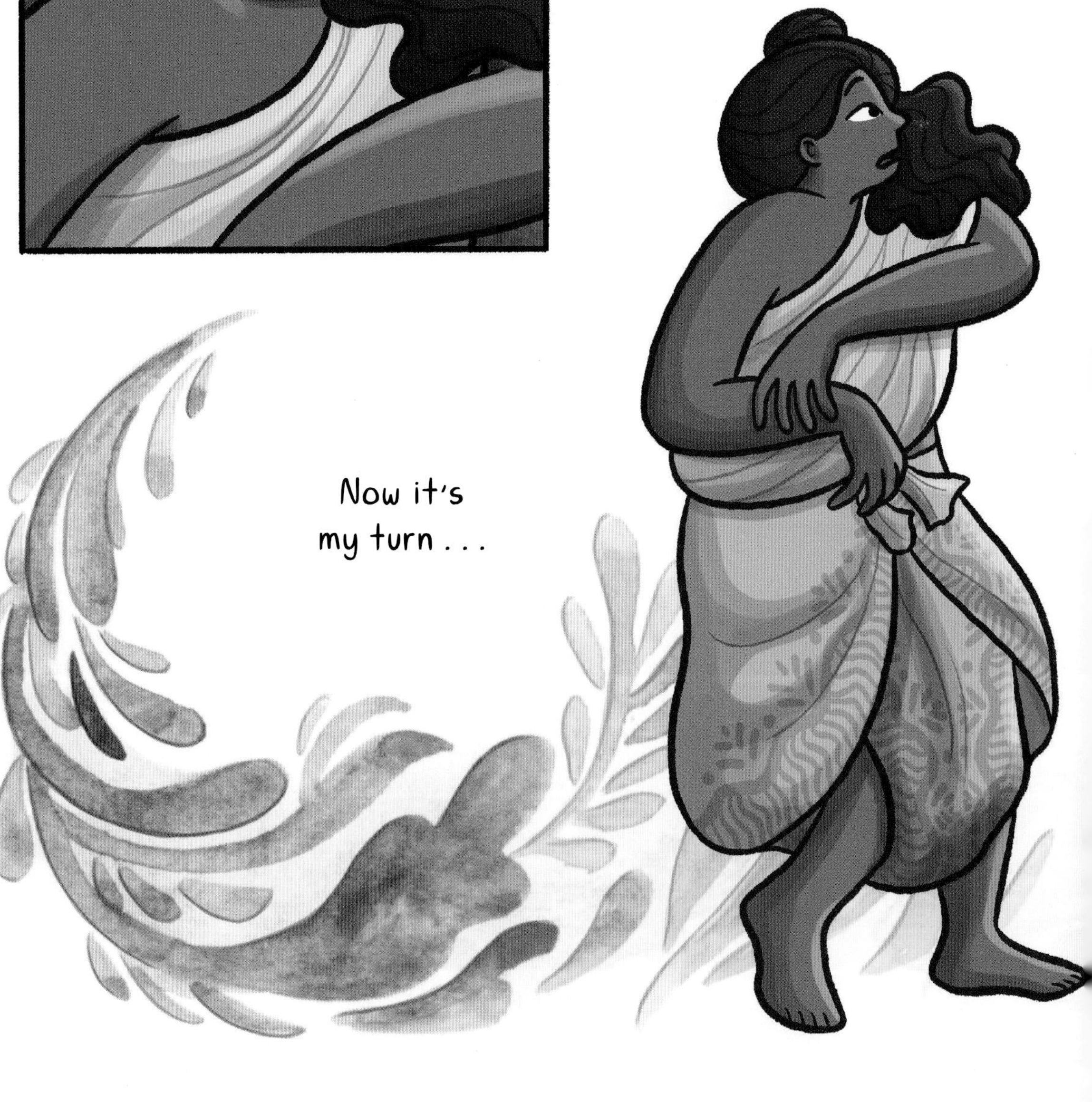
Now it's
my turn . . .

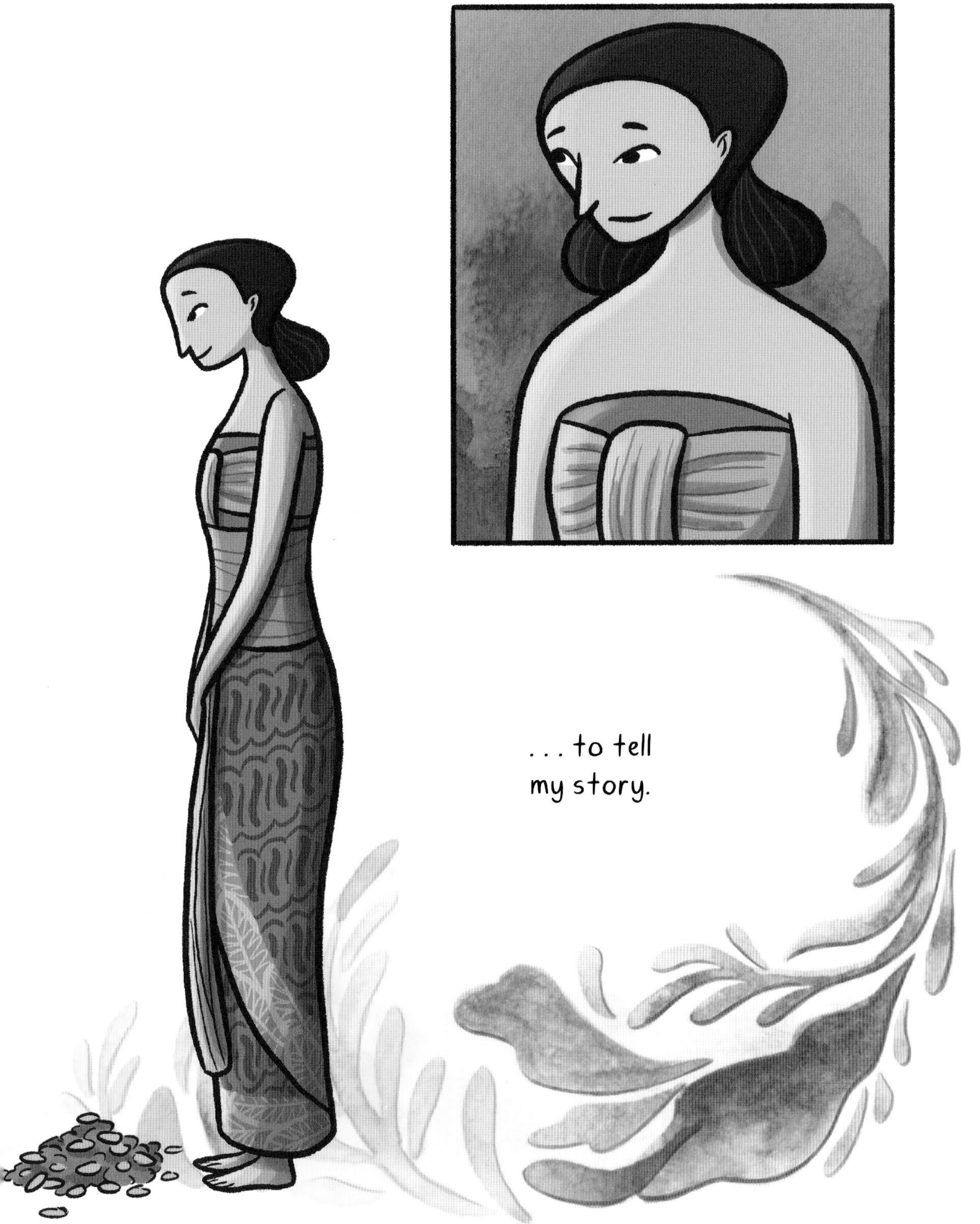
. . . to tell my story.

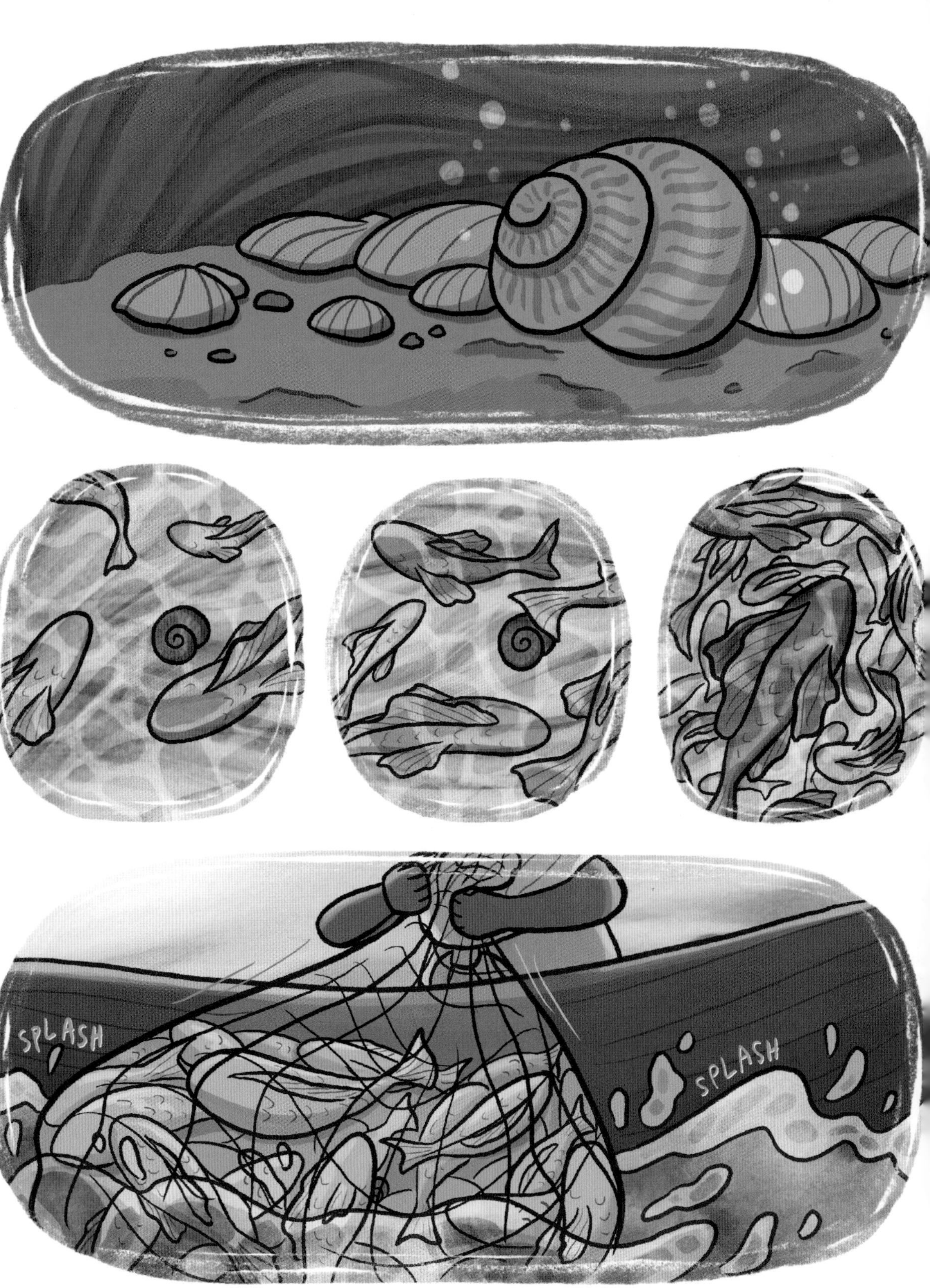
SPLASH
SPLASH

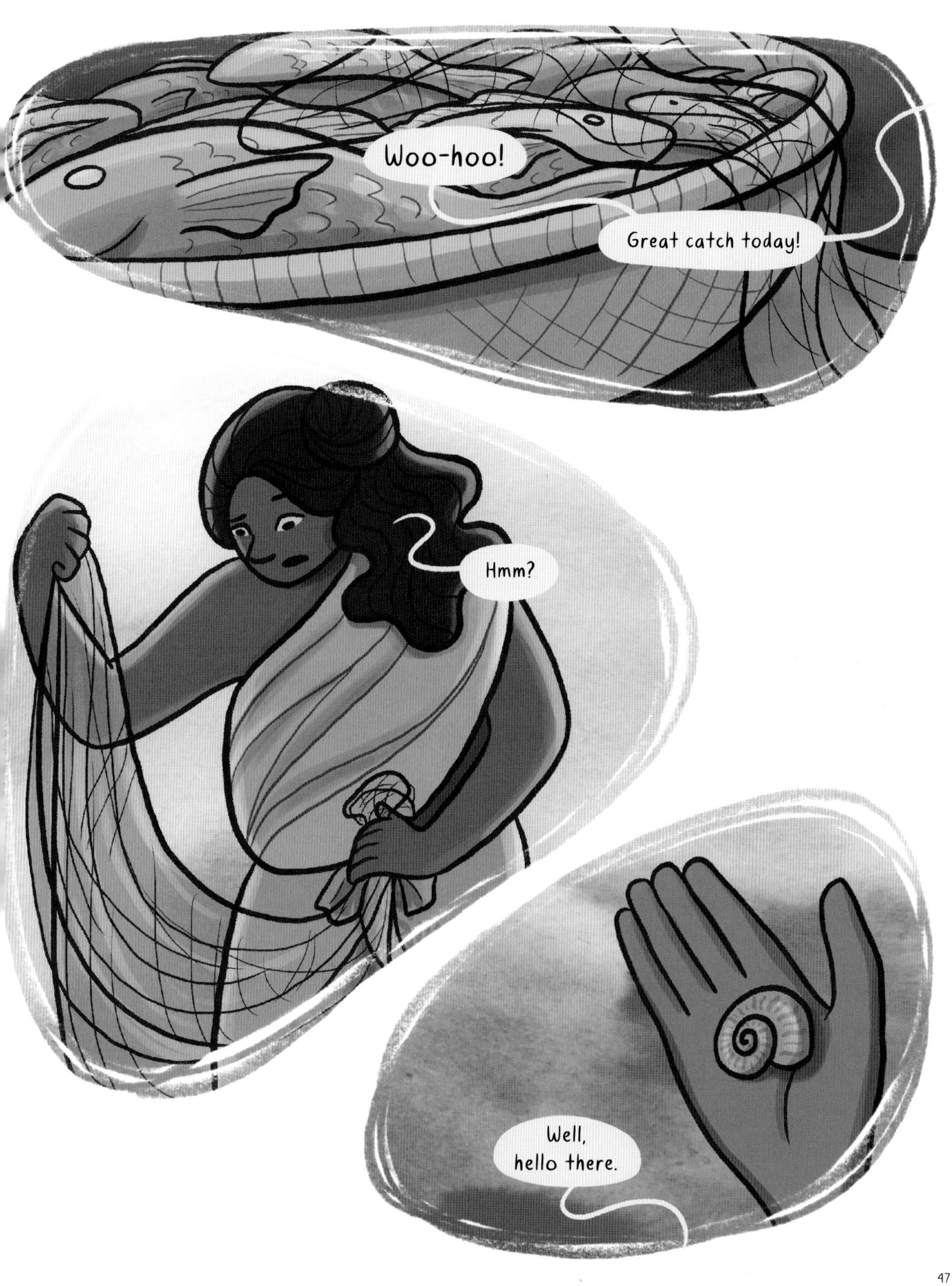
Woo-hoo!
Great catch today!
Hmm?
Well, hello there.

Hello.

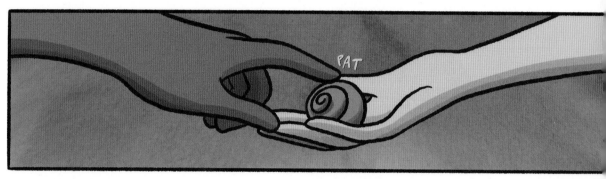

PAT

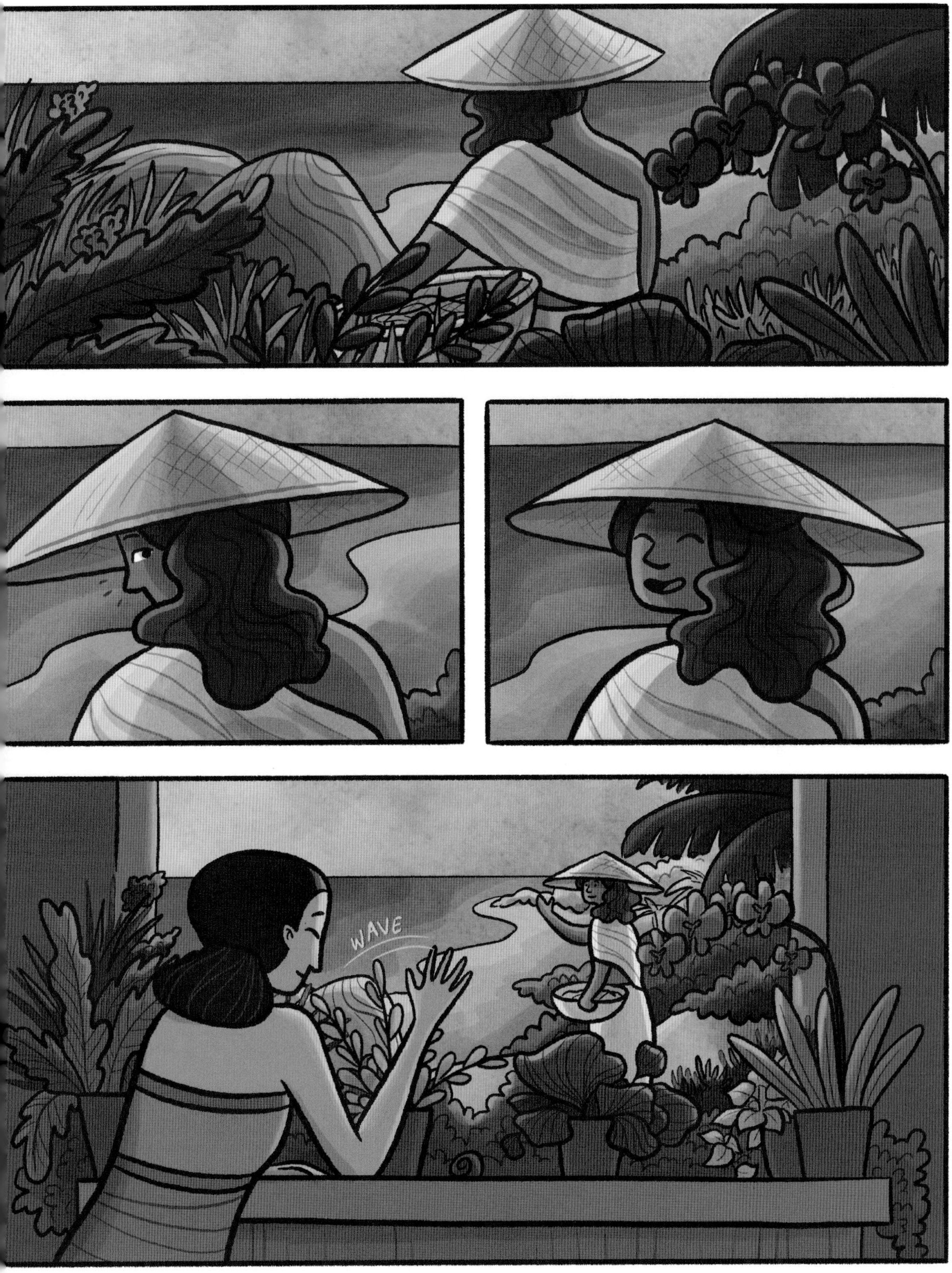
WAVE

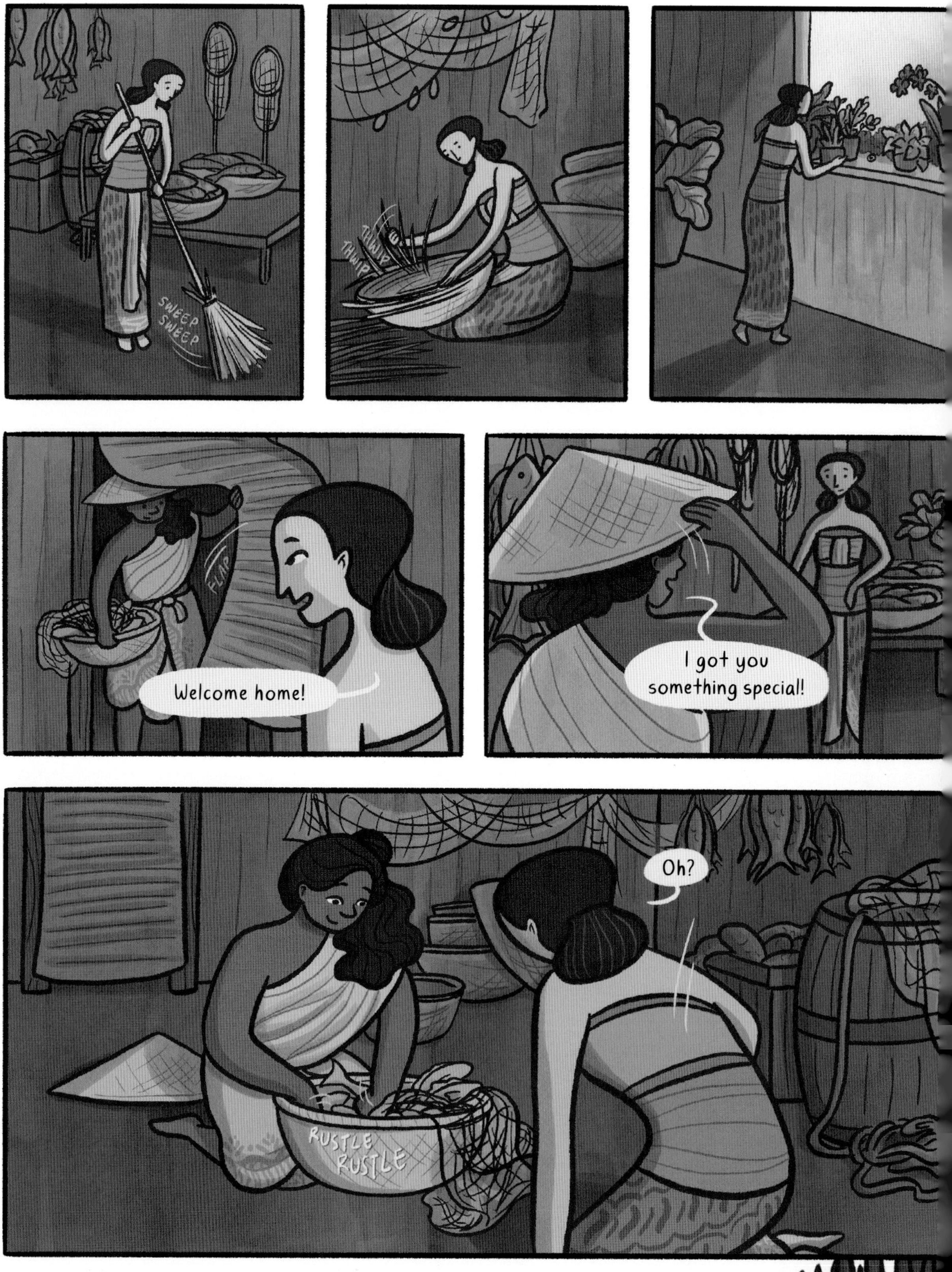
SWEEP
SWEEP
THWIP
THWIP
FLAP
Welcome home!
I got you something special!
Oh?
RUSTLE
RUSTLE

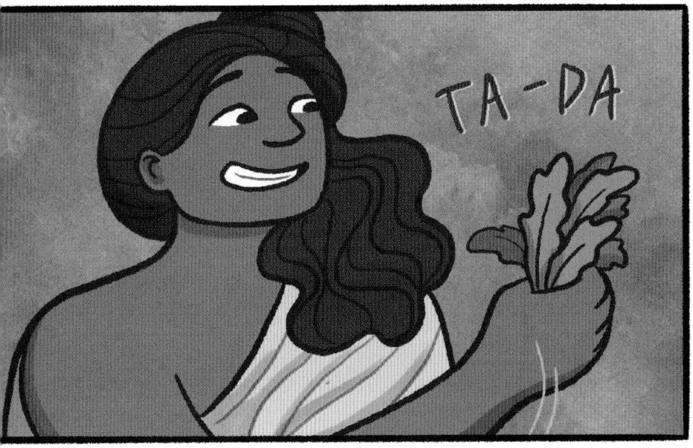
TA-DA

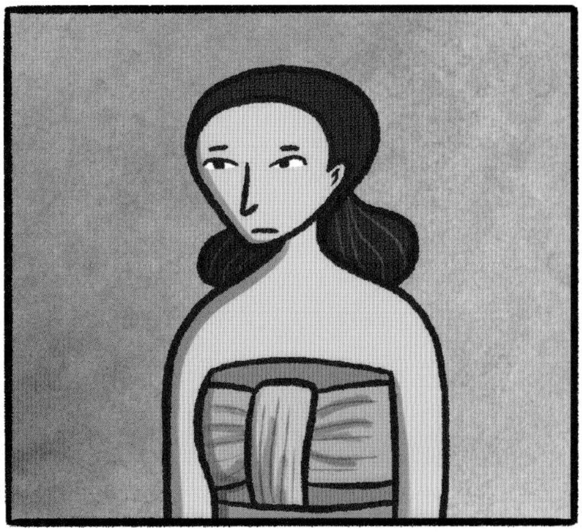

The gods were listening this whole time.

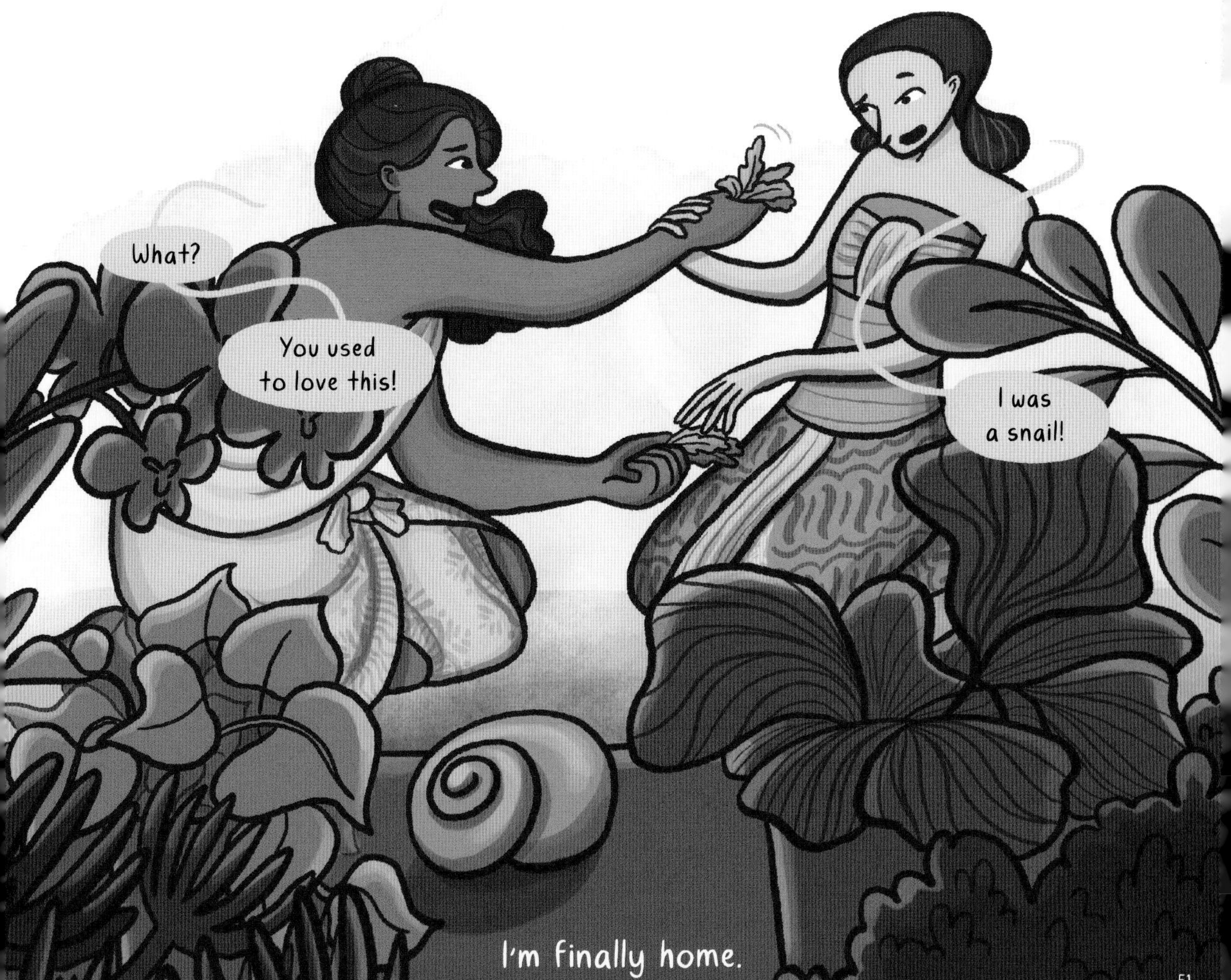
What?
You used to love this!
I was a snail!
I'm finally home.

Bawang Merah

Bawang Putih

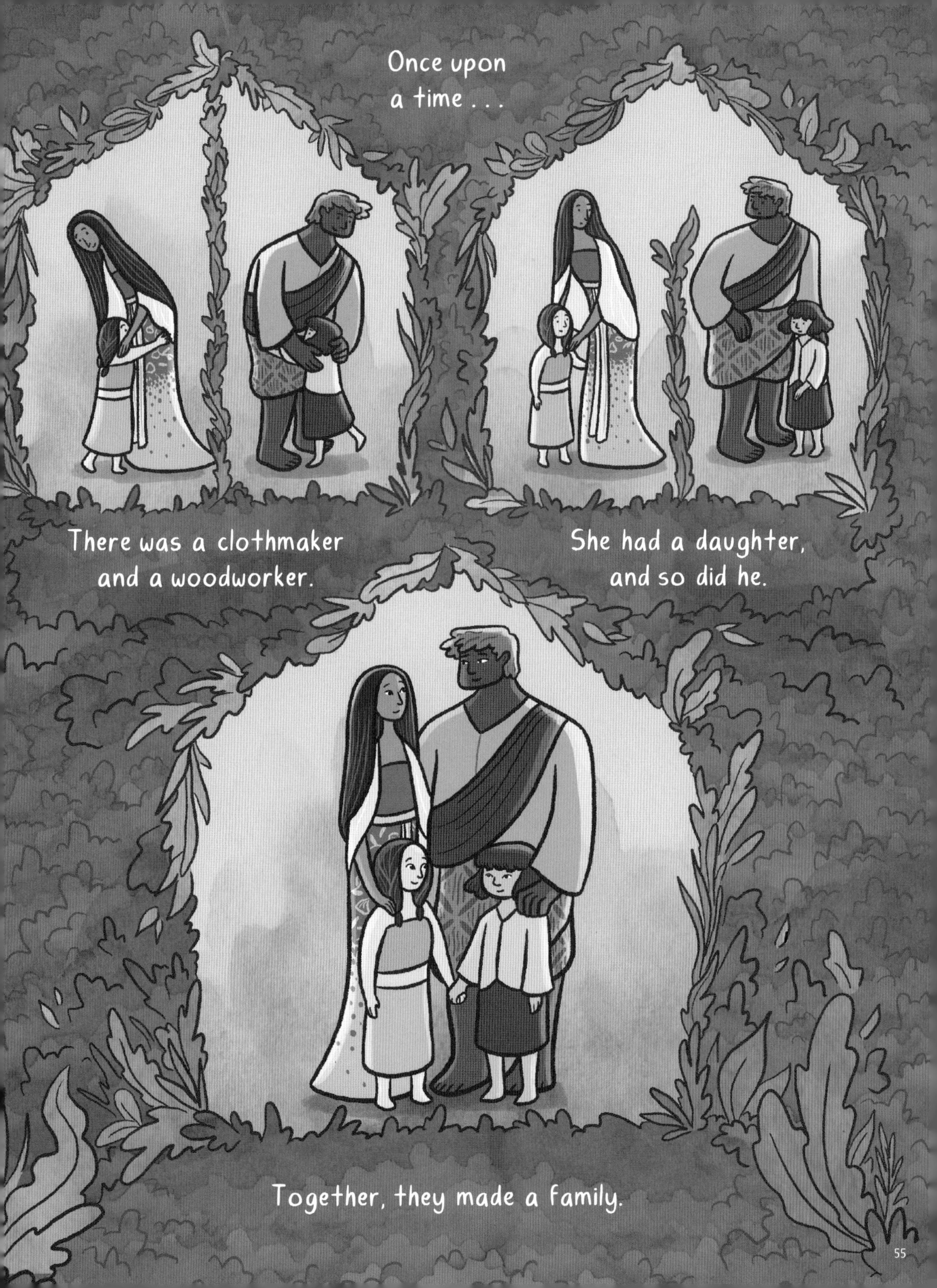
Once upon a time . . .
There was a clothmaker and a woodworker.
She had a daughter, and so did he.
Together, they made a family.

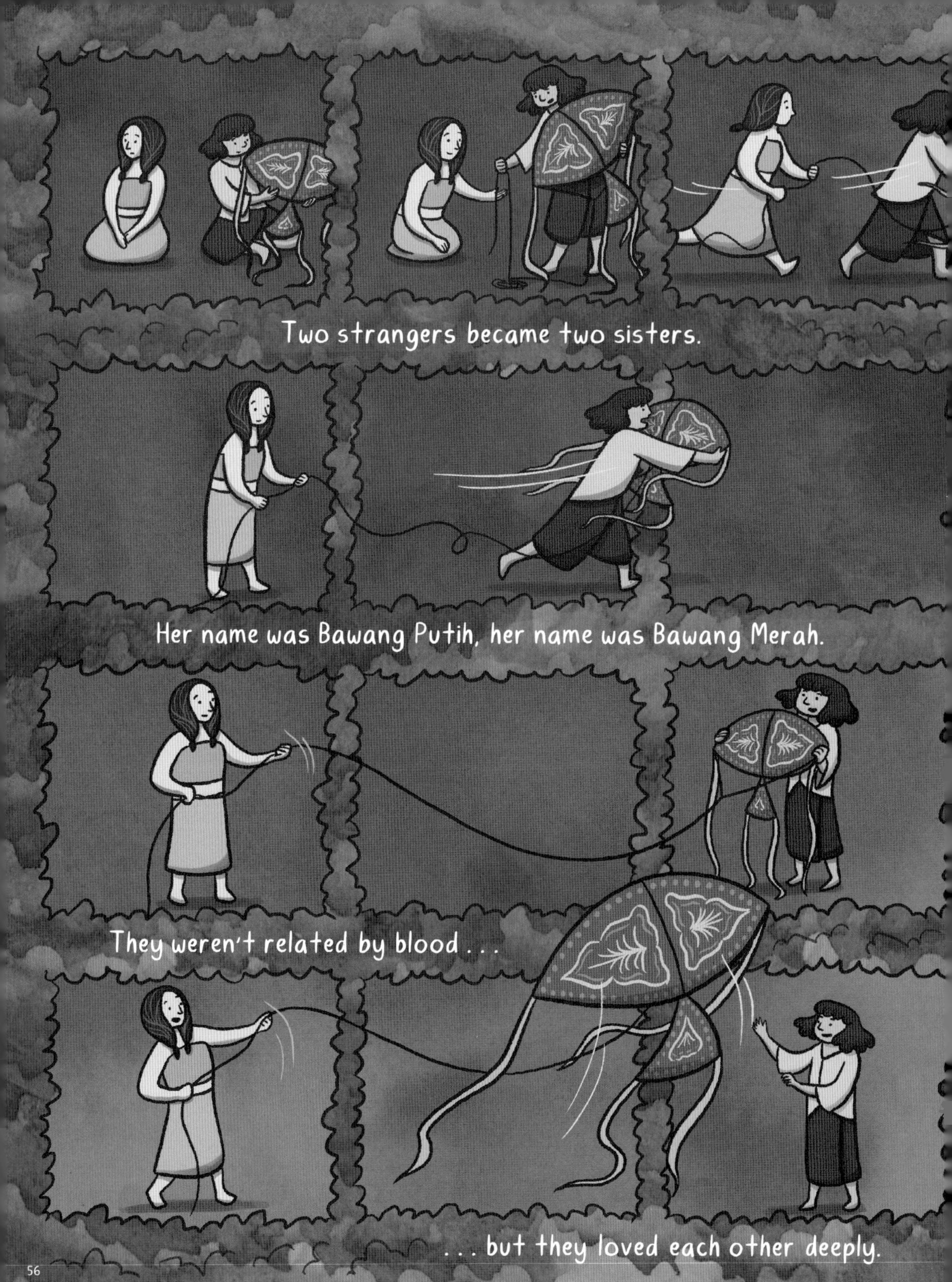
Two strangers became two sisters.
Her name was Bawang Putih, her name was Bawang Merah.
They weren't related by blood . . .
. . . but they loved each other deeply.

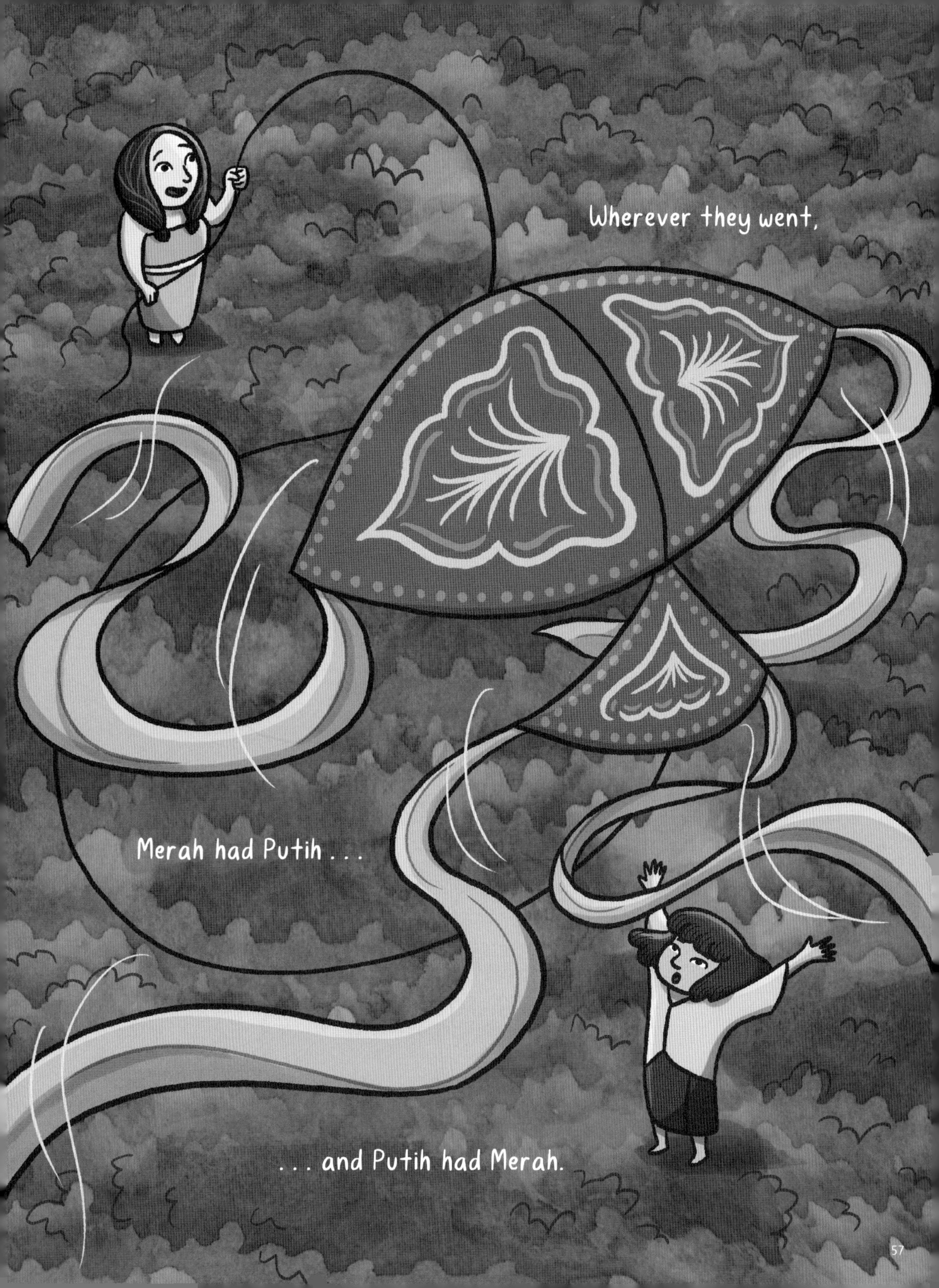
Wherever they went,
Merah had Putih . . .
. . . and Putih had Merah.

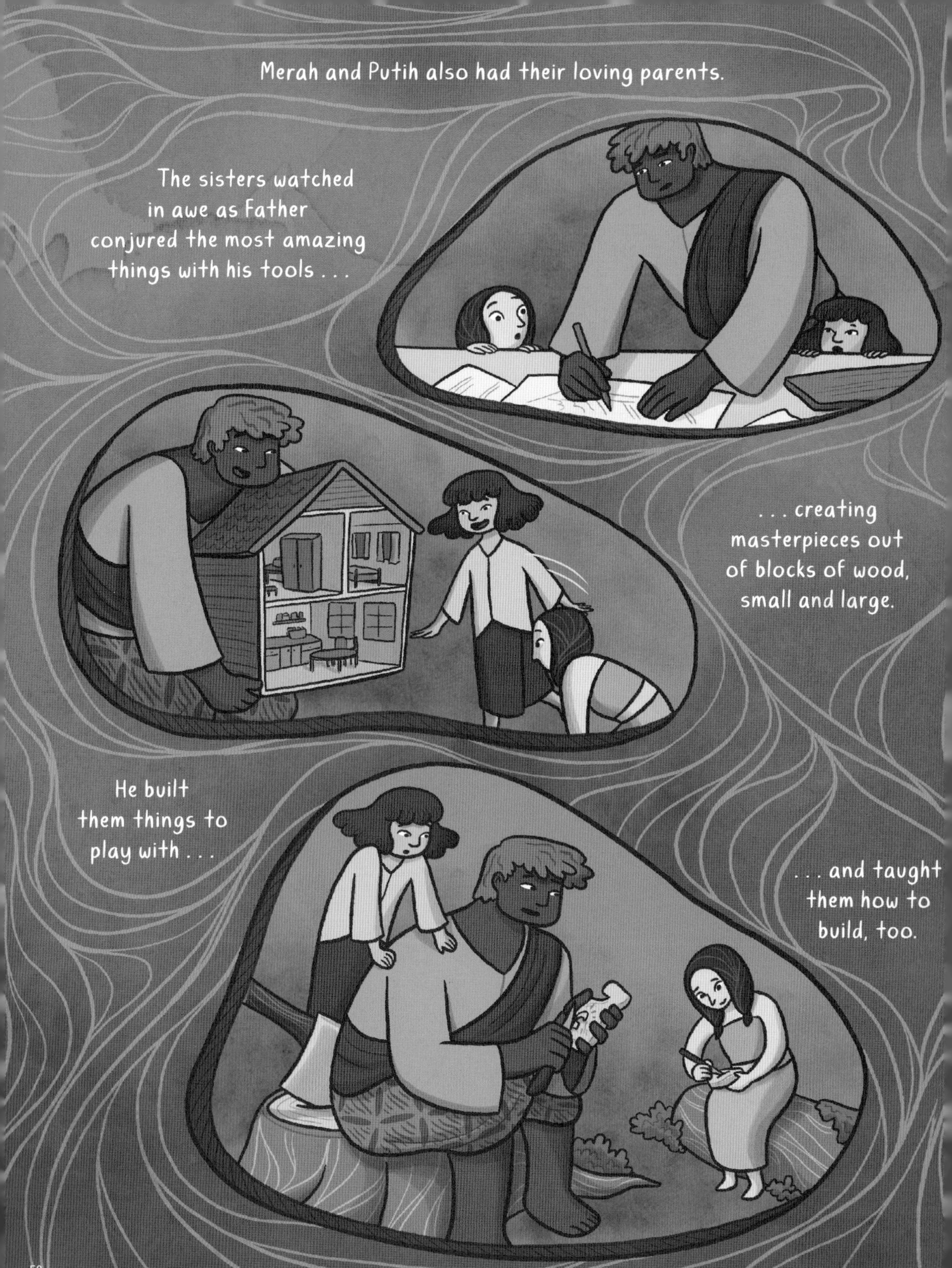
Merah and Putih also had their loving parents.
The sisters watched in awe as Father conjured the most amazing things with his tools . . .
. . . creating masterpieces out of blocks of wood, small and large.
He built them things to play with . . .
. . . and taught them how to build, too.

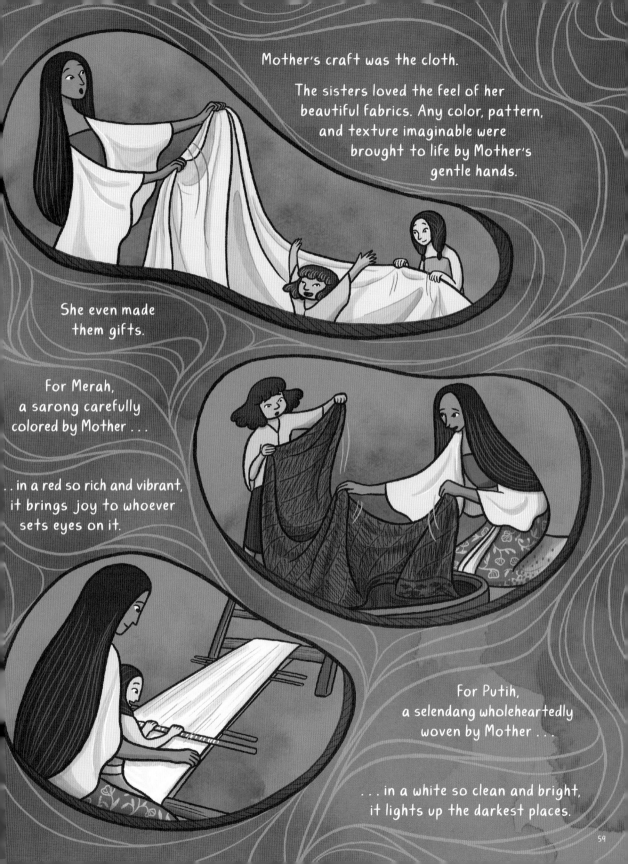

Mother's craft was the cloth.

The sisters loved the feel of her beautiful fabrics. Any color, pattern, and texture imaginable were brought to life by Mother's gentle hands.

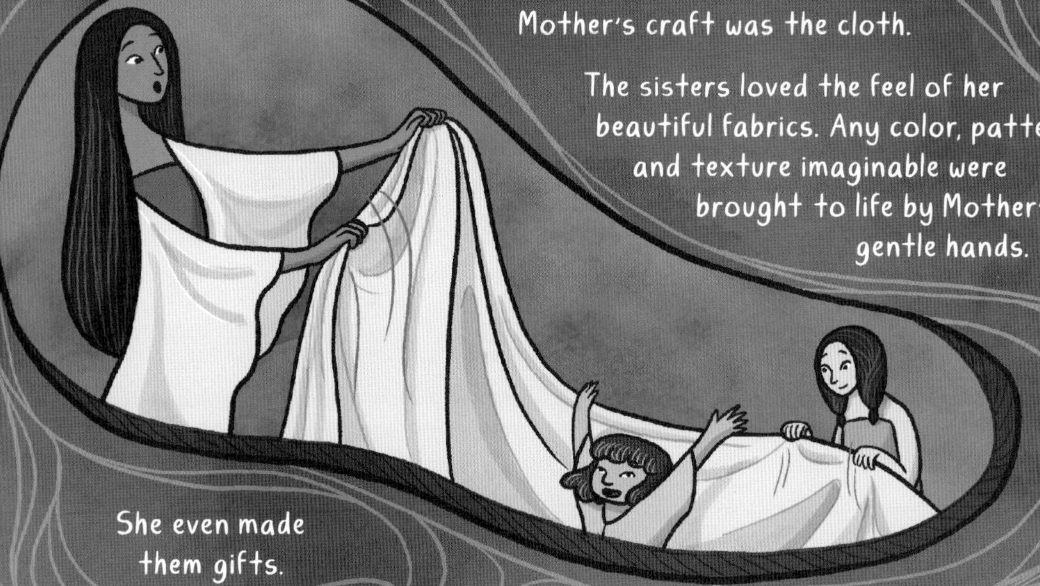

She even made them gifts.

For Merah, a sarong carefully colored by Mother . . .

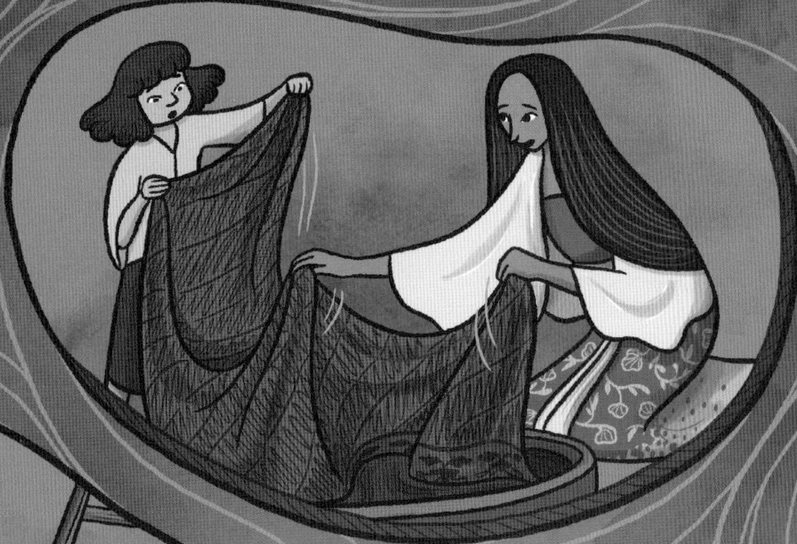

. . in a red so rich and vibrant, it brings joy to whoever sets eyes on it.

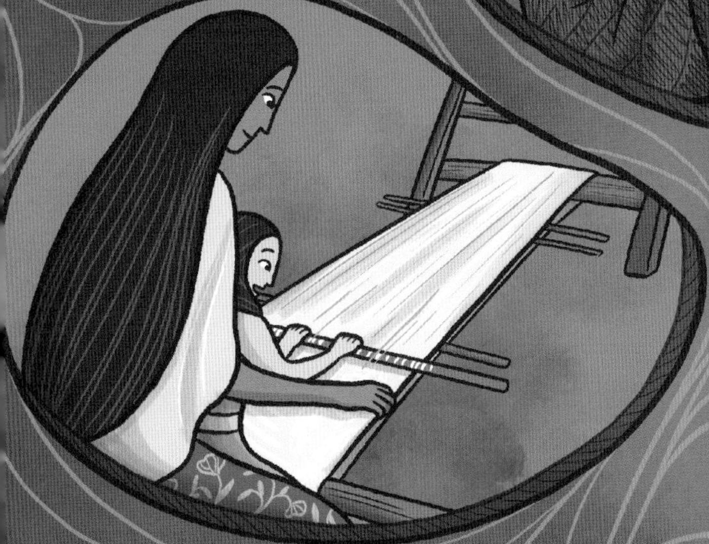

For Putih, a selendang wholeheartedly woven by Mother . . .

. . . in a white so clean and bright, it lights up the darkest places.

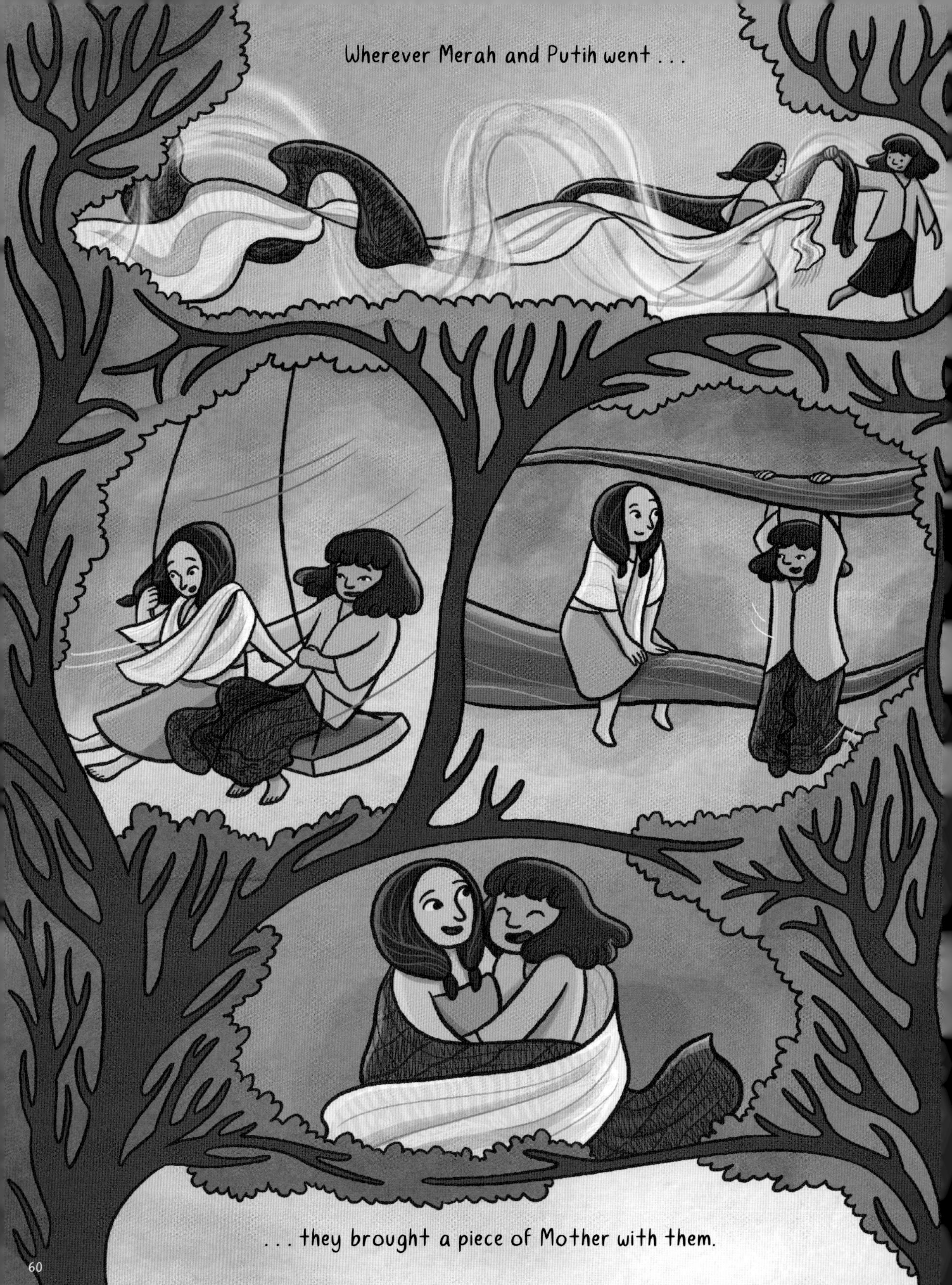
Wherever Merah and Putih went . . .
. . . they brought a piece of Mother with them.

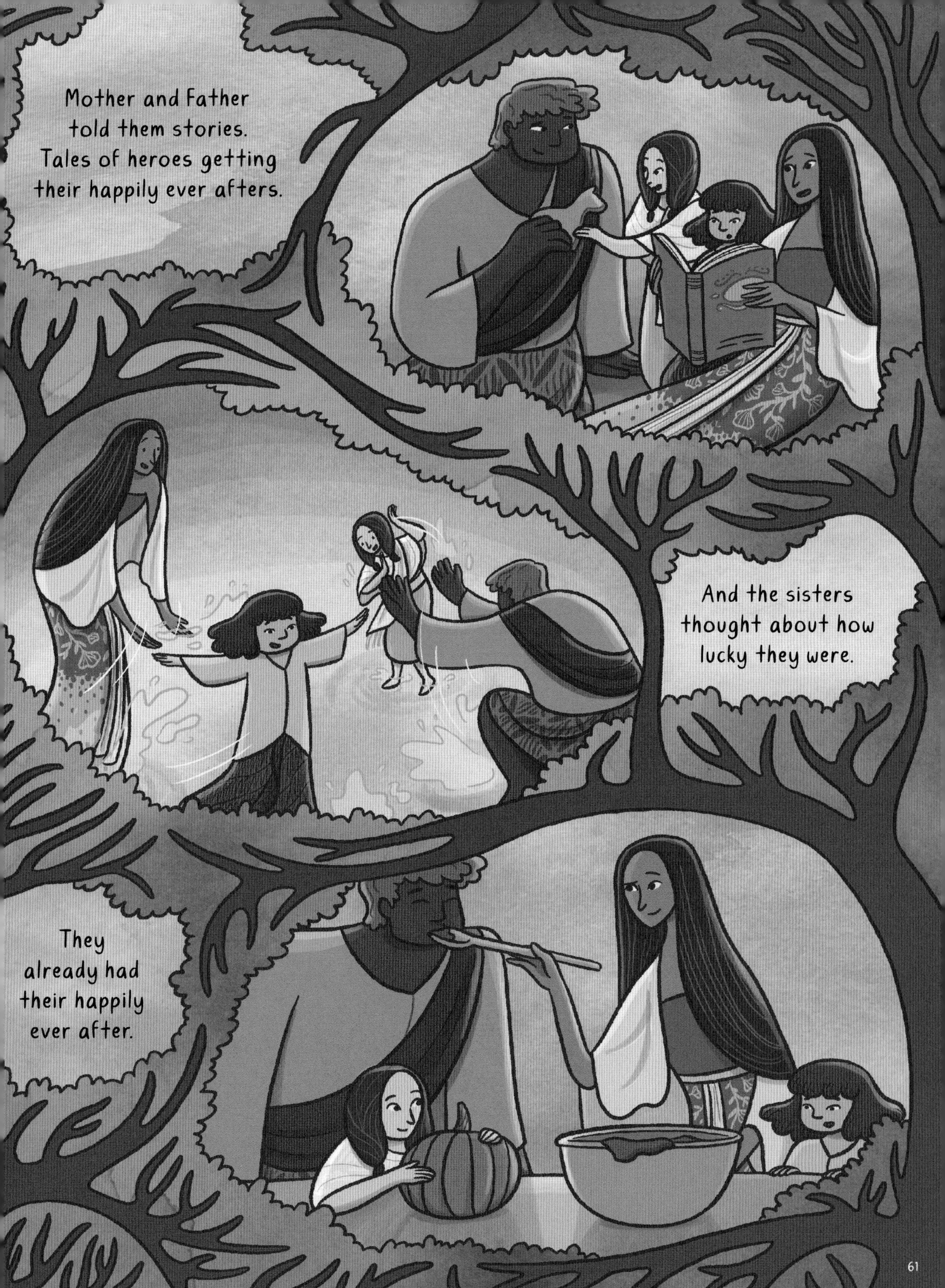
Mother and Father told them stories. Tales of heroes getting their happily ever afters.
And the sisters thought about how lucky they were.
They already had their happily ever after.

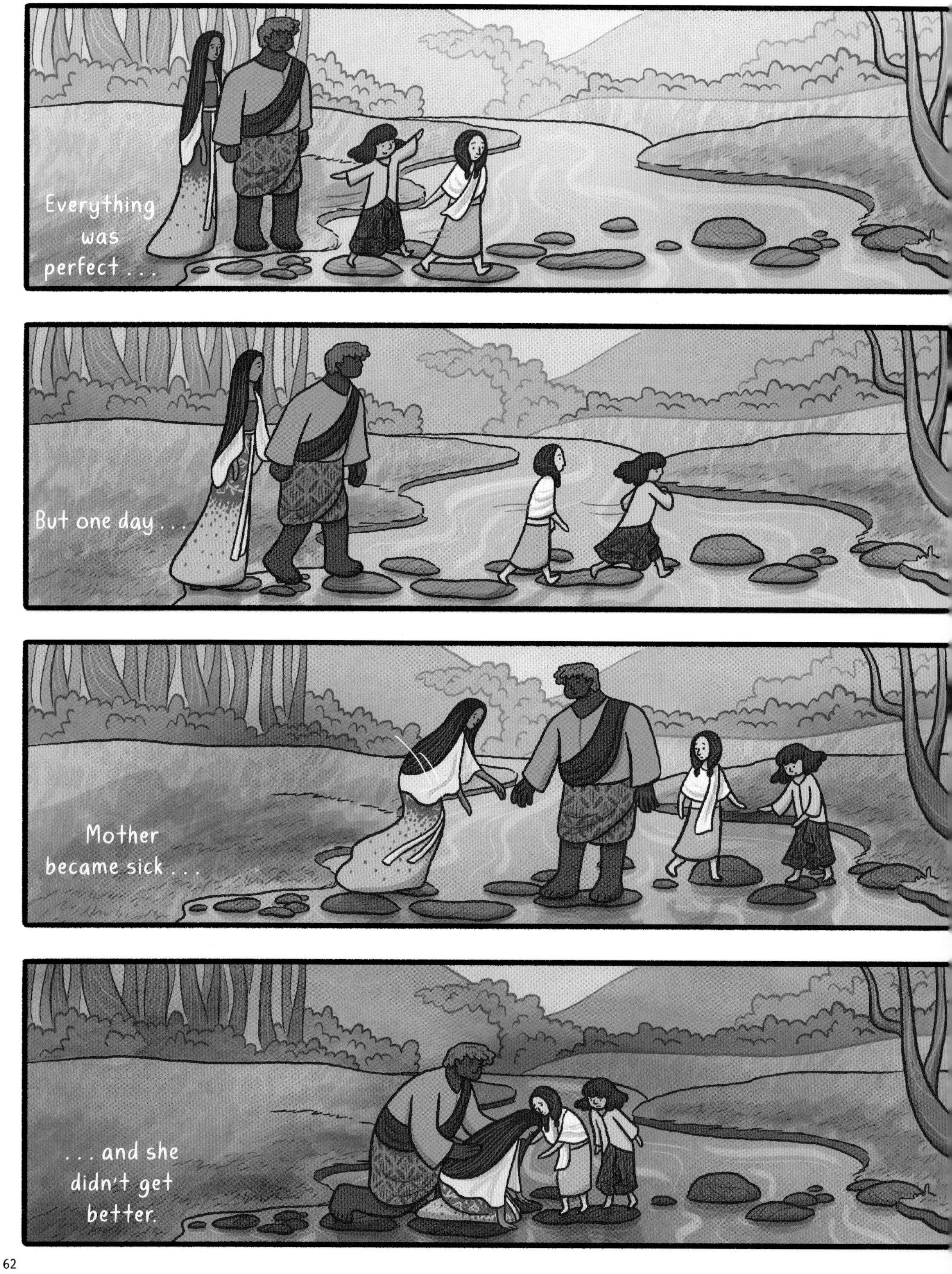
Everything was perfect . . .
But one day . . .
Mother became sick . . .
. . . and she didn't get better.

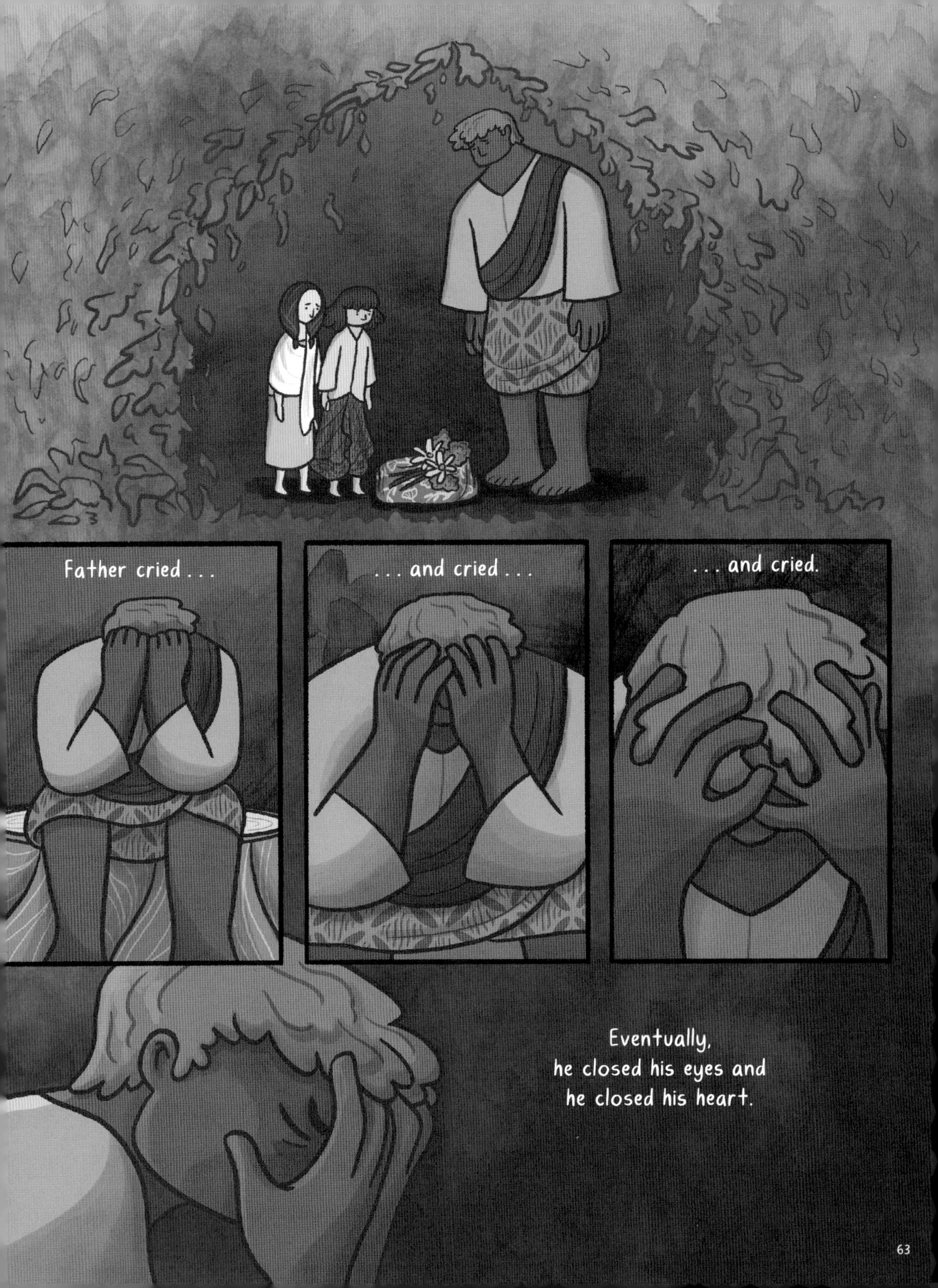
Father cried . . .
. . . and cried . . .
. . . and cried.
Eventually,
he closed his eyes and
he closed his heart.

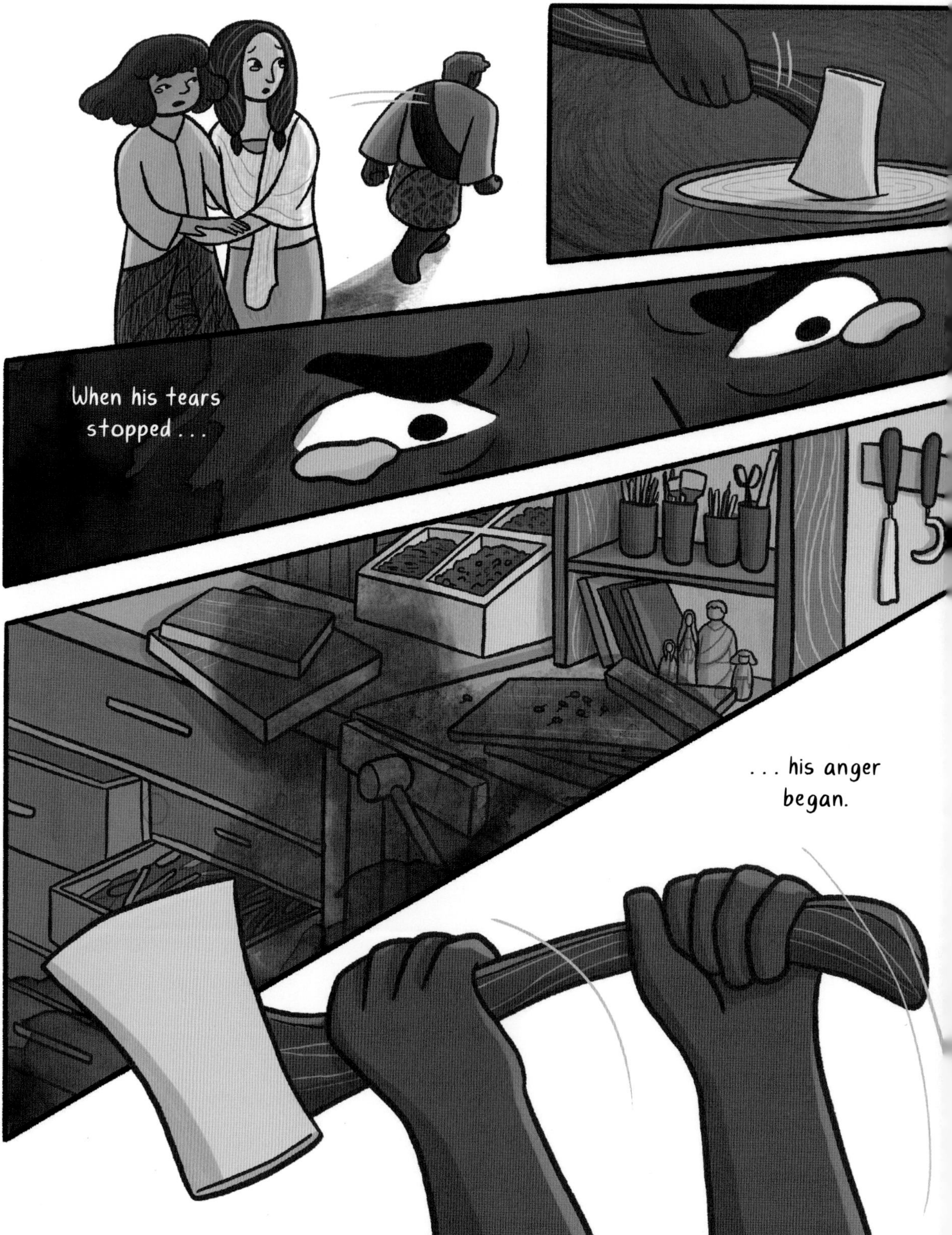
When his tears stopped . . .
. . . his anger began.

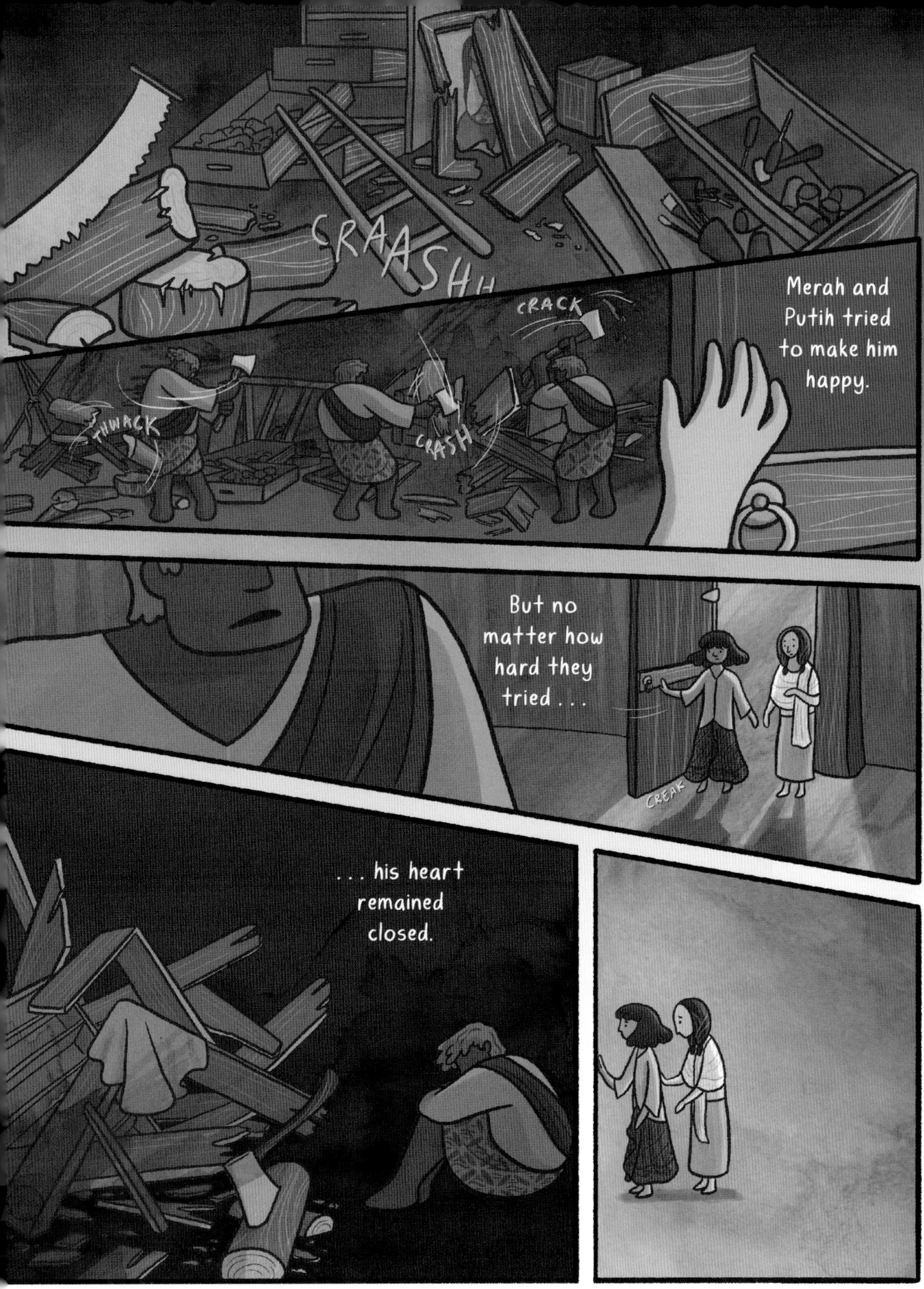
CRAASHH
CRACK
THWACK
CRASH
Merah and Putih tried to make him happy.
But no matter how hard they tried . . .
CREAK
. . . his heart remained closed.

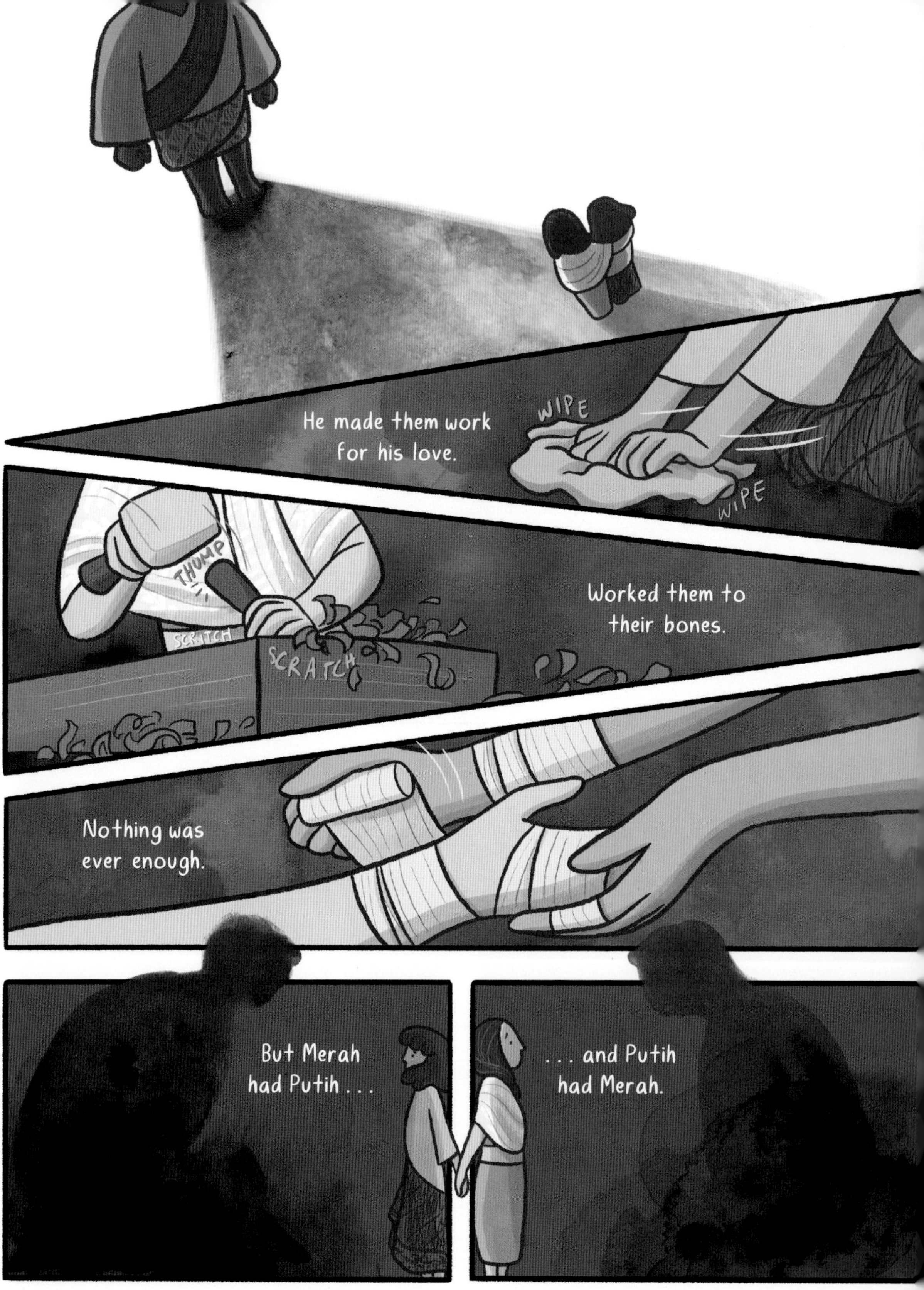
He made them work for his love.
WIPE
WIPE
THUMP
SCRATCH
SCRATCH
Worked them to their bones.
Nothing was ever enough.
But Merah had Putih . . .
. . . and Putih had Merah.

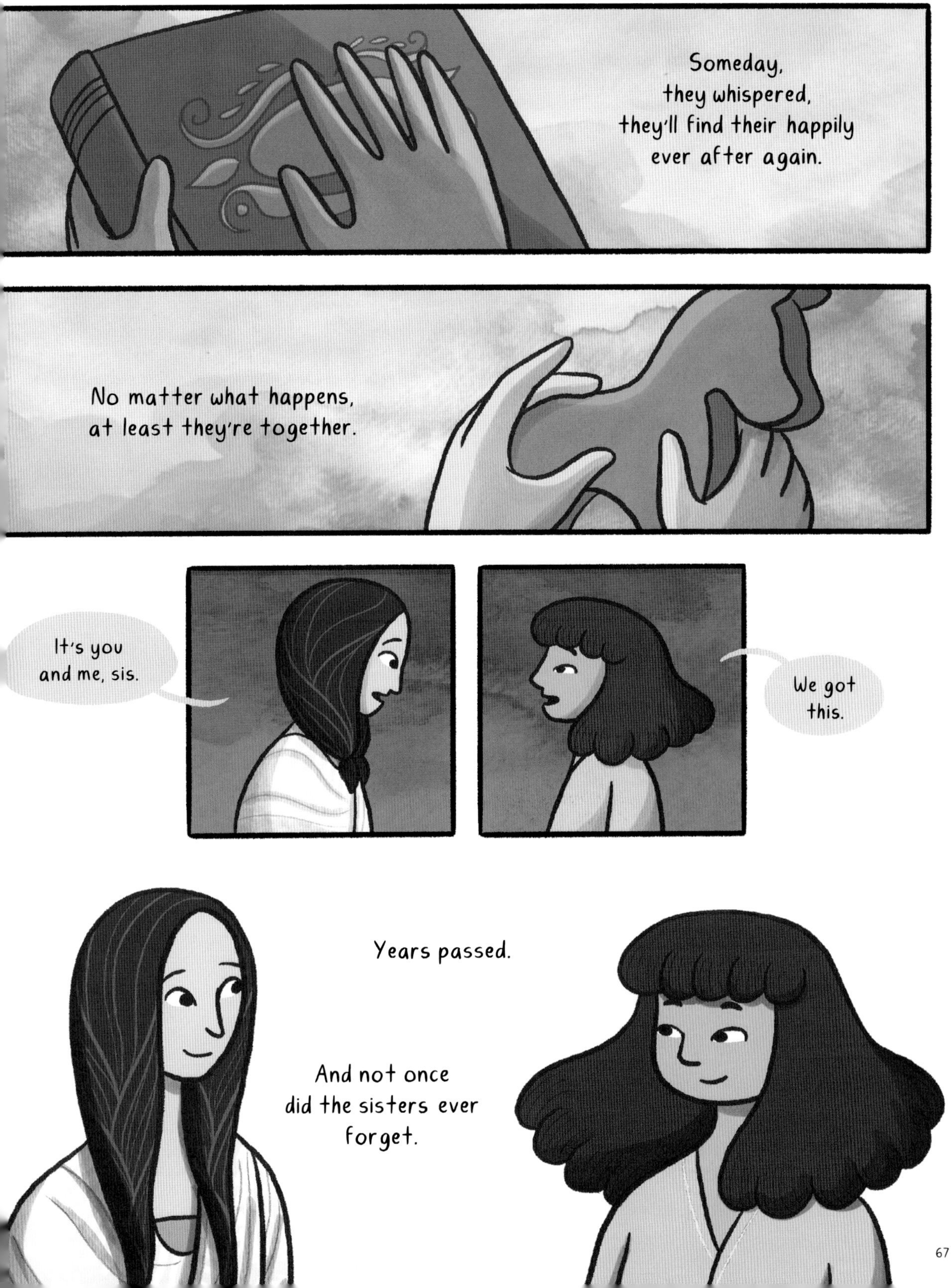
Someday, they whispered, they'll find their happily ever after again.
No matter what happens, at least they're together.
It's you and me, sis.
We got this.
Years passed.
And not once did the sisters ever forget.

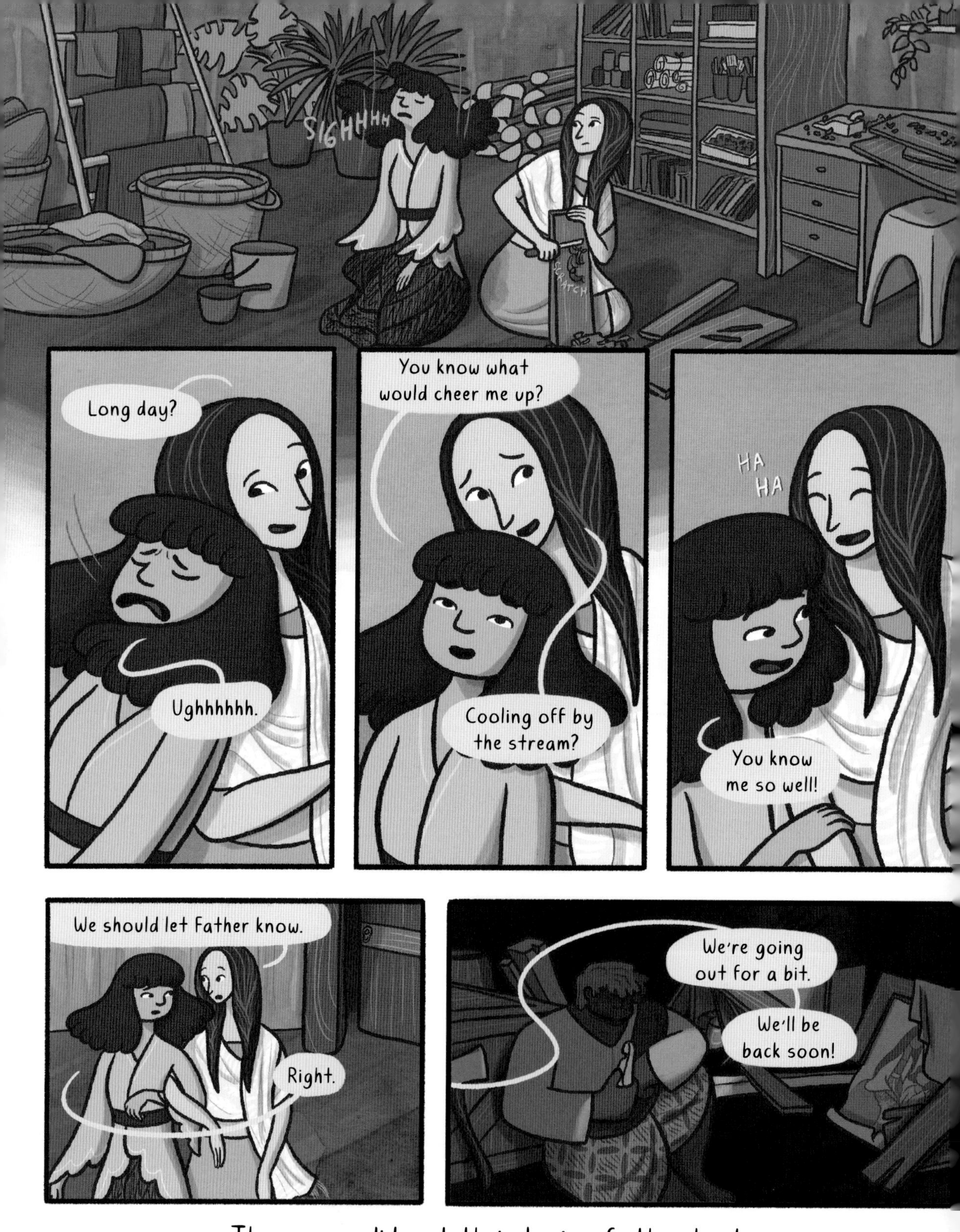
SIGHHHH
SCRATCH
Long day?
Ughhhhhh.
You know what would cheer me up?
Cooling off by the stream?
HA HA
You know me so well!
We should let Father know.
Right.
We're going out for a bit.
We'll be back soon!

They never did get their loving father back.

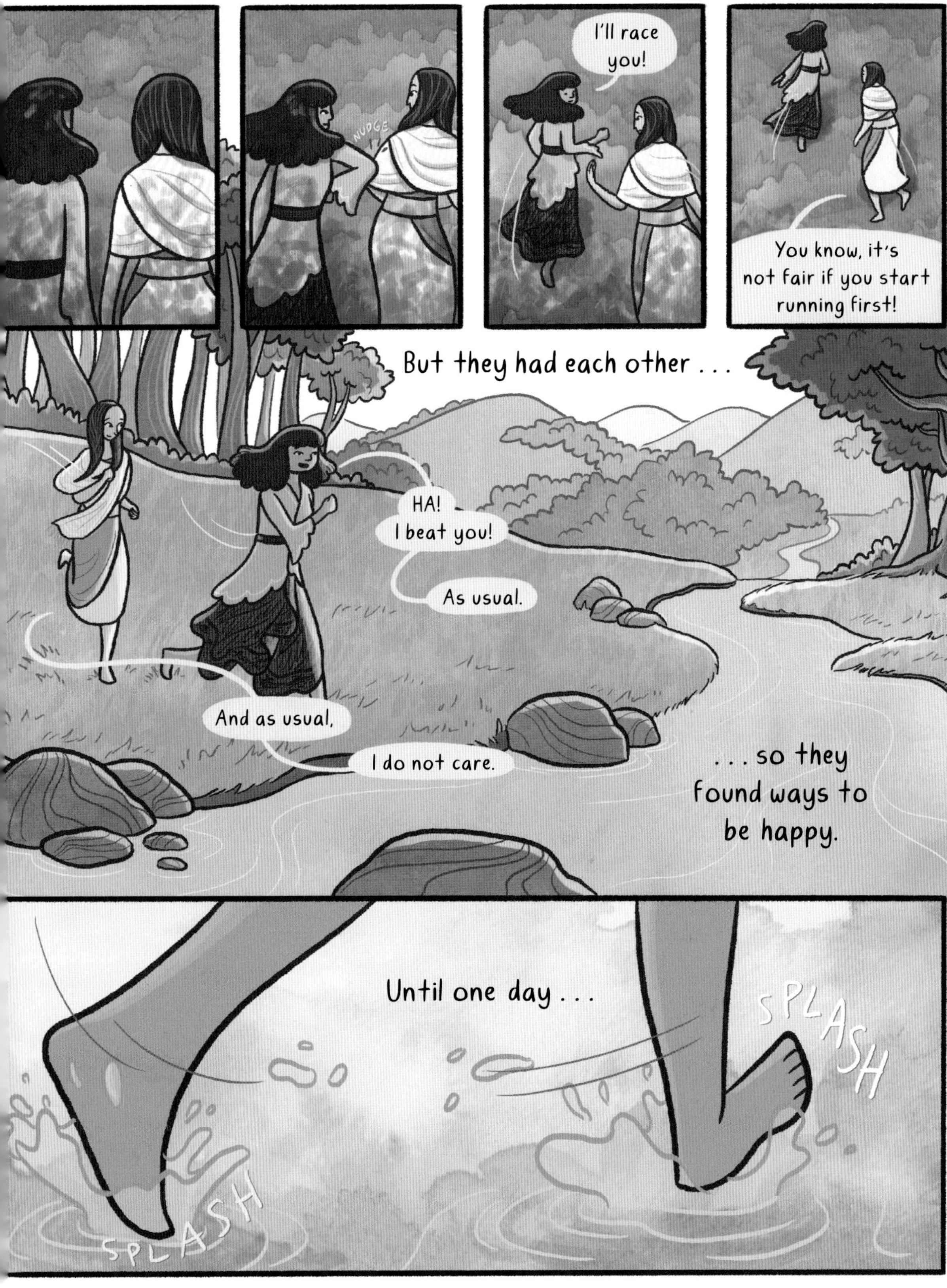
NUDGE
I'll race you!
You know, it's not fair if you start running first!
But they had each other . . .
HA! I beat you!
As usual.
And as usual,
I do not care.
. . . so they found ways to be happy.
Until one day . . .
SPLASH
SPLASH

They left their sarong and selendang on a nearby tree branch . . .

HA HA HA

SPLASH

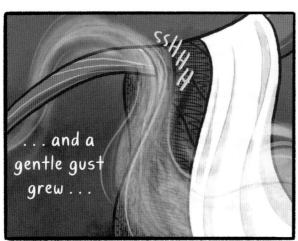

. . . and a gentle gust grew . . .

SSHHH

. . . into a wailing wind.

swISSHH

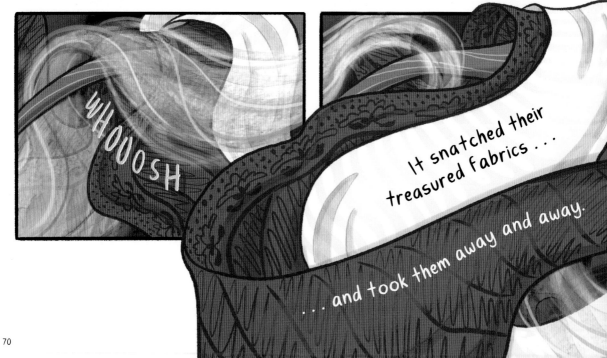

WHOOOSH

It snatched their treasured fabrics . . .

. . . and took them away and away.

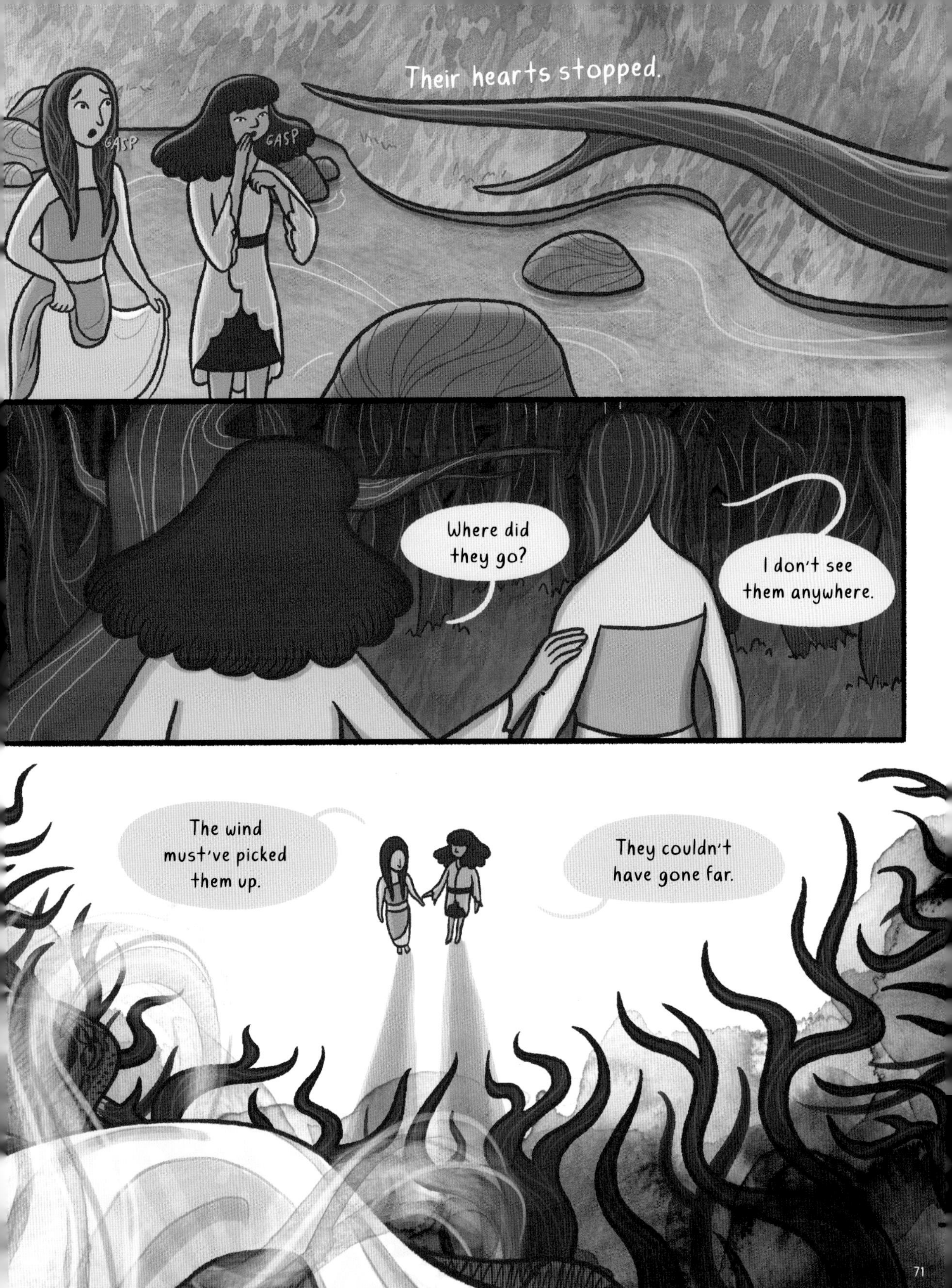
Their hearts stopped.
GASP
GASP
Where did they go?
I don't see them anywhere.
The wind must've picked them up.
They couldn't have gone far.

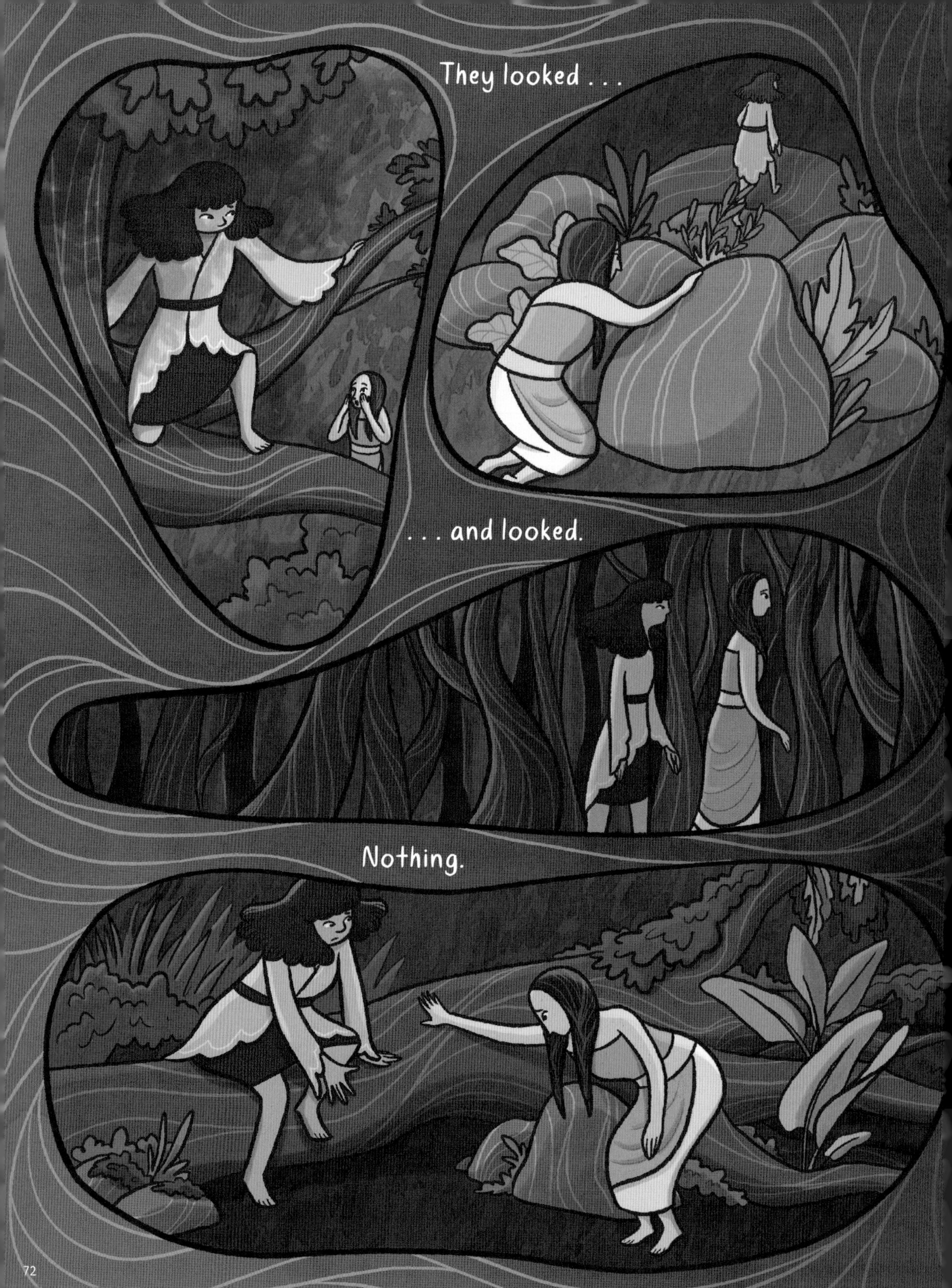
They looked . . .
. . . and looked.
Nothing.

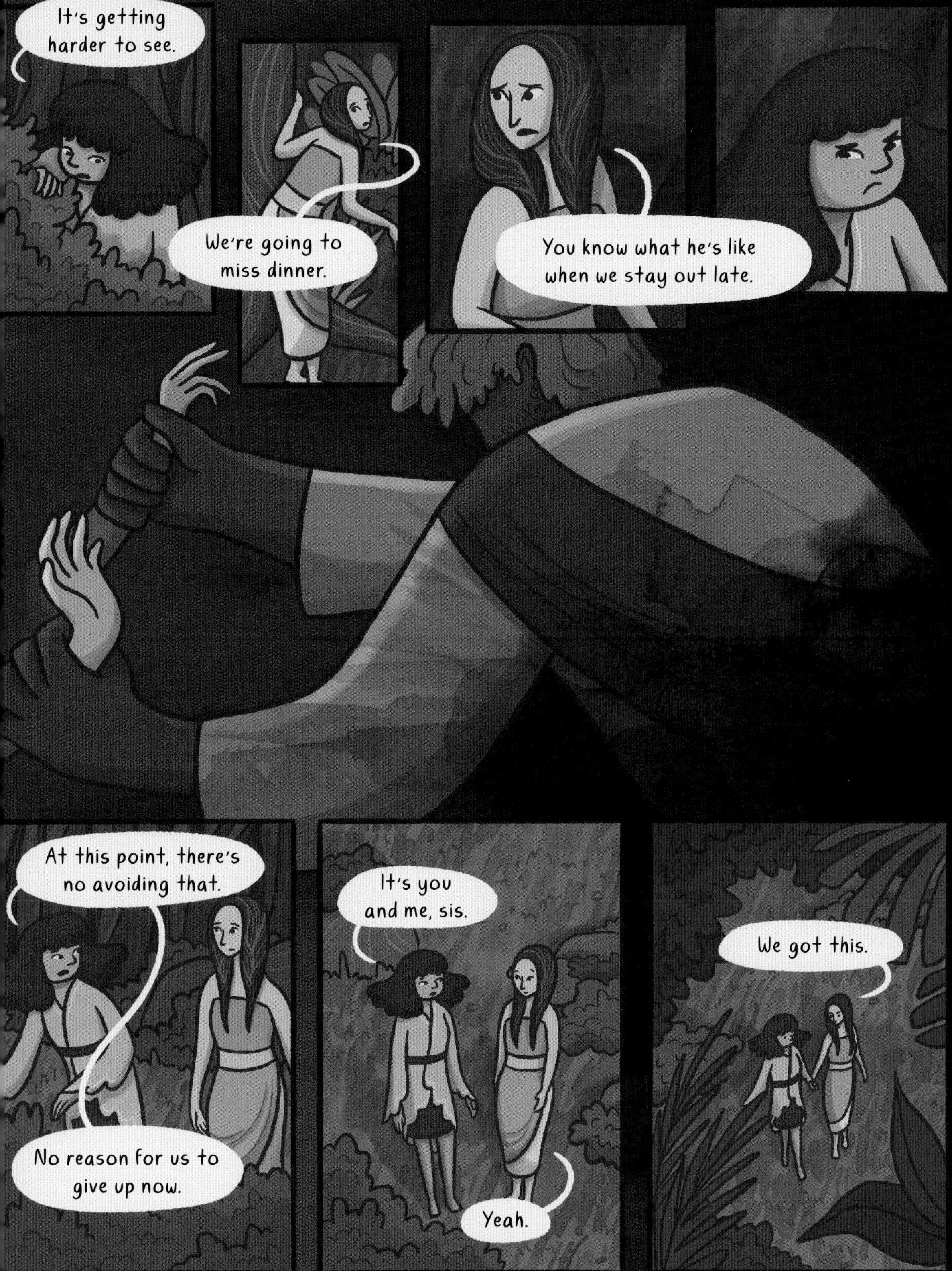
It's getting harder to see.
We're going to miss dinner.
You know what he's like when we stay out late.
At this point, there's no avoiding that.
No reason for us to give up now.
It's you and me, sis.
Yeah.
We got this.

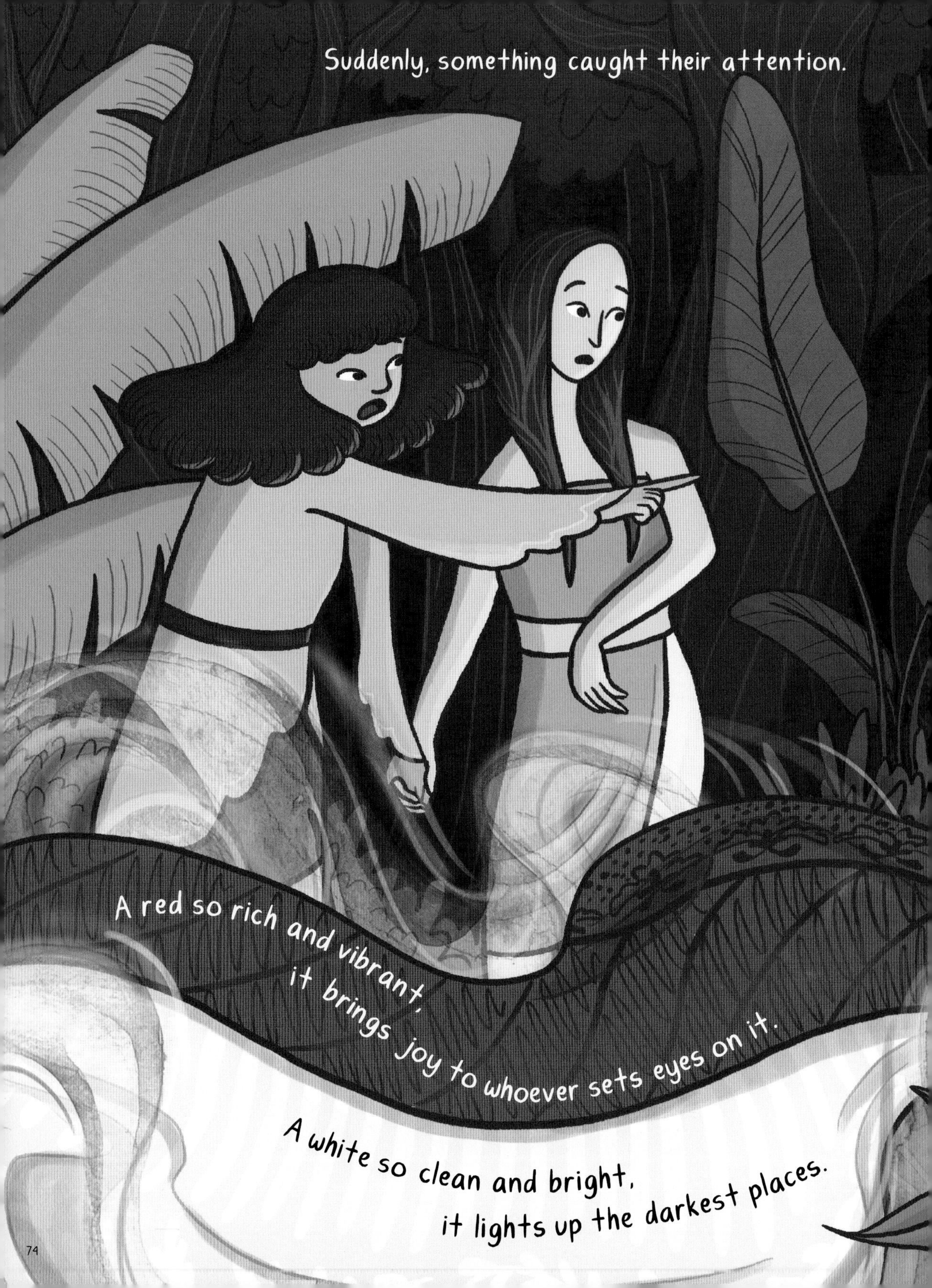
Suddenly, something caught their attention.
A red so rich and vibrant,
it brings joy to whoever sets eyes on it.
A white so clean and bright,
it lights up the darkest places.

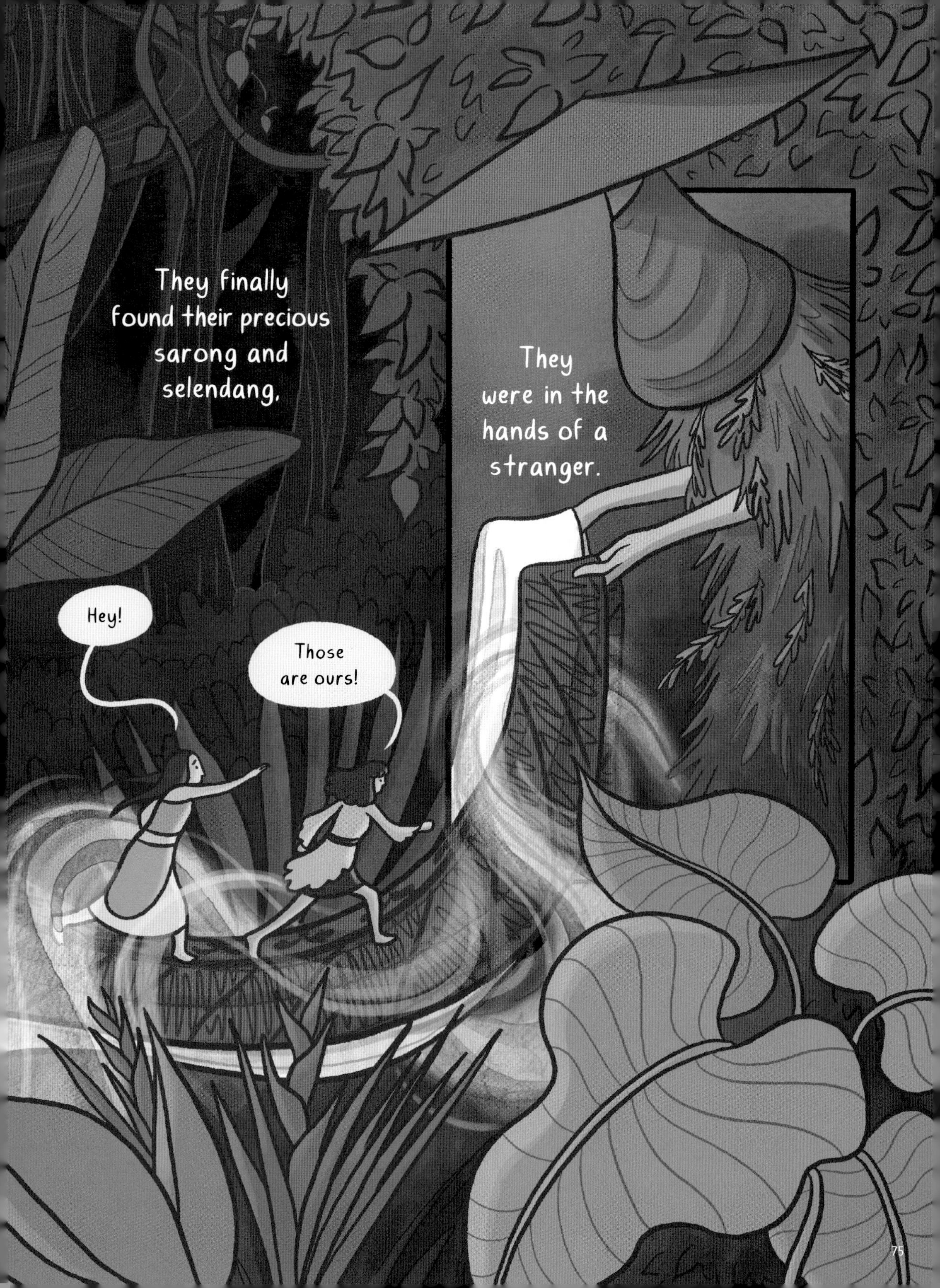
They finally found their precious sarong and selendang.
They were in the hands of a stranger.
Hey!
Those are ours!

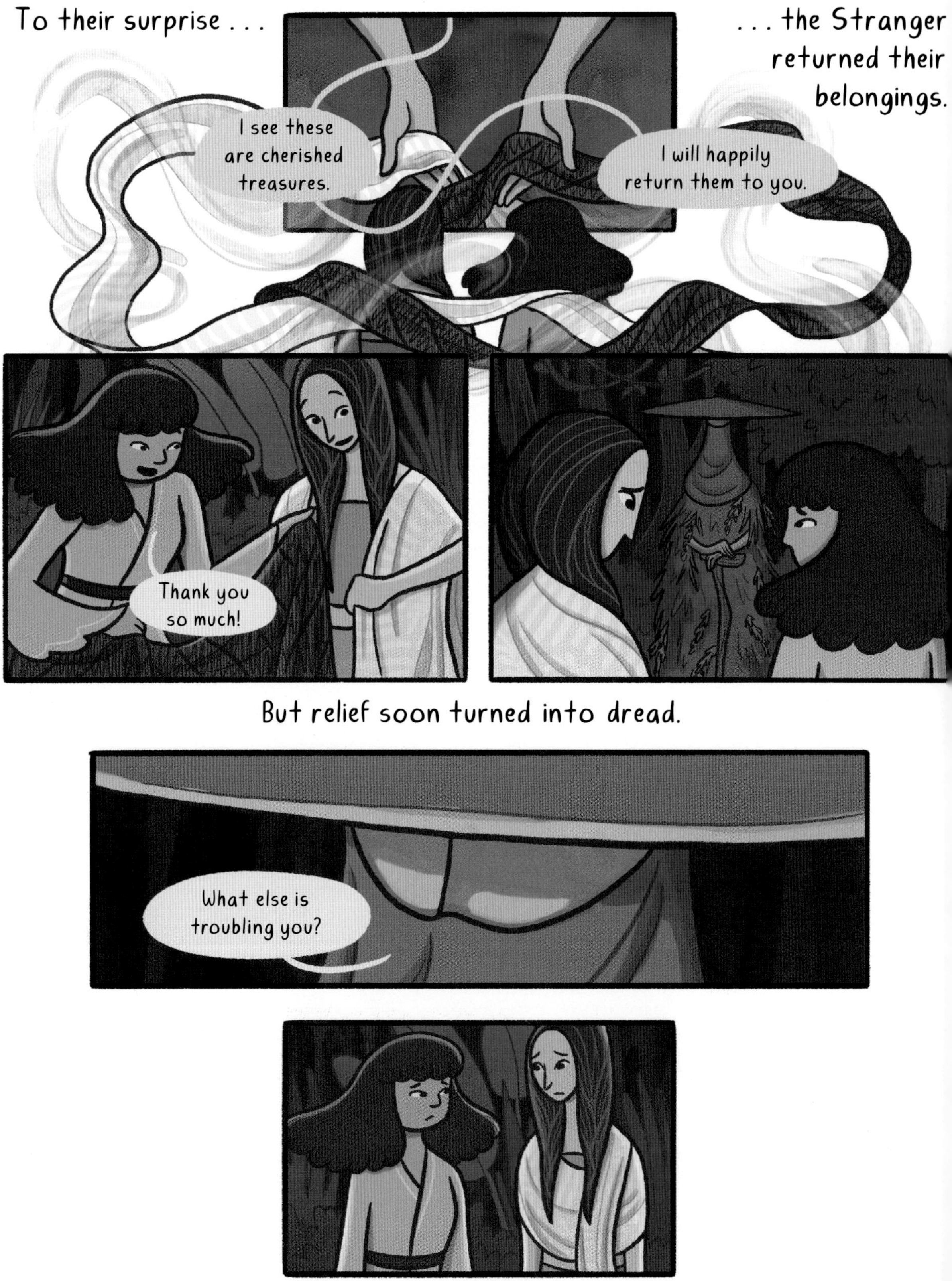
To their surprise . . .
I see these are cherished treasures.
I will happily return them to you.
. . . the Stranger returned their belongings.
Thank you so much!
But relief soon turned into dread.
What else is troubling you?

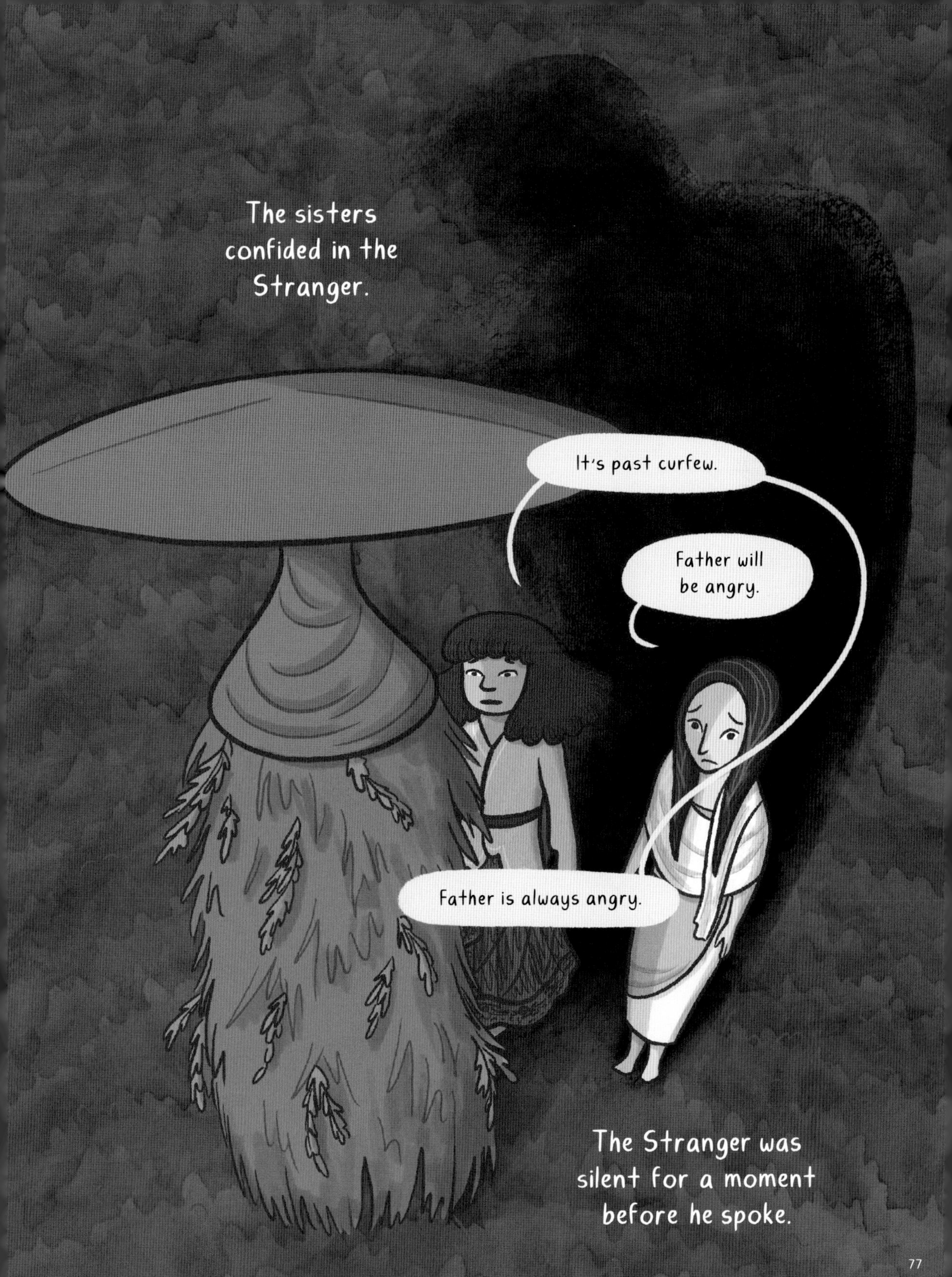

The sisters confided in the Stranger.
It's past curfew.
Father will be angry.
Father is always angry.
The Stranger was silent for a moment before he spoke.

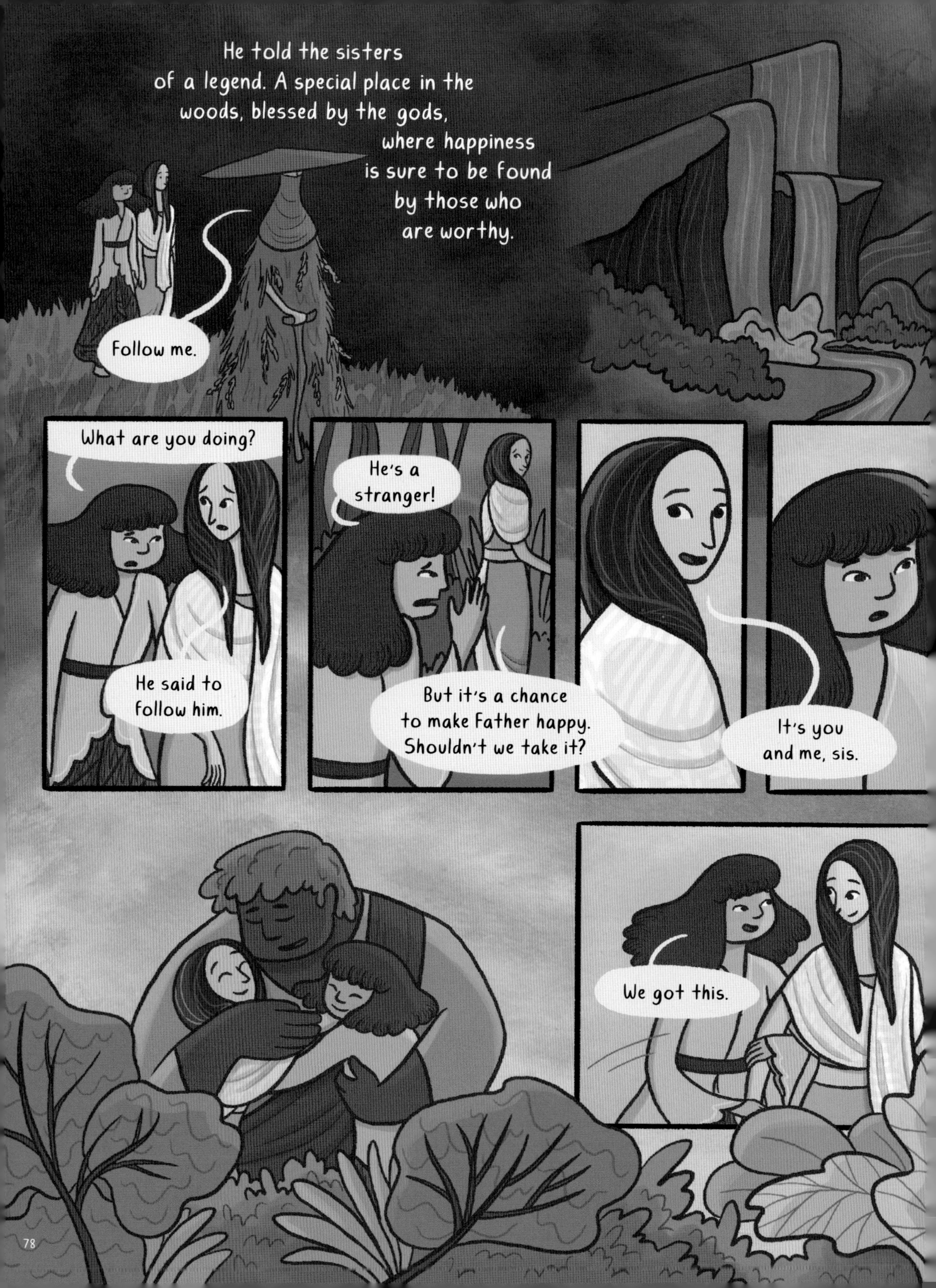
He told the sisters of a legend. A special place in the woods, blessed by the gods, where happiness is sure to be found by those who are worthy.
Follow me.
What are you doing?
He said to follow him.
He's a stranger!
But it's a chance to make Father happy. Shouldn't we take it?
It's you and me, sis.
We got this.

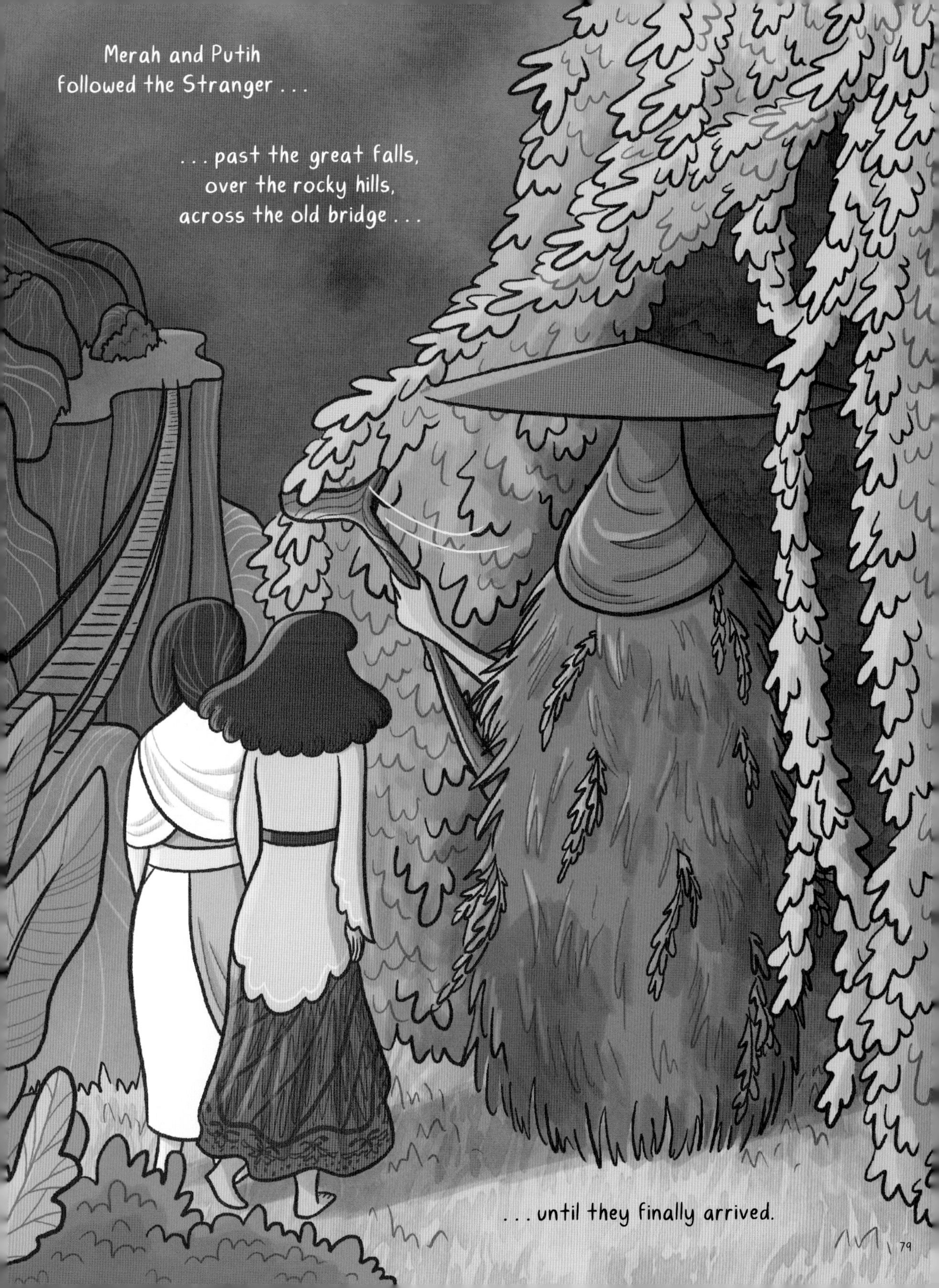
Merah and Putih followed the Stranger . . .
. . . past the great falls, over the rocky hills, across the old bridge . . .
. . . until they finally arrived.

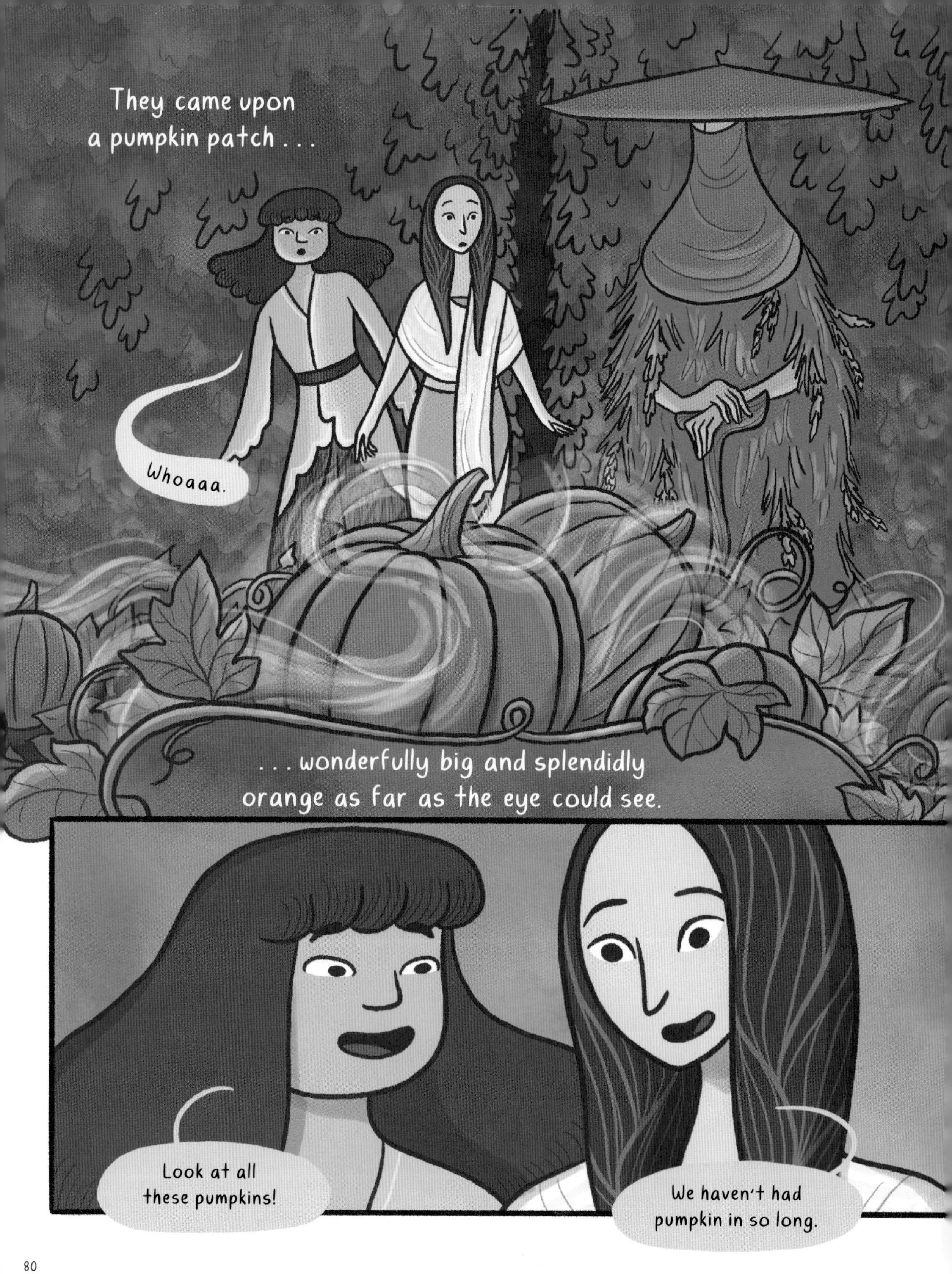
They came upon a pumpkin patch . . .
Whoaaa.
. . . wonderfully big and splendidly orange as far as the eye could see.
Look at all these pumpkins!
We haven't had pumpkin in so long.

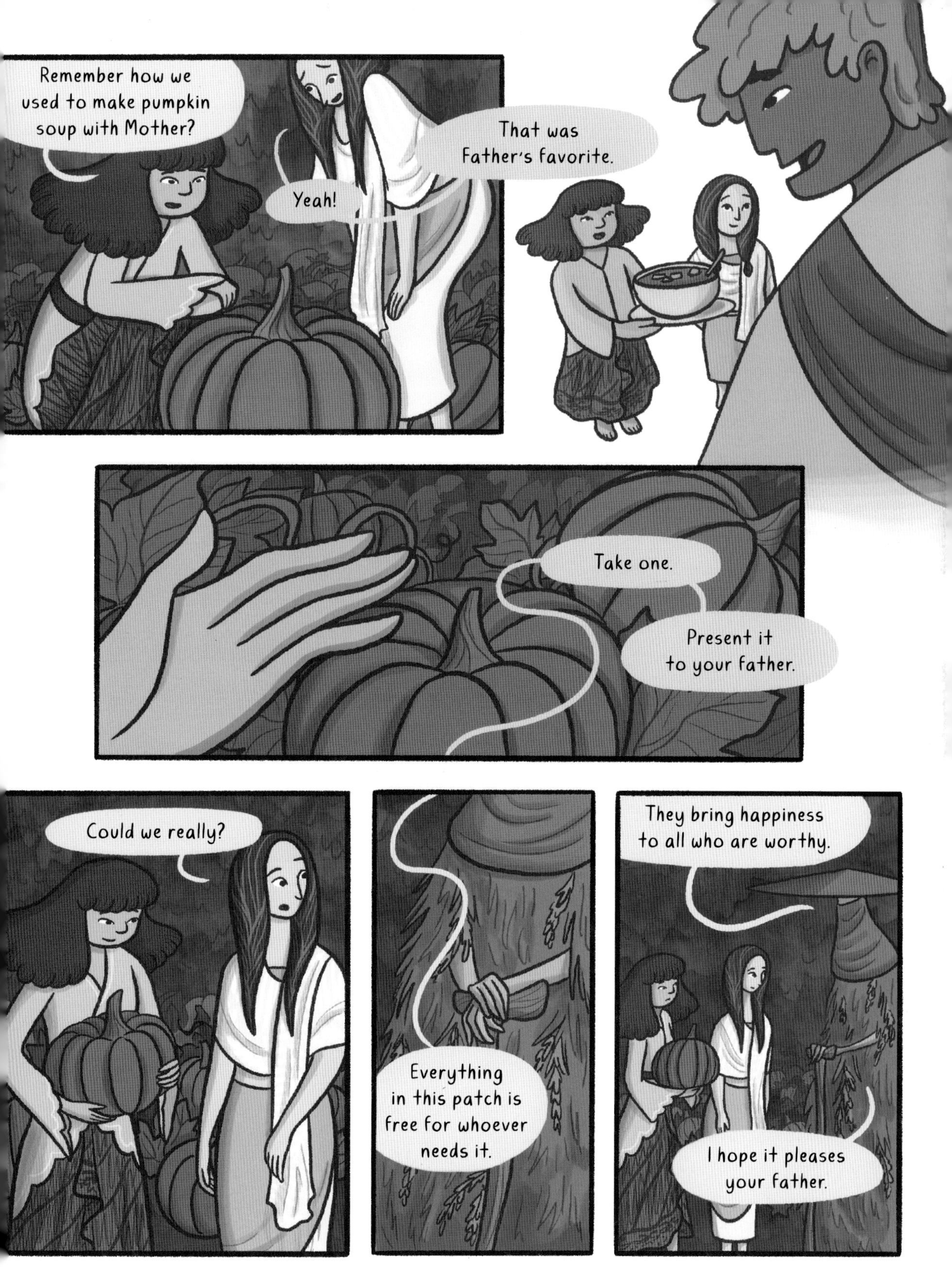
Remember how we used to make pumpkin soup with Mother?
Yeah!
That was Father's favorite.
Take one.
Present it to your father.
Could we really?
Everything in this patch is free for whoever needs it.
They bring happiness to all who are worthy.
I hope it pleases your father.

And so, Merah and Putih headed back home.

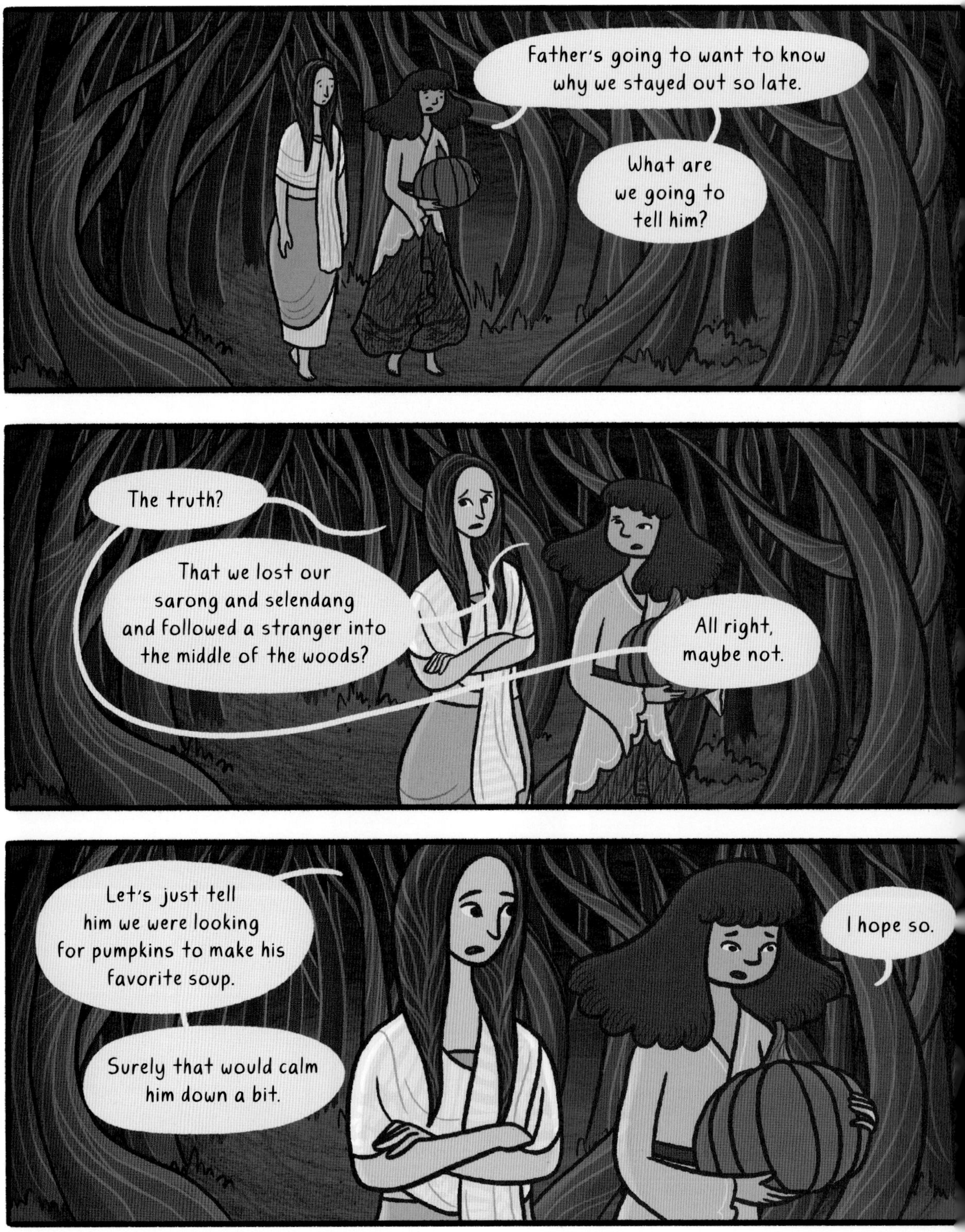
Father's going to want to know why we stayed out so late.
What are we going to tell him?
The truth?
That we lost our sarong and selendang and followed a stranger into the middle of the woods?
All right, maybe not.
Let's just tell him we were looking for pumpkins to make his favorite soup.
Surely that would calm him down a bit.
I hope so.

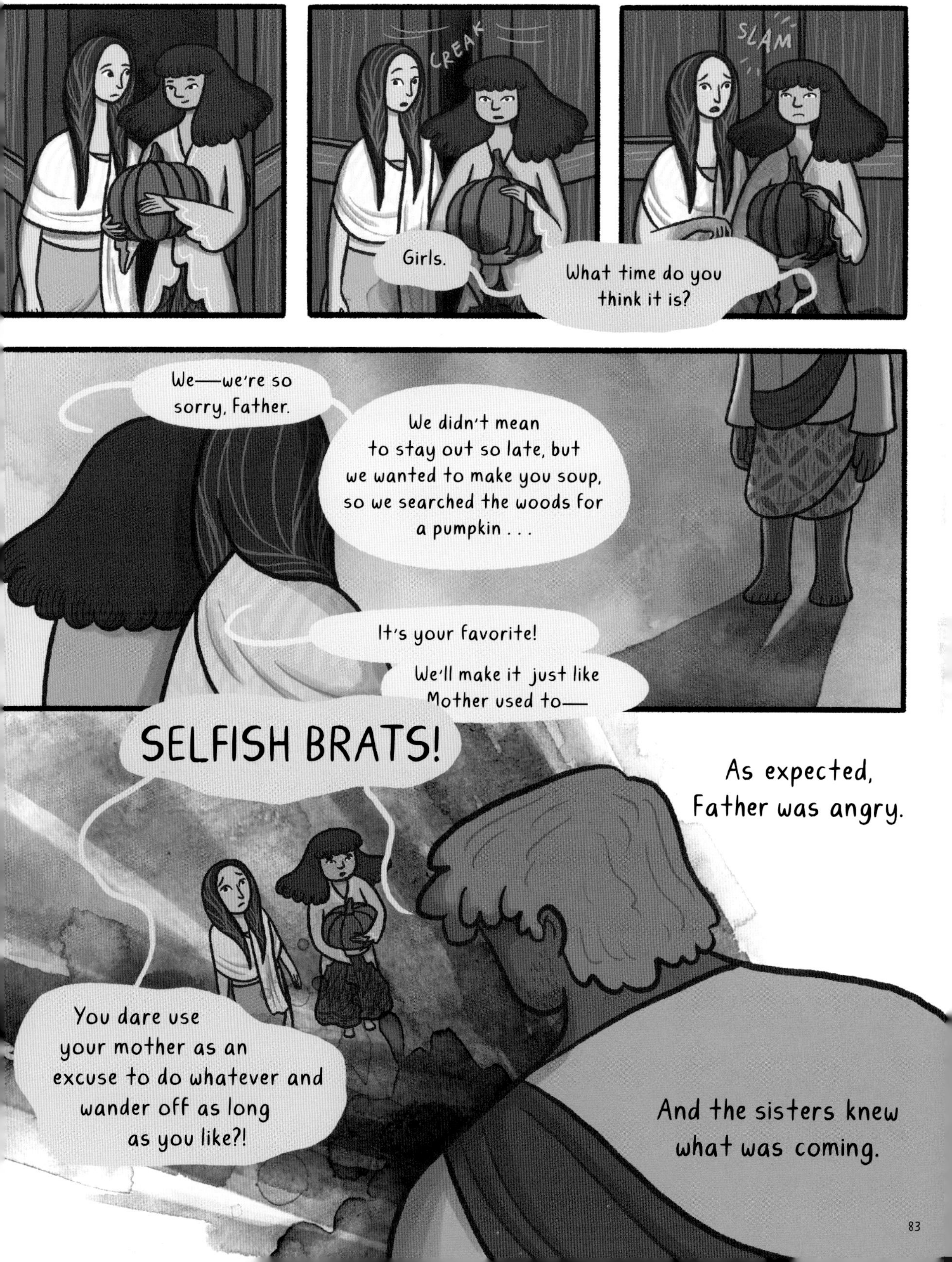
CREAK
SLAM
Girls.
What time do you think it is?
We—we're so sorry, Father.
We didn't mean to stay out so late, but we wanted to make you soup, so we searched the woods for a pumpkin . . .
It's your favorite!
We'll make it just like Mother used to—
SELFISH BRATS!
As expected, Father was angry.
You dare use your mother as an excuse to do whatever and wander off as long as you like?!
And the sisters knew what was coming.

Merah protected Putih, and Putih protected Merah.

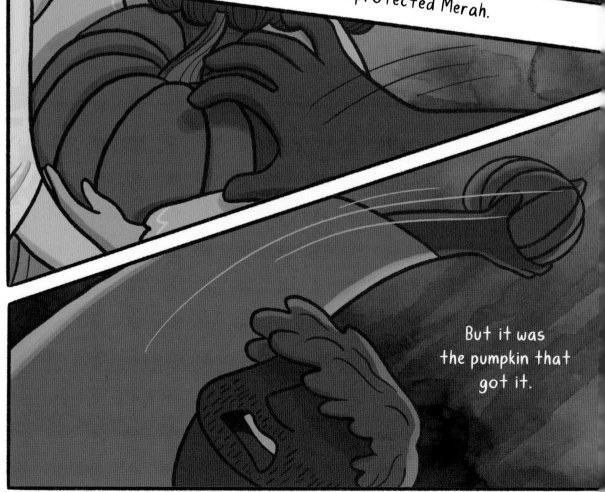

But it was the pumpkin that got it.

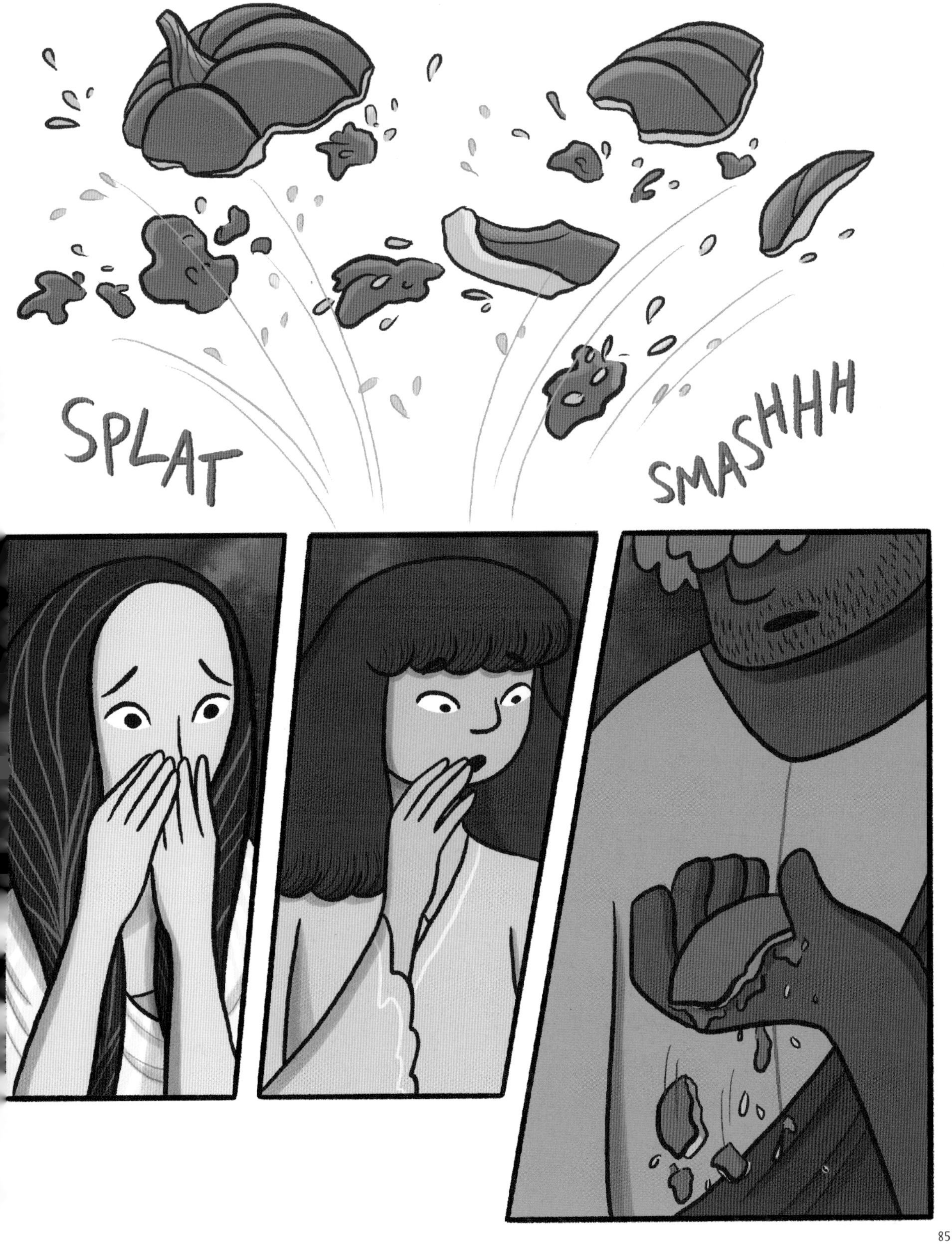
SPLAT
SMASHHH

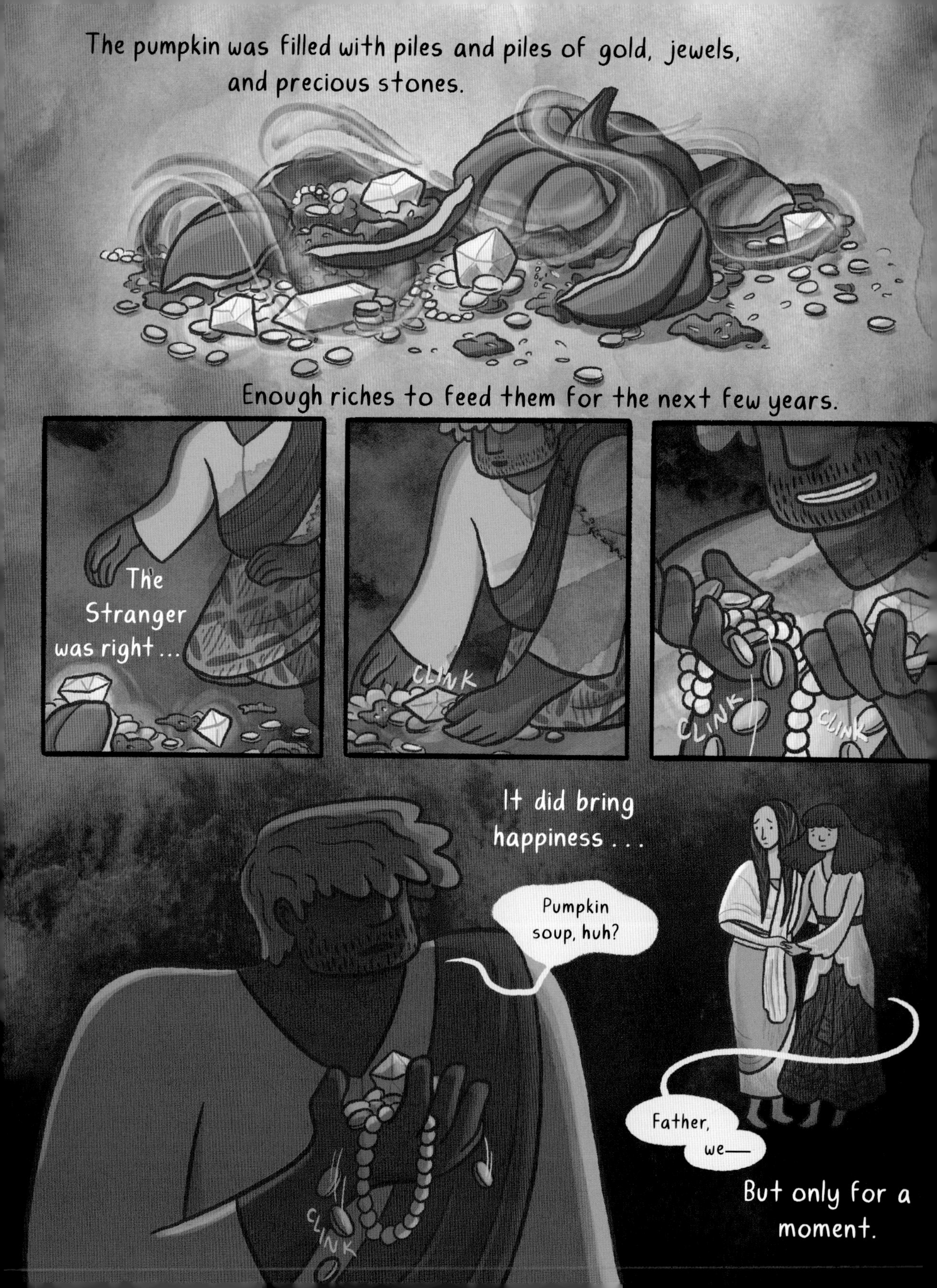

The pumpkin was filled with piles and piles of gold, jewels, and precious stones.
Enough riches to feed them for the next few years.
The Stranger was right . . .
CLINK
CLINK
CLINK
It did bring happiness . . .
Pumpkin soup, huh?
CLINK
Father, we—
But only for a moment.

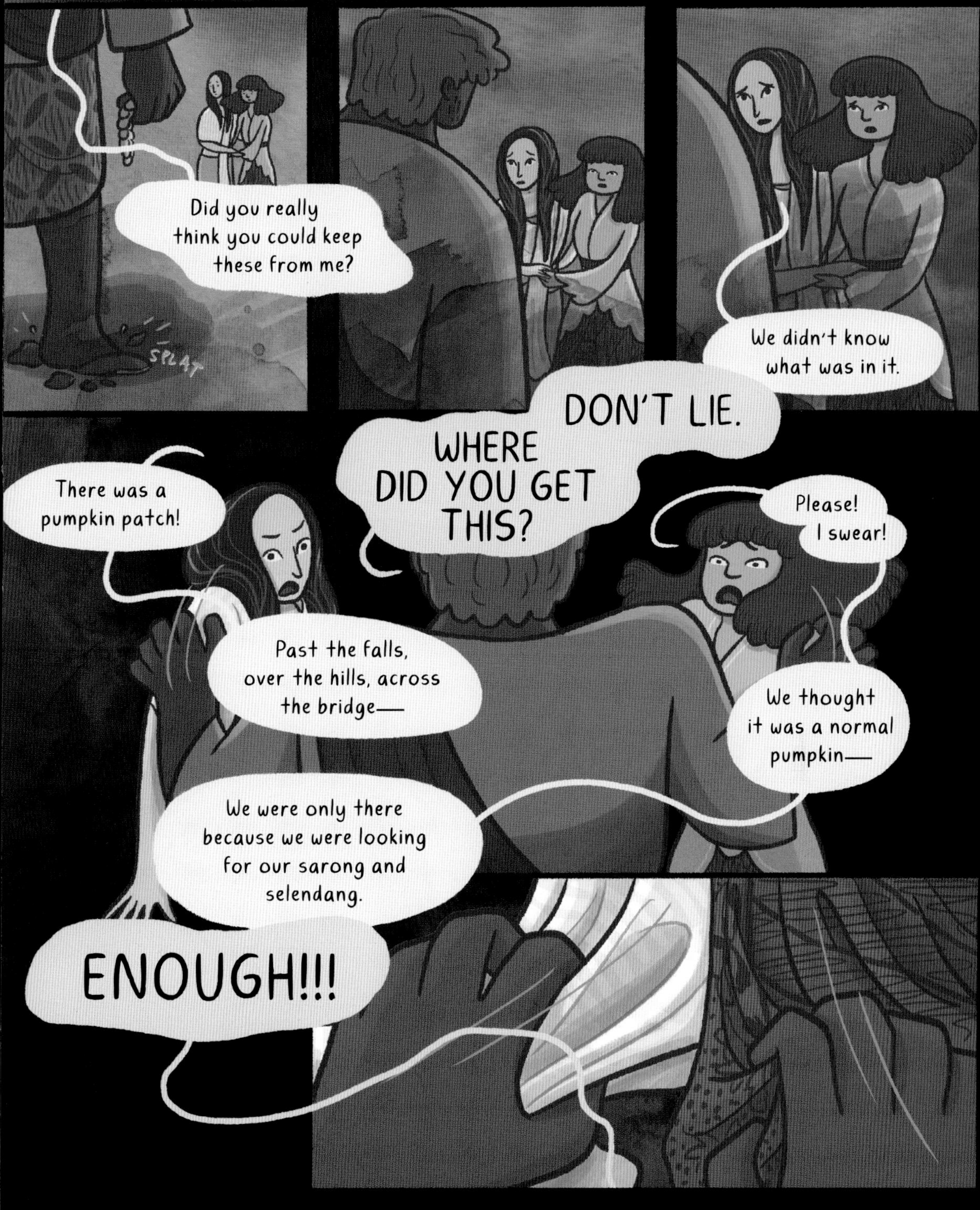
Did you really think you could keep these from me?
SPLAT
We didn't know what was in it.
DON'T LIE.
WHERE DID YOU GET THIS?
There was a pumpkin patch!
Please! I swear!
Past the falls, over the hills, across the bridge—
We thought it was a normal pumpkin—
We were only there because we were looking for our sarong and selendang.
ENOUGH!!!

For the second time that day, the sisters lost Mother's gifts.

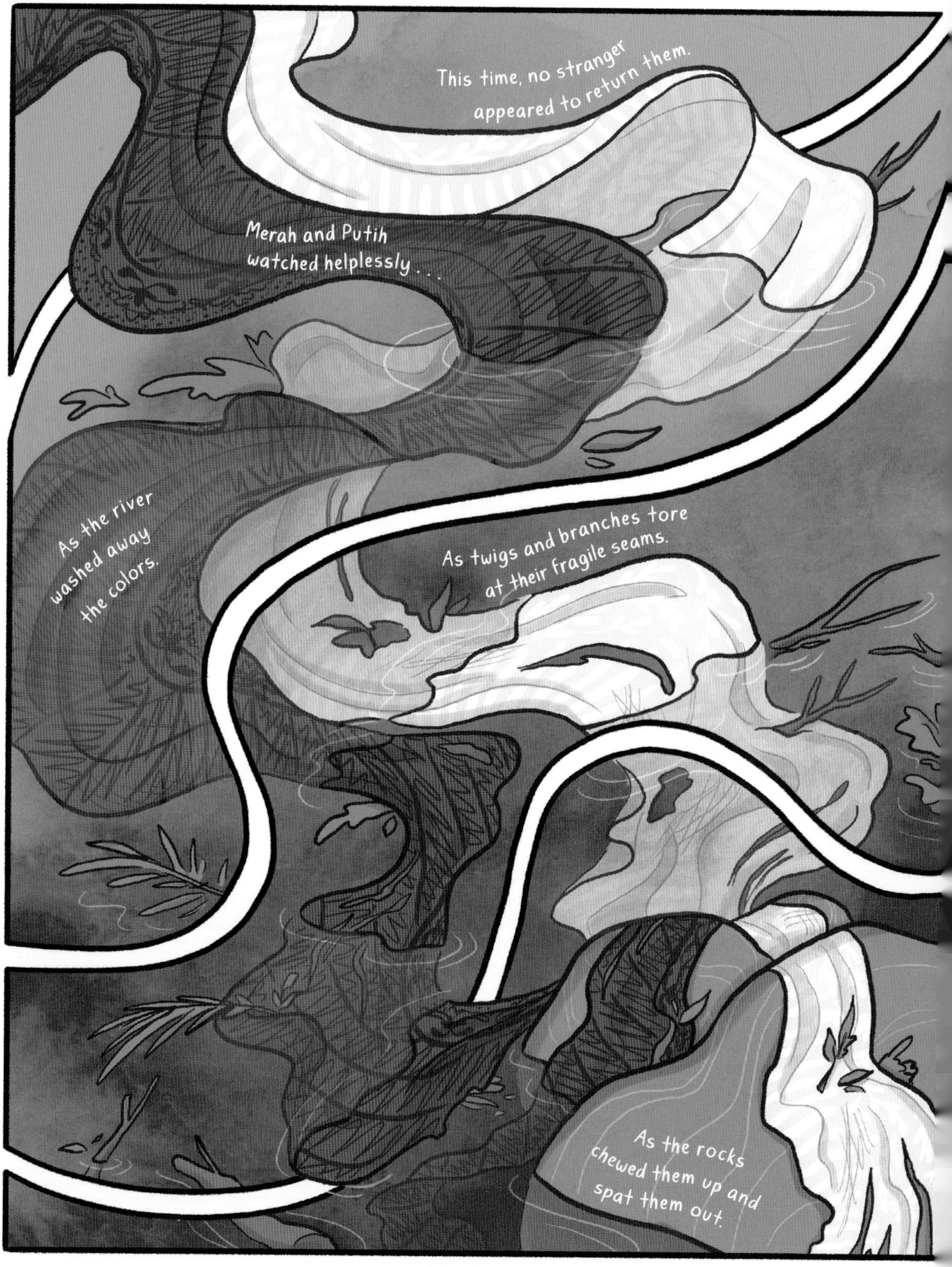
This time, no stranger appeared to return them.
Merah and Putih watched helplessly . . .
As the river washed away the colors.
As twigs and branches tore at their fragile seams.
As the rocks chewed them up and spat them out.

The sisters realized . . .

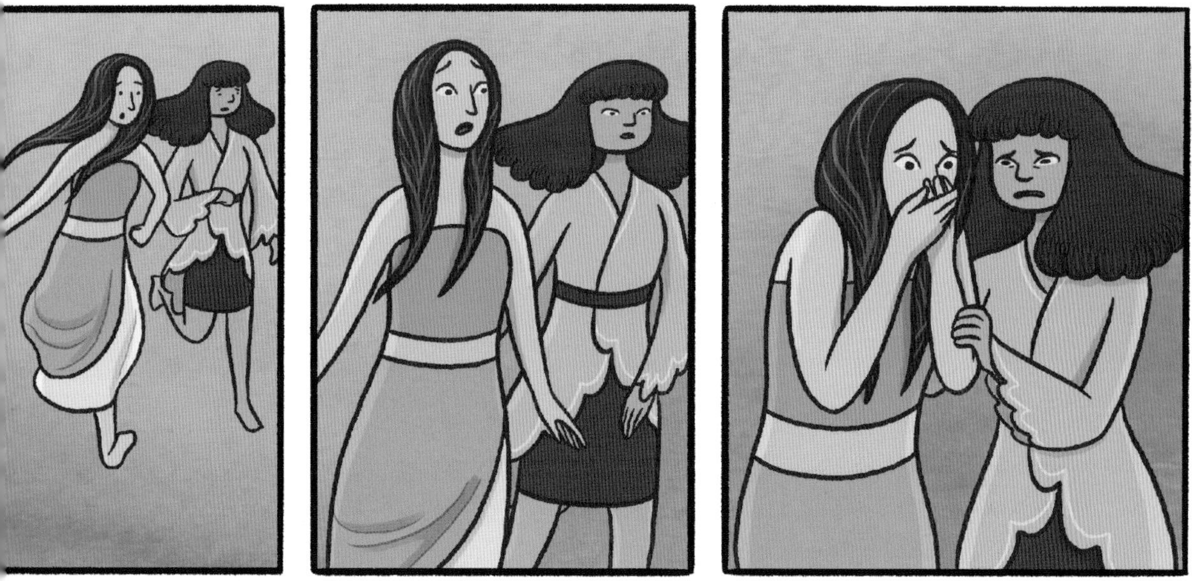

. . . they couldn't keep patiently waiting for their happily ever after.

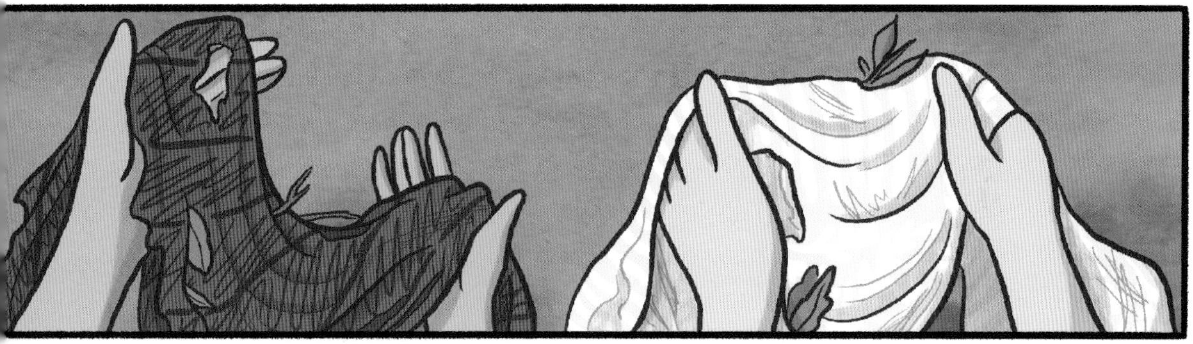

They needed to make their own happy ending.

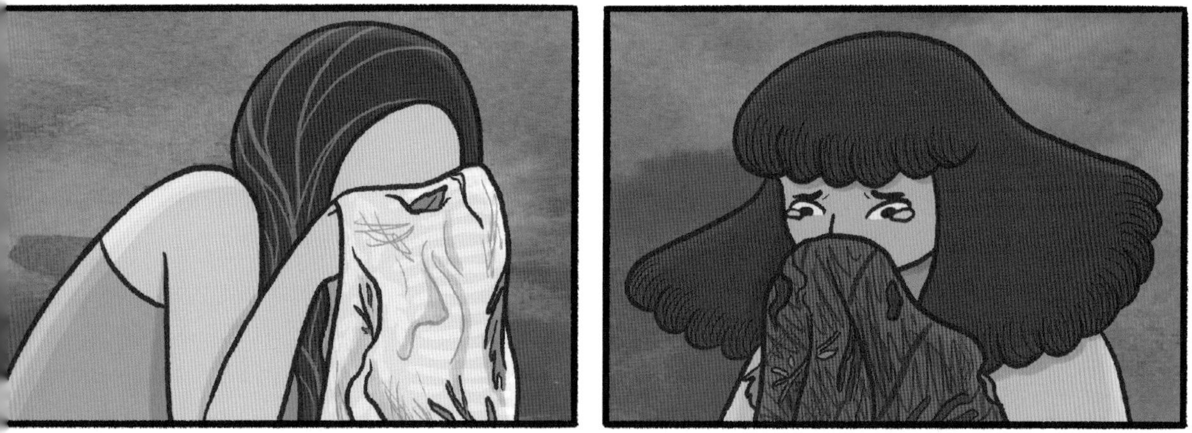

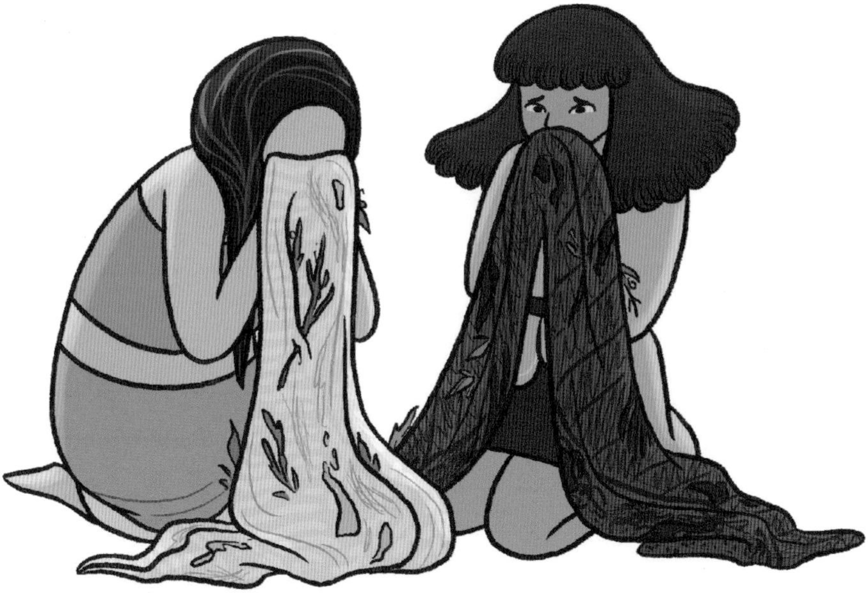

And it was time to accept
that they wouldn't find it here.

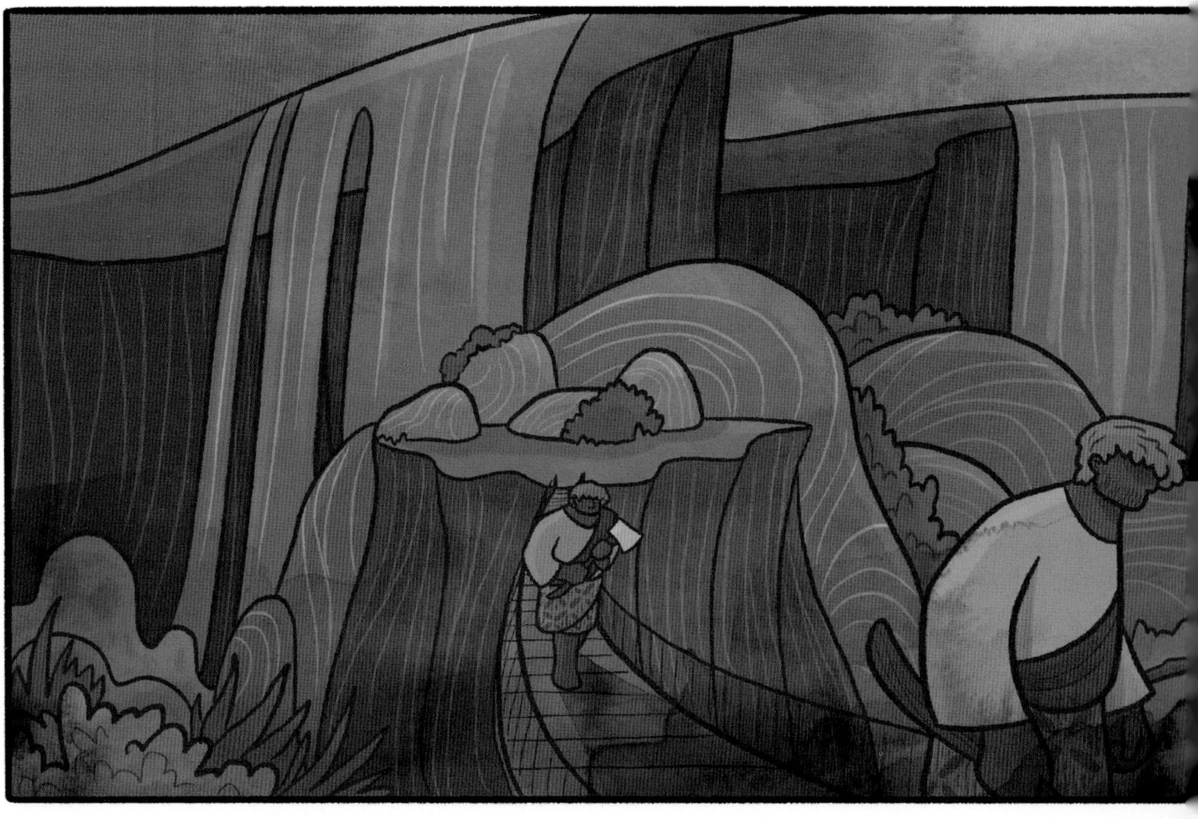

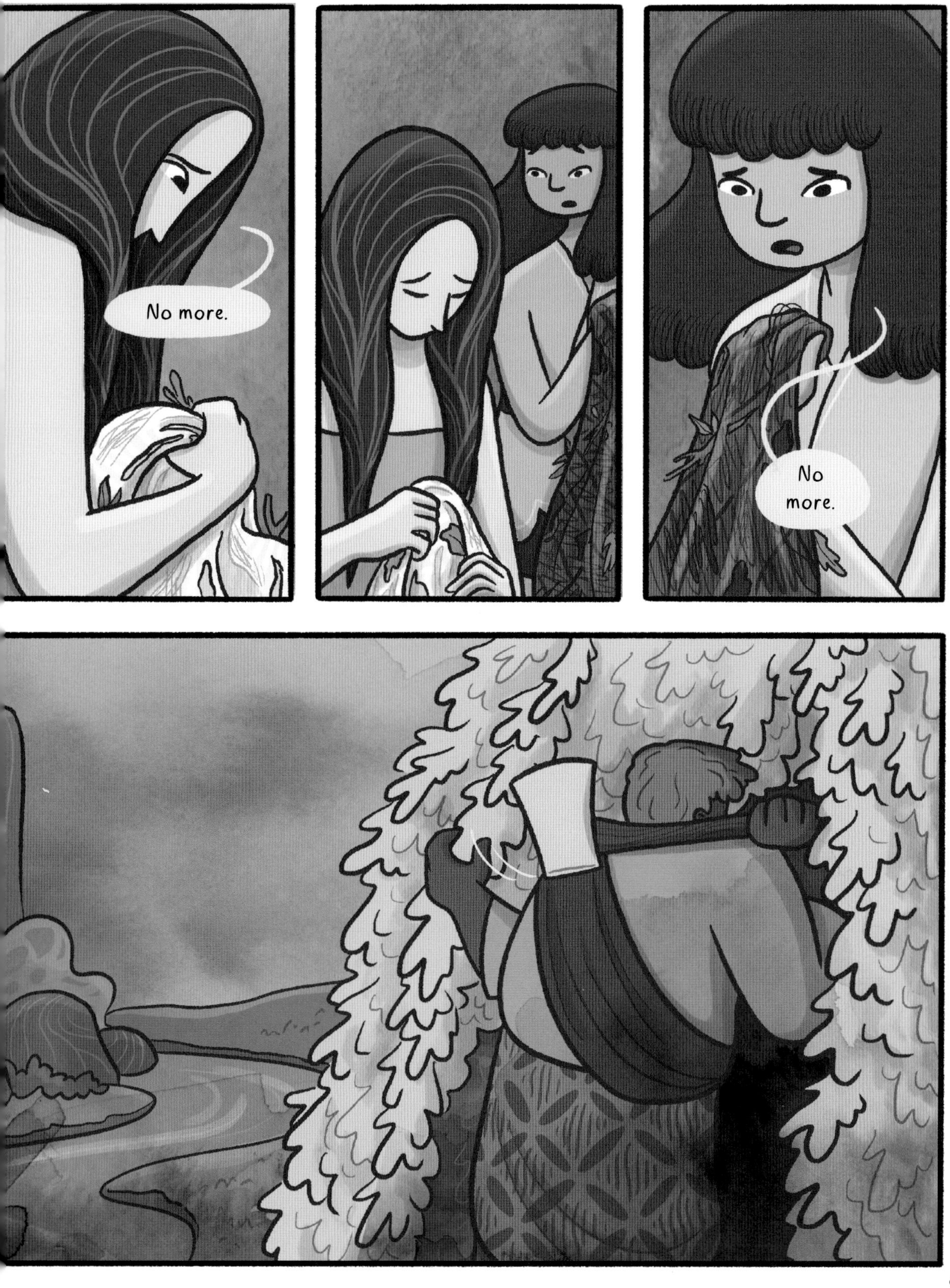
No more.
No more.

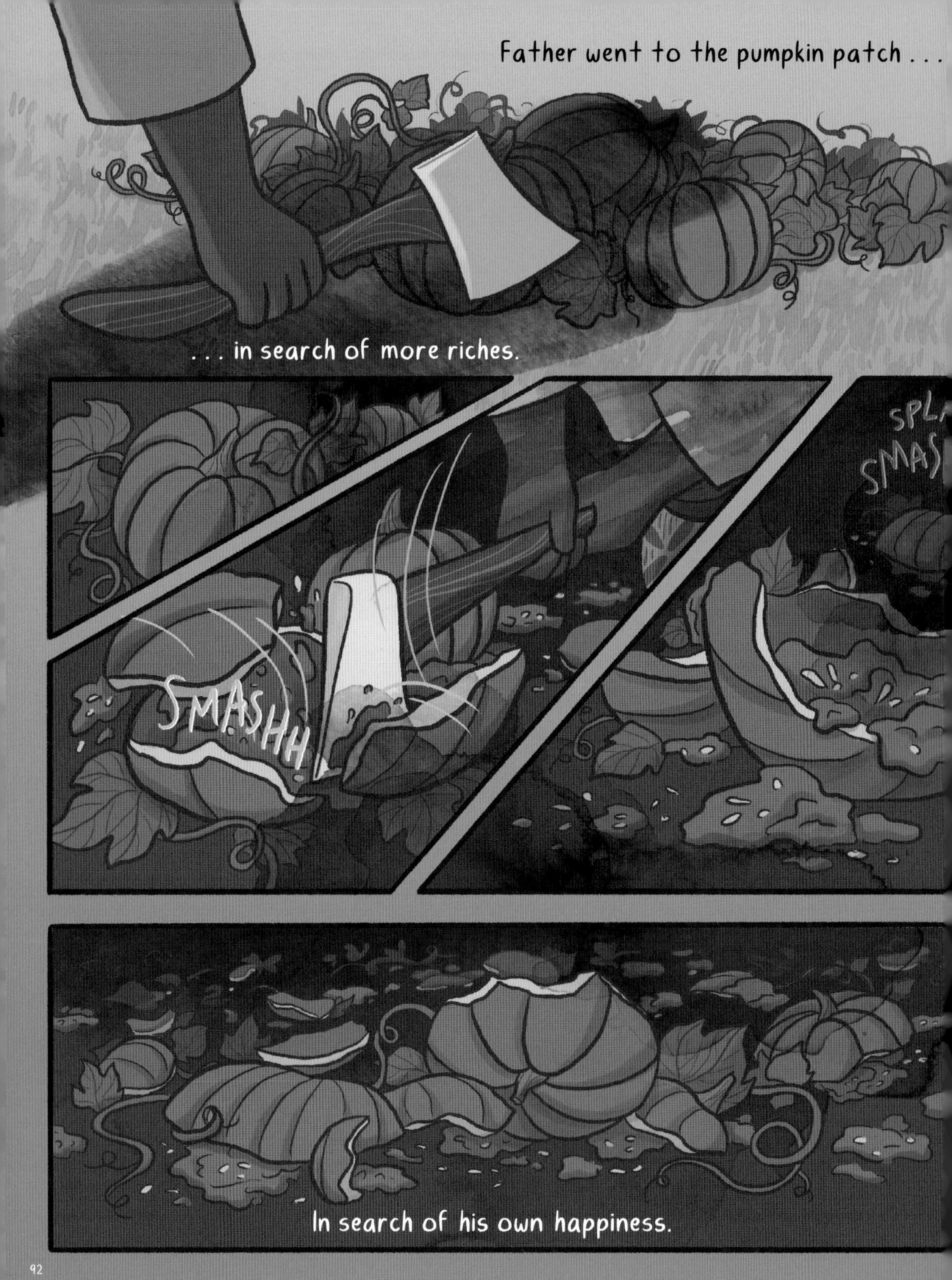
Father went to the pumpkin patch . . .
. . . in search of more riches.
SMASHH
In search of his own happiness.

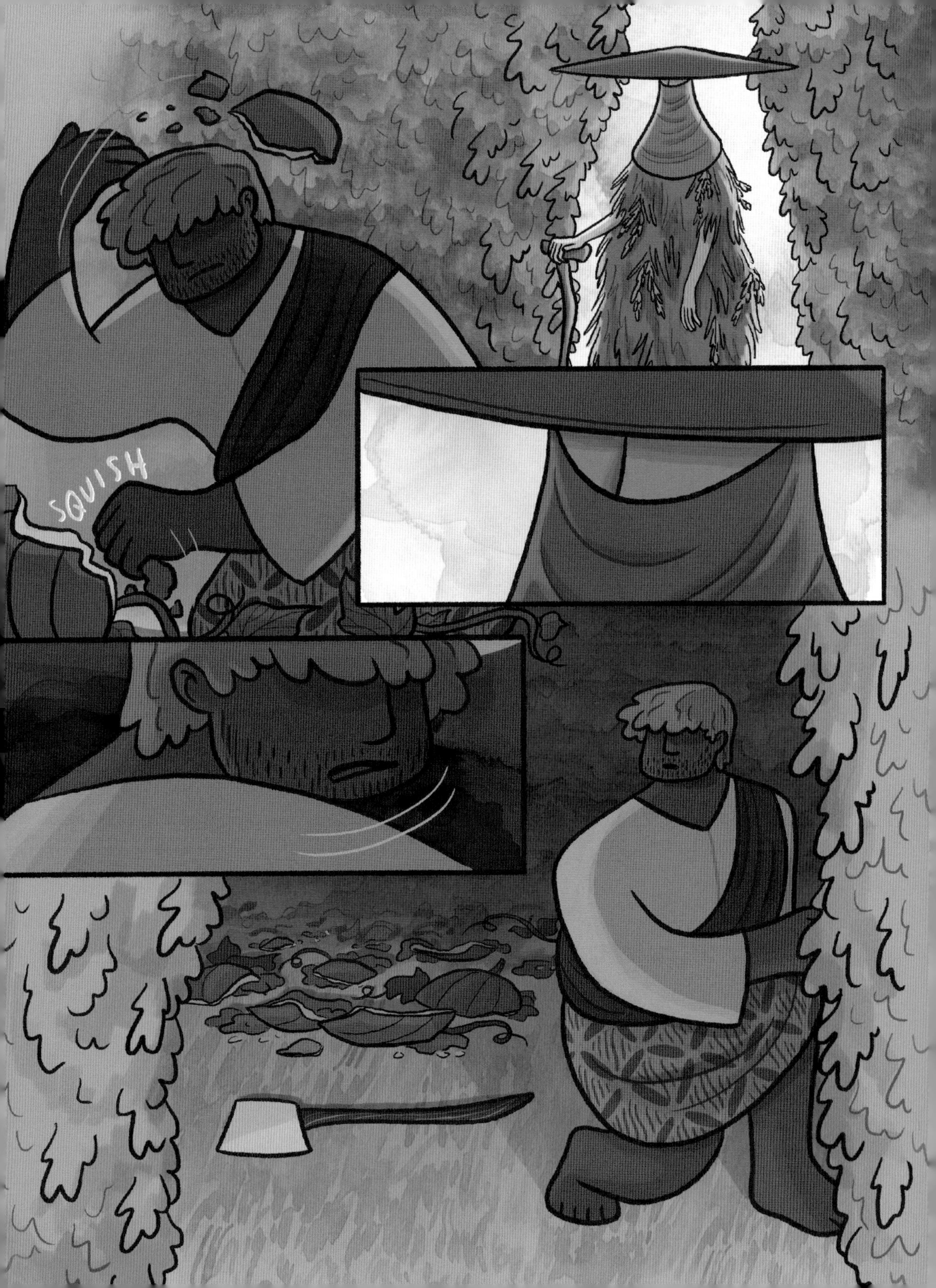
SQUISH

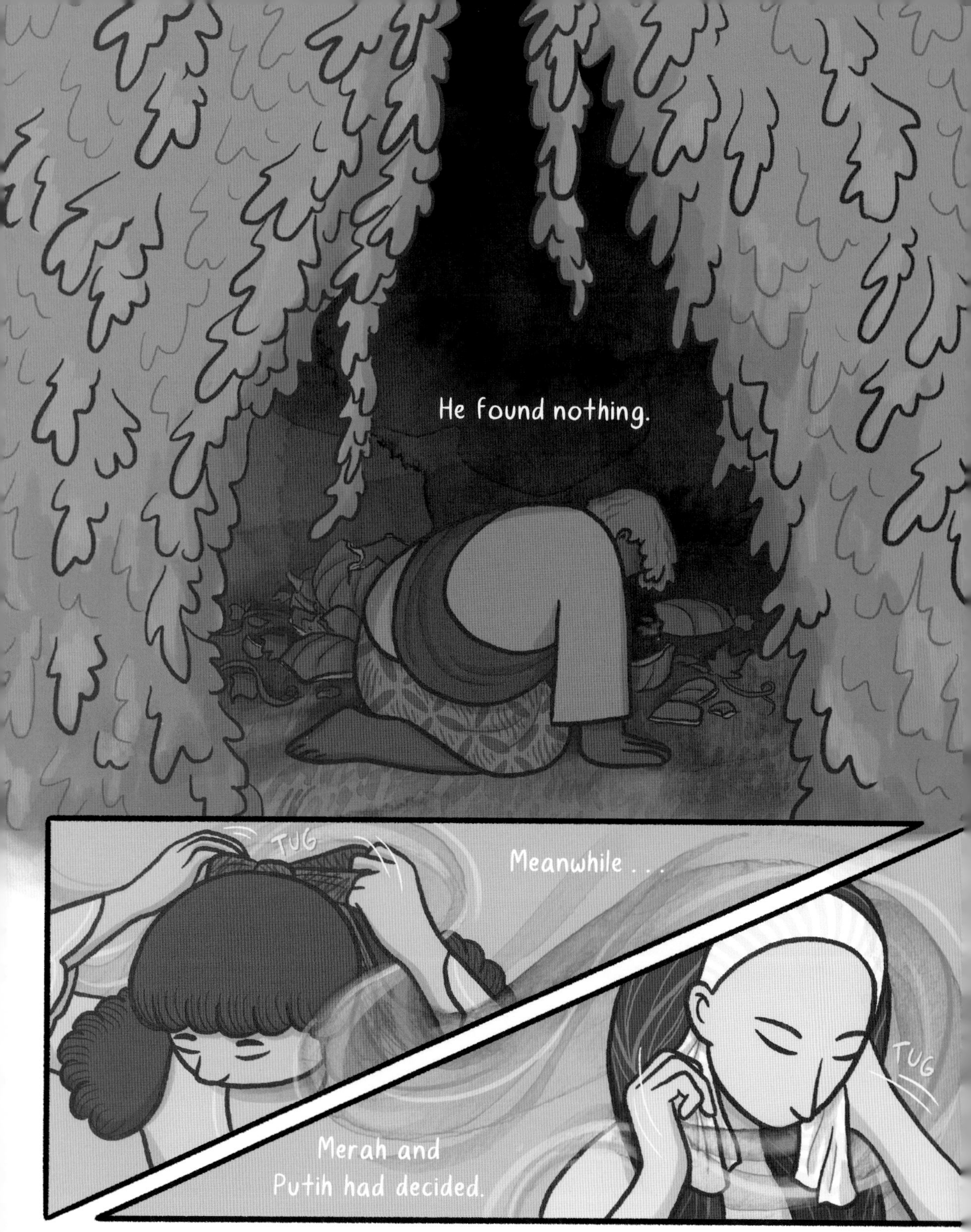
He found nothing.
TUG
Meanwhile . . .
Merah and
Putih had decided.
TUG

It was time to move on.

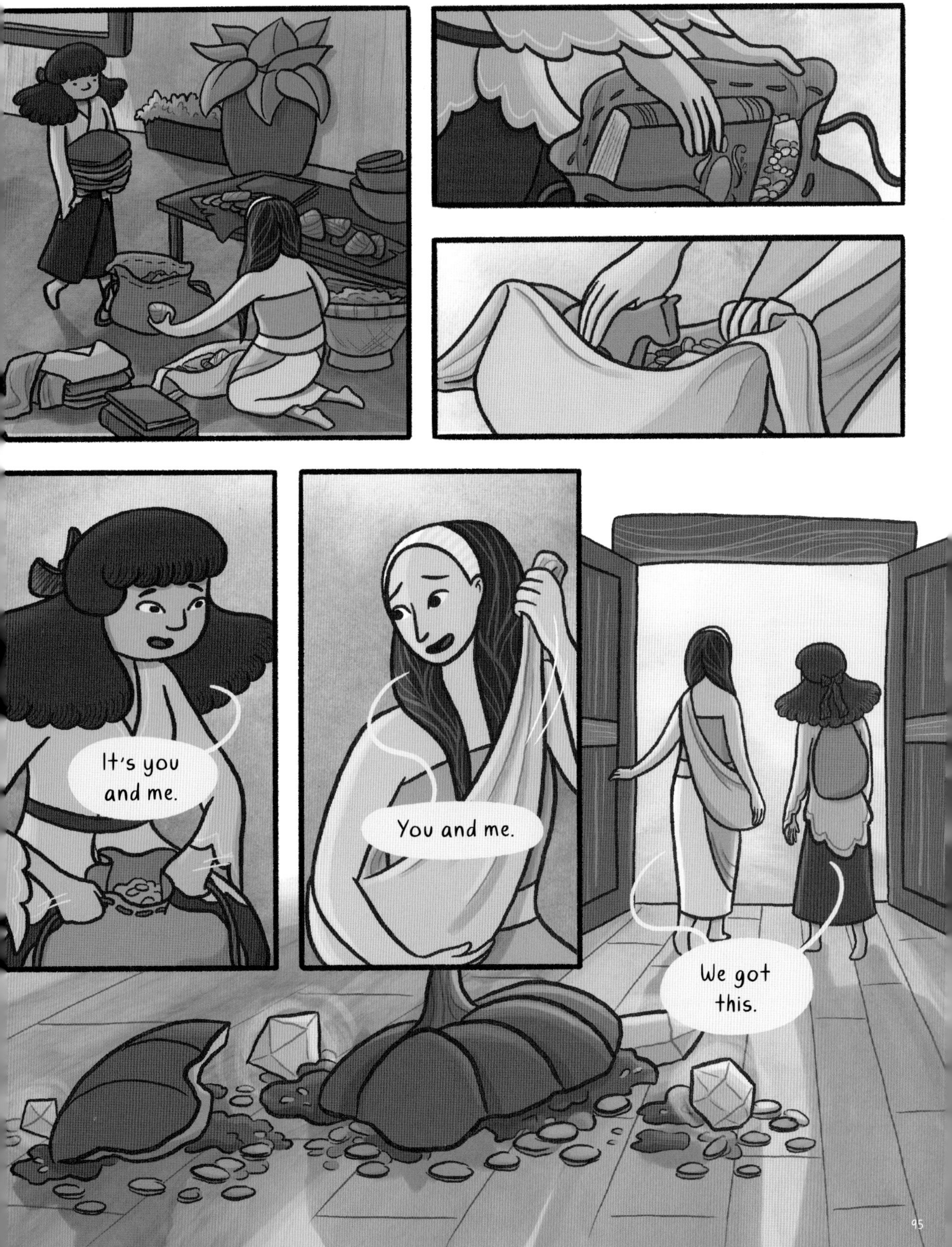
It's you and me.
You and me.
We got this.

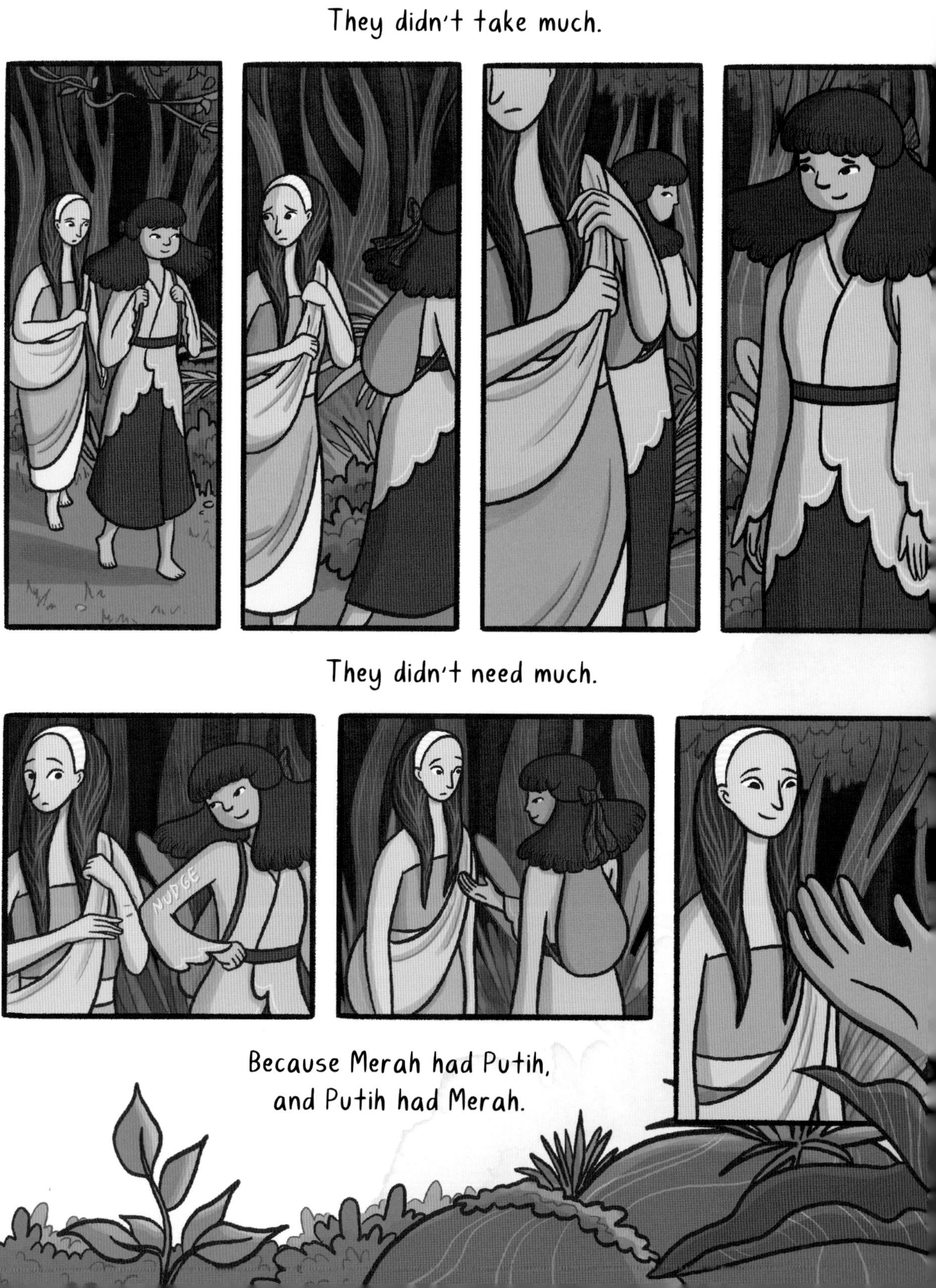
They didn't take much.
They didn't need much.
NUDGE
Because Merah had Putih,
and Putih had Merah.

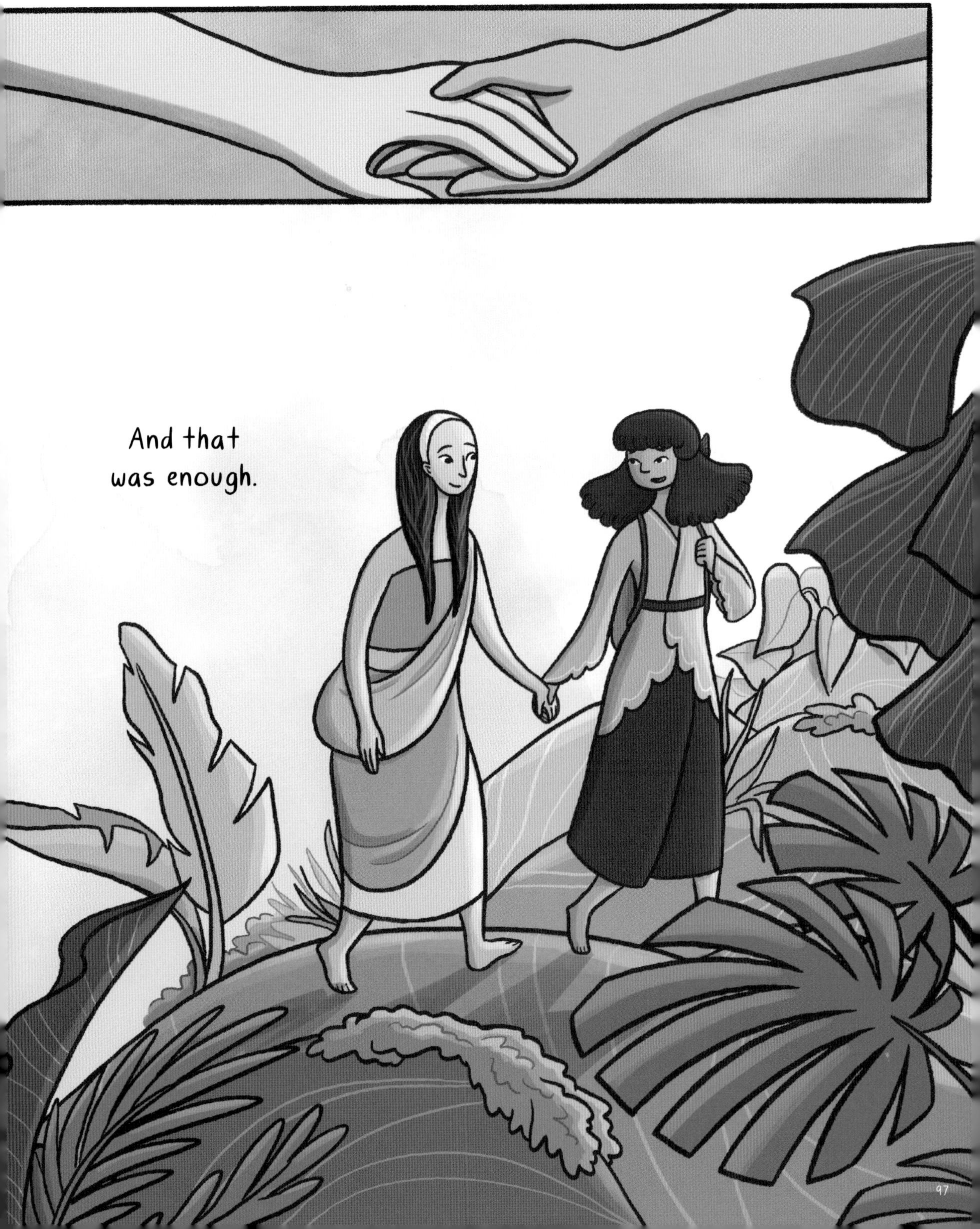
And that
was enough.

Timun Mas

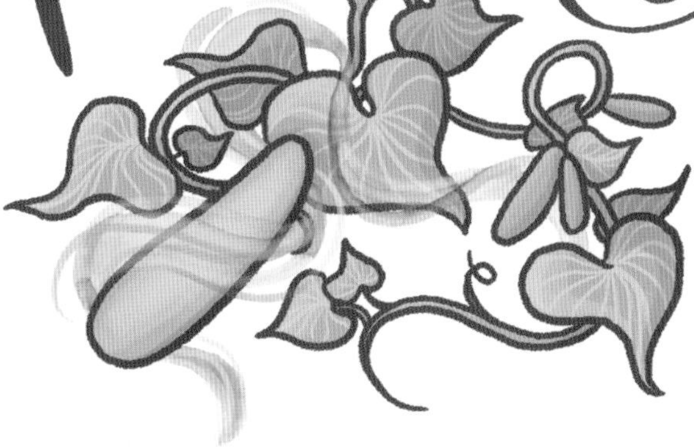

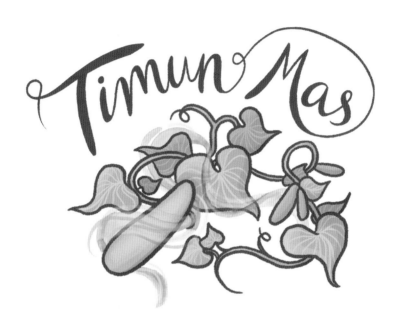

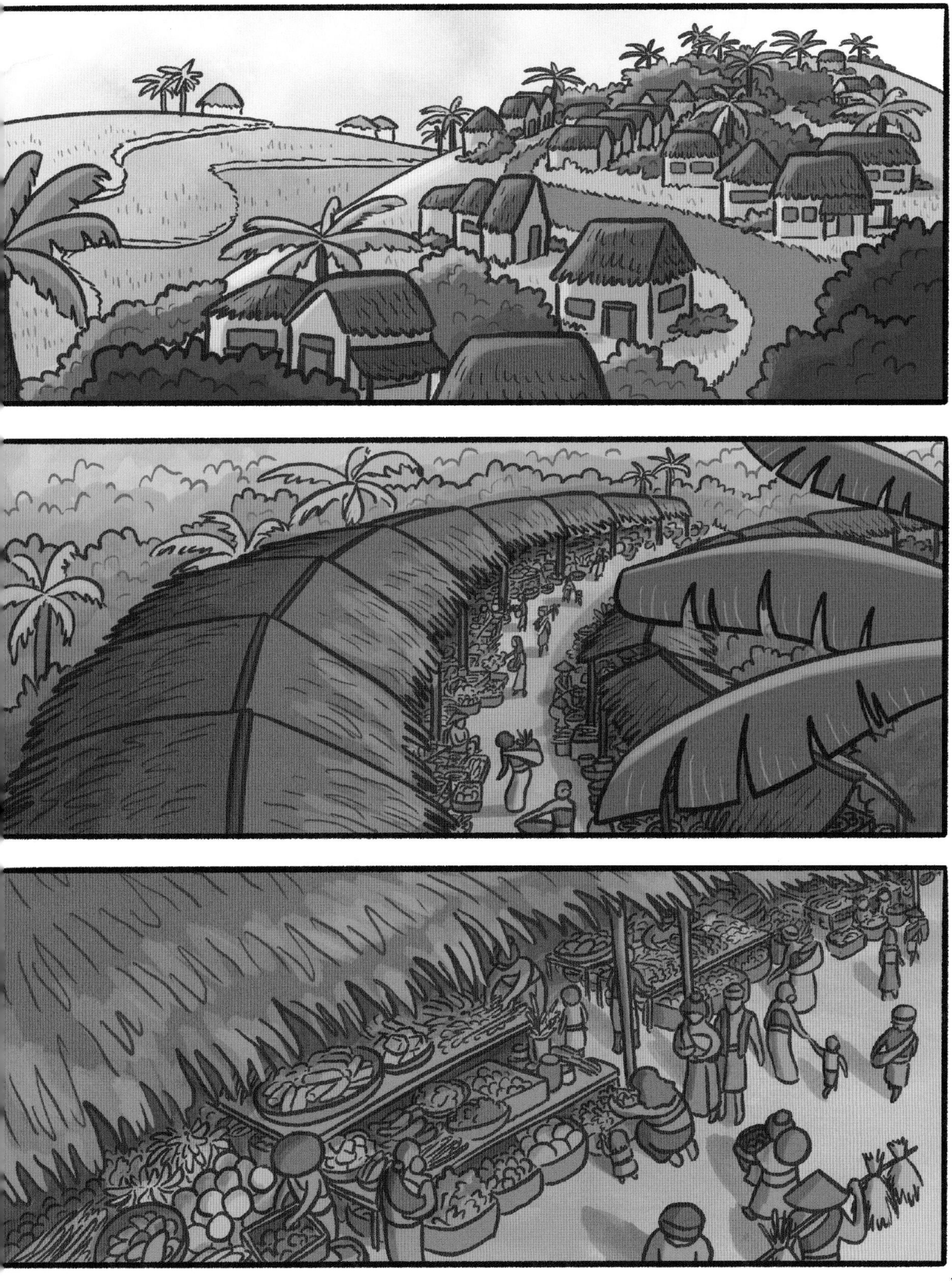

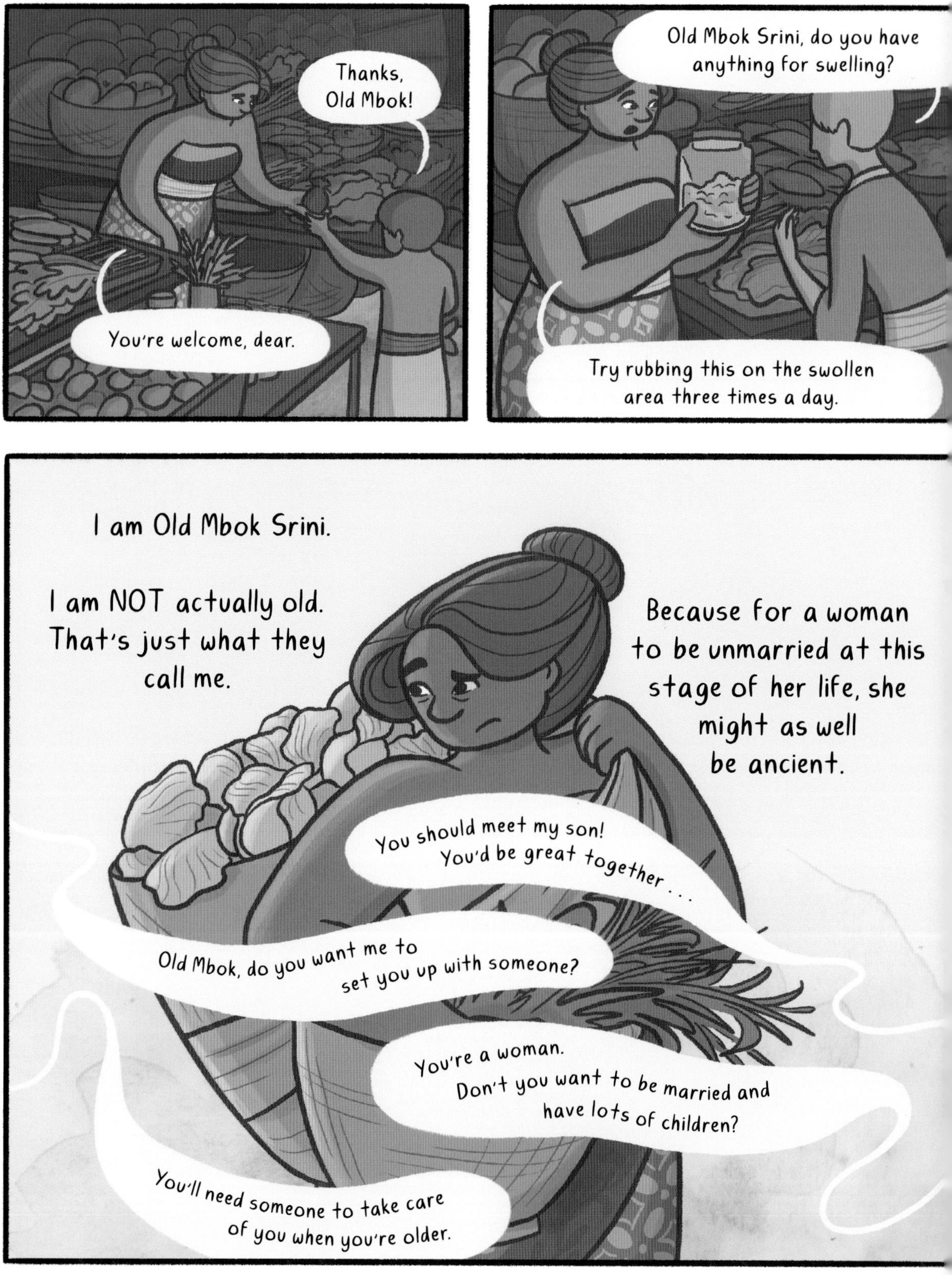
Thanks, Old Mbok!
You're welcome, dear.
Old Mbok Srini, do you have anything for swelling?
Try rubbing this on the swollen area three times a day.
I am Old Mbok Srini.
I am NOT actually old. That's just what they call me.
Because for a woman to be unmarried at this stage of her life, she might as well be ancient.
You should meet my son! You'd be great together . . .
Old Mbok, do you want me to set you up with someone?
You're a woman. Don't you want to be married and have lots of children?
You'll need someone to take care of you when you're older.

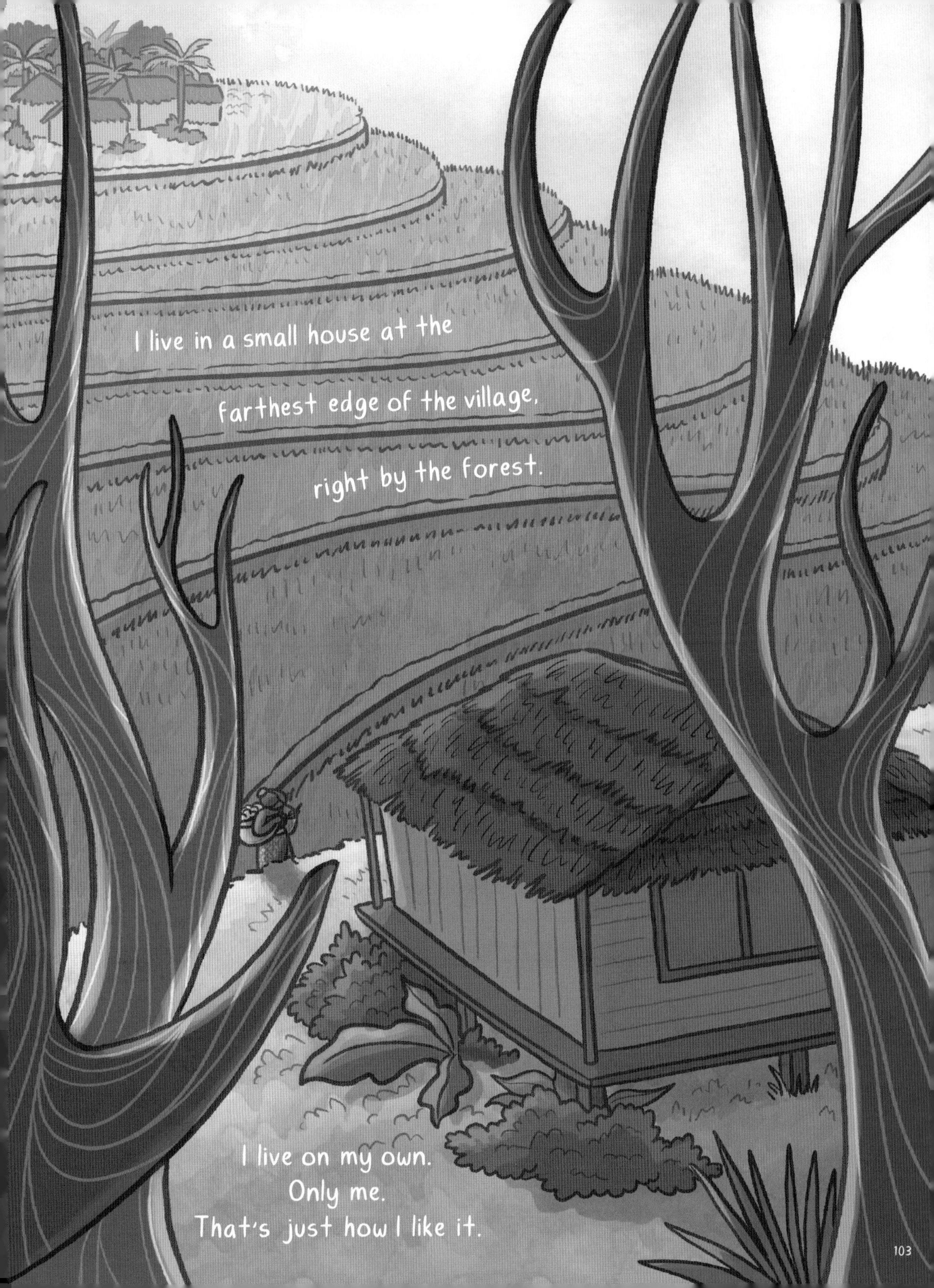
I live in a small house at the
farthest edge of the village,
right by the forest.
I live on my own.
Only me.
That's just how I like it.

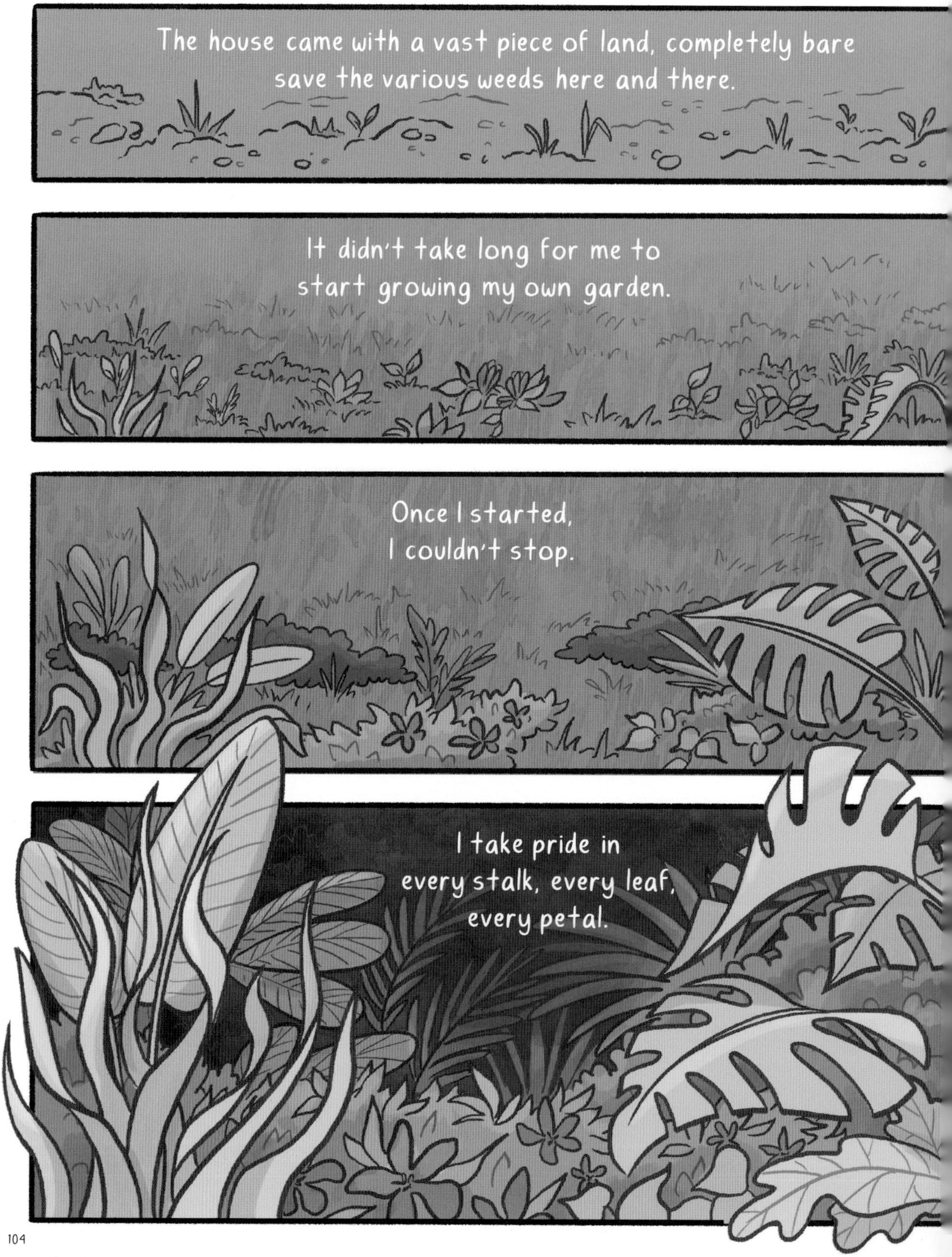
The house came with a vast piece of land, completely bare save the various weeds here and there.
It didn't take long for me to start growing my own garden.
Once I started, I couldn't stop.
I take pride in every stalk, every leaf, every petal.

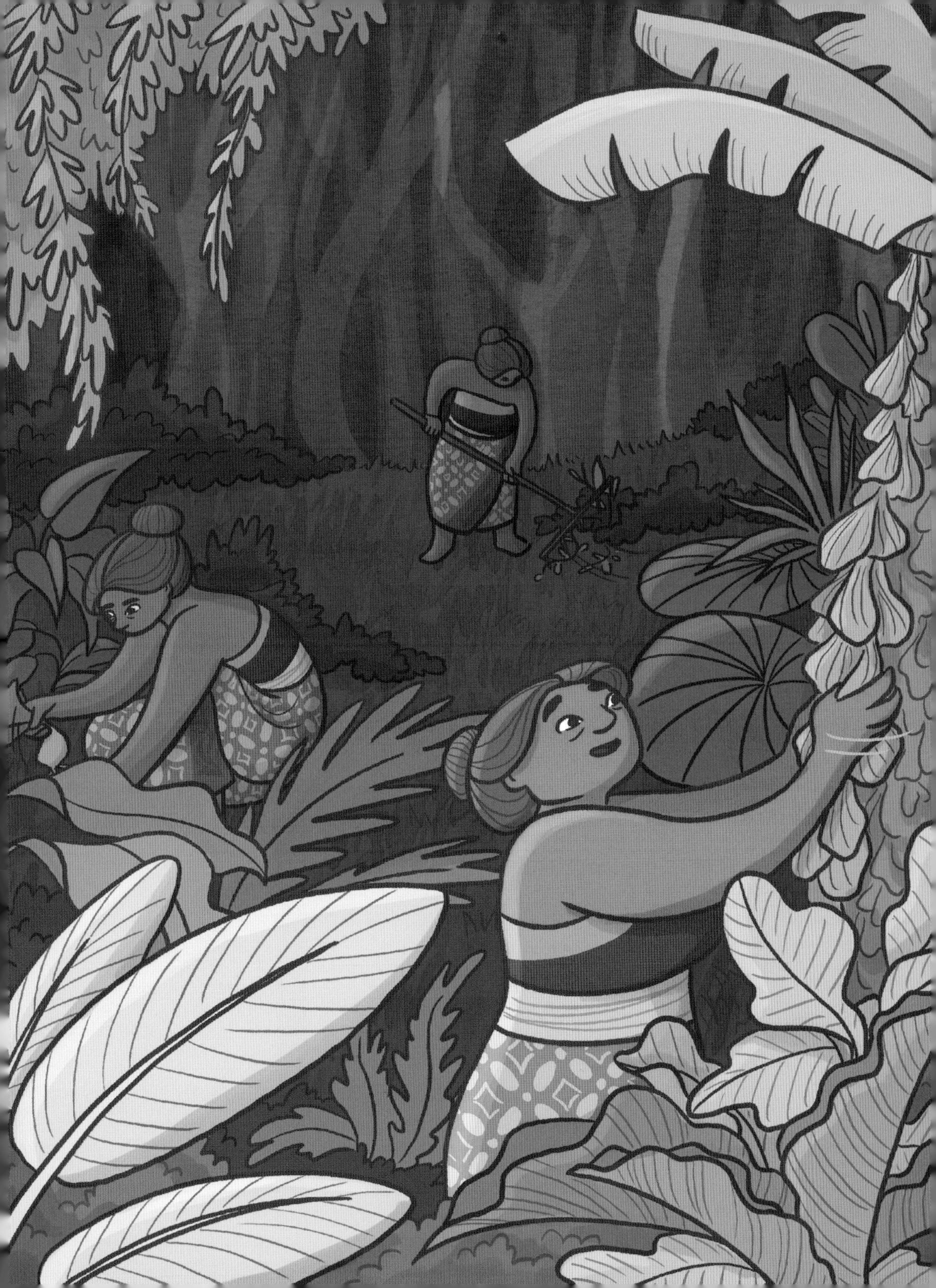

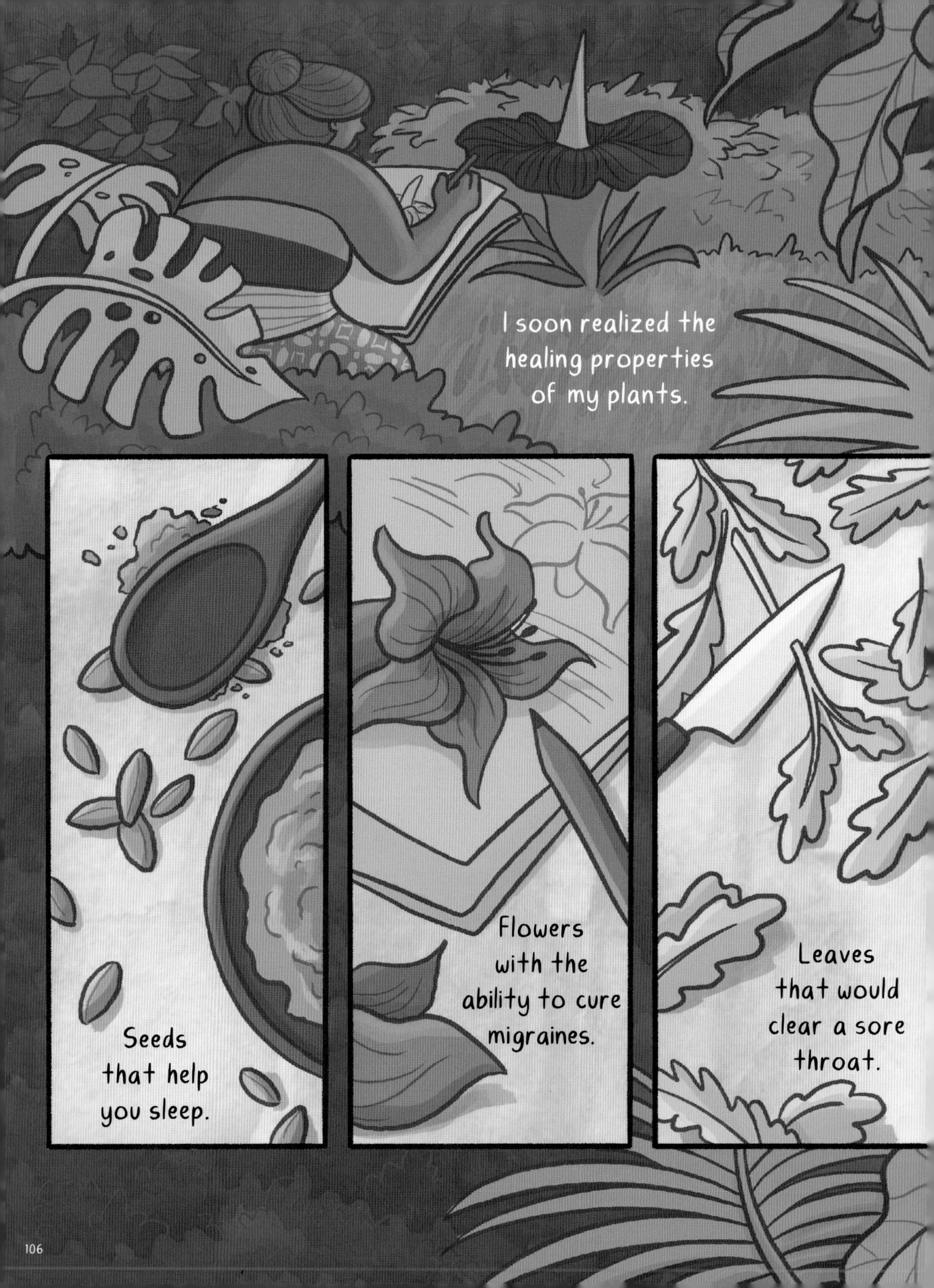
I soon realized the healing properties of my plants.
Seeds that help you sleep.
Flowers with the ability to cure migraines.
Leaves that would clear a sore throat.

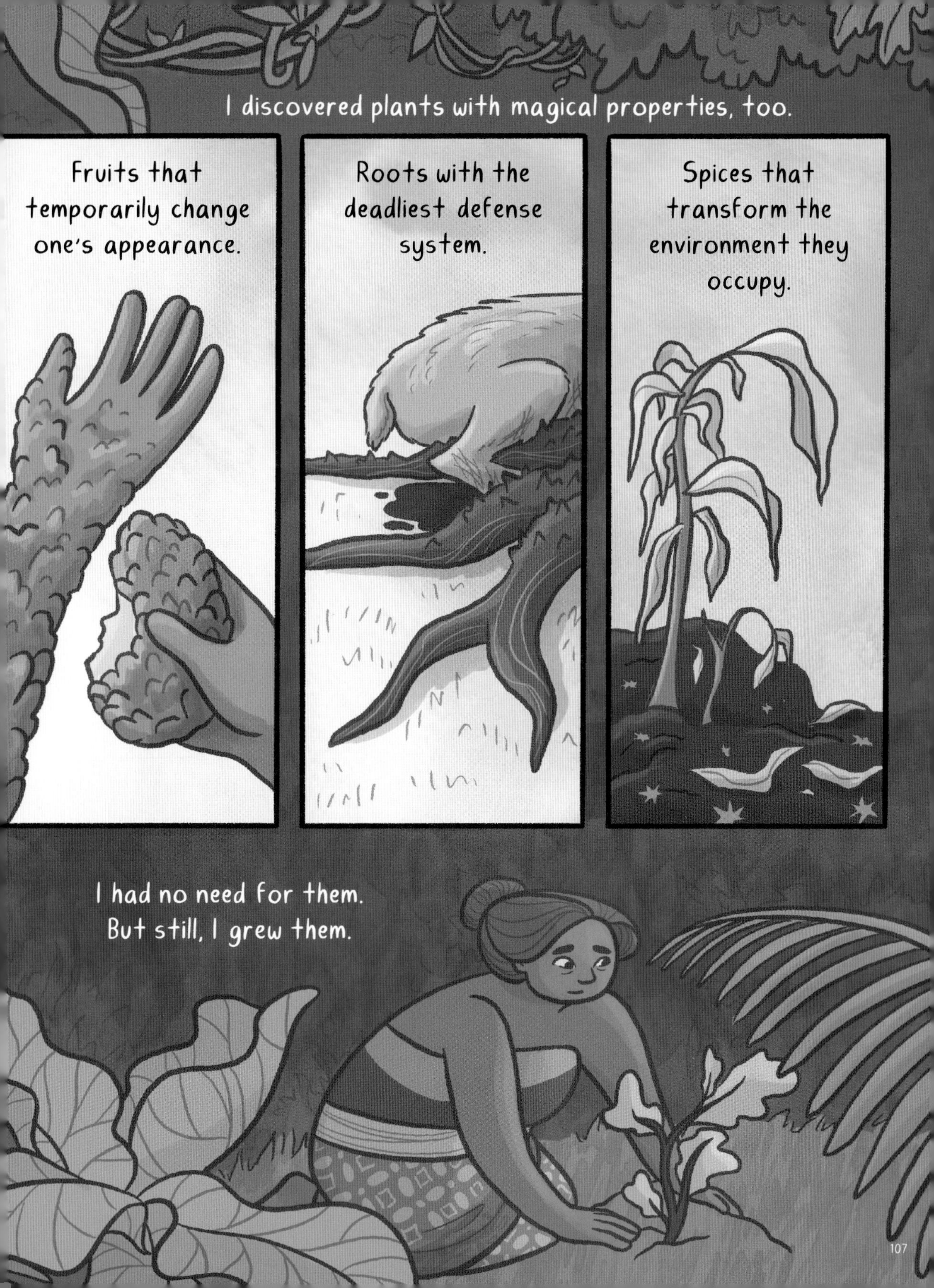
I discovered plants with magical properties, too.
Fruits that temporarily change one's appearance.
Roots with the deadliest defense system.
Spices that transform the environment they occupy.
I had no need for them. But still, I grew them.

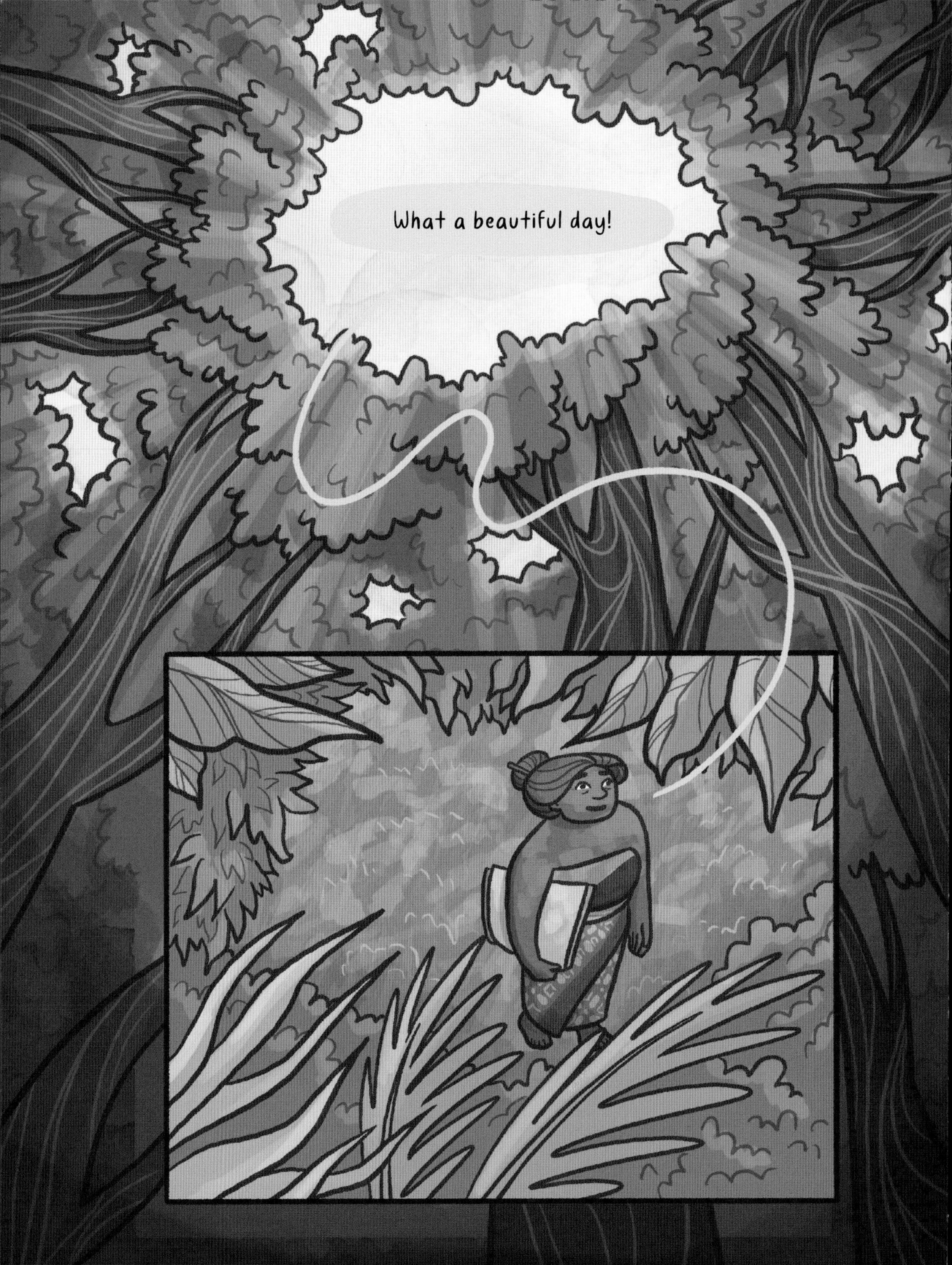
What a beautiful day!

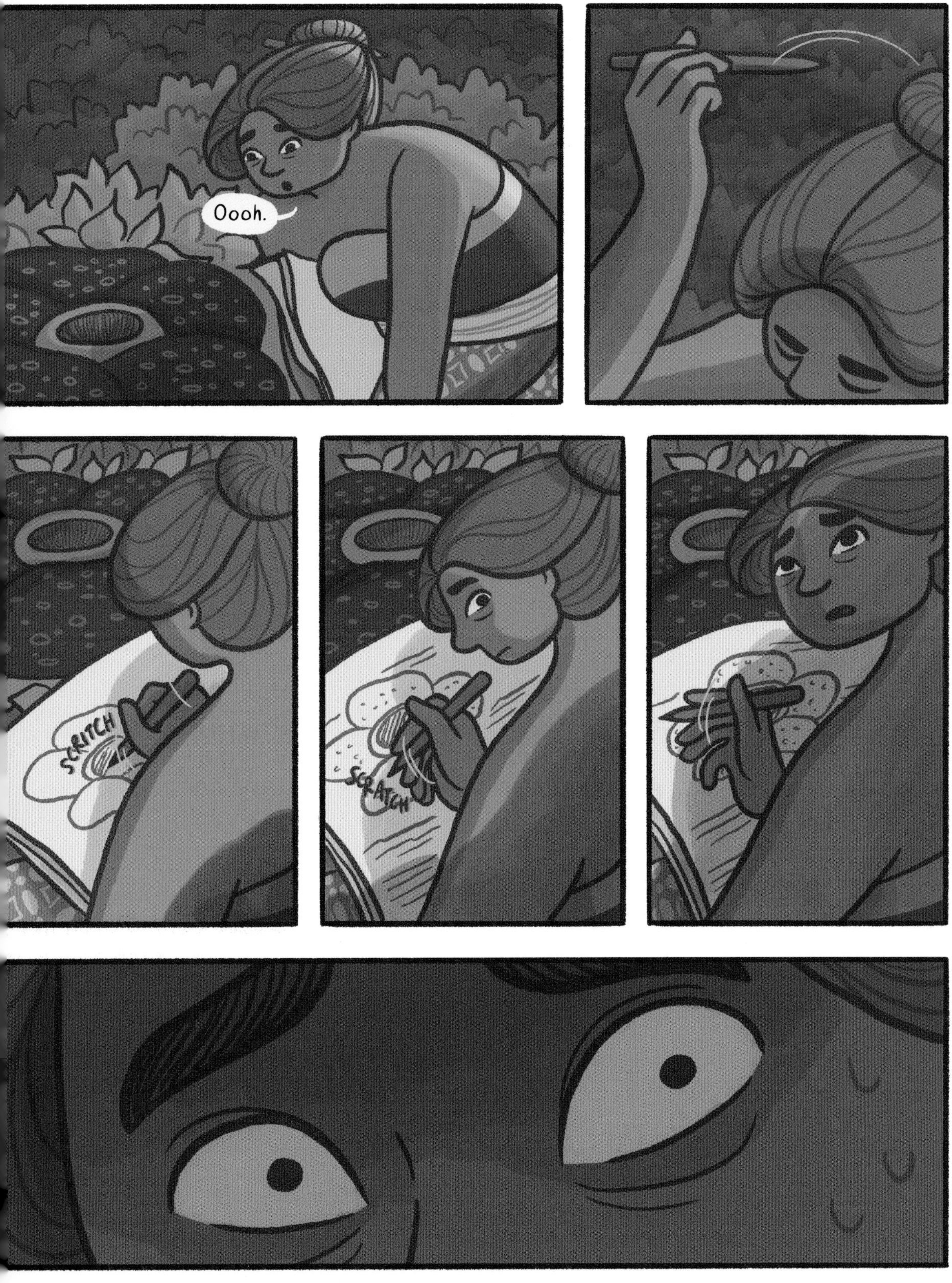
Oooh.
SCRITCH
SCRATCH

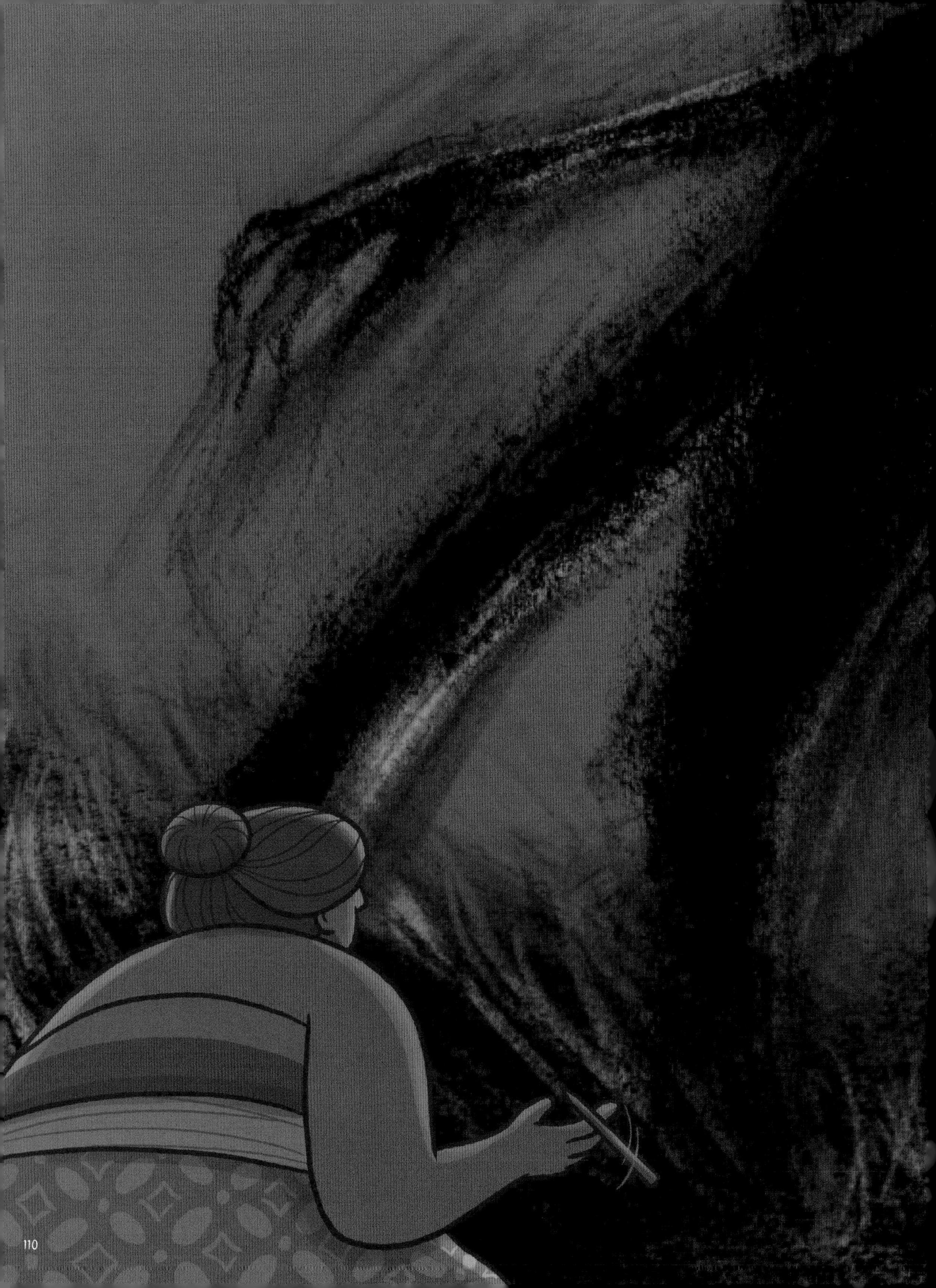

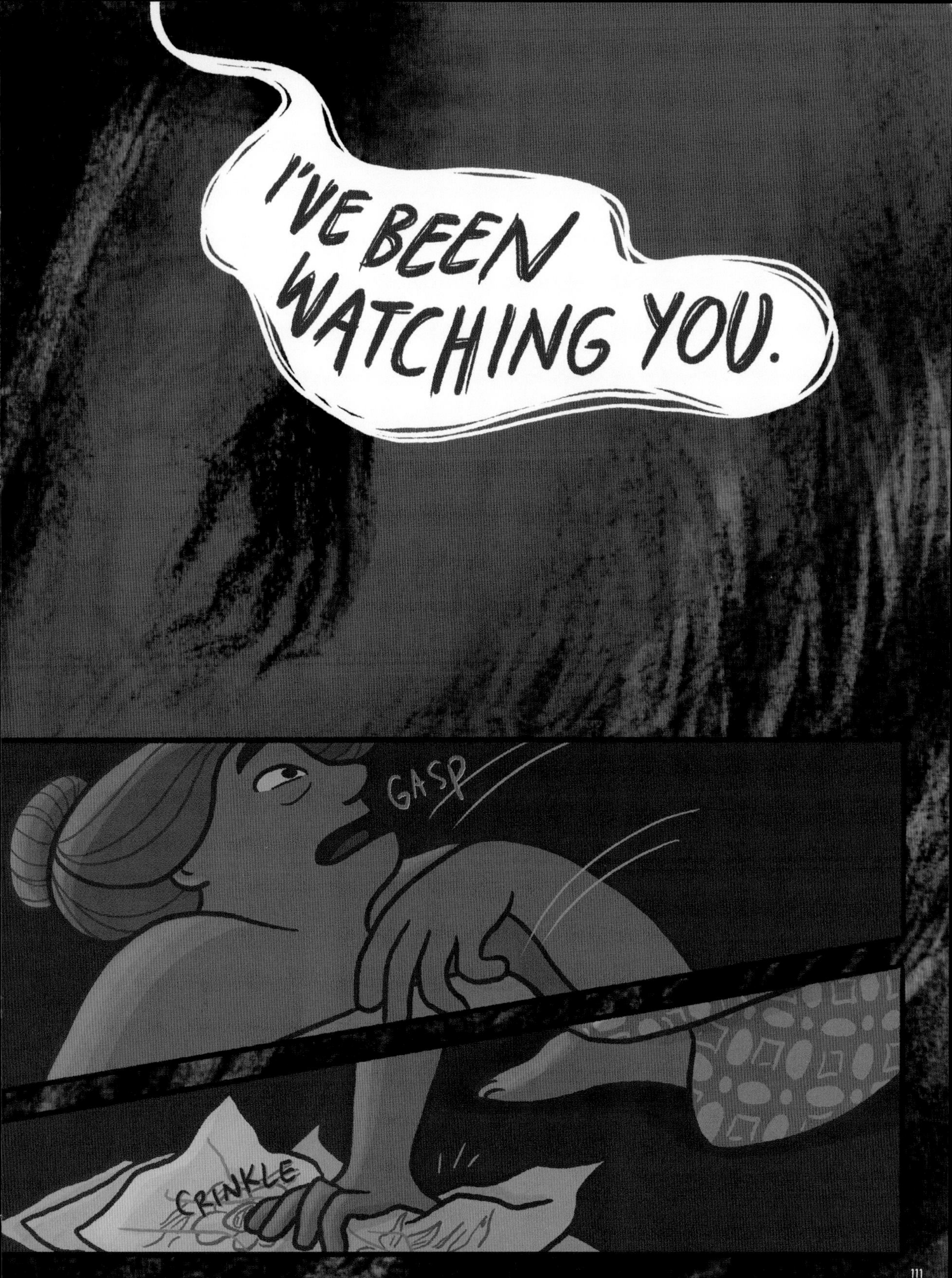
I'VE BEEN WATCHING YOU.
GASP
CRINKLE

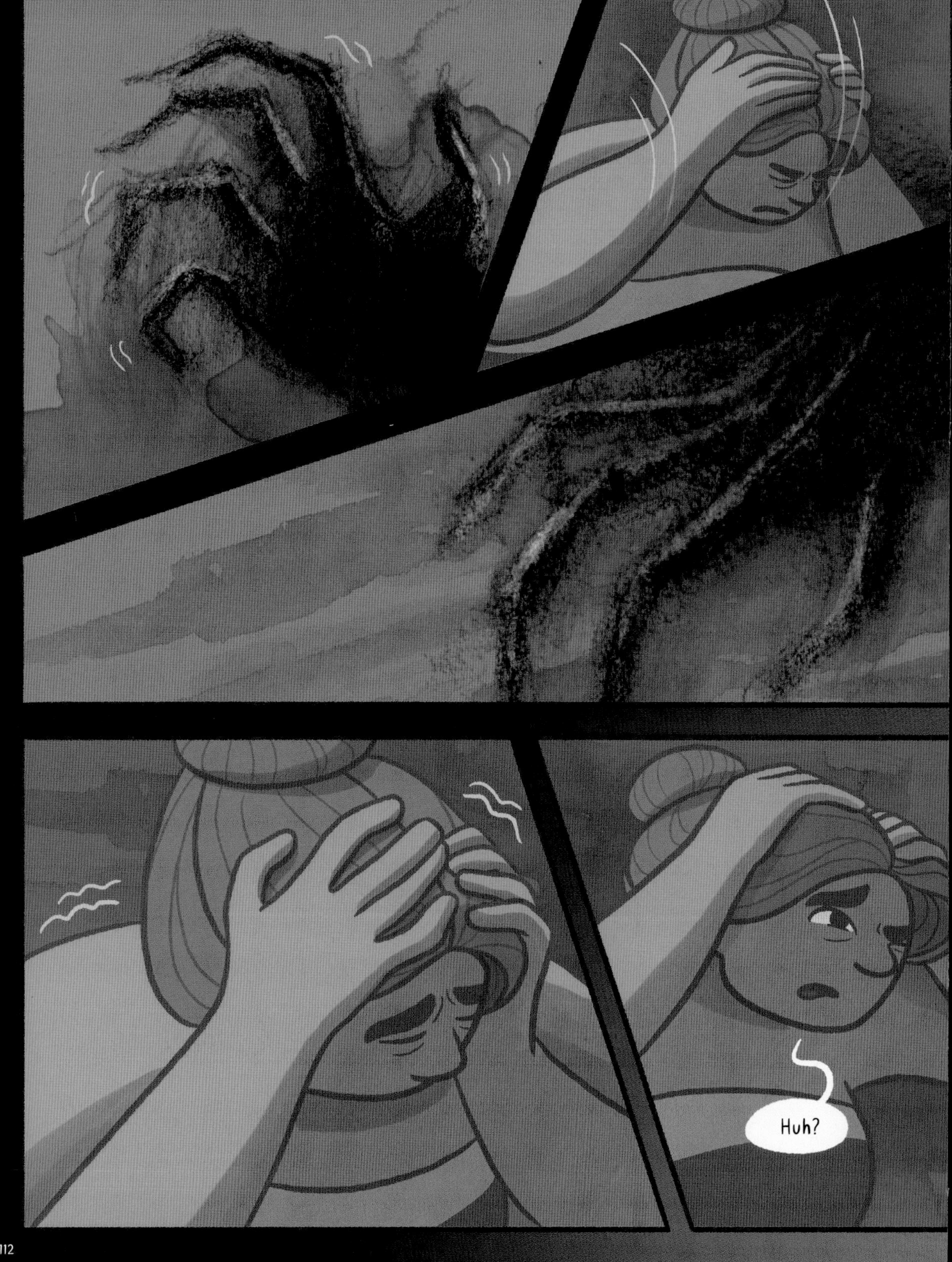
Huh?

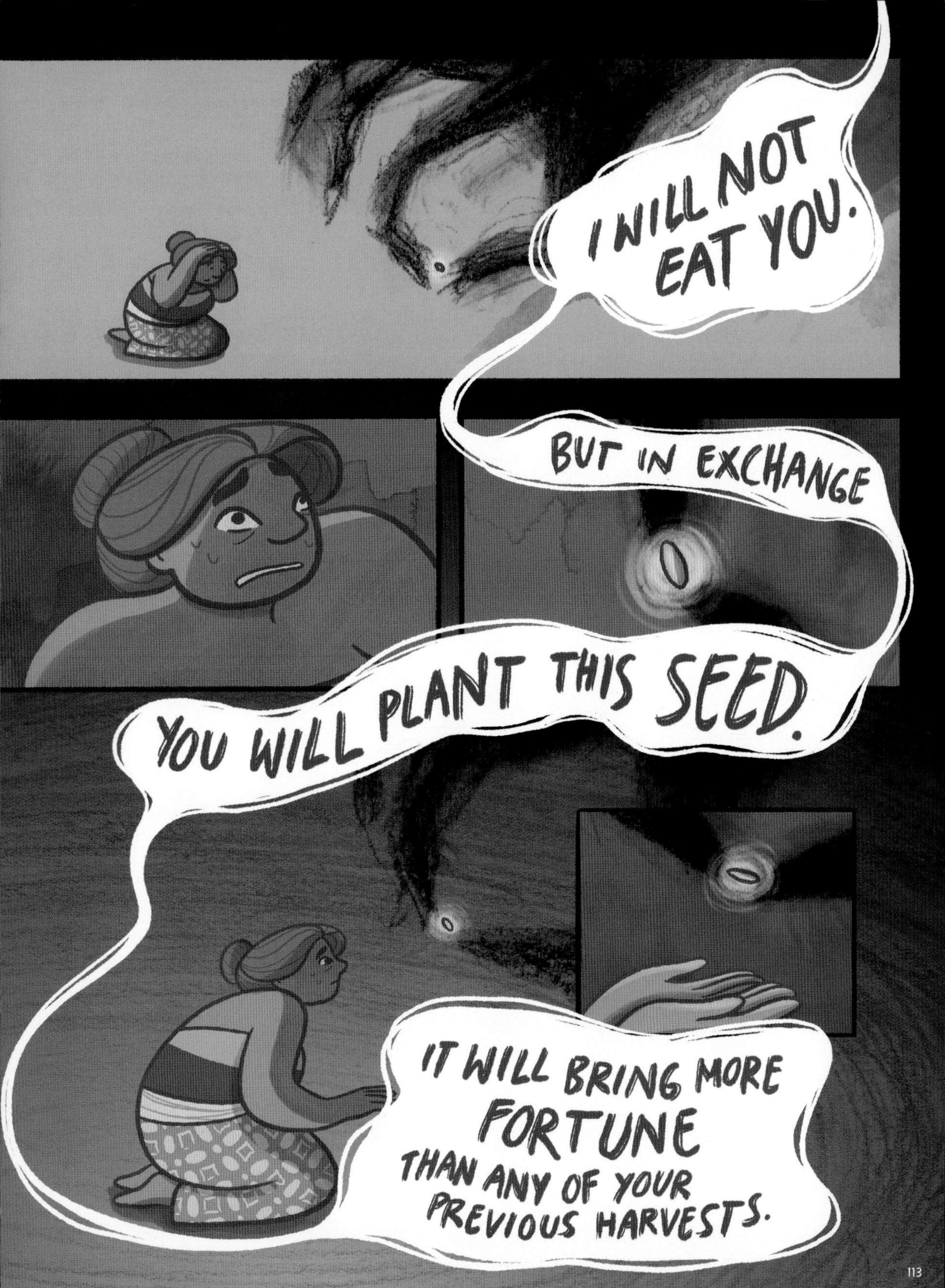
I WILL NOT EAT YOU.
BUT IN EXCHANGE
YOU WILL PLANT THIS SEED.
IT WILL BRING MORE FORTUNE THAN ANY OF YOUR PREVIOUS HARVESTS.

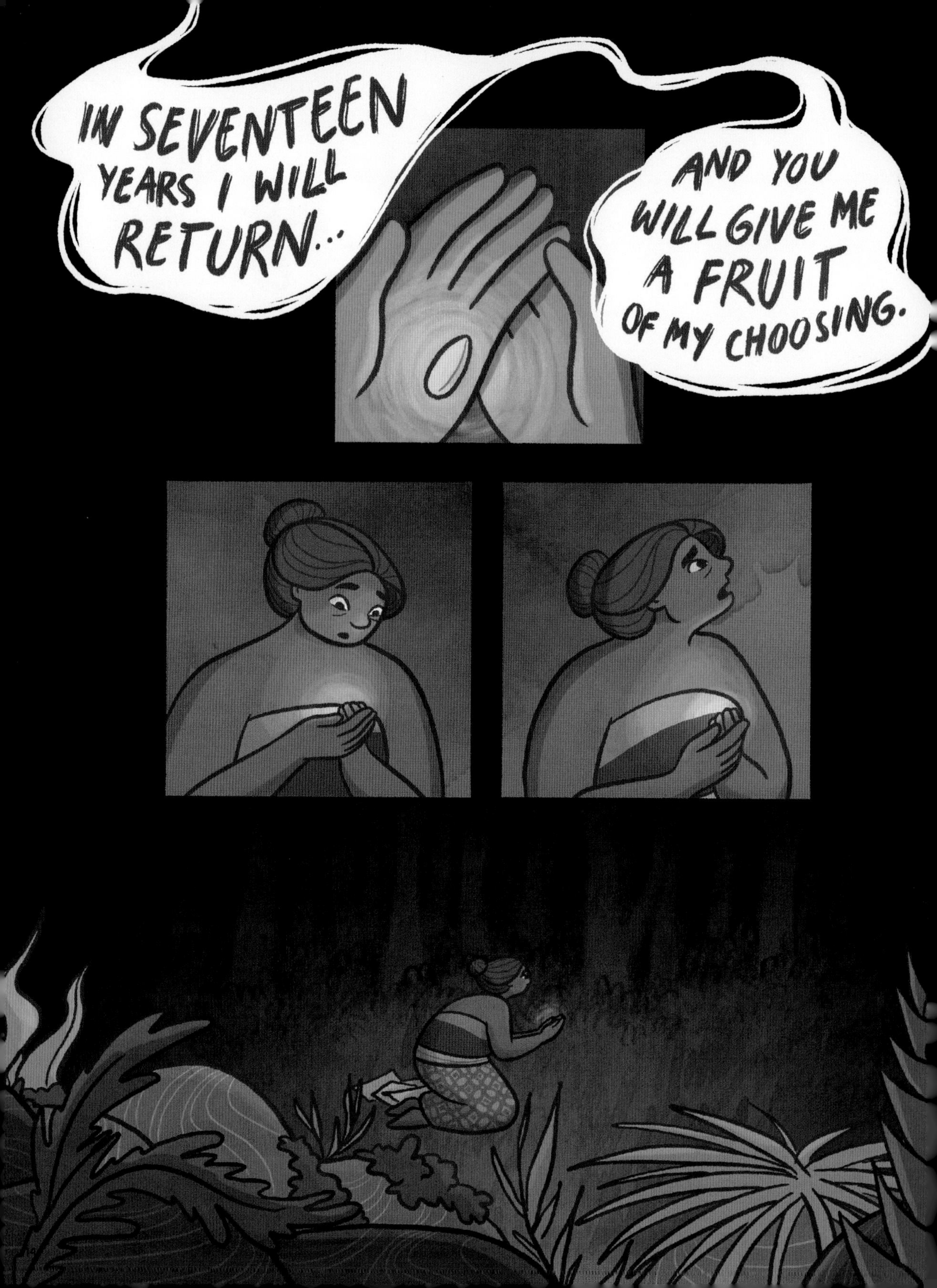
IN SEVENTEEN YEARS I WILL RETURN...
AND YOU WILL GIVE ME A FRUIT OF MY CHOOSING.

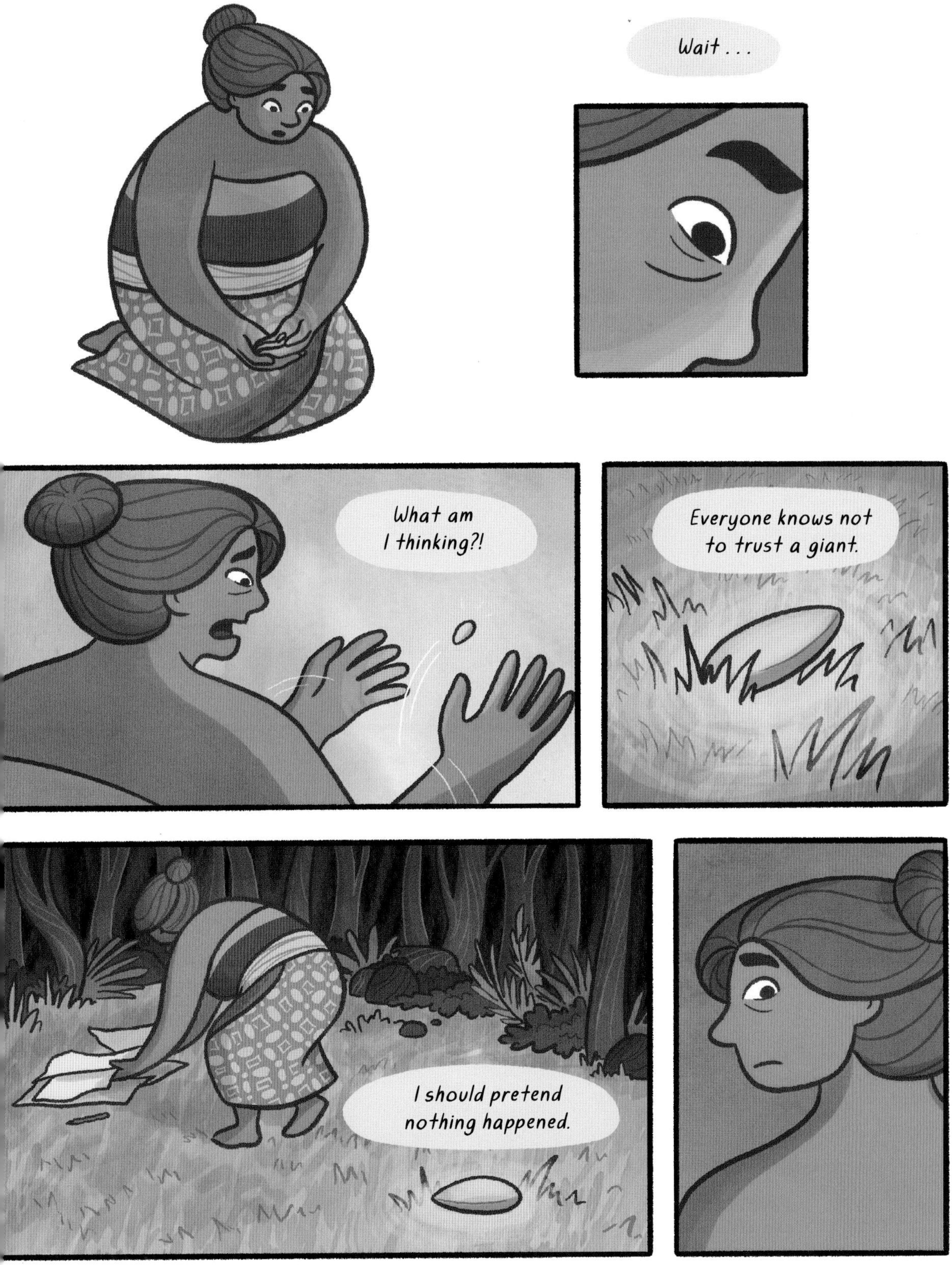
Wait . . .
What am I thinking?!
Everyone knows not to trust a giant.
I should pretend nothing happened.

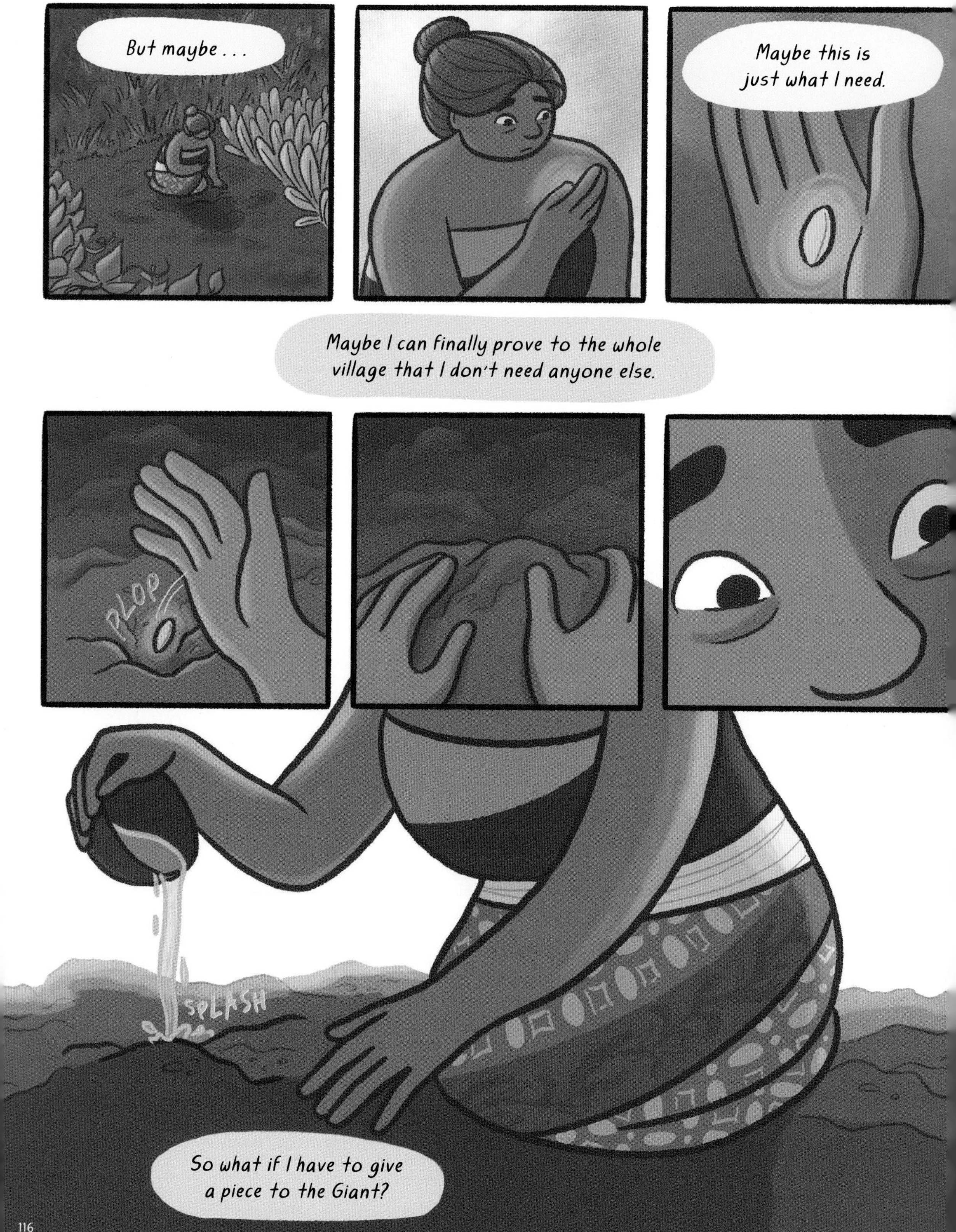

But maybe . . .
Maybe this is just what I need.
Maybe I can finally prove to the whole village that I don't need anyone else.
PLOP
SPLASH
So what if I have to give a piece to the Giant?

And so the seed grew . . .

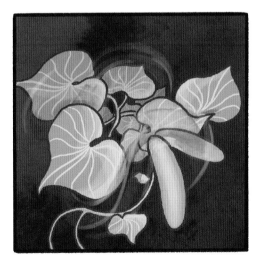

. . . into a cucumber plant.

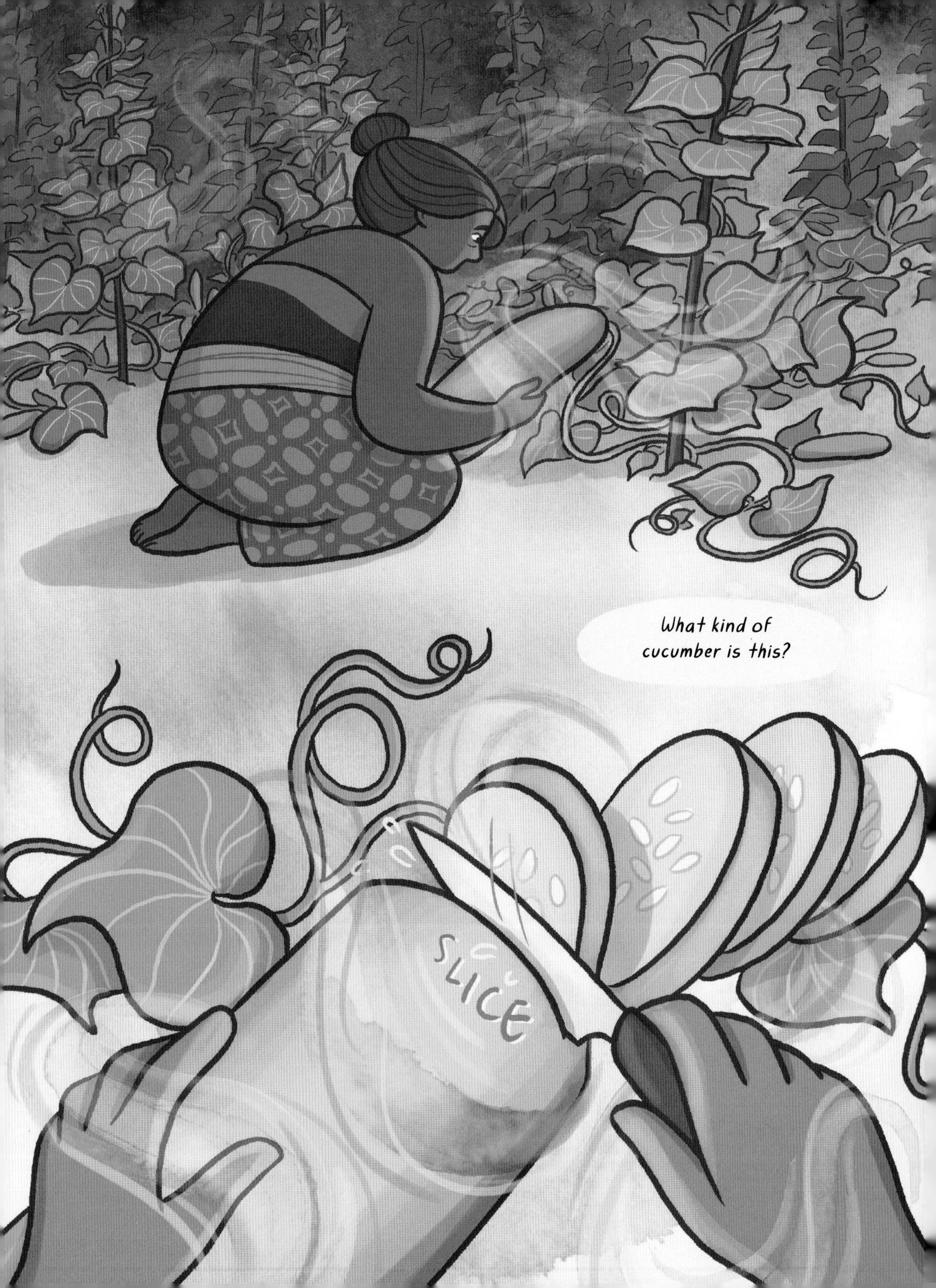
What kind of cucumber is this?
SLICE

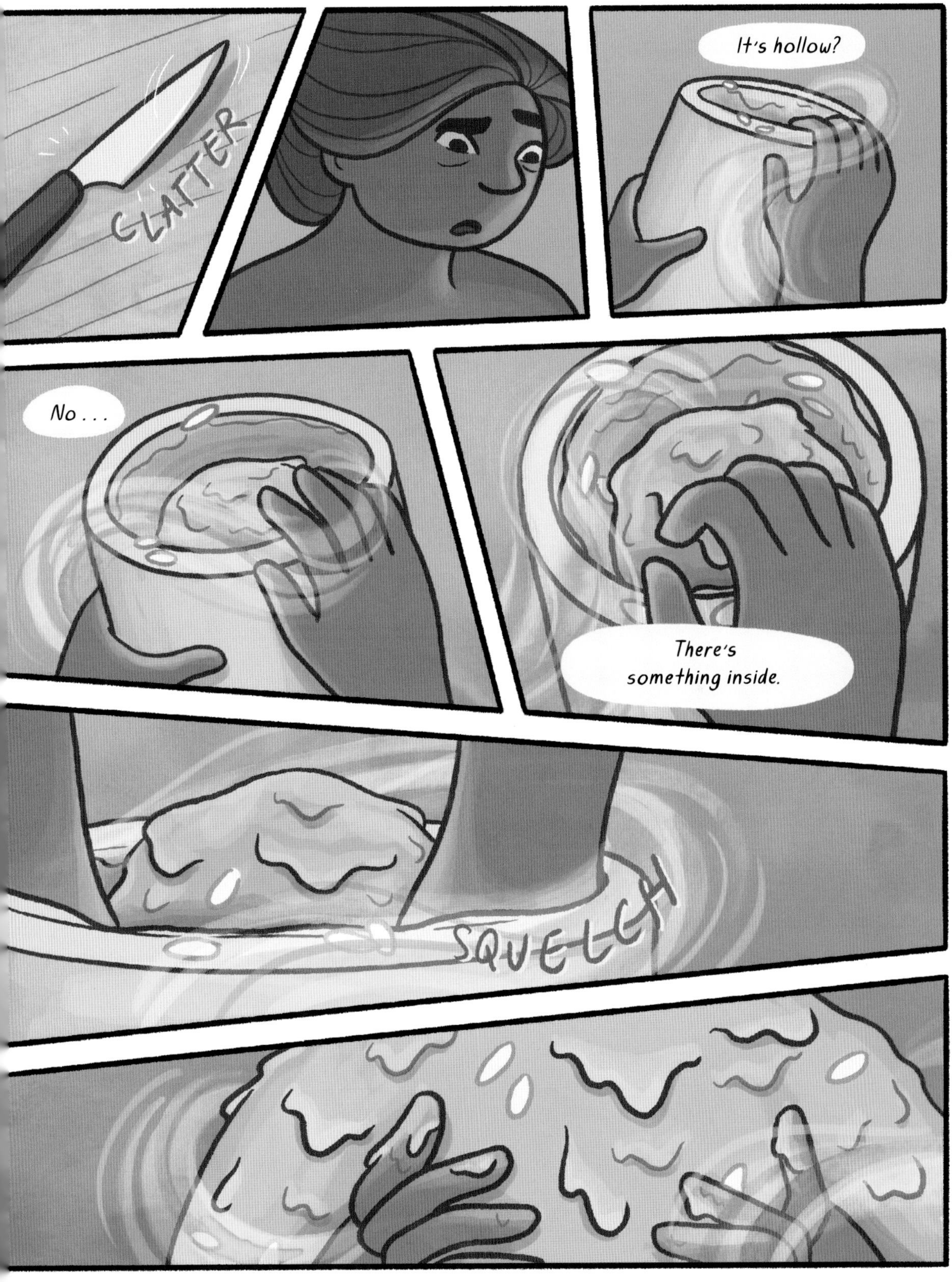
CLATTER
It's hollow?
No . . .
There's something inside.
SQUELCH

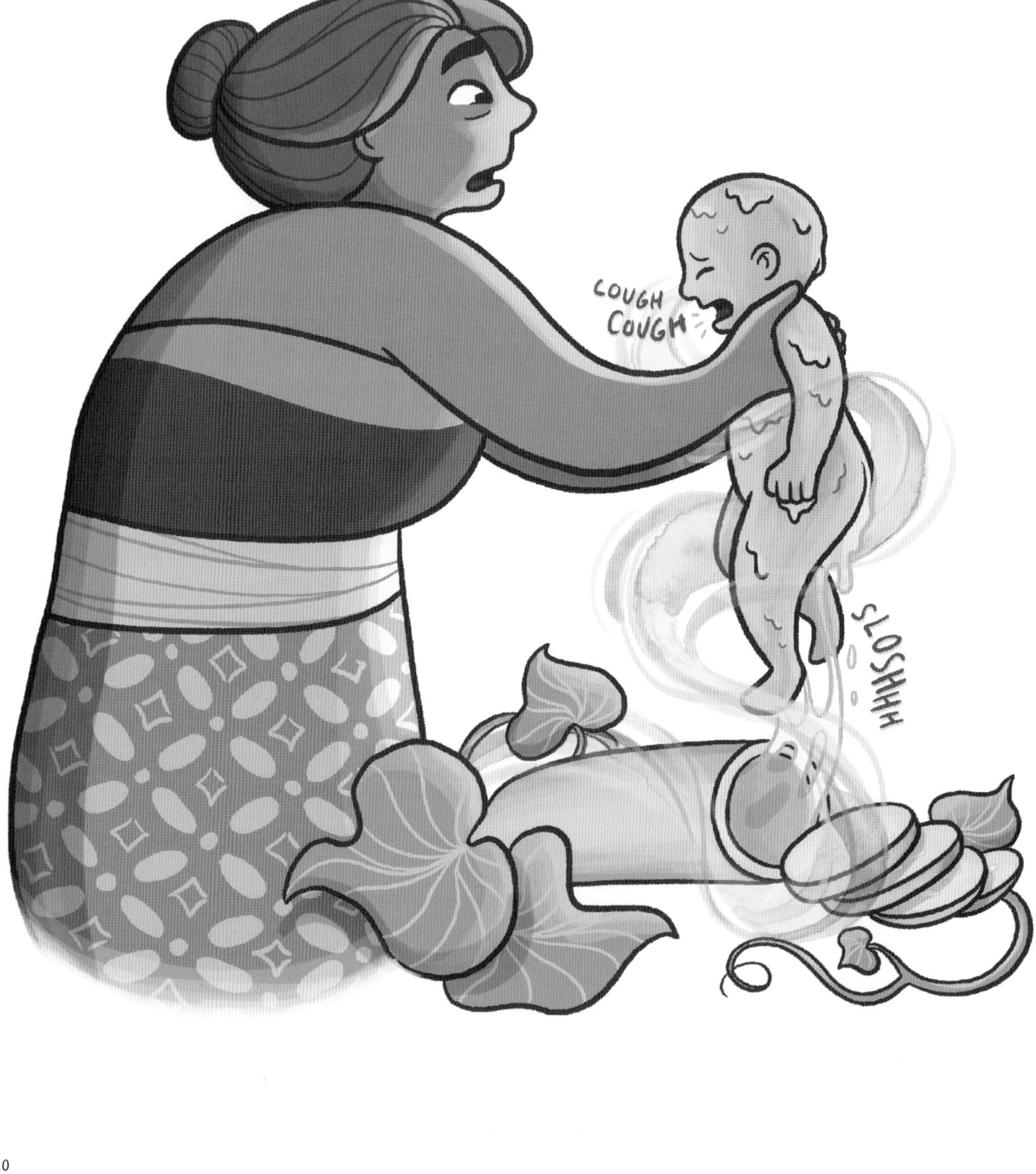
COUGH
COUGH
SLOSHHH

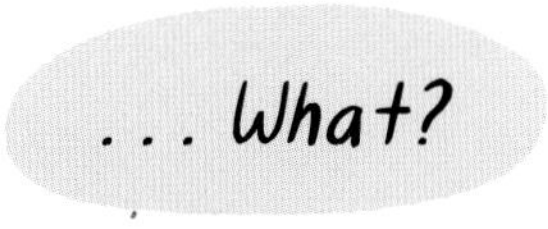
... What?

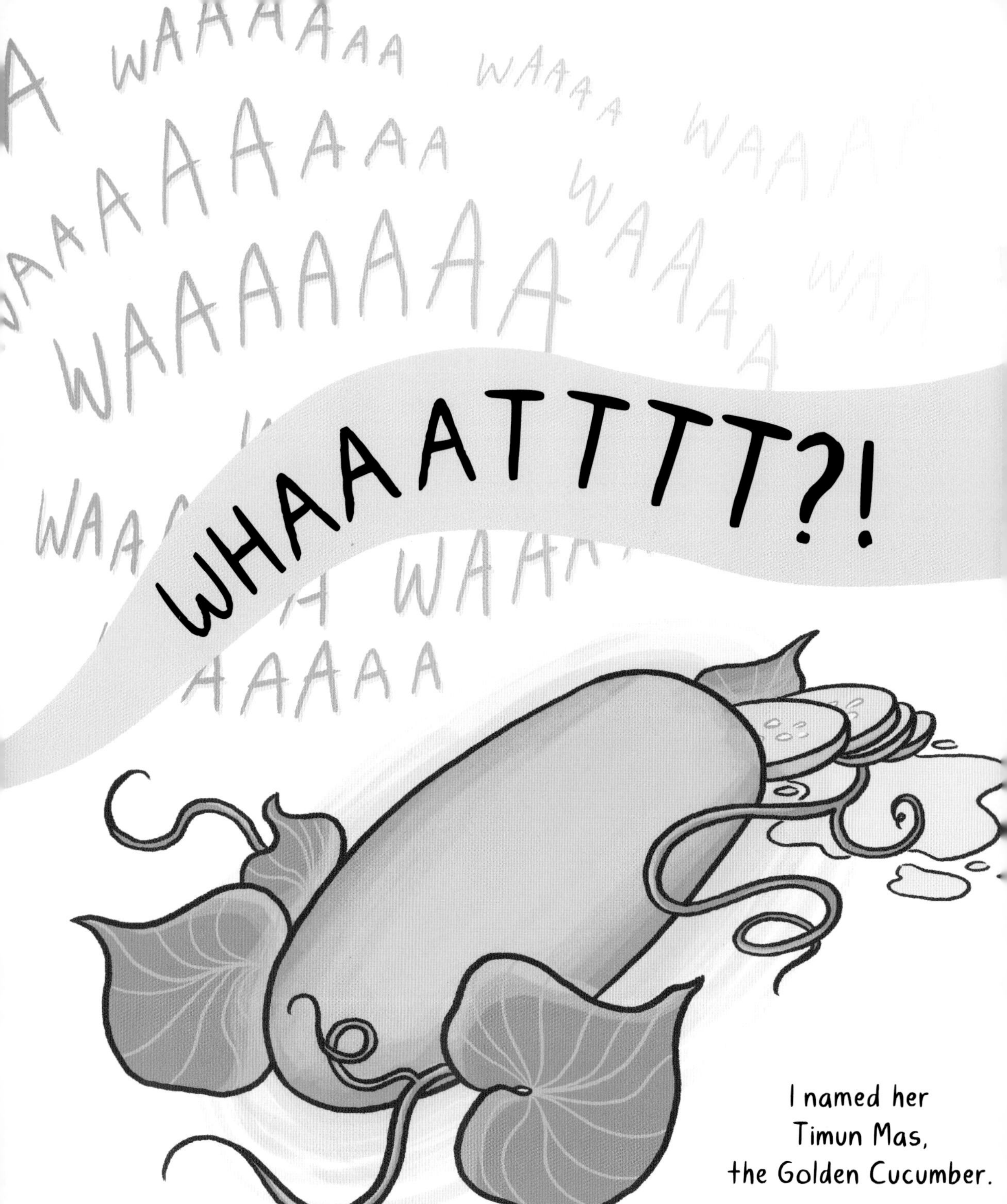
WHAAATTTT?!
I named her Timun Mas, the Golden Cucumber.

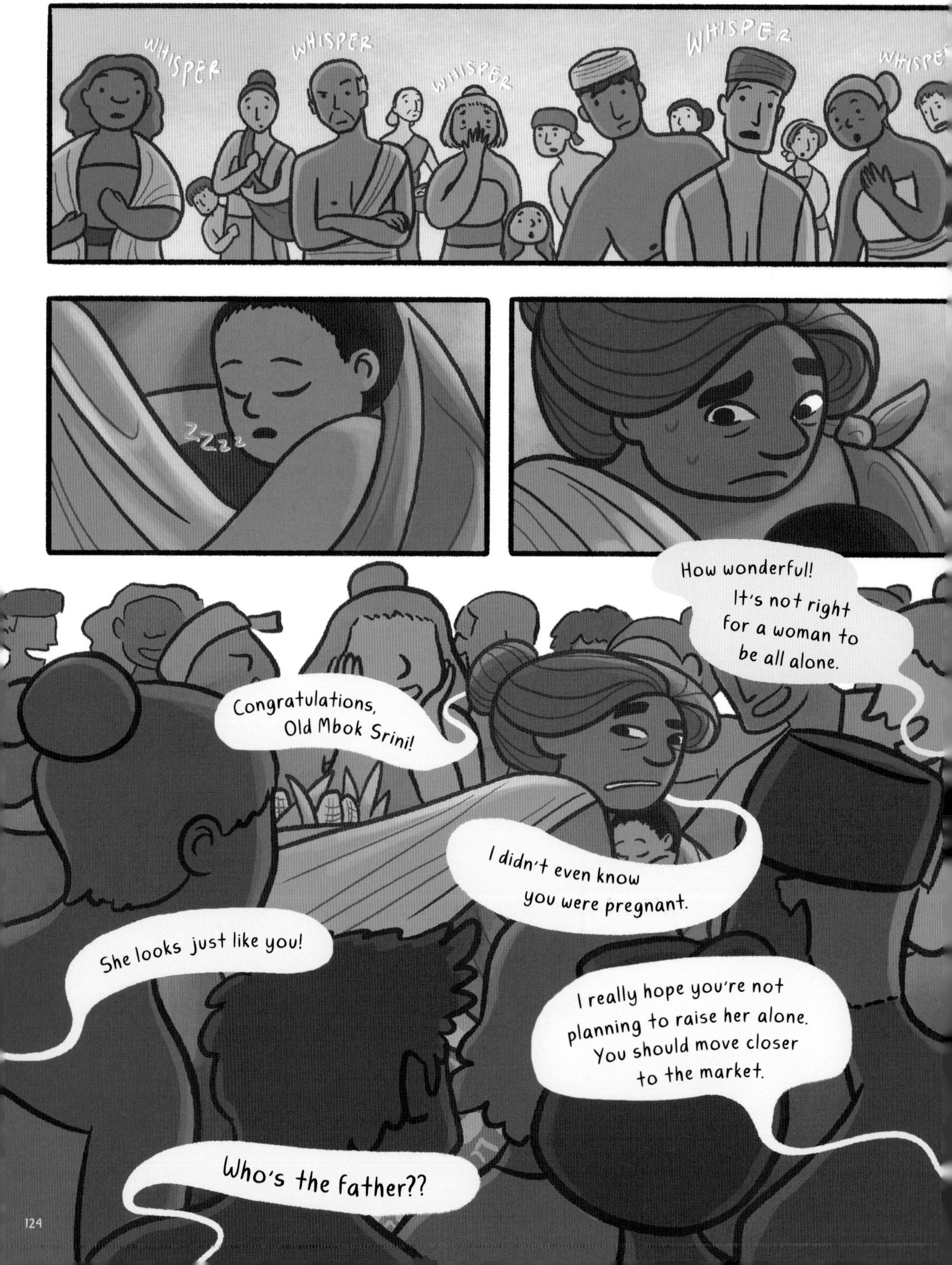
WHISPER
WHISPER
WHISPER
WHISPER
WHISPER
ZZZZ
How wonderful!
It's not right for a woman to be all alone.
Congratulations, Old Mbok Srini!
I didn't even know you were pregnant.
She looks just like you!
I really hope you're not planning to raise her alone. You should move closer to the market.
Who's the father??

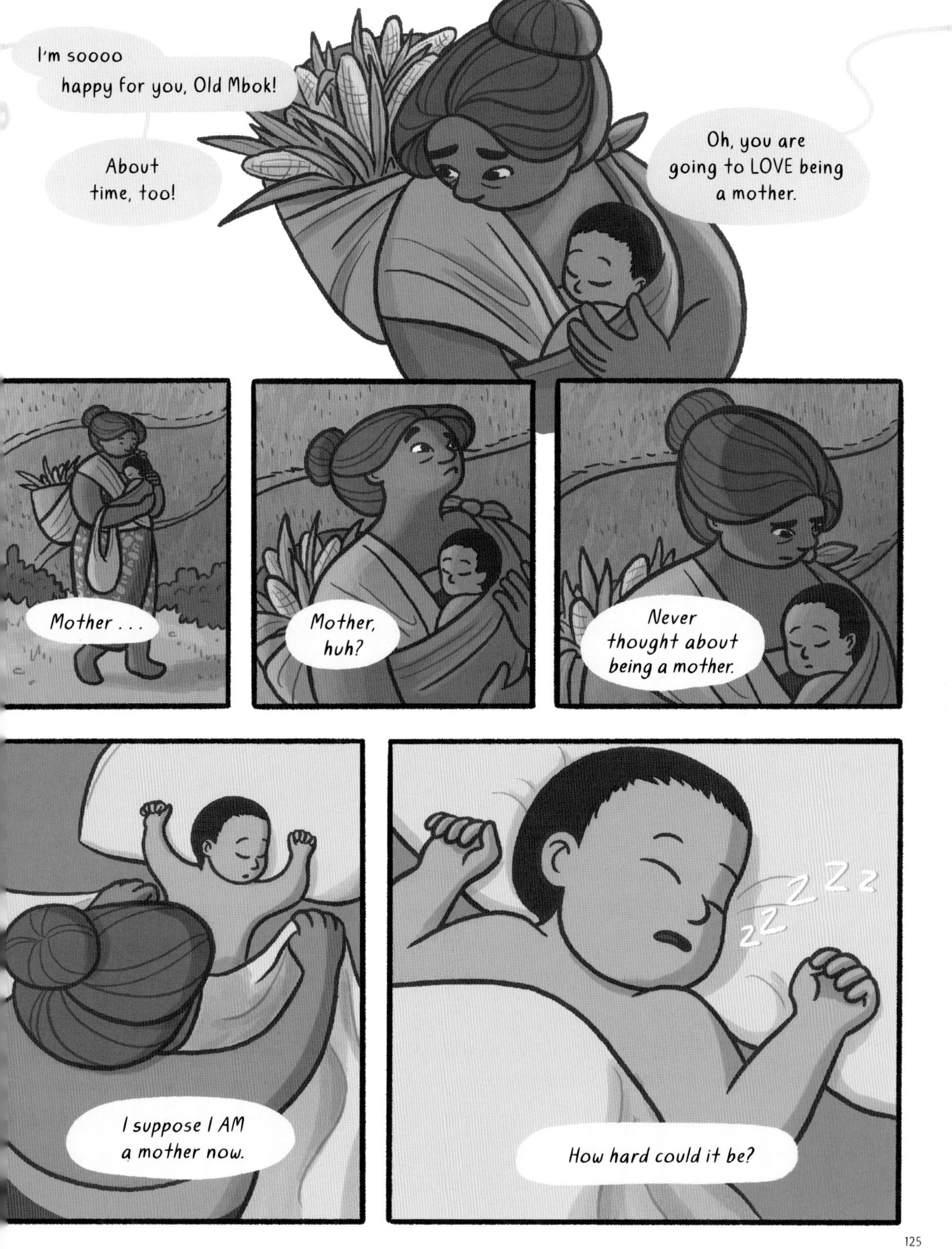

I'm soooo happy for you, Old Mbok!
About time, too!
Oh, you are going to LOVE being a mother.
Mother . . .
Mother, huh?
Never thought about being a mother.
I suppose I AM a mother now.
ZZZZZ
How hard could it be?

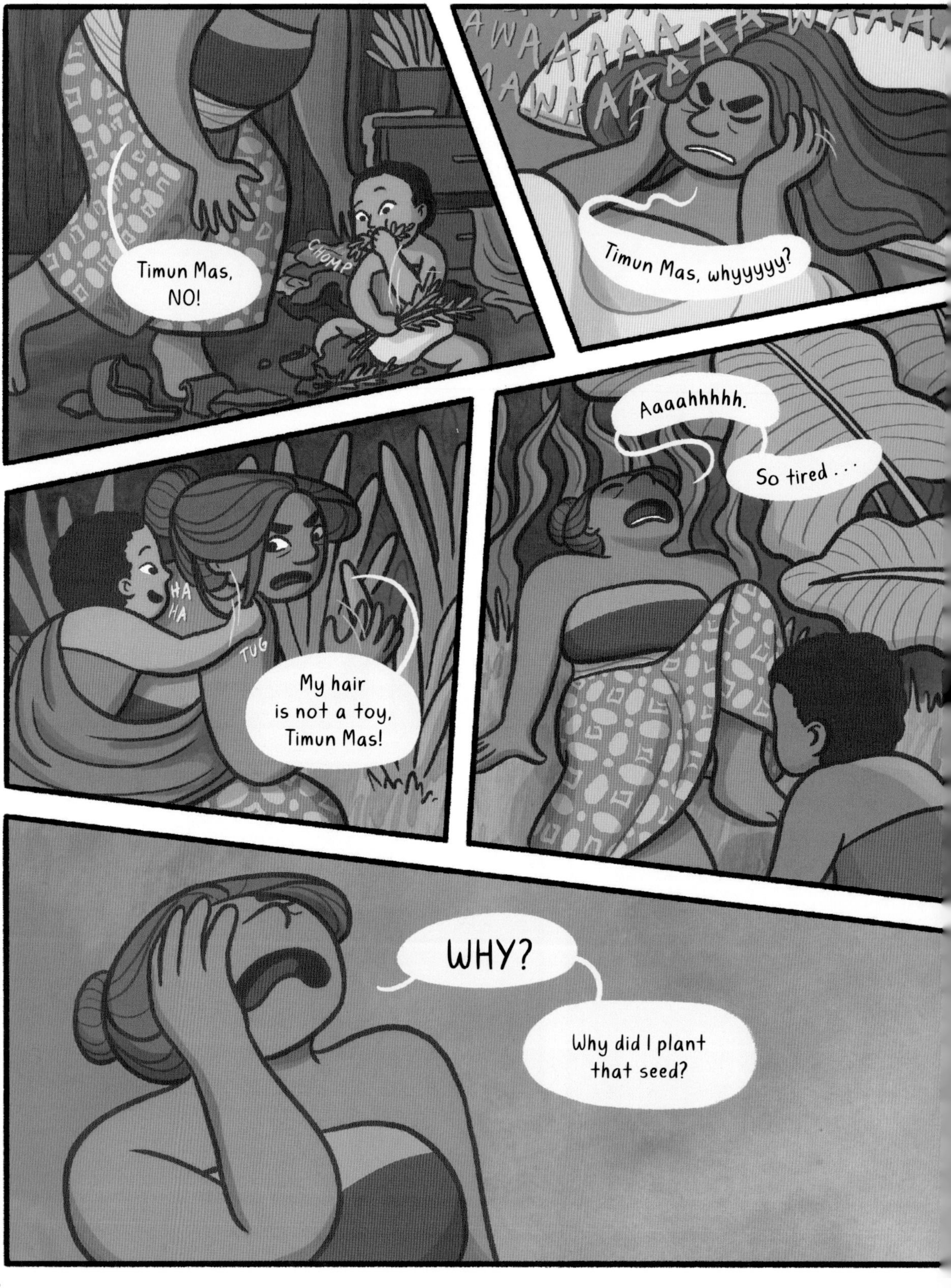

CHOMP
Timun Mas,
NO!
WAAAAAAA WAAAAA
Timun Mas, whyyyyy?
HA HA
TUG
My hair
is not a toy,
Timun Mas!
Aaaahhhh.
So tired . . .
WHY?
Why did I plant
that seed?

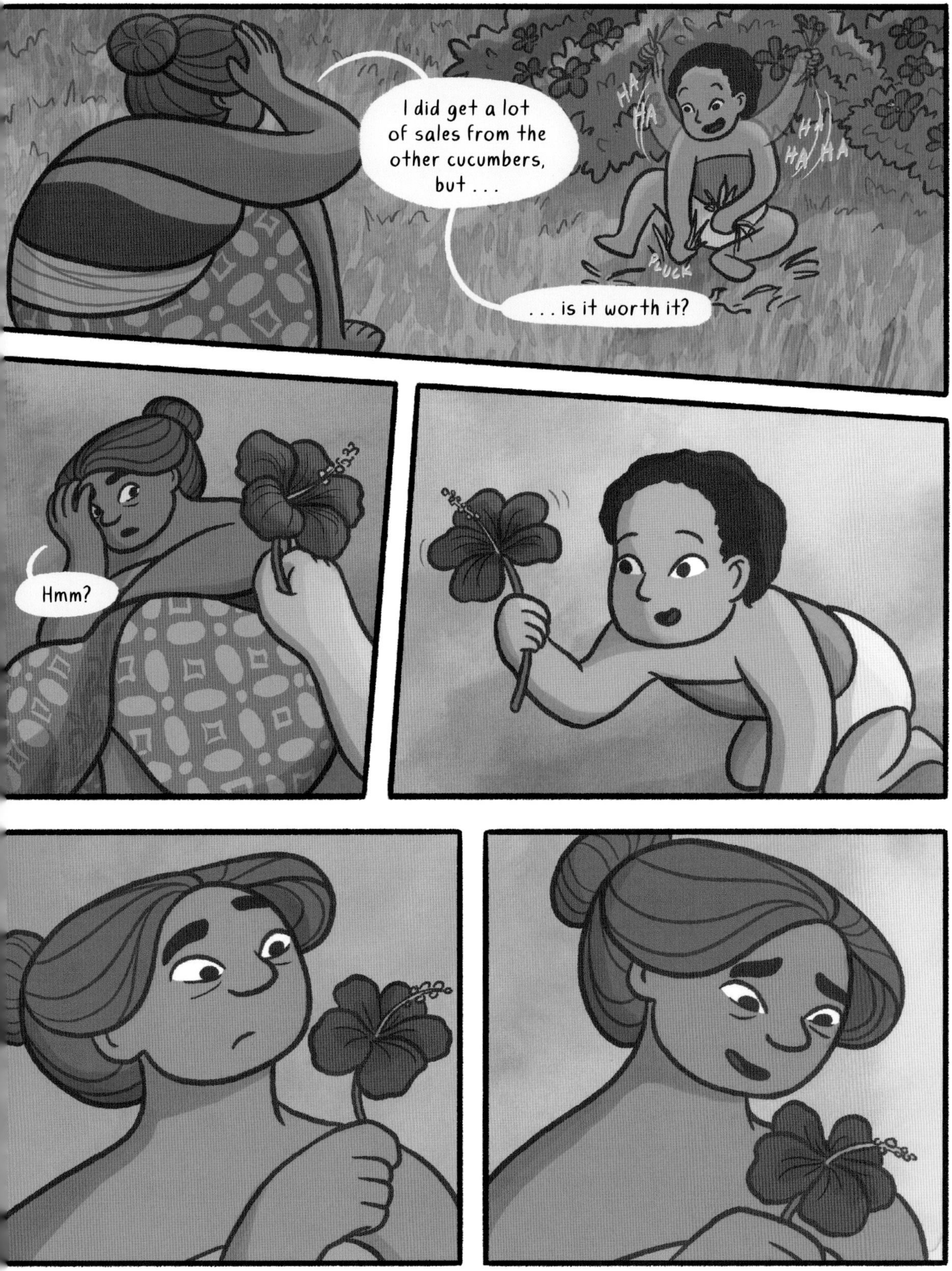

I did get a lot of sales from the other cucumbers, but . . .
HA HA
HA HA HA HA
PLUCK
. . . is it worth it?
Hmm?

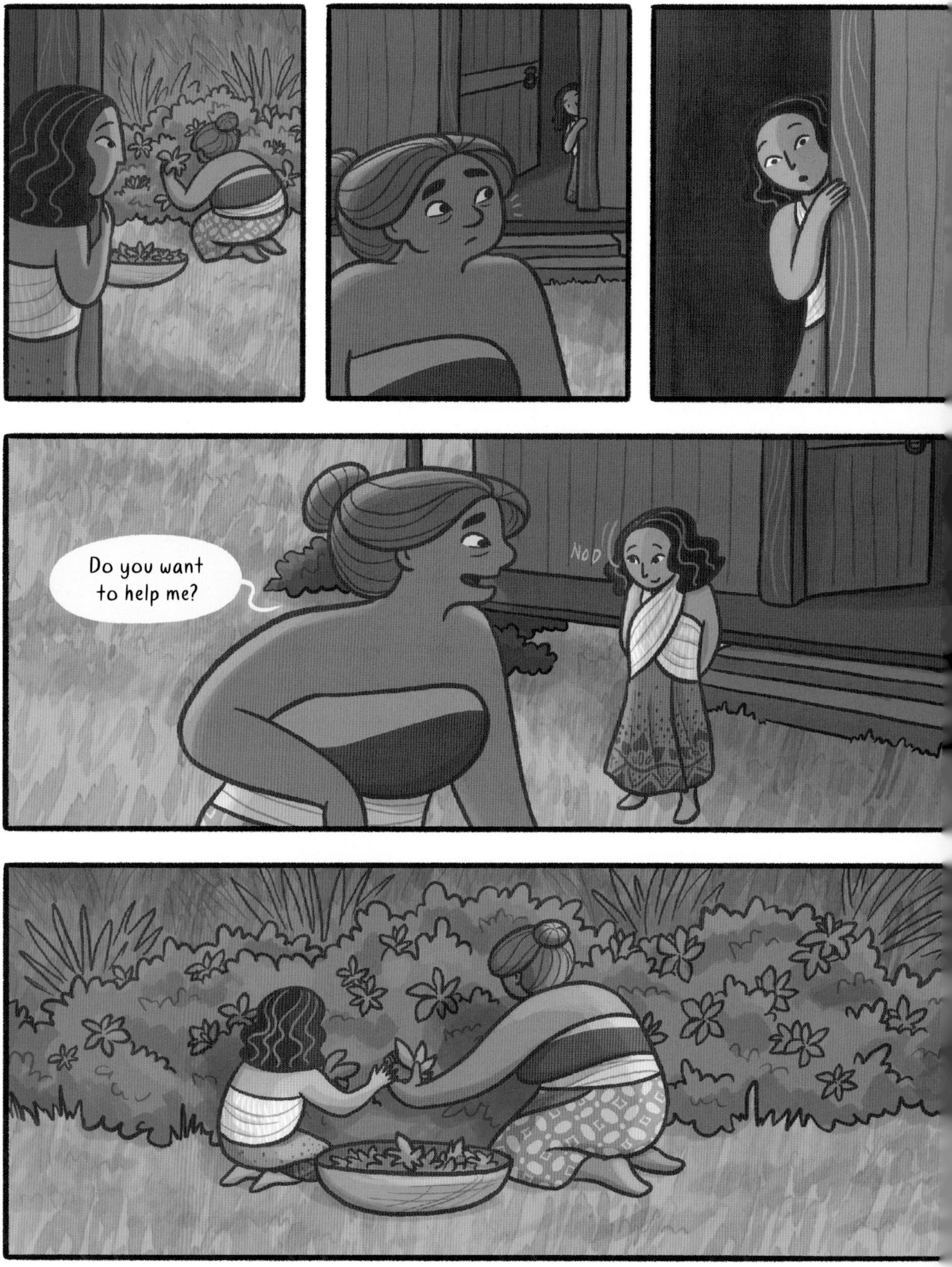
Do you want to help me?
NOD

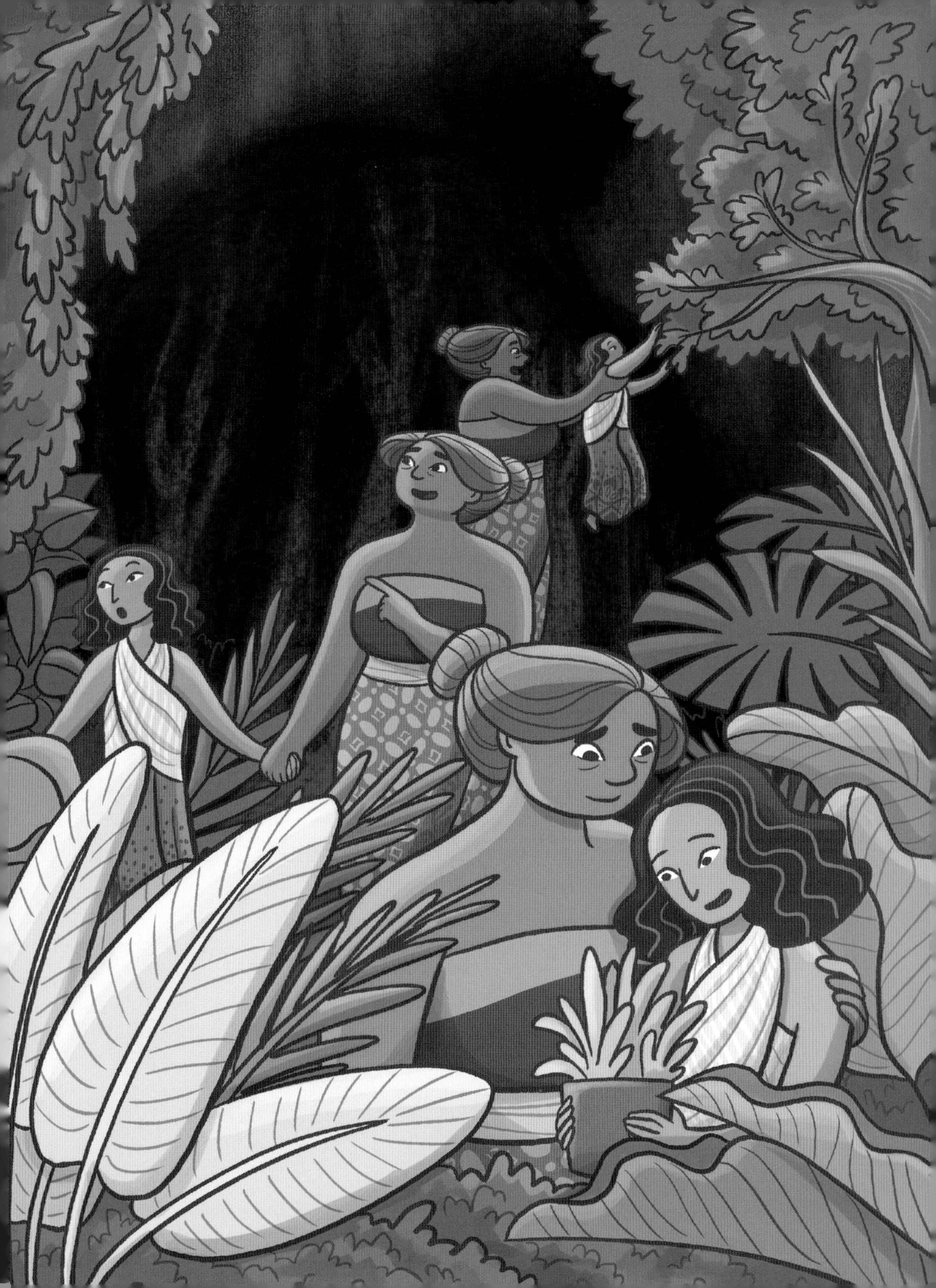

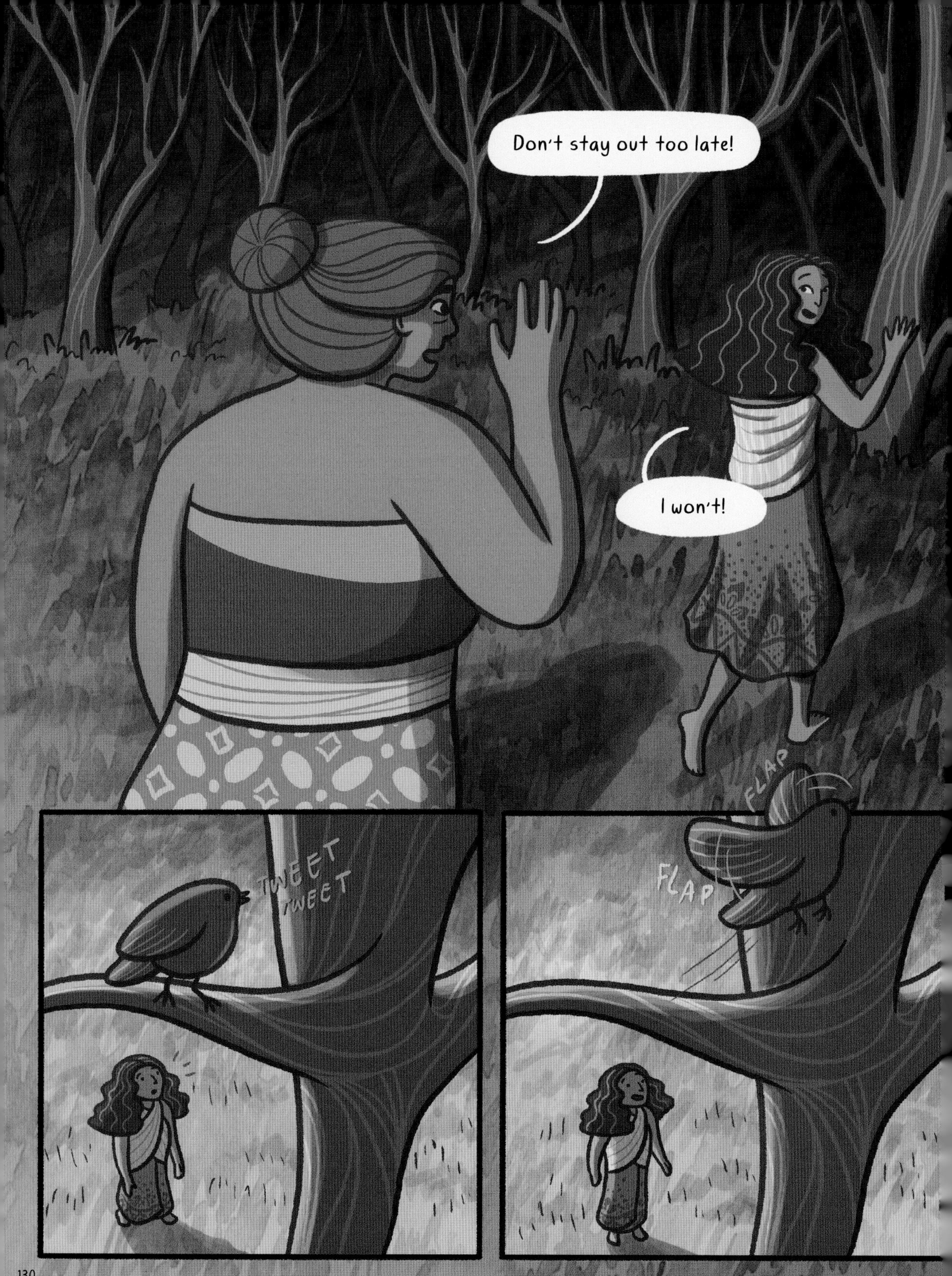
Don't stay out too late!
I won't!
TWEET
TWEET
FLAP
FLAP
FLAP

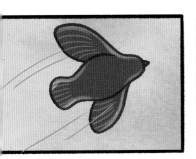
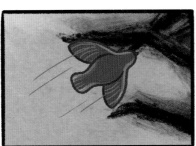

FFWISHH

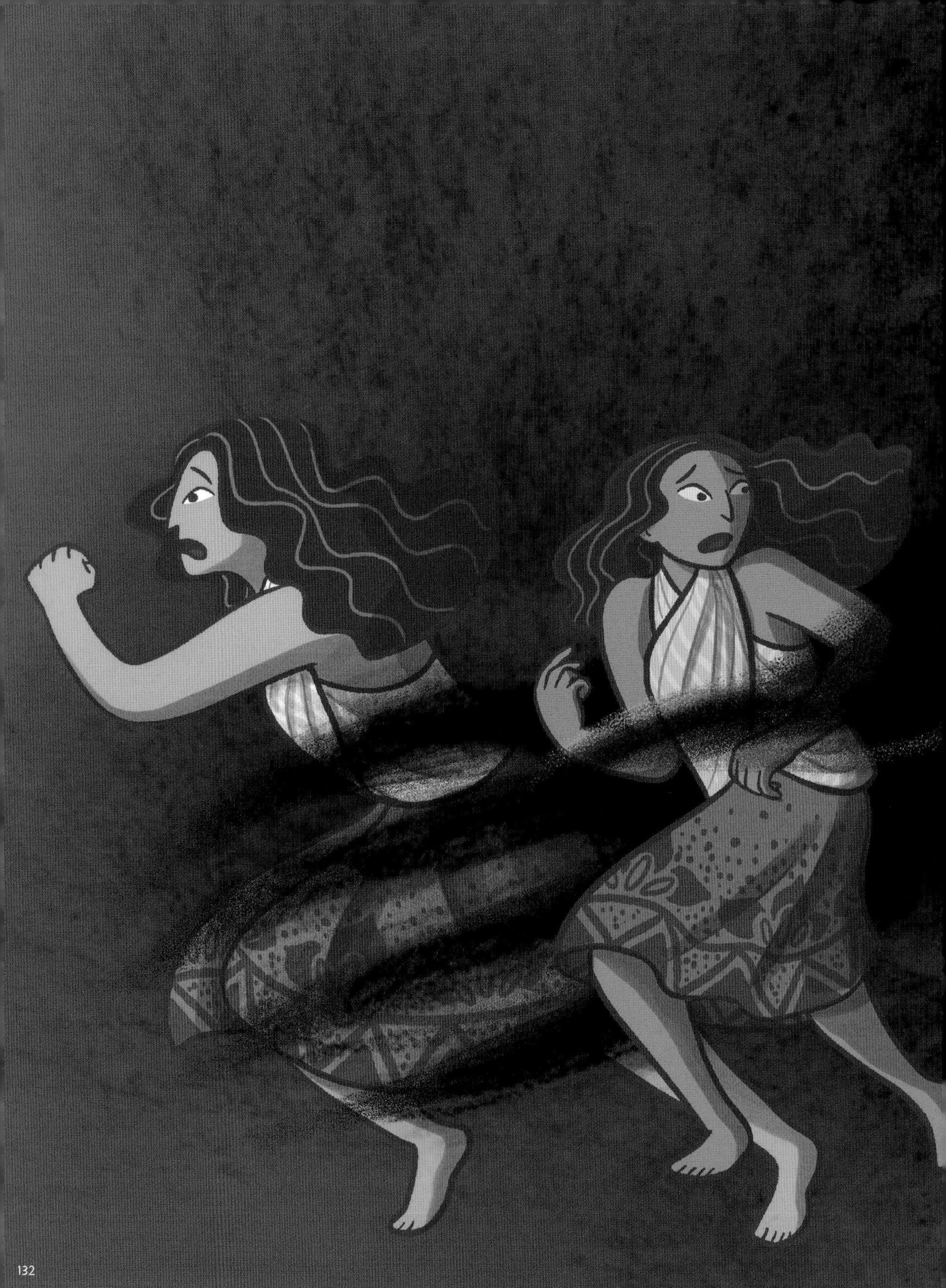

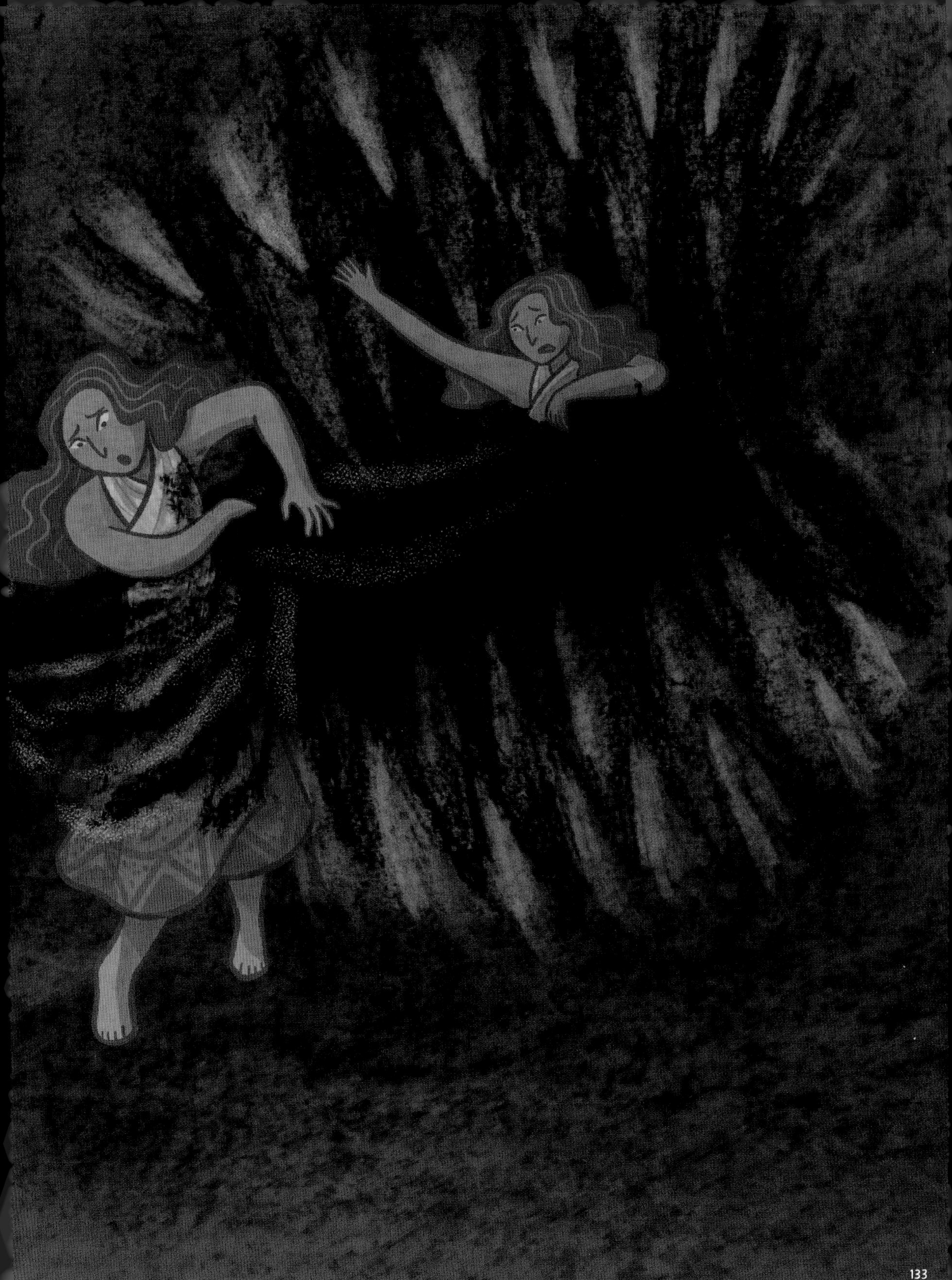

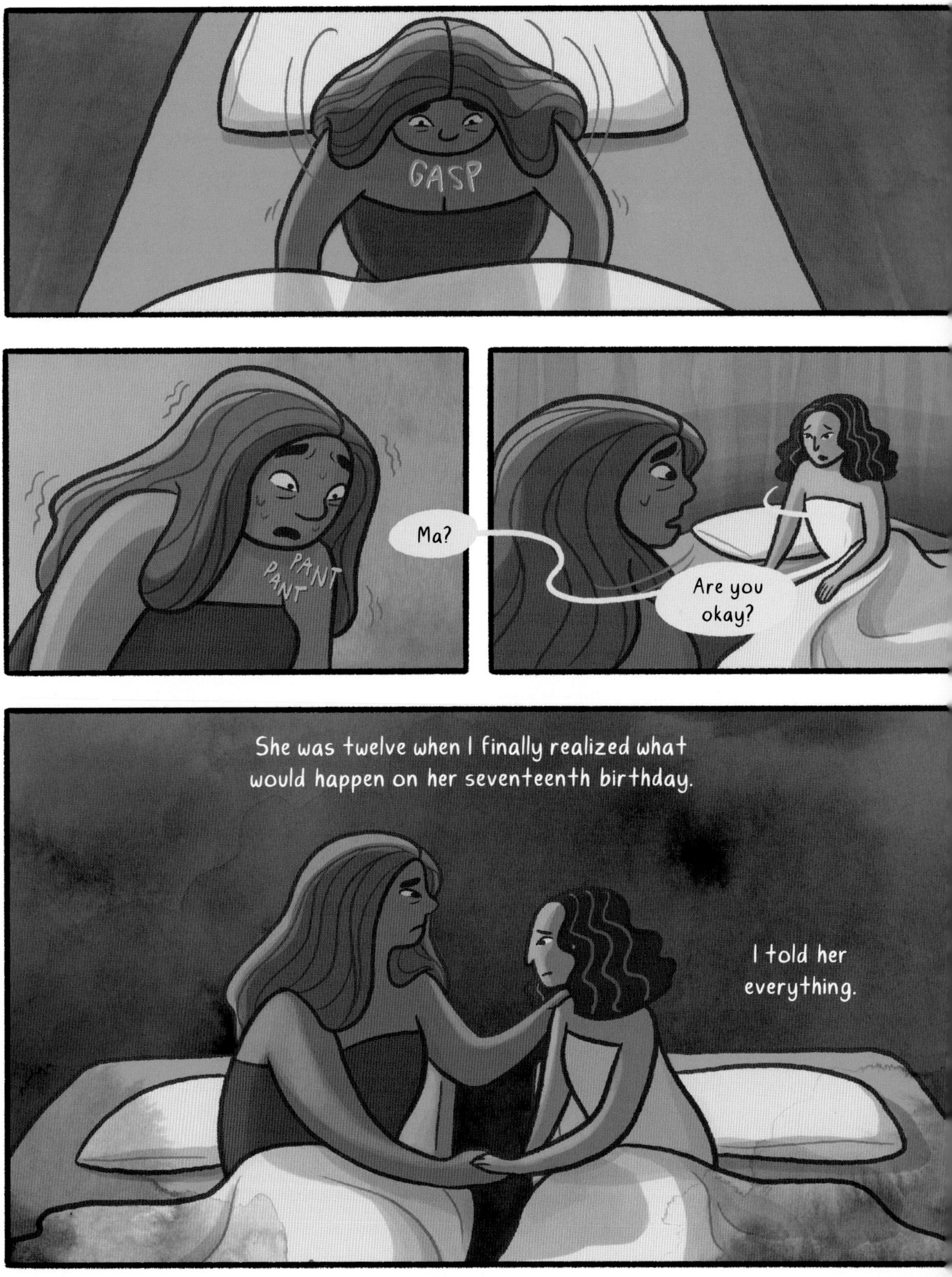
GASP
PANT PANT
Ma?
Are you okay?
She was twelve when I finally realized what would happen on her seventeenth birthday.
I told her everything.

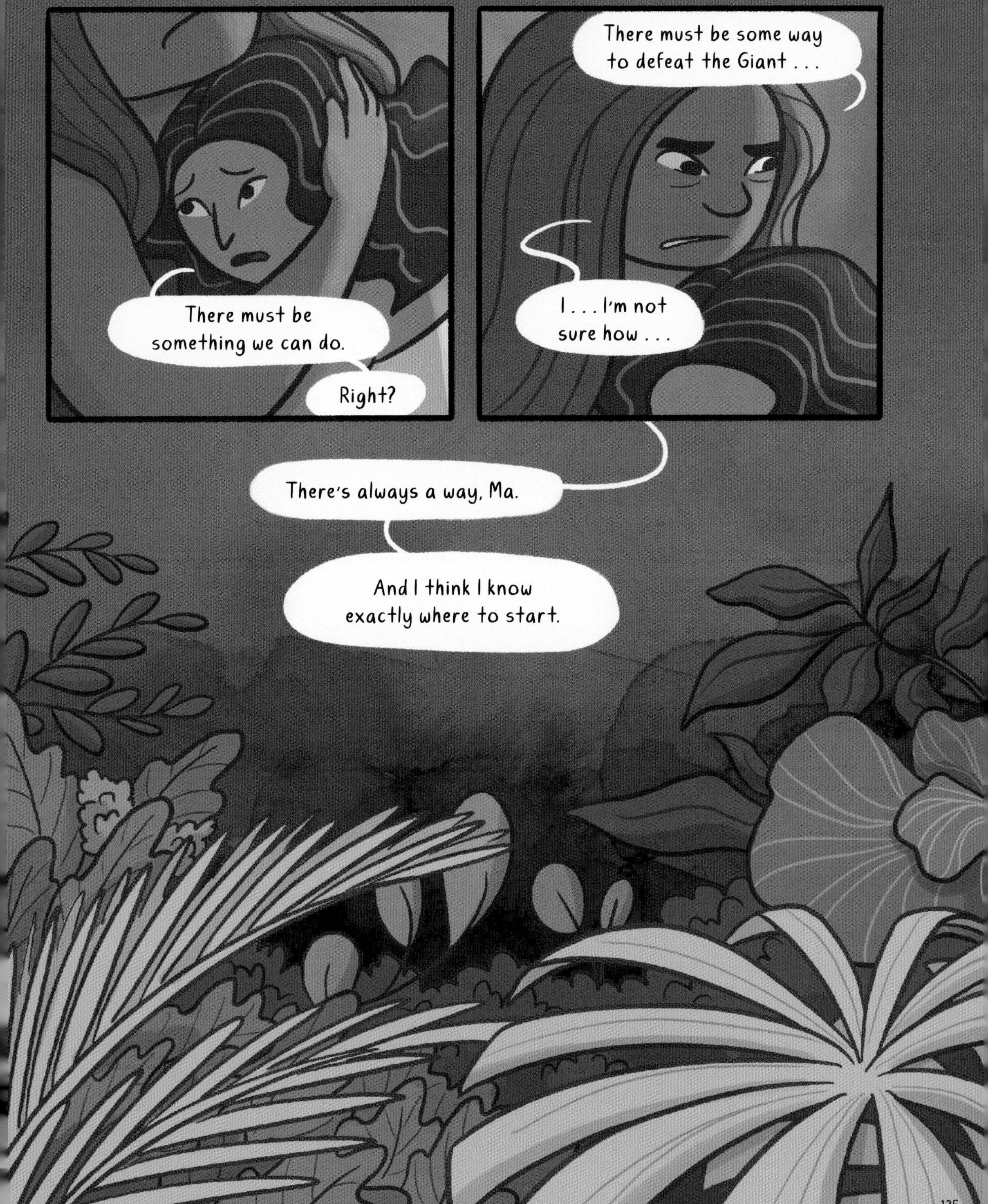
There must be something we can do.
Right?
There must be some way to defeat the Giant . . .
I . . . I'm not sure how . . .
There's always a way, Ma.
And I think I know exactly where to start.

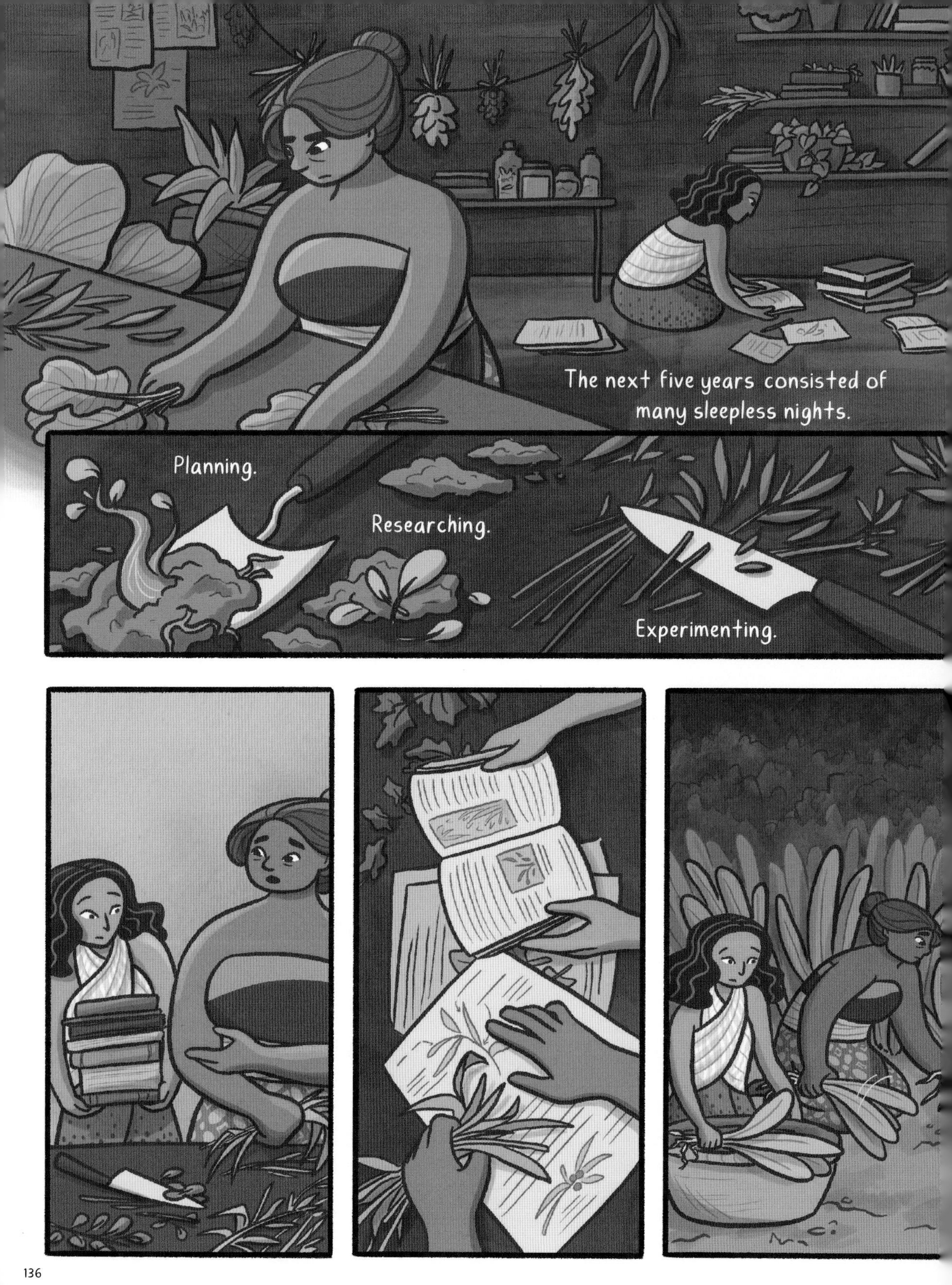
The next five years consisted of many sleepless nights.
Planning.
Researching.
Experimenting.

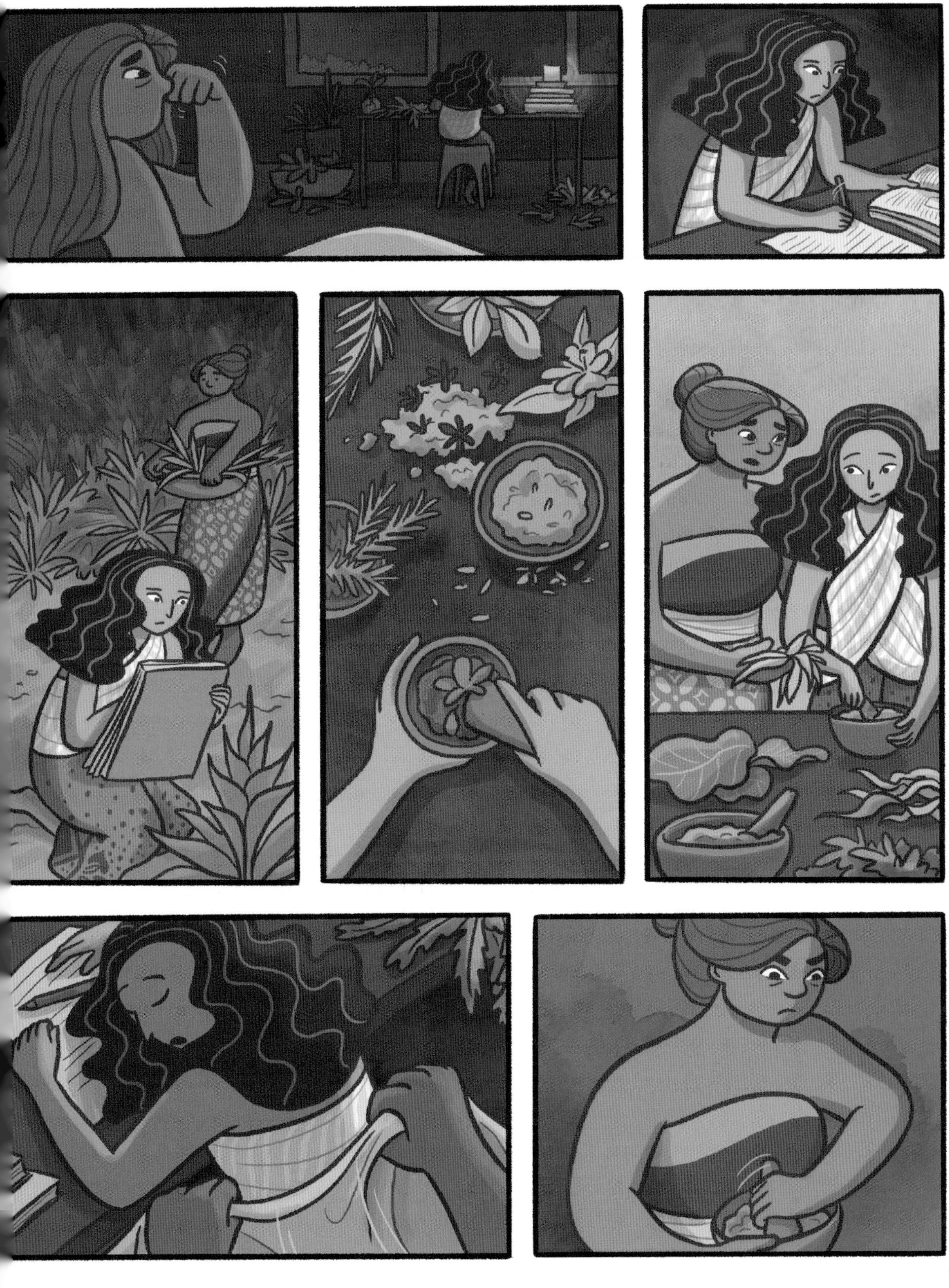

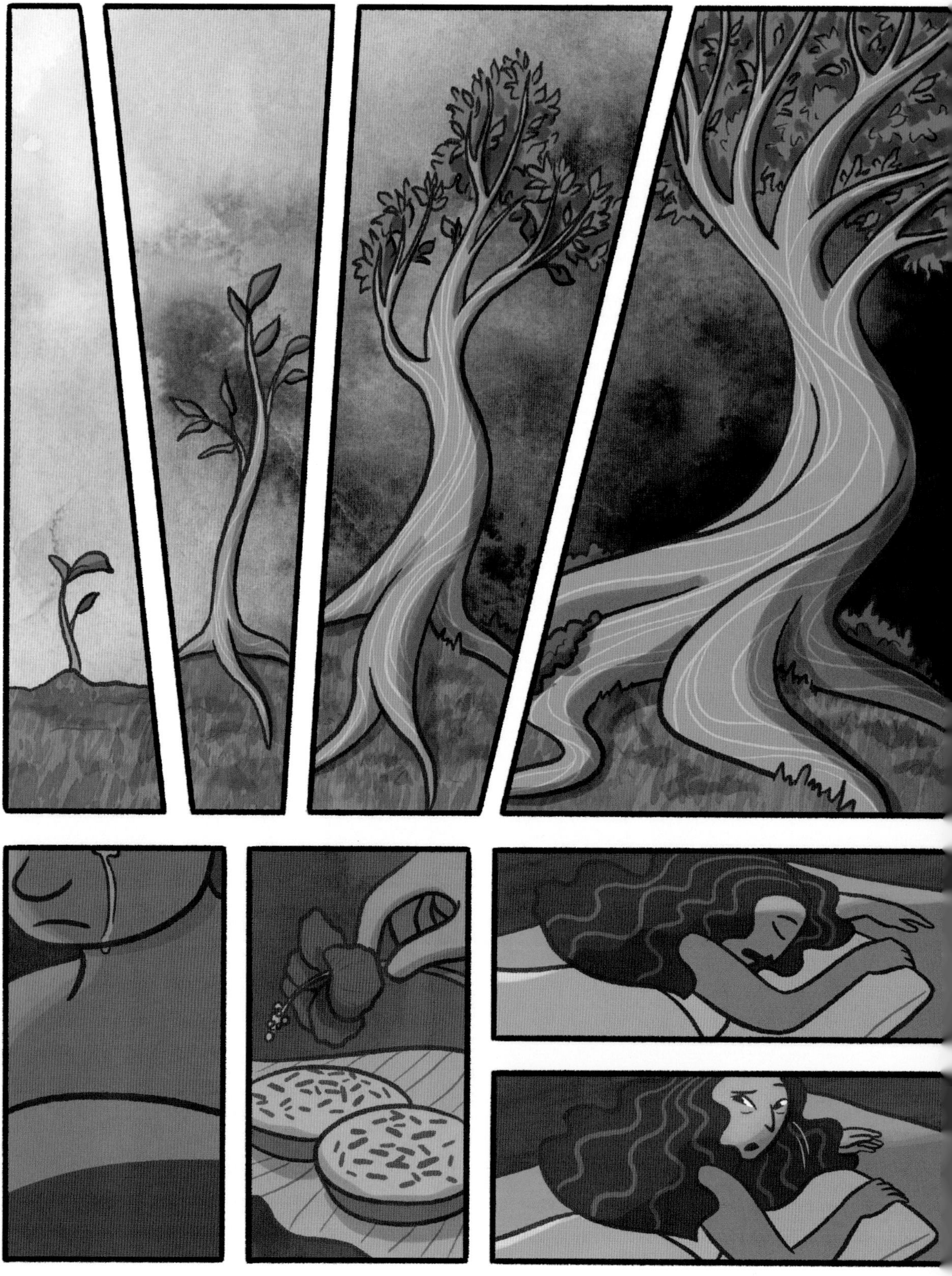

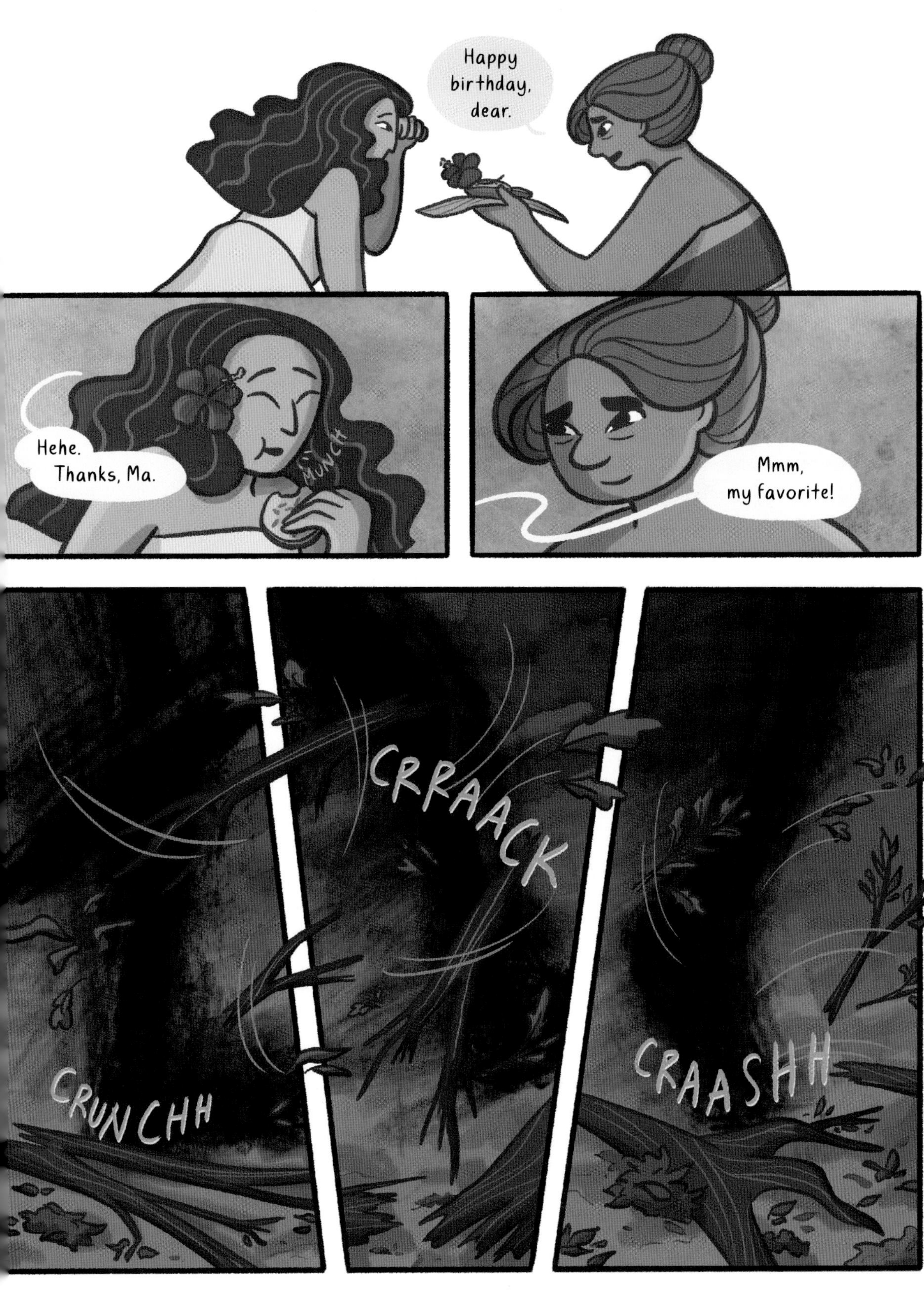
Happy birthday, dear.
Hehe. Thanks, Ma.
MUNCH
Mmm, my favorite!
CRRAACK
CRUNCHH
CRAASHH

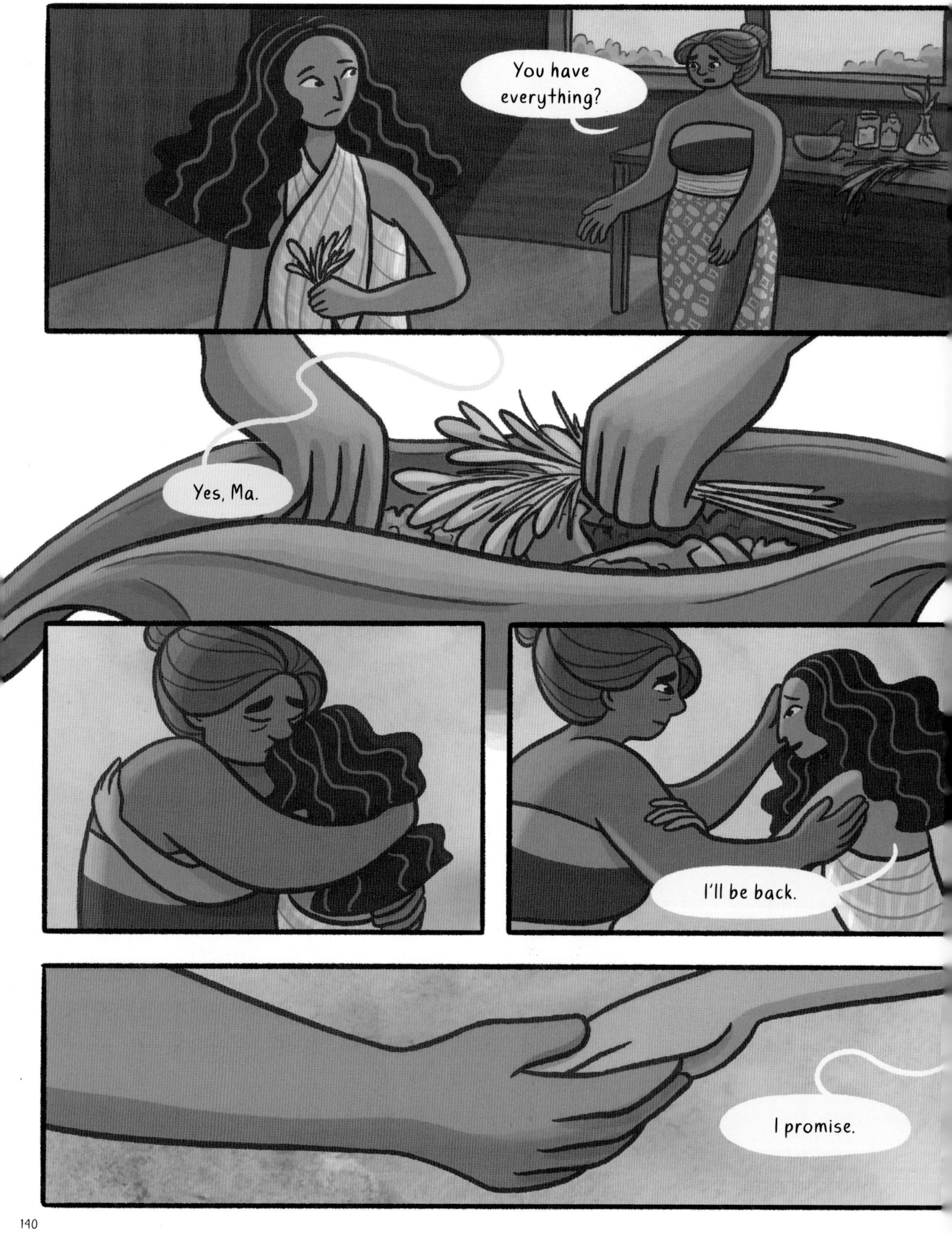
You have everything?
Yes, Ma.
I'll be back.
I promise.

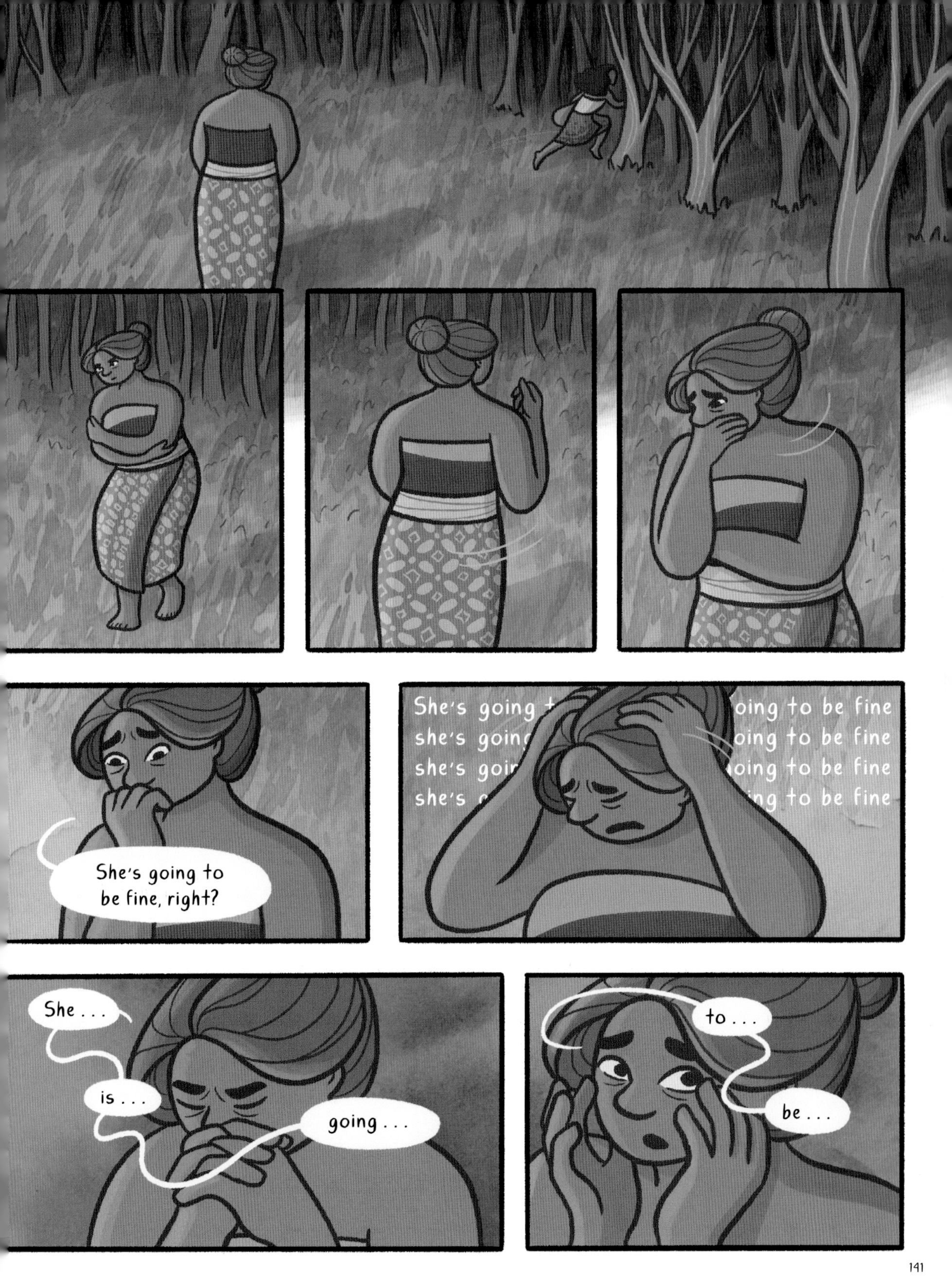
She's going to be fine, right?
She's going t
oing to be fine
she's going
oing to be fine
she's goir
oing to be fine
she's
ing to be fine
She . . .
is . . .
going . . .
to . . .
be . . .

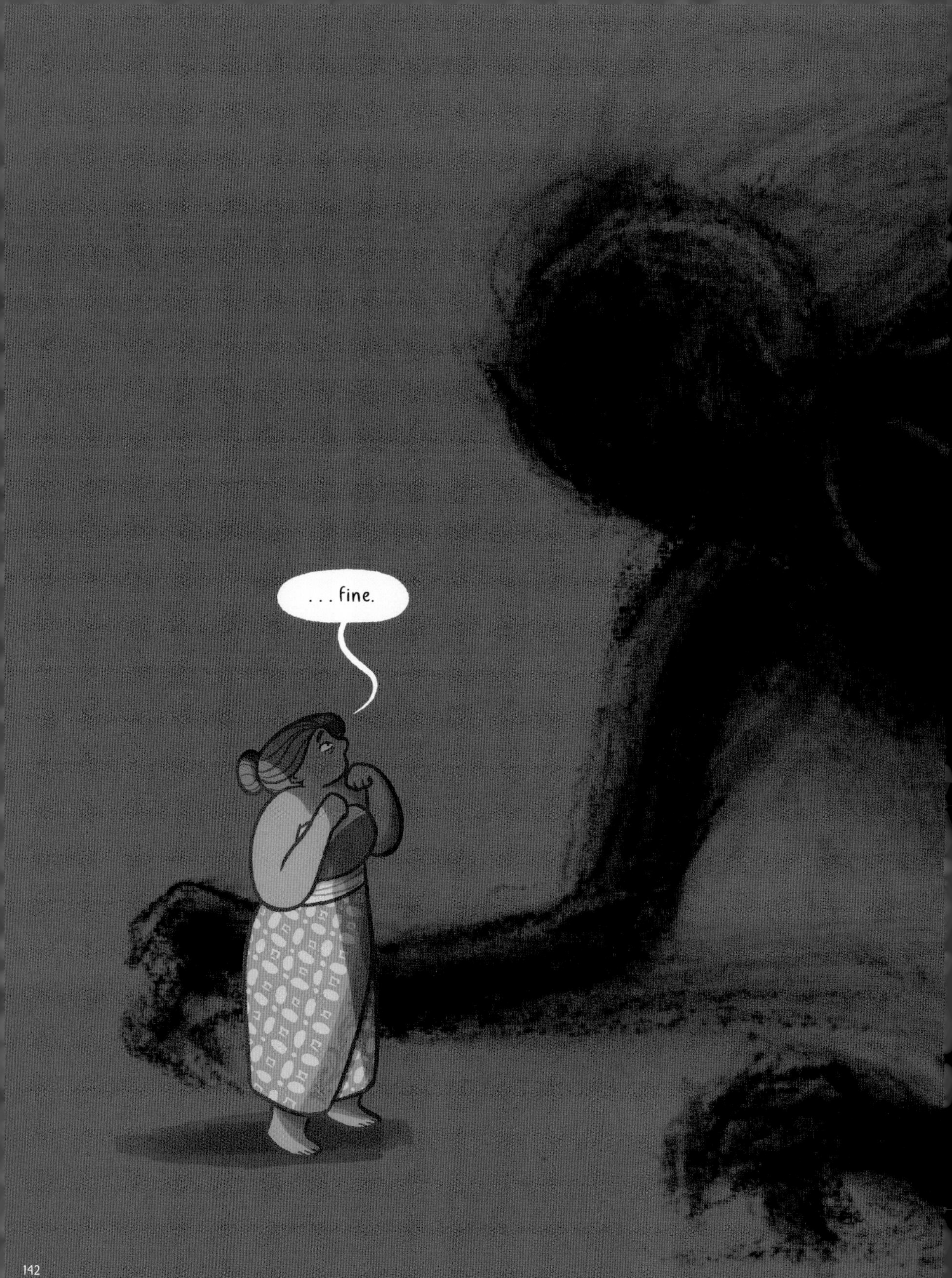
. . . fine.

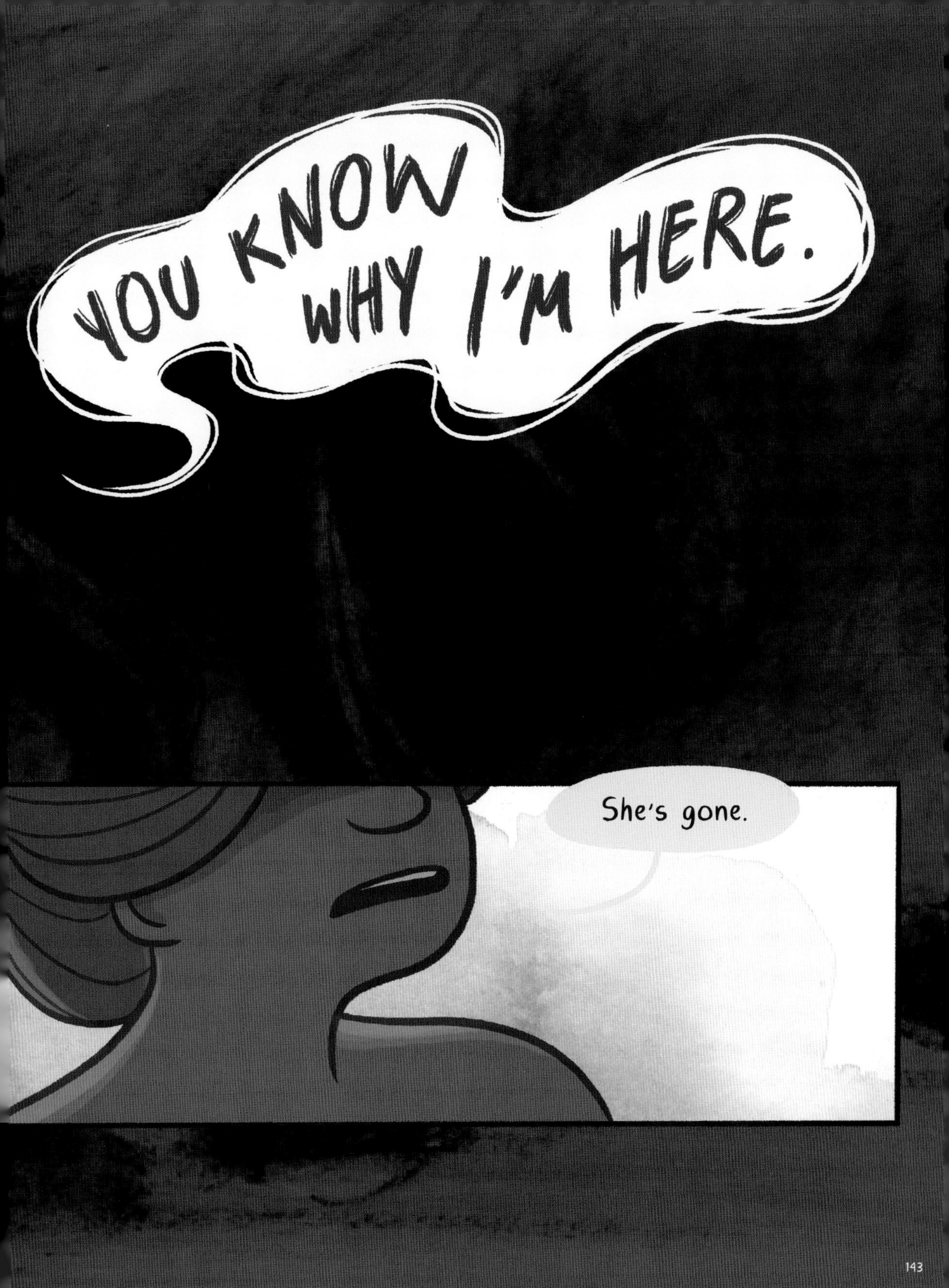
YOU KNOW WHY I'M HERE.
She's gone.

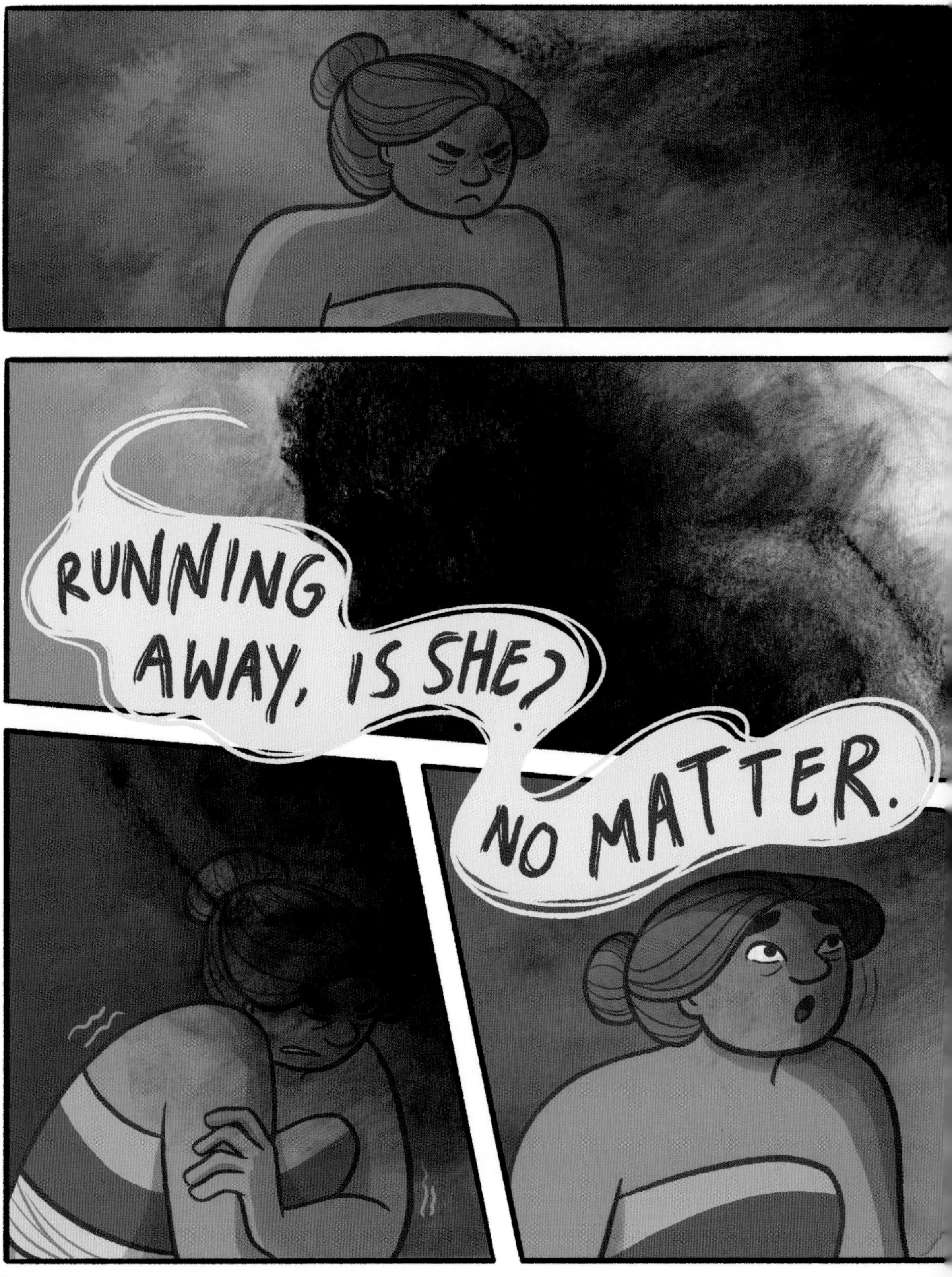
RUNNING AWAY, IS SHE?
NO MATTER.

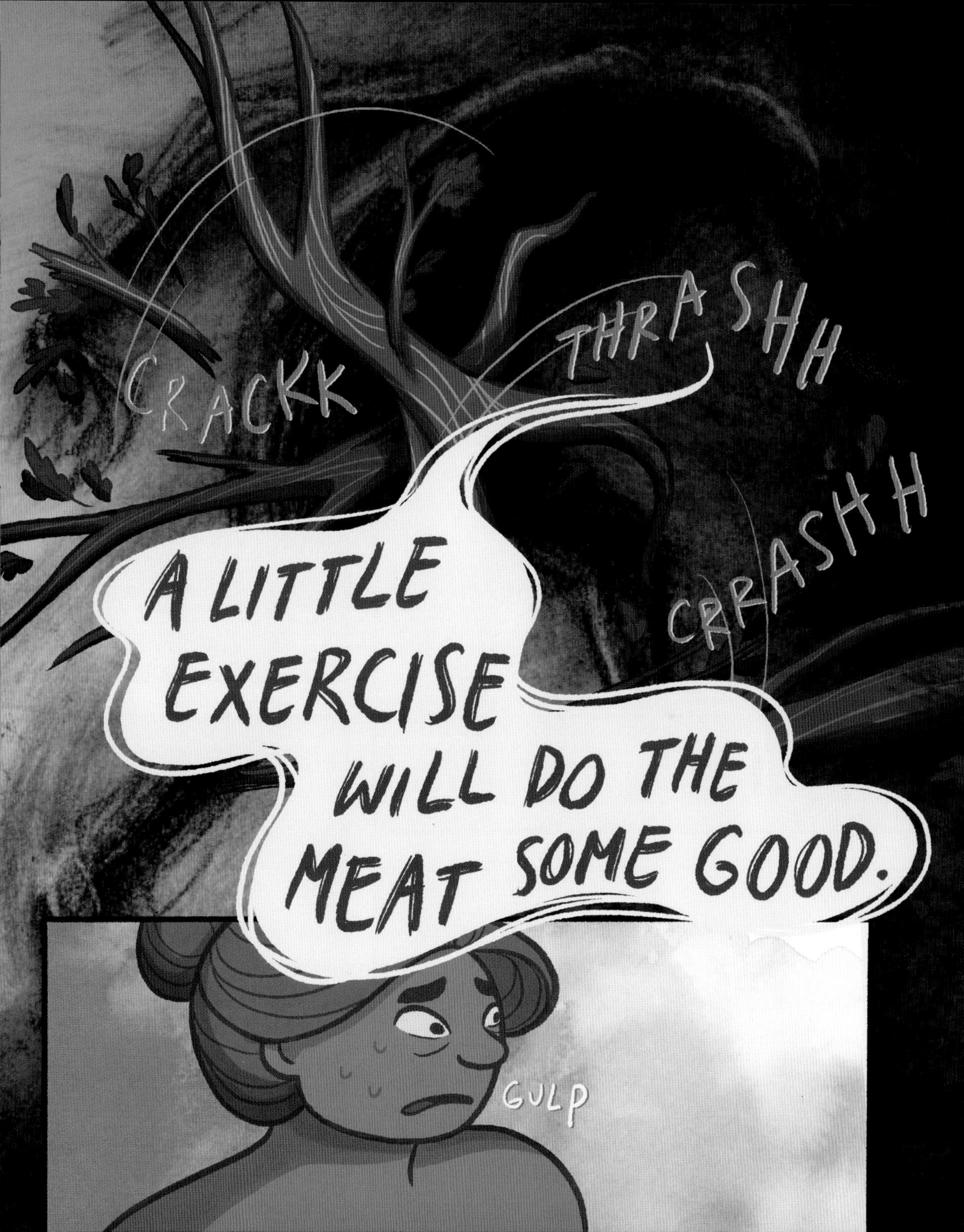
CRACKK
THRASHH
CRRASHH
A LITTLE EXERCISE WILL DO THE MEAT SOME GOOD.
GULP

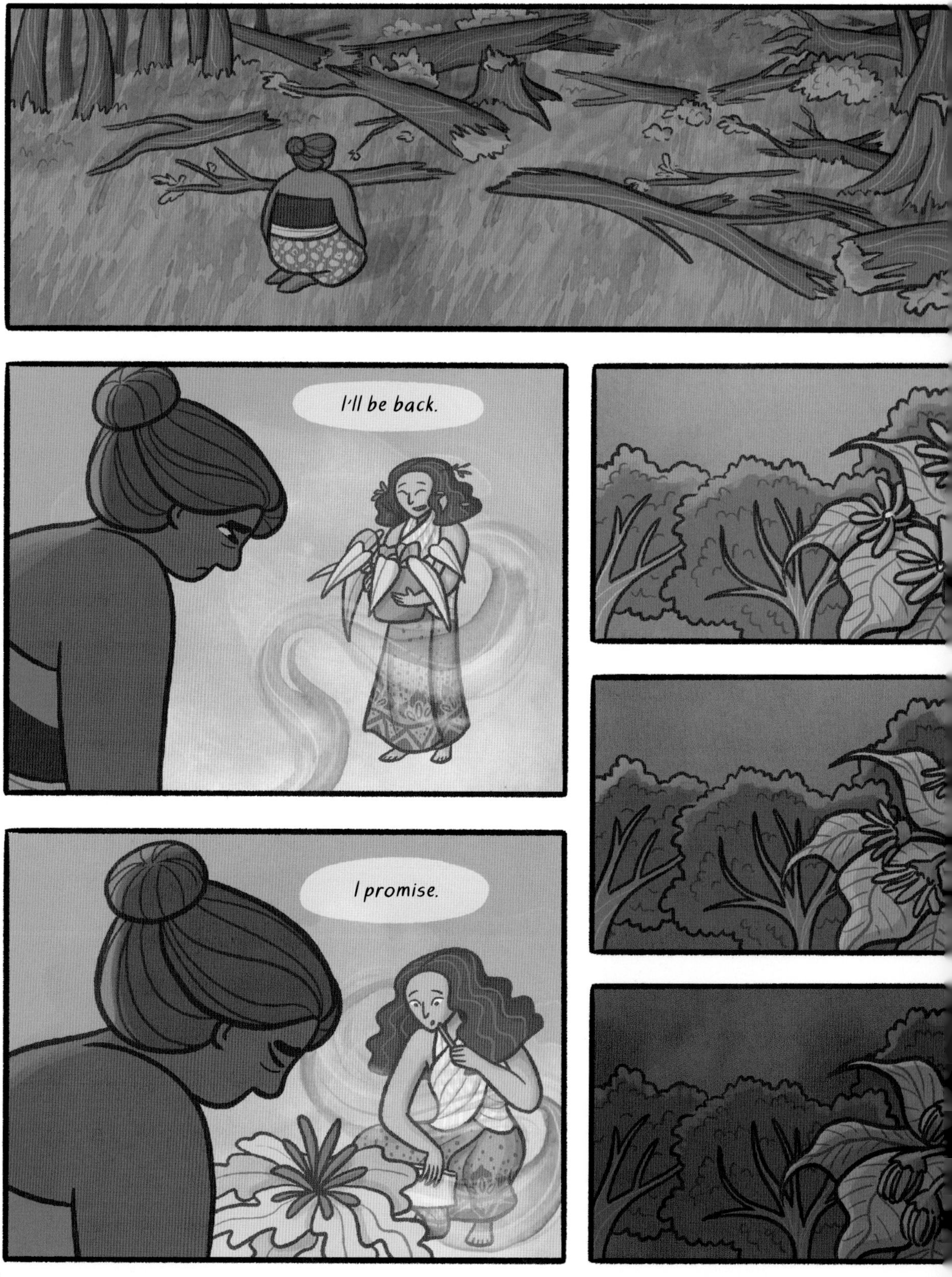
I'll be back.
I promise.

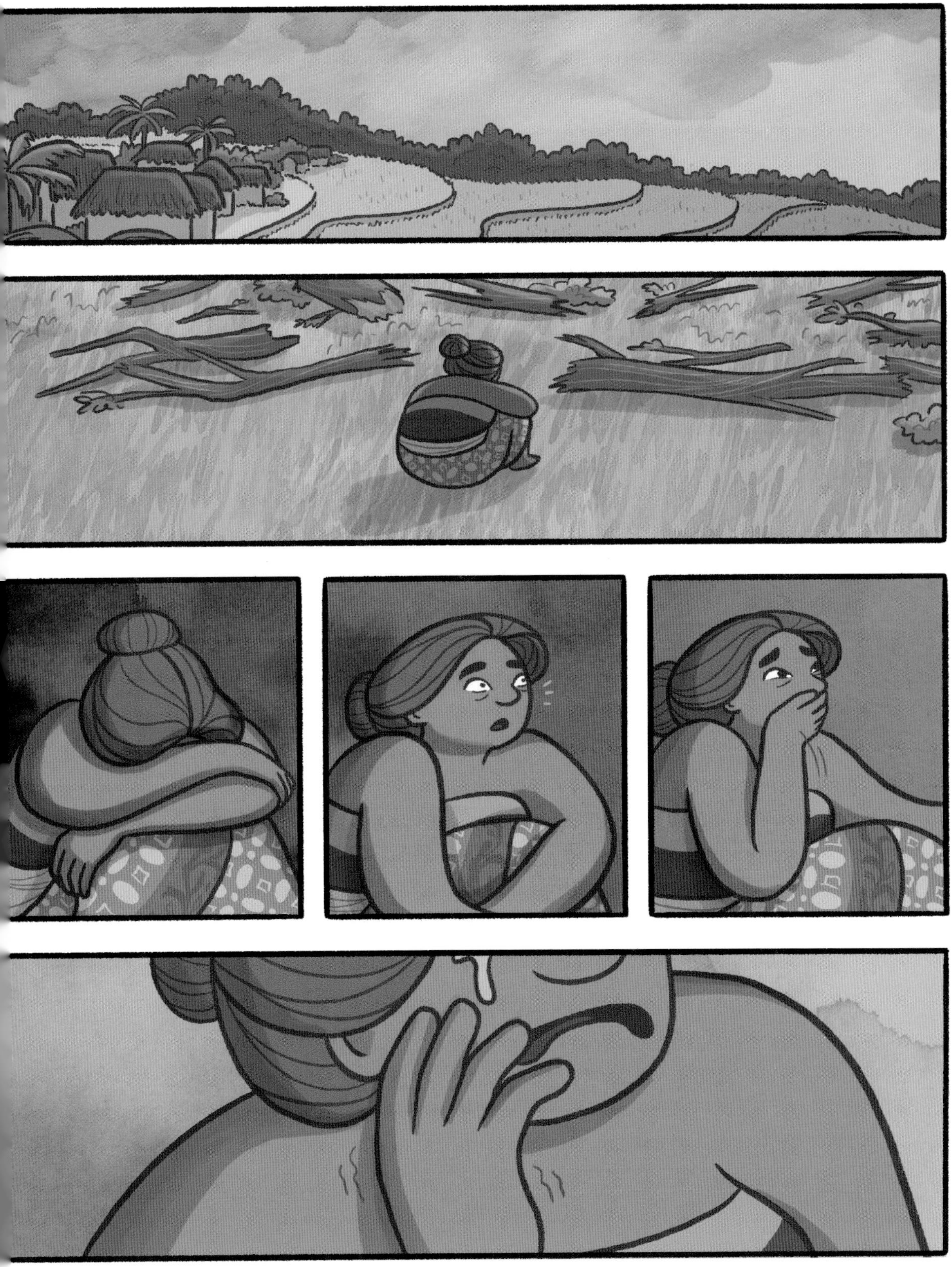

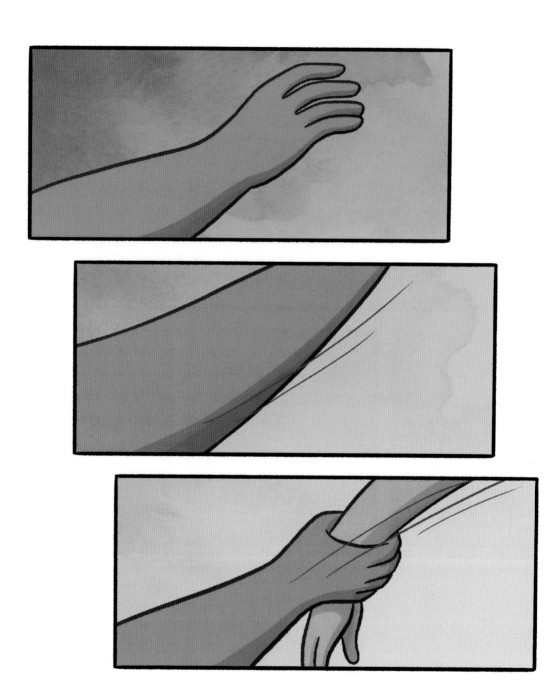

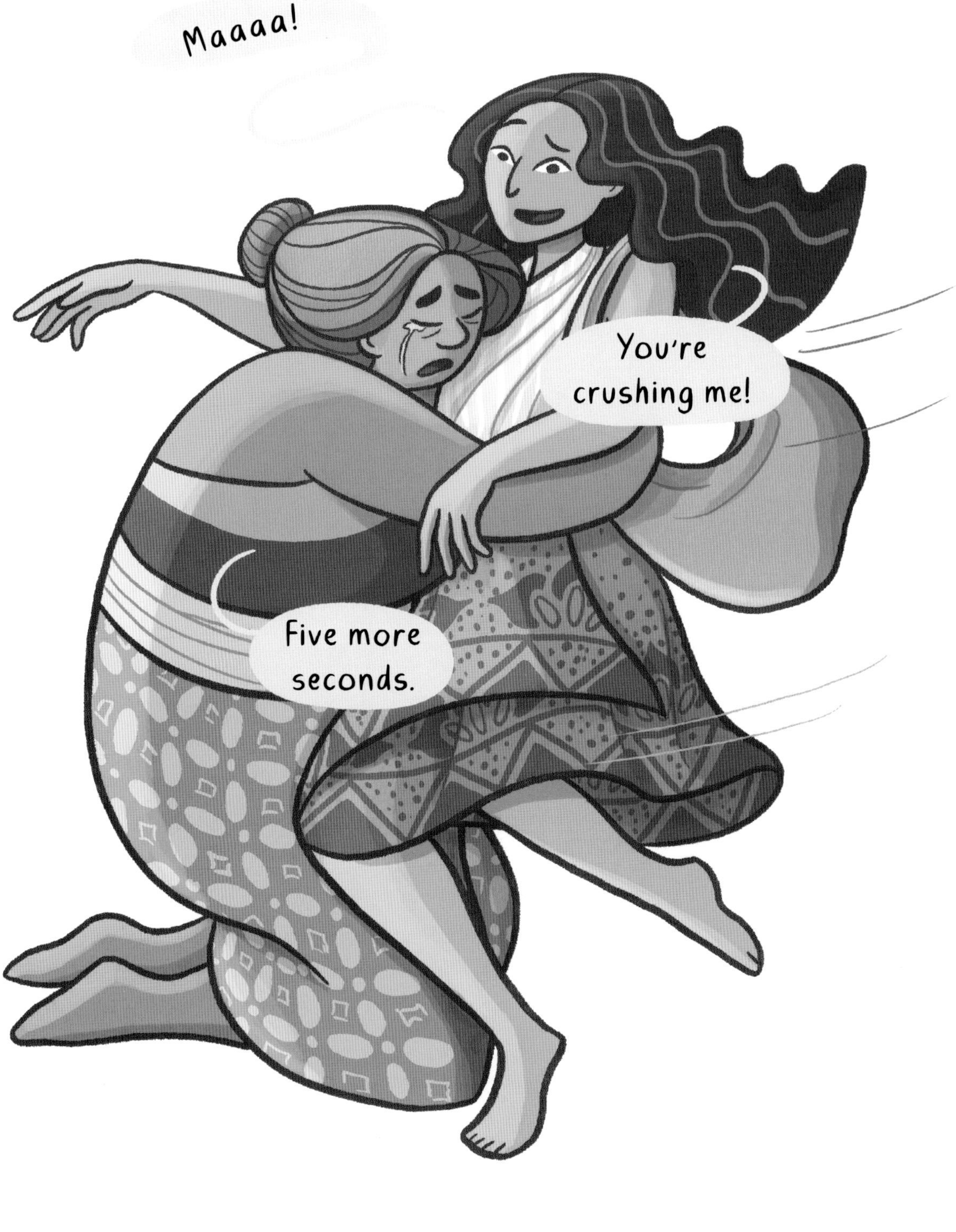
Maaaa!
You're crushing me!
Five more seconds.

And then she told me
how she escaped the Giant.

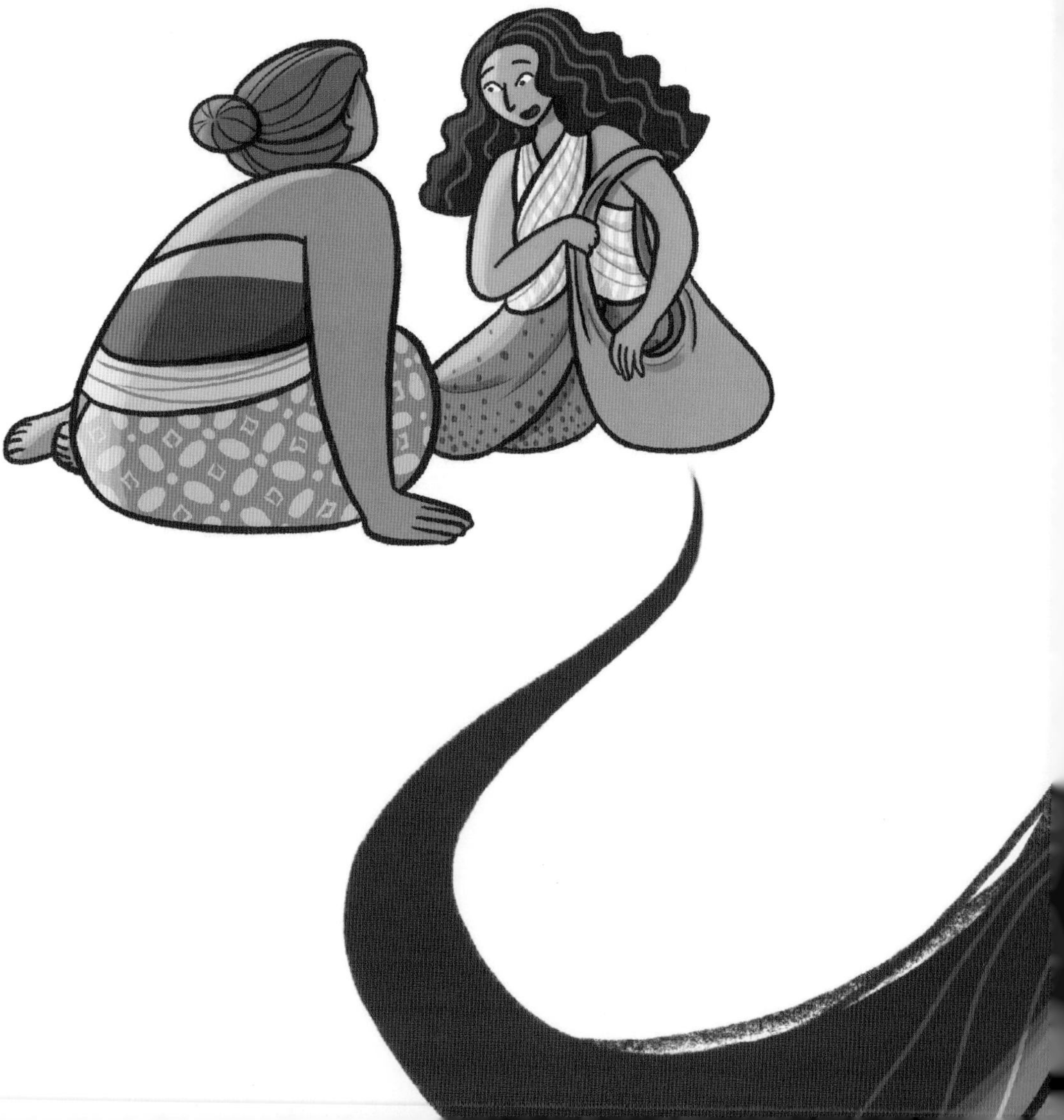

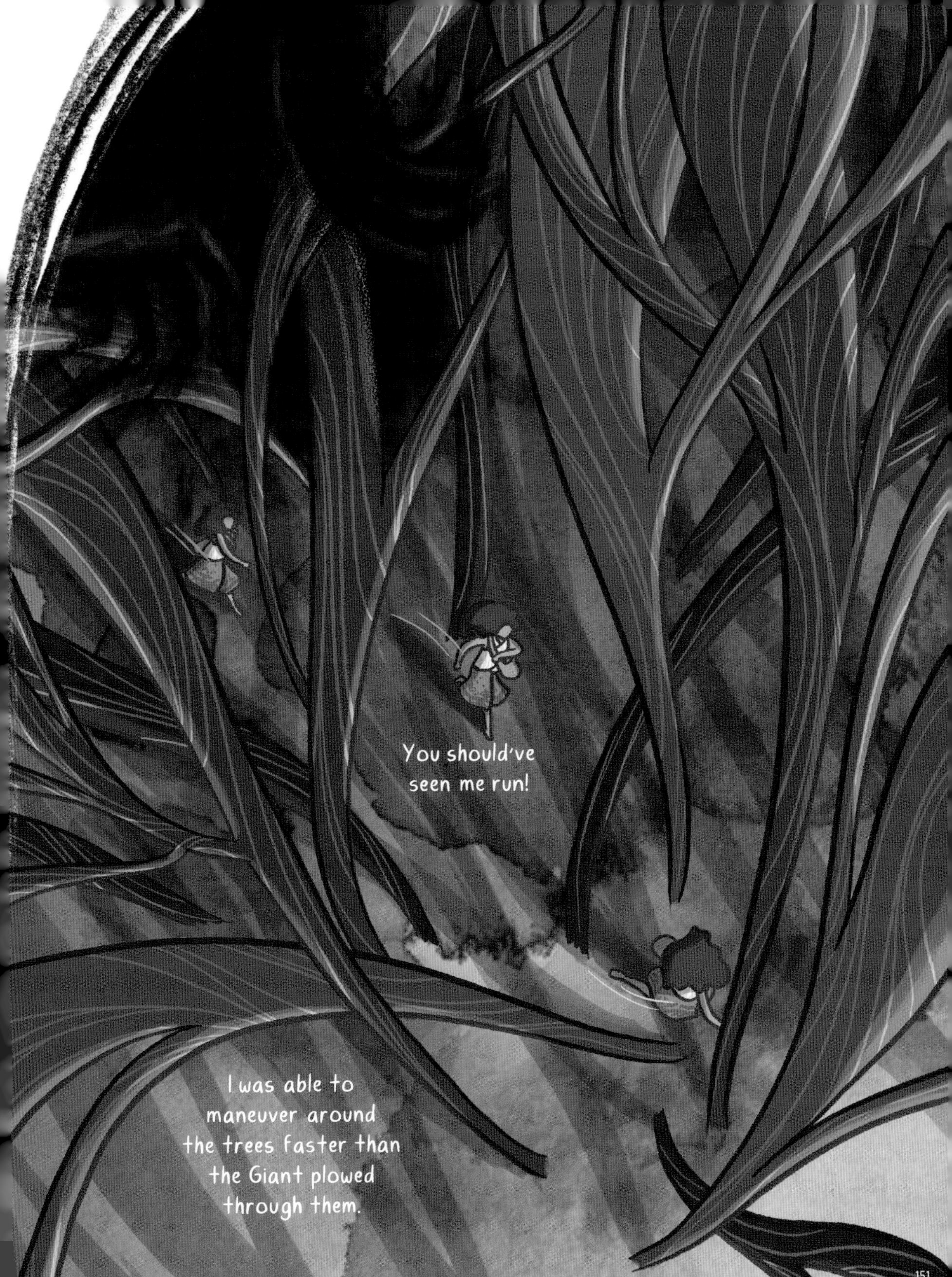
You should've seen me run!
I was able to maneuver around the trees faster than the Giant plowed through them.

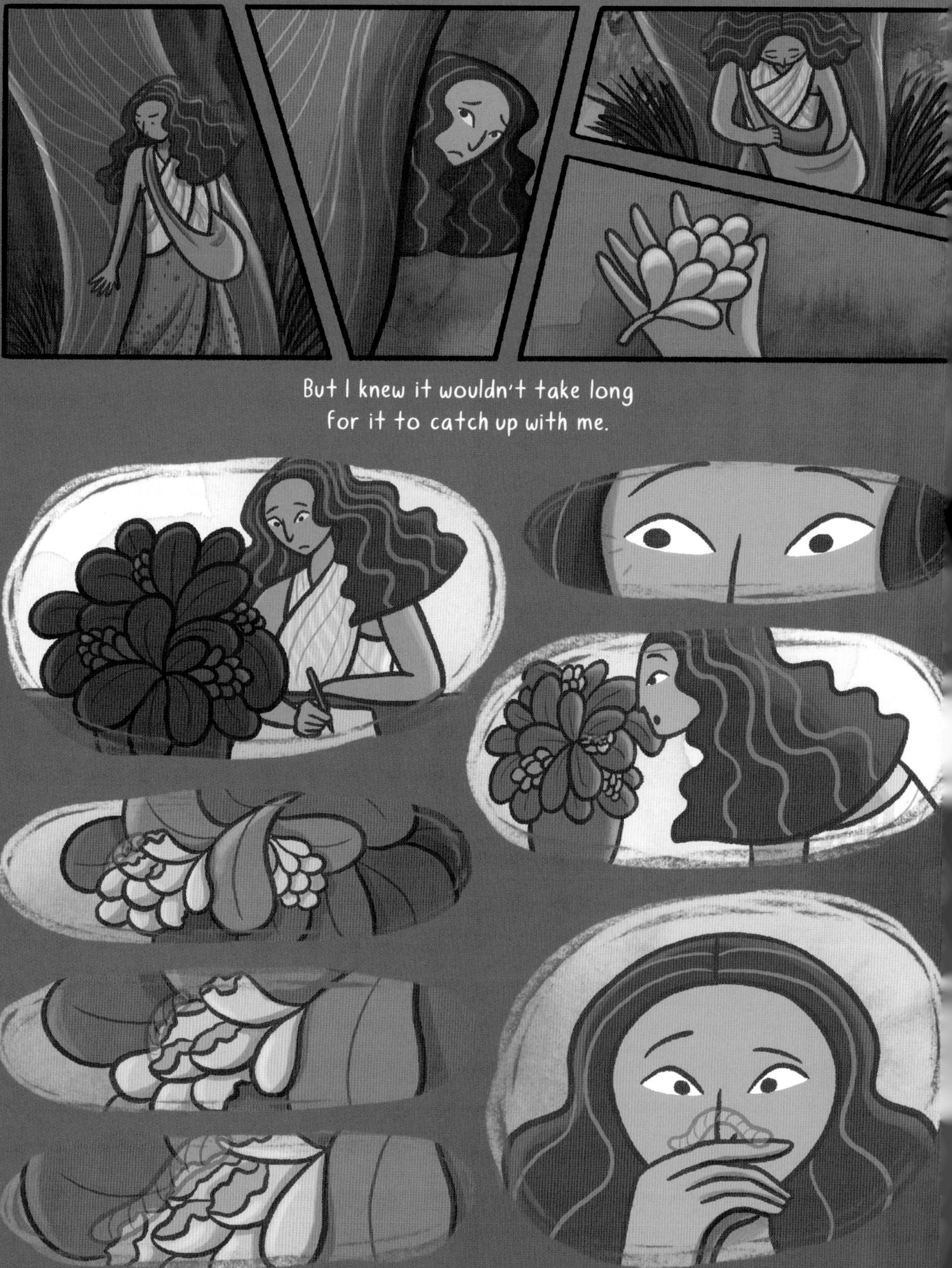
But I knew it wouldn't take long
for it to catch up with me.

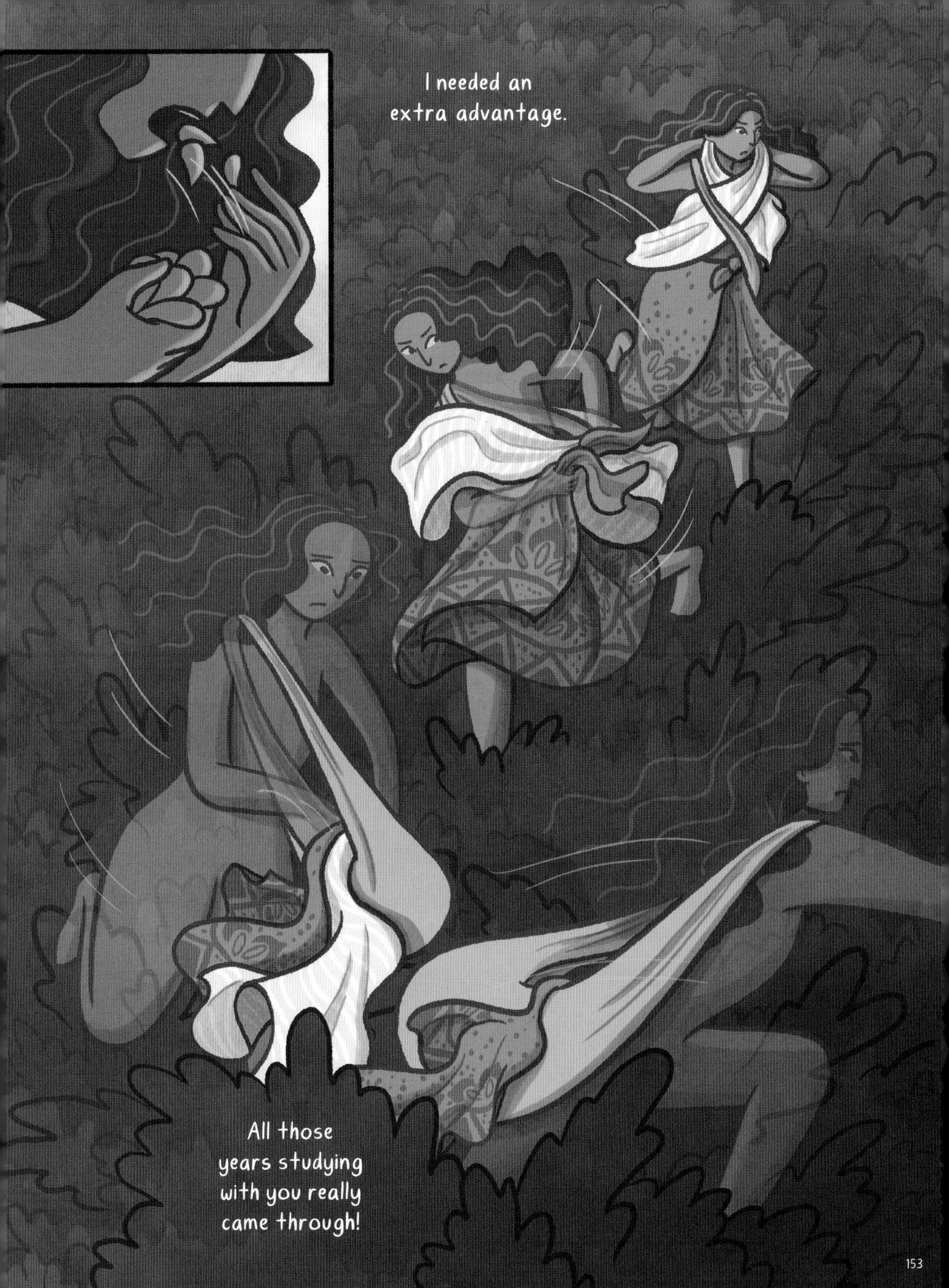
I needed an extra advantage.
All those years studying with you really came through!

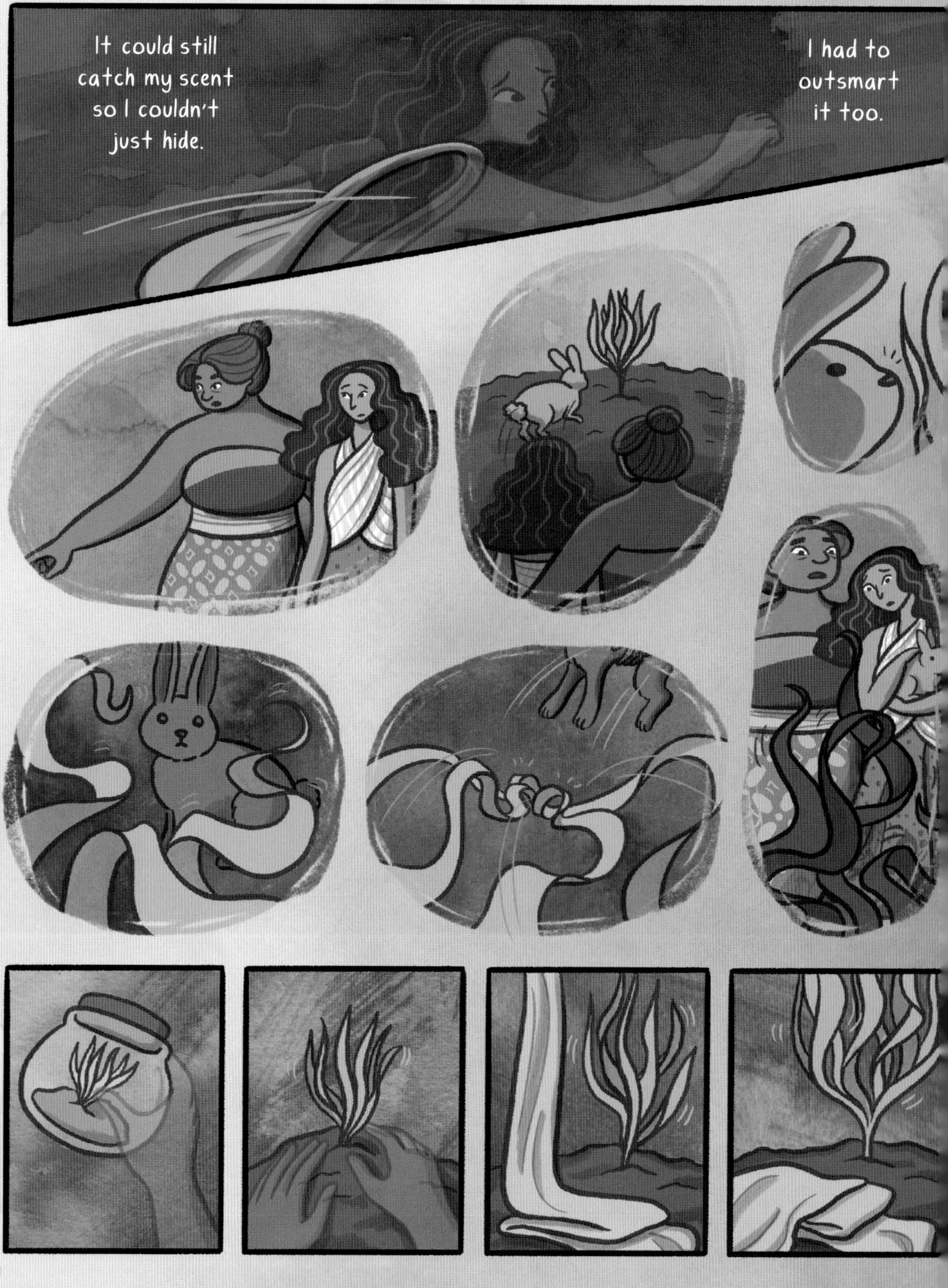
It could still catch my scent so I couldn't just hide.
I had to outsmart it too.

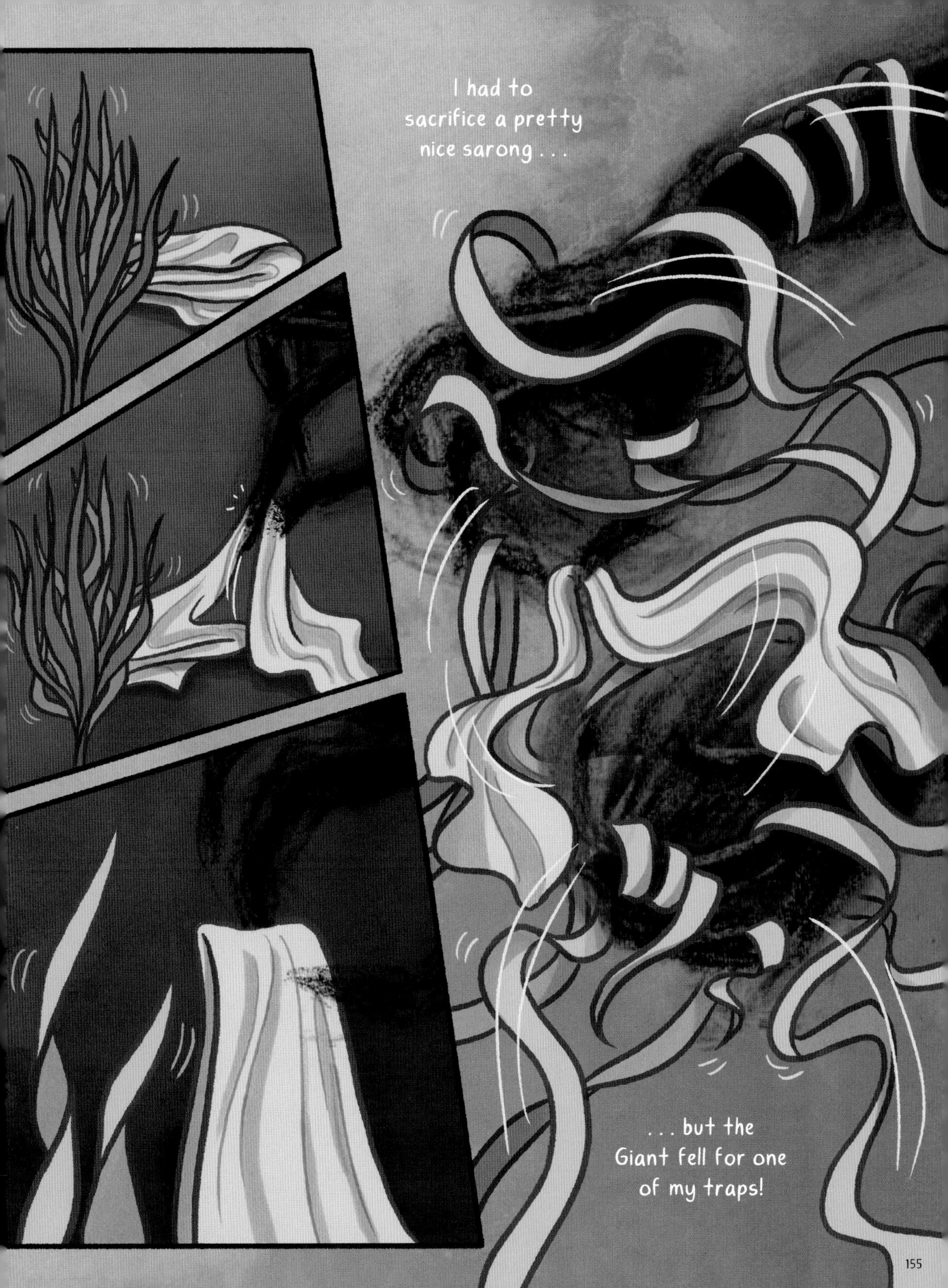
I had to sacrifice a pretty nice sarong . . .
. . . but the Giant fell for one of my traps!

Oh no.

I was starting to be visible again.

Still, the Giant kept chasing.

I was getting tired, but so was the Giant.

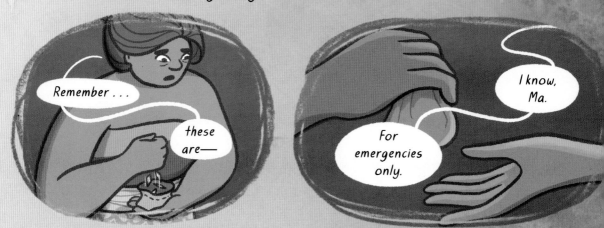

Remember . . .

these are—

For emergencies only.

I know, Ma.

It was finally time to use the secret weapon.

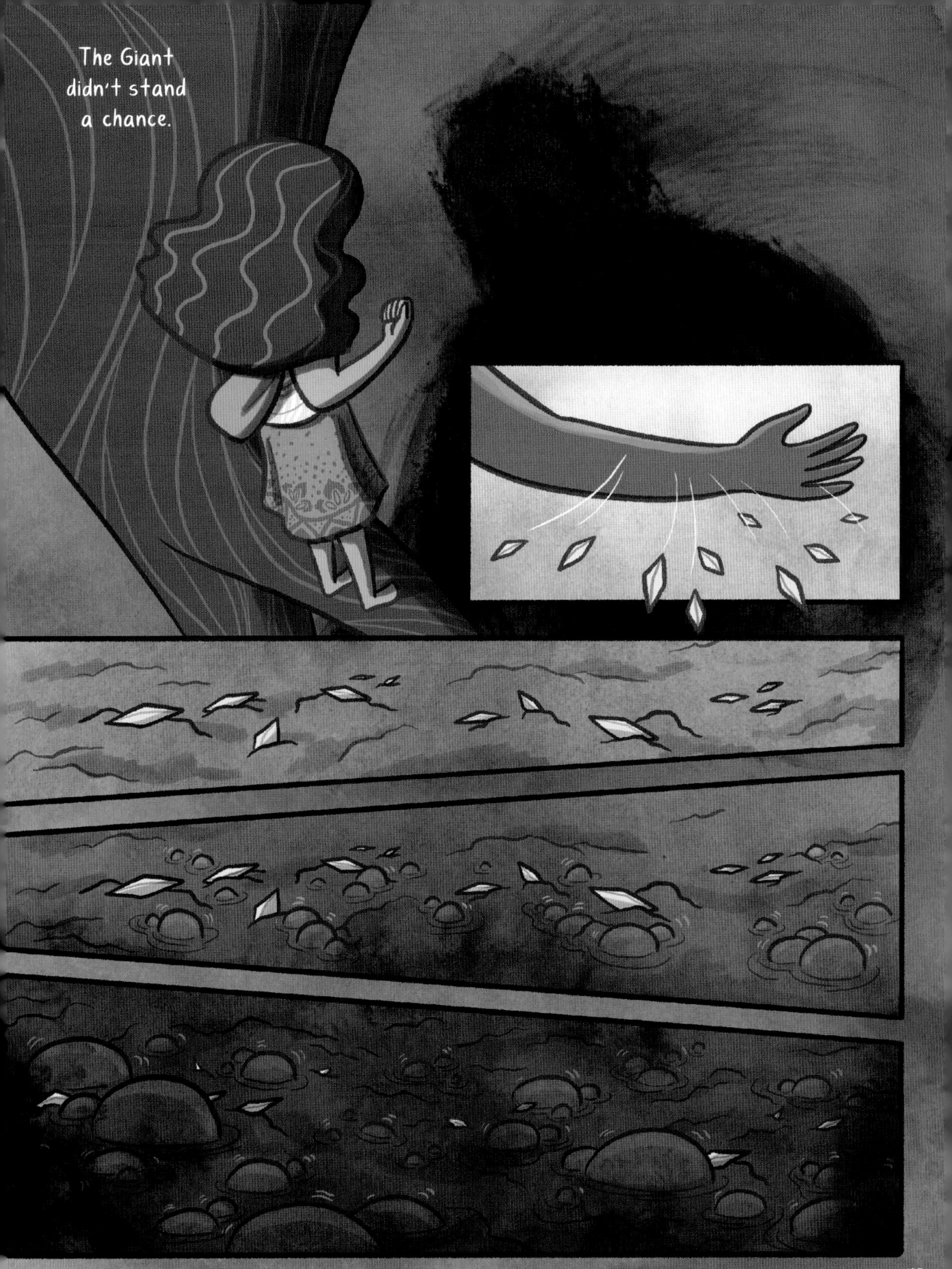
The Giant
didn't stand
a chance.

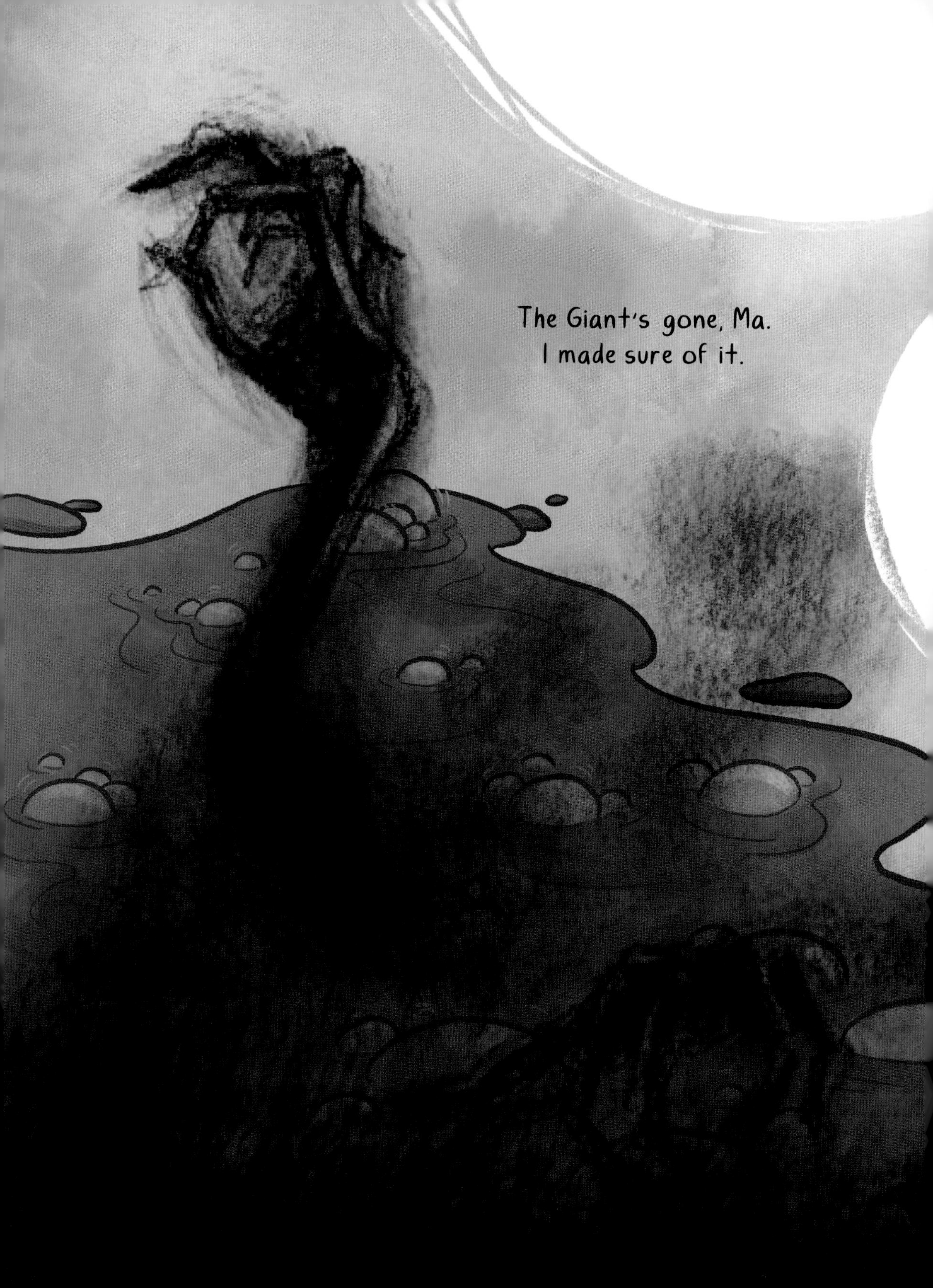
The Giant's gone, Ma.
I made sure of it.

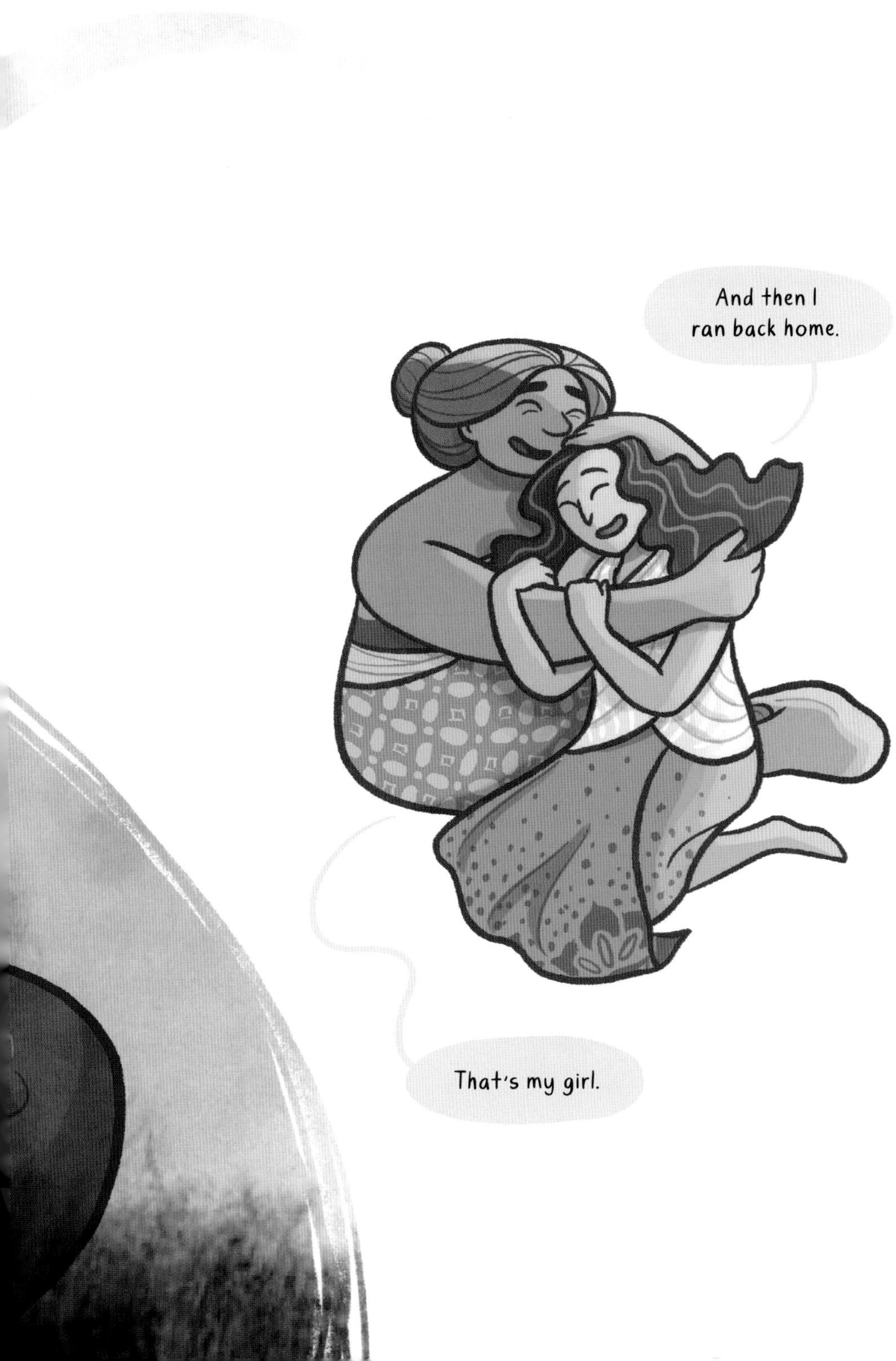
And then I ran back home.
That's my girl.

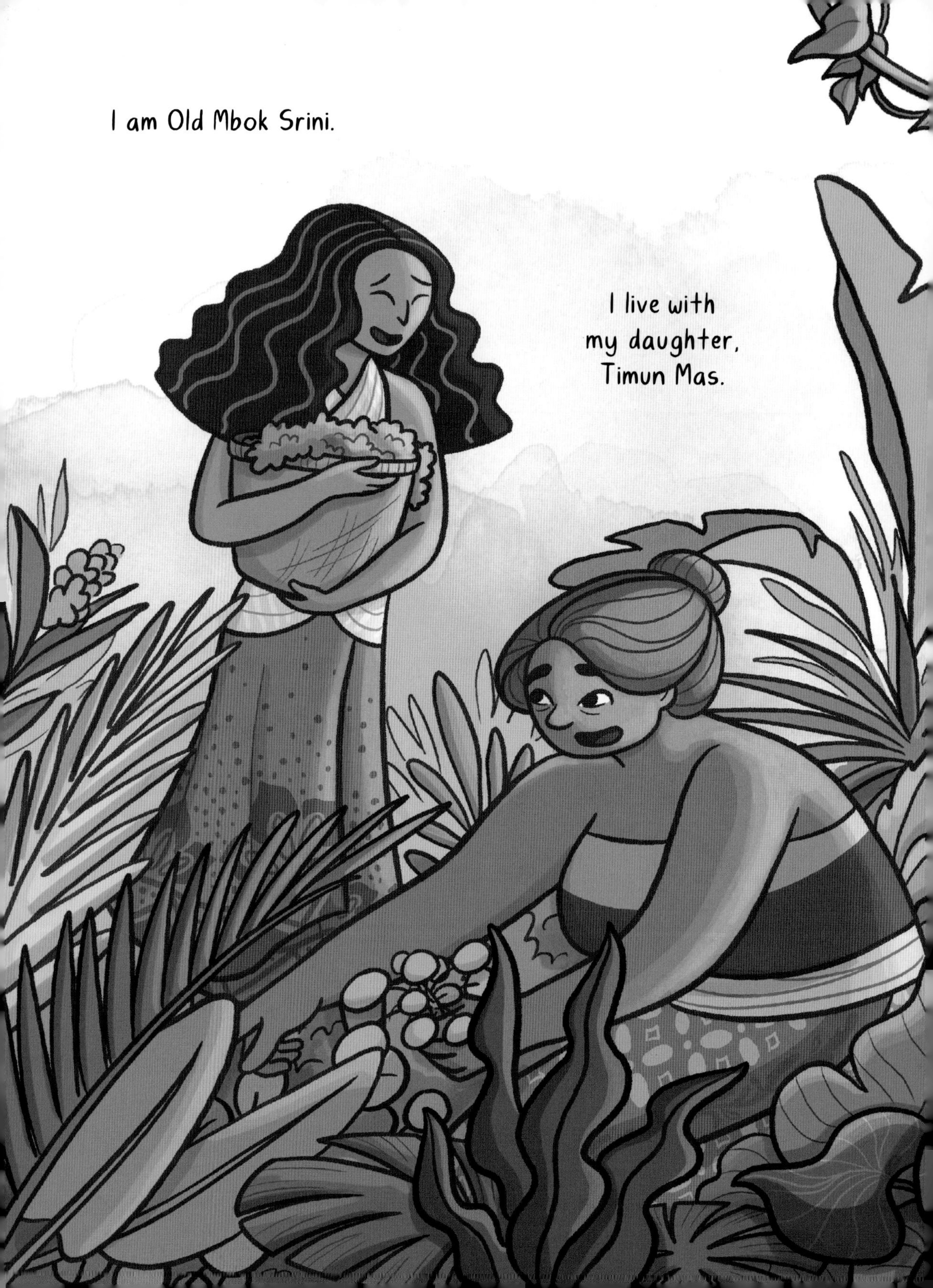
I am Old Mbok Srini.
I live with my daughter, Timun Mas.

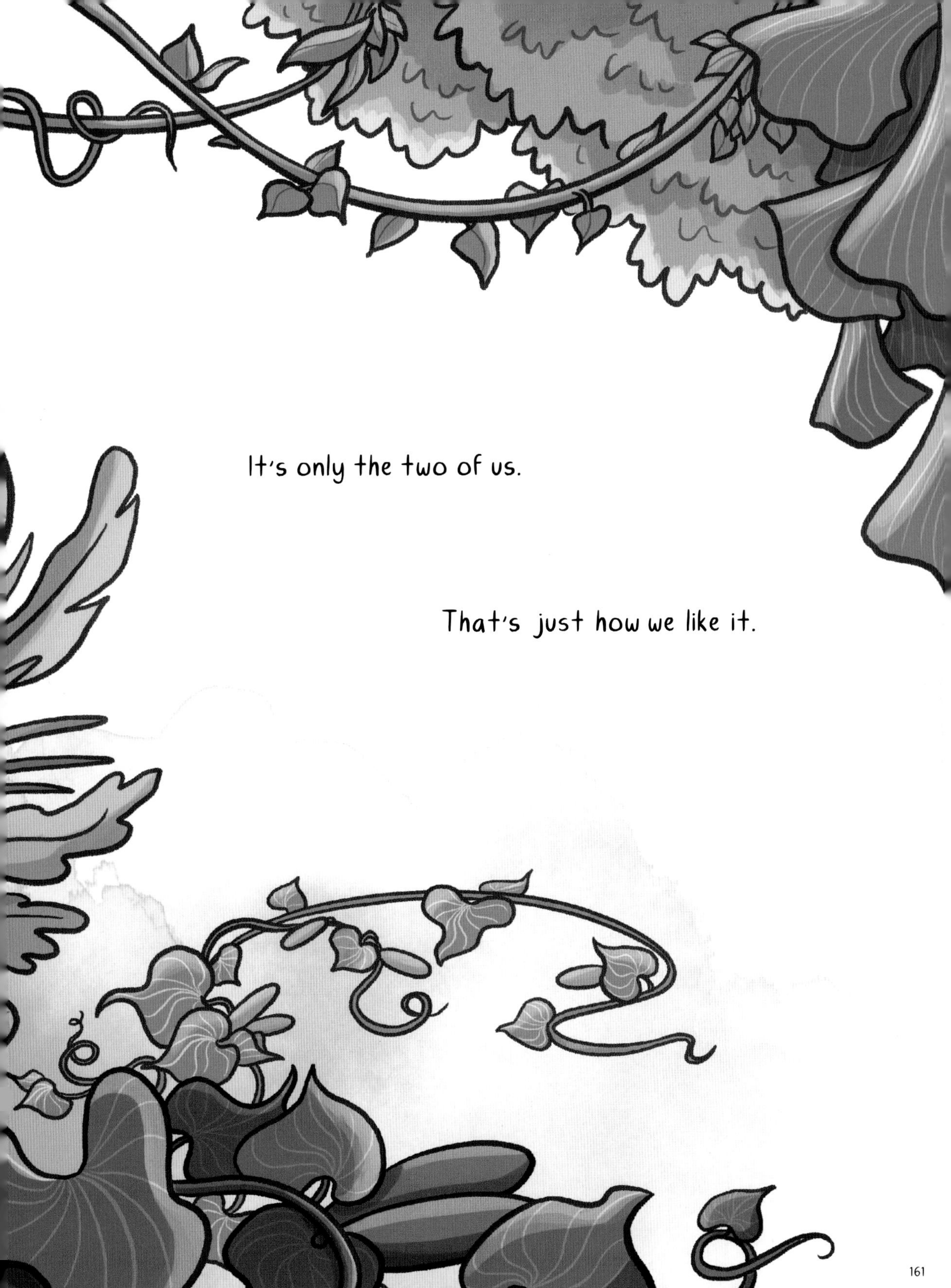
It's only the two of us.
That's just how we like it.

Author's Note

This book grew out of my fascination with traditional folktales. While I've always enjoyed these stories, I am sometimes bothered by how women are presented. They are often limited to superficial tropes like the damsel in distress, or the wicked and jealous stepmother, or the spinster wishing for a child, or the rags-to-riches-marrying-a-prince-they-just-met girl.

Stories of the Islands is a response to questions I'm constantly asking:

Who are these women beyond the hero's love interest? What are their hopes and dreams outside of what's expected of them? Why are they waiting for their saviors instead of just saving themselves?

I was raised by a single mother who is arguably the strongest person I know. I grew up watching her refuse to be defined by others as she struggled to make her own path. As a result, I have a strong distaste for narratives that perpetuate the concept that a woman is limited to what society expects of them. My mom taught me to challenge that idea and that's exactly what I did by rewriting the folktales I grew up with in Indonesia.

A country with over 17,000 islands, there were countless stories to choose from, but I decided to start with the three I was most familiar with. Thus, *Stories of the Islands* was born. I reimagined these folktales in a way I wish they were told to me when I was growing up. I want young girls to be exposed to a different kind of narrative, and be encouraged to break from stereotypes and the pattern of constantly being looked down on and underappreciated.

In reading my version of these stories, as well as the original tales in the following pages, I'm hoping you, reader, will be inspired to take control of your own life, regardless of the expectations and limitations imposed on you.

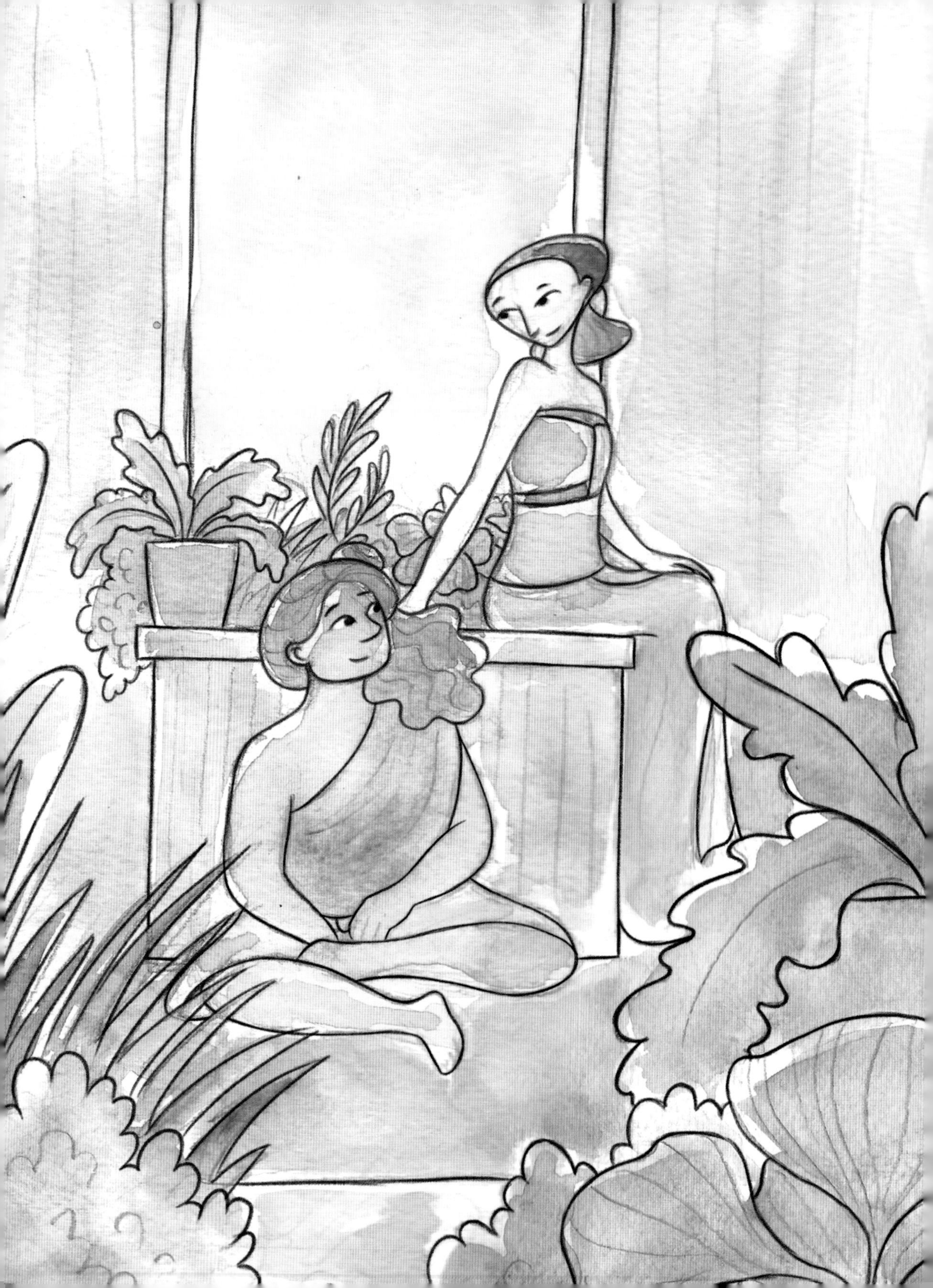

Keong Mas (Golden Snail)
THE ORIGINAL STORY

A handsome prince arrived at a kingdom with the intention of making one of the two princesses, Candra Kirana or Dewi Galuh, his wife. He chose Candra Kirana, and Dewi Galuh became so jealous she asked an evil witch to transform Candra Kirana into something disgusting to repel the prince. The witch transformed the princess into a snail with a golden shell and threw her in a river. The curse placed on her could only be broken if she was reunited with the prince.

The Golden Snail got caught in the fishing net of an old widow, who decided to bring the snail home with her. The next day, when the widow arrived home from the river after not catching any fish, she was shocked to find a feast prepared for her. This kept happening, so she pretended to leave one day, only to sneak back in to witness the Golden Snail transform into the princess.

Meanwhile, the prince never gave up on searching for the missing princess. The witch, trying to prevent him from ever finding her, transformed herself into a talking crow and gave him false directions. The Prince came across a hungry elderly man and stopped to give him some food. The elderly man turned out to be a warlock who then warned the prince that the crow was misleading him.

After being given the proper directions, the prince continued to walk for days. Tired and thirsty, he approached a house to ask for a glass of water, and saw Candra Kirana through the window. Reunited with her prince, the princess's curse was finally lifted. The prince brought Candra Kirana and the old widow back with him to the kingdom, where Dewi Galuh's evil deeds were exposed to the king. Candra Kirana and her prince got married, and they lived happily ever after.

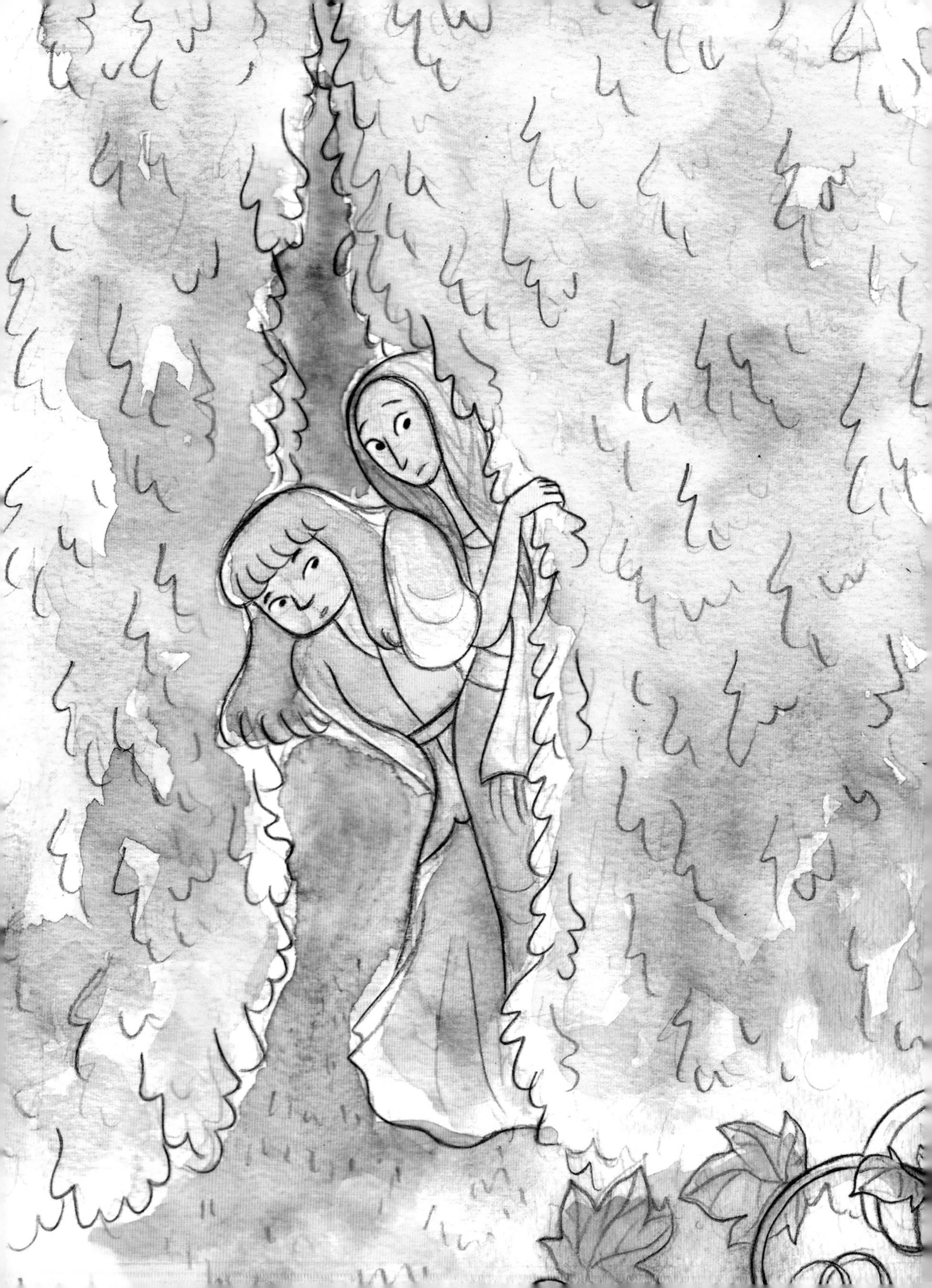

Bawang Merah Bawang Putih
(Shallot Garlic)
THE ORIGINAL STORY

There was a widow who lived with her lazy and selfish daughter, Bawang Merah, and her kind and honest stepdaughter, Bawang Putih. The Widow spoiled her daughter but abused her stepdaughter, forcing her to do all the work like a slave. One day, as Bawang Putih was doing laundry by the river, she realized that a piece of cloth was missing. She walked along the river in search of it. The river led her to the home of an old woman who revealed she knew where the cloth was but would only return it after Bawang Putih did all her household chores. Once the tasks were completed, the old woman returned the cloth, and then she asked the girl to choose between two pumpkins, one small and one large. She took the smaller one.

It was late when Bawang Putih returned home and the Widow and Bawang Merah were furious. The Widow snatched the pumpkin from Bawang Putih and smashed it to the ground. The pumpkin broke apart to reveal jewelry hidden within. Hearts filled with greed, the Widow and Bawang Merah yelled at Bawang Putih for choosing the small pumpkin over the larger one that probably contained much more jewelry.

The Widow ordered Bawang Merah to repeat Bawang Putih's actions, purposefully letting a piece of cloth drift away and following until it led to the old woman. Unlike Bawang Putih, Bawang Merah refused to do any work for the old woman and instead began demanding the larger pumpkin. The old woman gave it to the girl, who then brought it back home to her mother. Worried that Bawang Putih would want her own share of the pumpkin, the Widow ordered her stepdaughter to go to the river. The Widow and Bawang Merah smashed the pumpkin, but found no jewelry, only venomous snakes that proceeded to attack them.

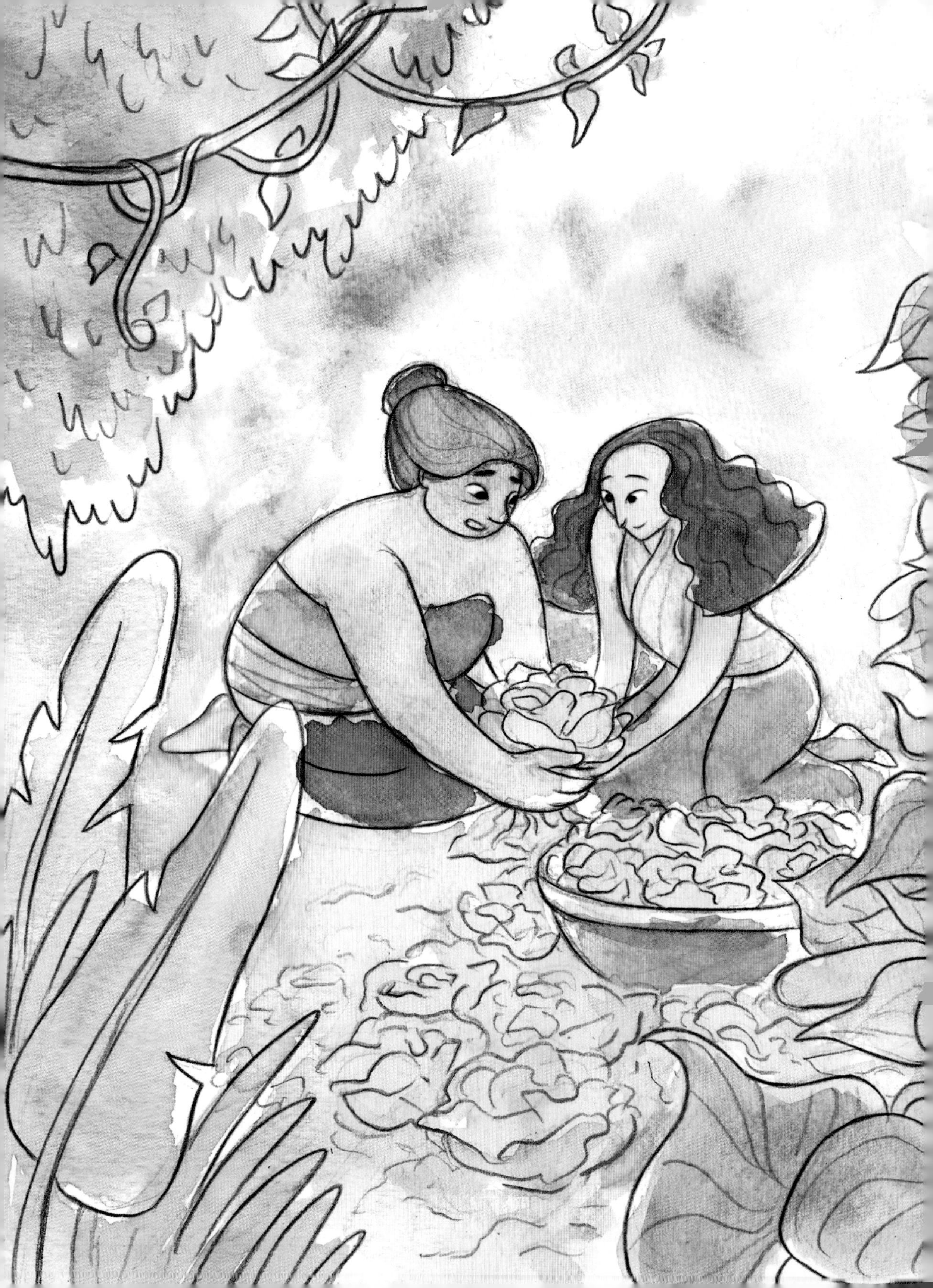

Timun Mas (Golden Cucumber)
THE ORIGINAL STORY

Mbok Srini was a lonely widow who wanted a child more than anything. One day, she met Buto Ijo (Green Giant) who gave her a cucumber seed that would give her a child. However, in return, Mbok Srini must give the child for Buto Ijo to eat once she turned seventeen. Her desire for a child was so strong that the widow agreed.

After deciding to take the Giant's deal, Mbok Srini planted the cucumber seed, which grew into a golden cucumber. Inside the cucumber was a baby girl, whom she named Timun Mas. Years passed, and a week before Timun Mas's seventeenth birthday, Buto Ijo paid Mbok Srini a visit to remind her that he will take Timun Mas on her birthday. Mbok Srini sought help from a dukun (witch doctor), who gave her four small bags, each filled with different magical objects to fight off the Giant: cucumber seeds, needles, salt, and terasi (shrimp paste).

Timun Mas turned seventeen, and Buto Ijo came to eat her. As the Giant chased her, Timun Mas threw the magical objects at him. The cucumber seeds grew into a large cucumber vine that strangled Buto Ijo, the needles transformed into a bamboo forest with sharp tips that wounded him, the salt became a large pool of seawater that forced him to swim across, and finally, the terasi turned the land into boiling volcanic mud, which finally killed the Giant. Timun Mas returned to her mother, and they lived happily ever after.

Special Thanks

To Della, my editor who randomly found my work while browsing through a random art site, thank you for tracking me down and giving me this opportunity

To the Holiday House team (Chris, Kerry, Lisa, Rebecca, Jill, Sara, Bree, Terry, Michelle, Alison, Elyse, Mary, Melissa, Kayla, Annie), thank you for helping me bring this project to life.

To Antoine and Kelly, this book's first supervisors, thank you for giving me guidance when this was just an untitled art school project that I truly didn't think would ever go anywhere.

To Jen and Ans, the ones who have stuck by me for over 12 years, thank you for our bimonthly New York-London-Sydney Skype sessions and for keeping me sane (or at least reminding me I'm not the only insane one).

To Sophia, the roommate who has witnessed many of my breakdowns, thank you for reminding me it's alright to take breaks and for being there when I was at my lowest.

To my family, who could've guilted me into becoming a doctor/lawyer/engineer/etc., thank you for the continuous support and encouragement.

To Akong, my grandpa who was taken too soon, thank you for giving me my first colored pens and for being the reason I started drawing in the first place.

To Patrycja, my therapist who has dealt with "my crazy" for the past two years, thank you for calling me out on my toxic work habits and for keeping me accountable in my attempts at self care.

To all of the men who have ever disappointed me, thank you for being one of the reasons I threw myself completely into this book as a way of coping—the results are pretty great.

And to anyone who's ever asked how my book was going and gotten a whimper and panicked look in response, thank you for believing in me when I couldn't.